# Ghost Bird

Harbingers, Book IV: Child of Sky

## Jane M. Wiseman

Shrike Publications
Albuquerque, New Mexico

**Shrike Publications**
Albuquerque, New Mexico

Publisher's Note: This is a work of fiction. Names, characters, places, and incidents are a product of the author's imagination. Locales and public names are sometimes used for atmospheric purposes. Any resemblance to actual people, living or dead, or to businesses, companies, events, institutions, or locales is completely coincidental.

Book Layout © 2017 BookDesignTemplates.com

**Ghost Bird/ Jane M Wiseman** . -- 1st ed.
ISBN 978-1-7328141-7-2

For Will and Wallace

*One for sorrow,*

*Two for mirth,*

*Three for death,*

*Four for birth,*

*Five for silver,*

*Six for gold,*

*Seven for secrets never told.*

*Eight for Ghost Bird, eight for Owl*

*underneath the Nine Spheres' bowl.*

# Map of the Unknown Lands

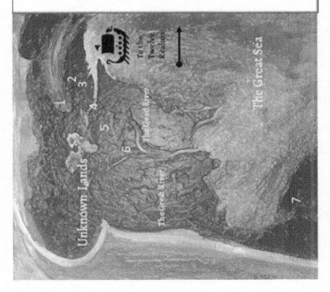

1 The Great Comet of 1066
2 The village of The People
3 Fishers' Bay
4 Three Rivers
5 Falls Village
6 The Great City of the Sun
7 The City of the Temples

# The Stormclouds/Harbingers Fantasy Series

## Stormclouds: The Prequel Series

Book I, *A Gyrfalcon for a King*
Book II, *The Call of the Shrike*
Book III, *Stormbird*

## The Harbingers Series

Book I, *Blackbird Rising*
Book II, *Halcyon*
Book III, *Firebird*
Book IV, *Ghost Bird*

## Betwixt and Between: The Companion Series

Book I, *The Martlet is a Wanderer*
Book II, *The Nightingale Holds Up the Sky*

## And now:

*Dark Ones Take It*
Being the origin story of Caedon and his brother, Maeldoi

All ten novels available in paperback from amazon.com and in ebook format for Kindle and Kindle-enabled devices.

# Contents

# PROLOGUE

The mage named Merlin, or maybe Myrddin, or—on at least one of the planes, Mervin, a trucker out of Asheville—lounged at his ease on his golden chair, watching his friend John Dee with amusement.

"Dee, you're a fine mage. But you get much too involved with the beings underneath the Spheres," he told his friend. "You know it's not allowed. The Three frowns on it most decidedly."

On the plane where Mervin was a trucker, Dee practiced neurology in St. Louis. On a different plane, a different time, he was instead a powerful alchemist and advisor to a mighty queen.

Just as, on a different plane, Mervin himself waved a wand and helped young boys pull swords out of stones so that they might go forth and found ideal communities of noble knights.

On both of those planes, the mages sported white pointy beards. Up here in the clouds, they didn't bother.

There, the resemblance between the two mages ended. Mervin was tall, with an imposing physique. His eyes were intense dark pools, his skin as dark and burnished as mahogany.

Dee was reedy and slight, his eyes a piercing blue, his skin (usually, depending) a dead-fish white.

Mervin was considered and calm.

Dee was volatile, tending to fly off the handle.

Or so Mervin thought.

"I can't help myself, Mervin," said Dee with a sigh. "I try to stop. But somehow, it always happens. I get too involved. It's just the way I'm made."

"I know." Mervin, or whoever he might be, looked fondly on his friend.

"For instance—" said Dee, and then he hesitated.

Mervin came to the edge of their cloud platform to look over, and down, to the land beneath the Spheres. "What?"

"Not there," said Dee. He indicated with his eyes another place, across a broad and unnavigable river. "There."

Mervin looked. He looked again, with a sharp intake of breath. But here it was, John in his usual state of consternation, and even though he felt himself shaken, he knew his most immediate task was to settle John down.

Something like this, though.

It would set John off, and Mervin needed John. Needed him to have a cool head in the struggle ahead of them.

"No, John," said Mervin firmly. "Step away. There's nothing you can do for that man. Nothing you can do about him. Not a thing." After a moment, when Dee had looked uneasily away but then back to the dark and bent-over figure of what once had been a man, Mervin took Dee by the sleeve and tugged. "Why would you even want to? The man is irredeemable."

"Then why is he over there, standing under that tree?"

"Why indeed?" muttered Mervin. He was staring now, too. "Can't look, can't look away," he said, disgusted with himself.

"Everything we know about that man tells us that, after death, he wouldn't have gone across that river." Dee was starting to get worked up. Mervin knew the signs too well.

"May as well go ahead and name him," said Mervin.

"Caedon," said Dee, and he practically snarled.

"No," said Mervin. "I agree with you, John. After that young apprentice mage of yours burnt Caedon to a crisp, he shouldn't have been allowed to go across that river. He should have tumbled into the dark and bottomless pit beneath the lands. Even after all this time, he should still be falling."

"Yet there he stands."

"Crouches."

"There he crouches, underneath that tree. What do you make of it?" said Dee, getting a grip.

After a moment, Mervin shrugged. "Beats me. These decisions aren't ours to make." He tried hard to speak in a calm and even tone.

"The Three makes them."

"They do, and we're not to question it."

"Perhaps. . ." Dee hesitated. "Perhaps Gilles appealed to The Three on Caedon's behalf. Got him a reprieve."

"How strange would that be? Think about it, Dee. I know your young mage did a mighty act, but she had help. At the last moment, just as she moved in to fry him with that uncanny fire of hers, Gilles appears to have removed his protective wards from Caedon. Why would he do that and then somehow finagle a reprieve for the scurvy fellow? But anyway," said Mervin soberly, feeling a terrible sinking of his spirits, "If that were to be the case, John." He heaved up a deep breath. "Then I wouldn't know what to think about anything. Anything at all. My whole view of the world would be upended. The world, this plane, all the planes, and everything in them, if somehow Gilles had that kind of clout with The Three. After what Gilles has tried to do."

"And yet, for the sake of balance—" Dee began.

Mervin shuddered. "I don't even want to think about a balance that would require us and the other mages of good will to be counterbalanced by Gilles. What universe that, in order to function properly, would require Gilles?"

"Talking about me behind my back?"

The two mages whirled around.

"Hello, Gilles," said Mervin carefully.

Gilles stepped to the edge of the platform and stared across the river. "There's my boy," he said softly.

"There is no justice," said Dee, with a bitter laugh, and stalked away.

Gilles glanced at Mervin. "Control your dog, Merlin, or something bad will happen to him."

Mervin did not reply. He too, went away, leaving Gilles alone on the platform. Looking across the river to the isolated and blackened creature he had made. Gilles stood alone and yearning across that vast gap, the tears glittering in his eyes.

# I KEERA: Two

## Dis-orderly

Keera watched as Gwyl scanned the horizon, the stiff ocean wind blowing his dark hair back off his face, his gray Sea-Child eyes keen. He called out a command to his men as the seas, running higher, hurled the ship up the steep side of a wave. Gwyl served as his own kendtman, and Keera knew she should trust him. She did trust him. He knew what he was doing. The dragon ship ran smoothly down the back side of the wave into the deep trench. And here came another. Kerra was afraid.

A snatch of one of her mother's songs came to her. "One for sorrow, two for mirth," she hummed to herself. It was a song about the owls. Ghost birds, some called them. She'd always loved the owls, and usually, the song gave her comfort. But today, it seemed somehow ominous to her. There was mirth, but there was also sorrow. The two were paired. *You can't have one without the other*, she whispered to herself.

"We'll outrun that ship, whoever she is, never fear," Gwyl murmured into Keera's ear, pulling her to him. He seemed to know when she was troubled. He always seemed to know. "We're fast," he reassured her.

"Is it the same one?" Keera stared back at the vessel coming up behind them. It had been following them for days.

"Looks like it."

"That ship has kept up with us."

"Yes. They're fast, too." He began flipping his sun-stone over and over in his left hand, a habit she knew he had when he was worried about something. "Her master knows what he's about." The respect in his voice was grudging.

"So we didn't lose them, back there."

"No." He bent down and kissed her.

"What does that mean? If they're just pirates . . ."

"Well," he said, and she looked up into his face as he thought it over. "Whoever they turn out to be, it might mean they know who we are and where we're going. Not many come out here, this far to the westward."

Keera shivered, pulling her cloak tighter about herself. Pirates wouldn't, she thought. They'd stay close to a harbor where they could run their loot quickly to land and exchange it for good solid coin. She'd never considered before actually hoping for pirates. The mysterious ship that seemed to be following them might be worse than pirates. Her imagination kept harrowing her. What would be worse than pirates? She recalled the time Caedon's ships intercepted hers, and the danger it meant. But Caedon was dead. Thank the Children, he was gone to the Dark Ones who surely must have taken his twisted spirit, one of Their own, to Themselves. Who, then?

*Ansgar*, she decided. The unscrupulous king who had stepped into the power vacuum Caedon left behind him. As her parents' diplomat, she had learned a lot about the more unsavory corners of the politics of the Twelve Realms. But she didn't want to share this uncomfortable insight of hers with Gwyl.

She was feeling a little sick again, and finally that's what stopped her dwelling on these possible enemies. She kept her hands clamped hard on the topmost strake of Gwyl's skeid, trying to keep her eyes on the horizon. That way she hoped to steady her stomach and not lose her breakfast. The fresh breeze kept her feeling a bit better than she had five days before, when they headed out from her parents' rocky outpost for this long voyage. By now they were well past the boundary where, sailors claimed, the Northern Sea gave way to the unknowns of the Great Sea stretching far off to westward.

Keera felt a bit foolish, getting sick like this. She was the Fire Child's own, not the Sea Child's, as Gwyl was, but she was familiar with water, since her mother also reverenced the Sea Child. Keera had spent her entire childhood in and around water. So she couldn't easily account for the queasy feeling she felt as the big skeid cut through the waves.

Giving her a quick embrace, Gwyl left her side to stride the deck, calling out to his mariners as they managed the billowing black sail with his insignia woven in white wool: a triple spiral, each spiraling stripe ending in the fierce head of a bird of prey. His skeid was called Dragon Wind, and he was hugely proud of the painted dragon's-head prow. He'd hired a master wood-worker for the fine carving of it, and he had clambered all over it and around it, helping to paint it himself: golds, blues, reds.

The skeid's hull was riven oak, clinker built, a ship to make a man of the Ice-realm proud. Gwyl was not from there. He was the Sea Child's for sure, as many of the Ice-men were, but he had grown up eastward on the promontory of the Baronies that ex-tended its rocky topmost corner into the choppy waters of the Narrows dividing the Eastern Baronies from its rival kingdom, the Sceptered Isle.

During his young manhood, the misfortunes of war and fam-ily had driven Gwyl from his home to roam the islands sprinkled between the northern reaches of the Sceptered Isle and the Ice-realm. There he'd apprenticed himself to a master mariner and shipwright of the Ice-realm. There he had encountered Keera's father, Walter I, exiled monarch of the Sceptered Isle, the last of Ranulf's line (if you didn't count the usurper Audemar). And there, kendtman on one of Wat's ships, Gwyl had met Keera. She remembered half-fondly, half with a shudder the time he had pulled her out of a barrel and released her from a bad fate to the terrified arms of her mother, Mirin, Wat's beloved wife, a queen in her own right.

None of them would have believed, in that moment, that Keera and Gwyl would one day wed. None but Gwyl, that is.

"I knew the moment I saw you," he whispered to her once. "I knew I needed you more than life itself."

Keera had laughed at him. "I was thirteen! I was half-dead. I must have looked dreadful."

"You did," he assured her. "Dreadful. Filthy. Skinny. Your red hair all in a mop of tangles. I knew it right away. It was you I had to have."

"Did you know you'd find me when Father sent you off to the Fire Isle?"

"Of course. We figured out that's where you must have gone. I volunteered right away. I wouldn't let anyone else take on the task. Here's my chance with the king's beautiful daughter, I told myself."

"I don't know if I believe that," said Keera. "You and your sugared words." But she hadn't had time to say anything more about it, because then Gwyl had dragged her down under the furs with him, and then the music their bodies made was so delicious she forgot what they'd been talking about.

Body music. Part of the music of the world. That's what the Old Ones meant, in their treatises about music. The music of the Nine Spheres arching over all, and then, the corresponding music of the creatures crawling beneath those crystalline Spheres, reflecting their harmony. If those creatures were very lucky, that is.

Keera felt very, very lucky. She did when she and Gwyl first realized what they felt for each other, and she did now, even though, Dark Ones take it, she knew her body was dis-ordered and out of harmony altogether. She knew she was about to lose her breakfast.

Gwyl came to stand beside her after she finished retching over the side of the skeid. "Child of Fire, this girl's Your own. What possessed me to take one of the Fire Child's on board my gorgeous ship?"

Keera wiped her mouth and took the firkin of water he handed to her. She managed a small sip. "I don't know what's wrong with me."

He folded her to his chest into his own cloak and soothed her hair off her forehead with a finger. "Better?"

"Kind of." She leaned her head against him. He was solid and reassuring.

"Don't lie down. Keep looking at the horizon line. I'll be back. Dark Ones take it, that ship is gaining on us. I need to re-position the sail."

But Keera wasn't listening. Another snatch of her mother's song, the one about the owls, came back to her. *Three for death. Four for birth.* She had a moment of enlightenment, counting backward and thinking hard. What wretched timing. *Fire Child keep me*, she thought. *I'm going to have a baby.*

## Clean

I t's not like ladies don't have babies every day, Gwyl," Keera told him, trying to laugh.

They were lying side by side on the deck with all the others, huddling in their sealskin pouches and hoping to keep warm. Keera wished she were in Gwyl's pouch. It felt strange not to spoon with him in their bed piled with furs back in her parents' fortress. *How much longer?* she thought. She'd never been on a voyage this long, out of sight of land for so many days, and she was finding it pretty uncomfortable.

He reached across from his own snug cocoon and drew a finger down her cheek. As if answering her unspoken thought, he said, "We'll put in at the Far Western Outpost in the Cold Lands late tomorrow."

*Land under my feet,* she thought with relief. *Not this horrible heaving of the waves.*

"I'm thinking we should stay there for a while. Maybe overwinter. You'll need to have some help with the baby."

"Silly, no. We'll be to the Unknown Lands well before this baby comes into the world." Child knows she didn't want to spend any more time at sea, but best get it over with. Get to the Unknown Lands as fast as Gwyl could urge Dragon Wind. She thought about it. "Funny to keep calling them unknown. Now they're known."

"They're vast. We've seen only a little of them, and they don't have a name yet. But the part of it where we'll make landfall does. The people there call it the New Found Land." His eyes were somber in the bright moonlight. "But Keera. Suppose no one at this New Found Land knows much about—you know, about all those women's things."

"You forget. I know a lot about those women's things, as you call them. Although I'm thinking you might have had a wee bit to do with my condition, my man. Maybe just a bit."

Ignoring this sally, he kept on. "But you maybe won't be able to take care of yourself, not by yourself, and—"

"Fiona knows all about it. Hasn't she had two babes of her own?" said Keera. But she felt far from confident. Putting a hand on her middle, she thought she might have felt a faint fluttering. No, she decided. Just her imagination. It was too early. "Aren't you excited, though? A daughter," Keera breathed.

At the same time, she heard Gwyl say, half to himself, "A son. I won't let any son of mine go through what—"

She thought about the desperate circumstances of his childhood, and her heart, as always, gave a wrench. How he had suffered under the hands of his stepfather. If she let it, it made her cry out.

"I've sorely missed Pierrick," said Gwyl, interrupting himself.

She realized he was thinking the same sad thoughts, but his mind had circled around to his brother, and that was the bright spot in his upbringing. Not his terrible parents. Both of them. Keera could never decide which was the crueler, his step-father Maro, who had beaten Gwyl, or his mother Betrys, who had stood by and done nothing to stop her husband. She had even condoned it.

But Gwyl's brother was his best friend. His half-brother, actually. That didn't matter to Gwyl and Pierrick. Keera realized that her own father, Wat, half-brother to King Avery, must have had similar feelings. But he hadn't grown up close to Avery. Circumstances had brought them close, going to war together, working together in The Rising before Avery's brutal murder. Wat's older brother John, though. John was Avery's best friend from birth, and his half-brother too, close in exactly the way Gwyl and Pierrick were close.

Gwyl and Pierrick, only a year apart, had been inseparable from the instant Pierrick was born. Keera realized how hard the last few years had been on Gwyl—probably both of them, away from each other for the first time in their lives. There had been minor separations. Never like this one.

Keera stepped away from the top strake of the skeid and went to huddle in her sealskin pouch, miserable again.

Late the next day, they spotted the dark ridge of land on the horizon. Gwyl pointed it out to Keera. "Nearly there," he said, giving her a reassuring squeeze.

Keera looked reflexively over her shoulder. A dot in the distance showed her where their pursuers rode the whale lanes in their wake.

"Yes," he said. "They're still there. Still following us. But we've outrun them to the Cold Lands. I'll be interested to see what happens when we land. We're headed to the settlement everyone calls the Far Western Outpost. Will these strangers land there too? If they do, we'll see who they are."

The skeid made a bound as the wind came up.

Keera suppressed a little scream. "I'll be glad to set foot on dry land. You of the Sea Child revel in this. The rest of us, not so much."

"How are you feeling today, my darling?"

"Better. Maybe it's nothing."

He looked at her.

"But I think I'm right," she said.

Then Gwyl moved away from her to talk to the rowers about the safest way to angle the skeid in closer to land. Some among them had come into the harbor before, but Gwyl never had. It was actually not so much a harbor as the mouth of a fjord. The seas were rough because of the race of the tide through the fjord into the sea, and the cliffs on either side were high and forbidding. They'd have to move in toward the coast at exactly the right angle to keep the waves from overtopping them. Keera wasn't worried. Well, she was, but only the way those not of the Sea-Child always worry when they're on water or around it. She just wasn't particularly worried. Gwyl knew his business.

No one had the time to wonder about the strange ship just behind them. They were all too busy getting to shore without shipwreck. And so they did.

After they anchored, Gwyl carried Keera in his arms through the surf to the rocky shingle. When she set foot on land at last, she praised her Child.

Then he made busy securing the skeid. He left a group of his mariners on board to guard it. "That stranger ship is coming into the fjord, too. I don't trust it. I don't trust their intentions toward us," he told Keera.

Then he hustled Keera up the pebbled narrow path to the top of the cliffs, where a small town huddled, its stone and turf dwellings dwarfed by an immense mountain of ice just behind.

Soon Gwyl was settling Keera by a hearth fire and bringing her something hot to drink.

"My lady wife is with child," he told the hostess of the small inn. "Is there a healer in the town, someone who knows about such things?"

"A midwife in the Upper Settlement some leagues away," said the hostess.

"I won't need a midwife," said Keera. "It's not my time yet, not for a season or two. And darling," she said to Gwyl, "I don't need a healer either. Women's stomachs are unsettled at times like these. It's a natural thing."

He looked down at her doubtfully.

"Don't worry so," she whispered to him, smiling.

But then the door to the inn banged open and two men stepped in, their hands on the hilts of their swords.

Quietly Gwyl put himself between them and Keera.

"Gwyl, son of Maro?" said one of them.

"Who wants to know?" said Gwyl.

"You're under arrest."

"By whose orders? Under whose authority?"

"I want no trouble here," said the hostess, looking from the men to Gwyl and back.

"By the authority of His Majesty King Ansgar of the Ice-realm," said the man who seemed to be in charge, ignoring the innkeeper.

*So I'm right*, thought Keera, staring at them.

"Ansgar has no authority here," Gwyl said. Nevertheless, his hand strayed to the hilt of his own sword. The hostess shrieked.

"Oh, but he does. He claims this land."

"He may claim it," said Gwyl, "but he hasn't taken possession of it. Let me be. I'm a peaceable man."

"You're in receipt of stolen property. You're a thief," said the man of Ansgar.

"I think he means me, husband," said Keera to Gwyl. She had gotten a chill, listening. Just as her forebodings had told her, these were Ansgar's henchmen. She knew she needed to pay closer attention to this inner voice of hers.

Gwyl put a hand on Keera's shoulder. "This woman is my wife," said Gwyl to the two men. "If Ansgar thinks he's her owner because he kidnapped her years ago, he's sadly mistaken. No one owns my wife."

"Enough talk," said Ansgar's man, drawing his sword. His companion did likewise. "Come with us, and turn over the woman."

What happened next seemed, to Keera, to happen in a blur. The men of Ansgar stood astounded and disarmed. With a few deft moves of his own blade, Gwyl had flipped theirs out of their hands and across the room.

"And here I thought I was out of practice," he murmured to Keera.

"No fighting in my establishment," the hostess said, her face turning an angry red. "The lot of you, get out."

Gwyl bent to pick up the other men's swords and handed them each to Keera. "Keep those for me, will you, darling?" he said. "I apologize, hostess. These men are very rude, but we won't want to cause you any trouble." He bowed to her, nodded curtly to the men, and steered Keera by an elbow out of the inn.

Once they were outside, he took the swords from her, stepped over to the cliff's edge, and threw them both off.

The men were scrambling out of the inn after them now. Gwyl shoved Keera behind him and drew his sword again. "One step closer, good sirs, and you'll find yourselves without hands and maybe noses. Move down the path before I change my mind and come after you anyway."

"We'll return," blustered the man who'd done all the talking. But as Gwyl stepped toward them, they backed away from him in a hurry and hustled themselves down the path. They stopped and looked over their shoulders at him.

He stood watching them, his sword drawn. So, muttering, they continued down the path.

Gwyl waited until they had moved out of sight.

"Let's get to Dragon Wind," said Gwyl, guiding Keera down a secondary path, reconnoitering every turn to make sure they didn't come unexpectedly on the men of Ansgar. When they got to the shore, Gwyl took off his boots, strung them around his neck by a thong, and waded out to the ship with Keera in his arms. "You're as light as a little child," he murmured against her ear. The mariners left on board helped him get her into the skeid and tucked into her sealskin pouch.

*Dark Ones take it*, thought Keera. *I wanted to sleep in a real bed.*

"I'm going back on shore to find my men," Gwyl told her. "This village is tiny. I'll be right back."

Instead, Gwyl's foray lasted all night, and he had to fight his way back to the skeid with his mariners. While Gwyl and Keera had climbed the path to the inn, Ansgar's men had been busy rounding up any of Dragon Wind's mariners who had come on shore. Ansgar's men had begun marching them to the stockade in the settlement on the next fjord. Or that's what they meant to do. Gwyl, as he told Keera later on, leaped out at them from ambush, cut his mariners free of the rope tying them together, and then they'd all turned on the officers of Ansgar, chased them, laid them out bleeding on the rocky shore, and escaped.

Keera knew. She couldn't sleep at all and watched the whole thing from the deck.

By dawn Gwyl was aboard again, and all of the mariners, only one hurt. Keera saw to him. Just a flesh wound.

"We left two of those rascals dead," Gwyl said, giving her a satisfied smile.

"So bloodthirsty," she muttered.

"Thought you'd be happy to see me."

"I am," she told him, "only you know how much I hate it when you go off like that, leaving me behind to wait."

"Darling," he began. Keera recognized his reasonable tone, the one he took with her when he saw she had something reckless in mind.

"Stop right there," she said, giving him a quick kiss.

He stood in the early morning sunlight holding her in his arms and smiling at her.

"You are very stinky and dirty," she told him. "I am too. I know it. I was looking forward to one of those sweat baths they have here, the *badstu*. And I wanted to sleep in a bed."

"We'll have to put that off, my darling. I have a plan."

She frowned.

He glanced at her sideways. "I think some of your spooky qualities are rubbing off on me, Keera. I know exactly what you're thinking."

They were both remembering the last time he left her alone to wait. Went off to war, rode off with her parents to fight their bitter enemy, Caedon. And then Keera had taken action herself. And then Caedon lay dead.

"But my plan isn't to leave you here and go off fighting. It's to get out of here with our ship and head to the Unknown Lands as soon as we resupply. It's not safe here for us now," said Gwyl. "Especially now we've killed some of Ansgar's people. They'll be after us."

"What about Fiona and Pierrick?"

"They're at the Upper Settlement. We'll head there right away, resupply there, see them, and if they're not ready to go yet, let them know we're sailing on ahead of them."

"And while we're at this Upper Settlement, take a nice cleansing sweat in the badstu there?"

"If we possibly can," promised Gwyl.

But when they got to the Upper Settlement where Fiona and Pierrick were supposed to be waiting for them, Keera and Gwyl found them gone.

They had been cautious where they landed, this time. Gwyl pulled the skeid into a protected cove well before the main harbor of the settlement.

Then, while his men restocked the skeid with food and fresh water, Gwyl led Keera to the badstu, and they both emerged a candle measure later, rosy and scrubbed and clean. Gwyl had been able to shave his face clean of his scruff of a beard.

"I liked it, though," said Keera, stroking his cheek. "It was scratchy. It felt good."

He looked a promise at her then. But there was no time to fulfill it. "You're making me burn, Keera," he murmured to her before turning away.

"You'll just have to wait," she said, grinning.

He put out a hand to her face. "I love this little dimple of yours, when you smile like that," he said.

"Hush, man. We'll lose all our resolve, and we need to move fast," she said.

Their plan was to head straight to Pierrick's and Fiona's farmstead up above the settlement. They knew they needed to hurry, not tumble into the nearest patch of shrubbery.

Keera kept waiting for that urgent feeling she got around Gwyl to cool down a bit, to settle into comfortable familiarity, but so far, it never had. She wanted just as much to get him alone, and his clothes off him, as she ever did, and if actions reflect thoughts, he felt the same.

*Maybe when we get to the farm and can settle down for the night, safe with our friends,* she said to herself.

But when they reached the farmstead, it was deserted except for a single servingman.

He pulled his forelock. "Master and Mistress say to tell you they've taken ship already with a party that put in here a sen'night ago," said the servant. "You're to follow as soon as ye may."

"Why?" Keera said. She looked around her at the deserted farmstead, its stone and turf buildings isolated and lonely. The fence by the house, the one that enclosed the near field, was broken down. The stones of the entrance door looked blackened by fire; the door itself, of timber, looked like someone had stove it in and then hastily, badly repaired it.

The servant didn't reply.

"Why?" Keera asked again. "They were waiting here for us to arrive. Why did they leave?"

"That I cannot say, mistress."

"Cannot or will not?" muttered Keera as she and Gwyl followed the path back to the settlement.

"I don't like it," said Gwyl. "That house looked like someone attacked it. Let's get on board ship and out of this place as soon as we may. We'll catch up with Pierrick and Fiona at the New Found Land."

"Suppose something has happened to them. Suppose that man is lying. Suppose they never got the chance to leave." An icy hand of fear gripped her heart.

Gwyl stopped still. He began to nod. "Suppose it has," he muttered. A worried line appeared between his eyes. "I should ask around."

"But Ansgar's men might be about. They know who you are now. They might take you."

"They'll try. I've killed their men now."

They had come to the shore by then. A line of Gwyl's mariners stretched from shore to the skeid, handing supplies along in a chain and hoisting them aboard.

"Suppose Ansgar has taken Fiona and Pierrick," Keera fretted.

"But why would he do such a thing? I'm the one with the stolen goods, you know," said Gwyl.

"The stolen goods, meaning me?"

"Meaning you. Very valuable goods. I'm an important thief."

"And how did Ansgar's men know to follow us here?"

"I don't know," he said, thinking about it. "Someone knows about you. About us, and where we're headed." Then he said, "Keera. I'm going to ask you to do something very simple for me. Will you do it?"

"No," she said.

"Keera—"

"We'll both go," she told him.

They looked out over the sweep of the fjord to the high mountains, and to floating mountains of ice in the mouth of the fjord.

"This isn't a safe place for many reasons," said Gwyl. "Ansgar's men. Those ice mountains. They could tear a hole in Dragon Wind's hull."

"Let's go quickly, then," said Keera, and she began moving back up the path toward the settlement again. "The woman who ran the badstu seemed like a pleasant sort. Let's ask her."

After a moment, Gwyl moved up beside her. "I'm worried too, you know. I'm just worried about you and the baby."

"Then let's be quick," said Keera again. "And the baby is safely tucked inside. She'll be fine."

He reached for her hand and grasped it. Even through the sealskin mitt, his hand was reassuring to her. In spite of her bold words to him, she was afraid.

But nothing happened to them. At the badstu, the woman in charge said she knew Fiona and Pierrick.

"Aye, mistress," said the woman. "Nice folk. Too bad what those newcomers did to them."

"What did they do?" said Keera quickly. Her heart made a strange little skipping in her chest.

"Soldiers of that king, that Ansgar. They drove them from their farm. That's wrong, mistress," said the woman.

"Why would they do such a thing? These people are friends of ours," said Gwyl. "That's why we're worried."

She shrugged.

"And where did they go? Are they all right?" said Keera.

"For a bit, they hid up in the hills. When the soldiers left, they came back down to the inn over there." She pointed. "There was a man, gathering up settlers for the New Found Land."

"And our friends went with him?"

The woman looked from Keera to Gwyl, her eyes suddenly suspicious. "Why do you want to know that?"

"We're their friends. We were to meet them here and sail to the New Found Land with them," said Gwyl.

"And that's your ship, down there in the fjord?" she said, looking past them to the sea.

"Yes," he said.

Keera suddenly realized. She gave the woman a smile. "Gwyl," she told him, putting a hand on his arm. "We could be agents of Ansgar. Spies for him. This good woman won't betray our friends to any such."

The woman looked at them uncertainly.

"My man Gwyl is Pierrick's brother," Keera told her.

The woman looked over at Gwyl skeptically.

"We don't look much alike, I know," said Gwyl to her. "But Pierrick is my brother right enough."

"And Fiona his wife is my girlhood friend," said Keera. "We are all heading for the New Found Land, to settle there together."

"Even with a fast ship, you can't catch them now," said the woman slowly. "So it's safe to tell you, I'm thinking. Yes, they did set sail for those savage lands."

Keera had a sudden thought. "Surely Fiona would have left me a message. She knows her letters, mistress."

The woman beamed at Keera. "Ah, now I see it. You aren't lying. No one would know a thing as strange as that except one who was close acquainted with her." The woman disappeared into her small house and came back out with a parchment.

"Thank the Child," said Keera, taking it. "The goodwife has the right of it," she said, turning to Gwyl. "Fiona and Pierrick left a sen'night ago, just as their rascally servant said."

"He's a bad one, he is. I'm thinking he has probably taken your friends' farm for his own," the woman said placidly.

Keera handed the parchment to Gwyl, who ran his eyes over it rapidly. "They left with a man gathering settlers, just as the goodwife tells us. Our thanks, goodwife," said Gwyl. "We need to leave. Those men of Ansgar are after us too."

"It's a bad business, gentles," said the woman. "That king means to take us for himself, here in our settlement, and add us to his realm. Sea Child go with you."

"Stay safe, goodwife," said Gwyl, handing her some coin. "And thanks for your help. We weren't sure what had happened to our friends and didn't want to leave here without finding out."

"And thanks for your lovely badstu, too," Keera told her as they turned to go.

"You see?" said Keera, as she and Gwyl made their way back to the ship. "What would you have done without me? You might not have known to ask about a message."

"You're right, my darling wife," said Gwyl.

"Forever trying to protect me," she muttered, but she could see he was pretending not to hear.

On board, they could at last take an easy breath.

"Now we're ready for our voyage," said Gwyl.

Keera ran her finger down Gwyl's smooth-shaven cheek again. She always wanted to touch him. She remembered thinking how odd her parents were, always touching each other. They were inseparable. Now she understood. She kissed Gwyl.

"We're ready," she said, "And we're clean, too."

## Voyagers

The beginning of their voyage from the Cold Lands was pleasant. The sun shone brightly, and the breezes were favorable. It was easy to see the floating ice mountains and to steer the ship around them.

"I'm more worried about the growlers," said Gwyl, pointing one out to Keera. "They're much smaller, but see how they float just at the surface of the waves. They're easy to get too close to. If we're not watchful, they can rip a hole in Dragon Wind's hull and sink us."

Keera looked over the side of Dragon Wind at the growler and shivered.

Later on, he comforted her. By then, they'd been at sea a fortnight longer, after their unsettling time in the Cold Lands. "Don't worry. We're lucky. All the signs say we'll have a quick and easy voyage. Besides," said Gwyl. "I have this." He and Keera were standing at the top strake of Dragon Wind. He showed Keera the little needle, her magic needle that Old Dee had given her, the small sliver of metal that always pointed north when Gwyl floated it in a noggin of water dipped up from the butt at the mast.

"You and this needle. You're my luck," he told her.

The sun shone so warm that Gwyl and the other mariners were all bare-chested as they went about the work of keeping Dragon Wind steady on its course over the Great Sea.

Keera looked over at Gwyl enviously. She wished she were bare-chested too. Of course, a modest wife, she couldn't be.

But the next day, the air turned chill and the winds backed against them. Gwyl bundled Keera into his extra cloak, heavy wool permeated with animal fat so that it was waterproof.

"I'm fine," she protested. But she knew she wasn't. Her queasy feelings had just gotten worse. Many's the time she had to step to leeward to lose her breakfast over the side.

"Not much of a sailor, am I?" she gasped out to Gwyl during the latest episode.

"Silly Keera. Didn't we sail all the way from the shores around Lunds-fort to the Western Isle? Didn't we sail all the way from the Northmost Isle to the Fire Isle? Rough waters. And you never got sick. It's that pesky baby."

"Don't talk about her like that!" Keera protested.

"I plan to give that boy a good dressing-down, once he comes out into the light and air," said Gwyl.

"But she's safe inside," said Keera, going over to her sealskin pouch. Gwyl helped her in and sat down beside her to hold her hand.

He looked out to the horizon line, squinting against the sun, his gray Sea-child eyes worried. Keera sat up to look too. A dark patch the size of a man's fist lay low on the horizon to the north-east.

"Storm's coming," he murmured. He gave her shoulder a re-assuring squeeze, but then he sprang to his feet to stride the length of the ship, speaking to the mariners and adjusting Dragon Wind's trim. The ship began vaulting high into the air with the high waves, then dropping deep into the troughs between waves.

Keera crawled from her sealskin pouch and held on, making her way leeward and vomiting again.

"Keep a hand on the stays," Gwyl called back to her over his shoulder.

"I'm fine," she called back. But she didn't feel fine.

They were close-hauled, so the seas and chill spray were coming in on them. Keera's teeth began actually chattering. But down the deck, she saw Gwyl directing the mariners to unreef the sail and close up the oar holes. It gave her a solid feeling, watching him, watching his confidence.

One mariner was bailing in a fury, while others lay at full length, pulling on the backstay and shrouds with all their might. Gwyl was right there with them.

Keera knew how proud he was of Dragon Wind's rigging. He and the mariners had replaced the hempen ropes throughout the ship with ropes of walrus-skin once they'd gotten to the Upper Settlement of the Cold Lands. "Walrus skin ropes are best," he told Keera, "but Nine Spheres, they're hard to find at home. Now we're completely rigged out with them. They're the most durable. And if we're shipwrecked and lose our supplies, we can eat them."

Keera had looked over at him, trying to figure out if he was joking. It was not a happy thought.

"I know a lad who had to eat his walrus-skin ropes," he insisted, but then he was contrite when she had to rush to leeward to vomit yet again.

The small dark smudge on the horizon became a howling storm. Keera huddled miserably in her sealskin cocoon, wishing she were helping out. Everyone was except for her.

"Stay there. Stay warm, my darling," Gwyl told her. His sealskin cap was pulled firmly down, but the fringes of his hair were soaked. "You can't do anything. You'll just get in our way, and it might hurt the baby." He'd given her a rough kiss and then was away, bawling at the top of his lungs over the roaring of the gale, something to do about the sail. Then Keera heard him shout, "Don't let her get abeam." The burliest of the mariners leaned hard on the tiller.

It seemed an entire day went by as the storm struggled to end them, and they struggled to say afloat. But as the seas calmed, Keera saw there was plenty of daylight left. True, in high summer the days and nights melted together into one long shining expanse, but the sun was still well above the horizon.

Gwyl came to sit beside Keera again. "Thank the Child, we weathered it. But we're far off-course now," he told her.

She put her hand out to hold his. "You're exhausted, Gwyl."

"It was exhilarating," he said.

She shook her head at him when she saw how his eyes sparkled. "You of the Sea Child. The rest of us know all of you are crazy."

"Thanks to your magic needle, we'll soon be back on course again." He stripped off his wet things and burrowed around in his sealskin sack for some drier clothing.

The other mariners were doing likewise. Keera only had eyes for Gwyl, though. He gave her a wink.

"How much longer? I want to get you into a real bed with me," she said. He glanced over at her, his eyes fond, as he pulled his sealskin tunic and trousers on. She could tell he was glad she could joke about what they'd just been through. They'd been at sea well over a fortnight now.

"We're maybe halfway," he told her, and her heart sank. "We lost some time in the storm."

Now it was harder, because they were beating against the wind and the sea currents. The mariners sat down on their sea chests along the sides of the ship and ran the oars out, Gwyl among them. *No wonder his muscles are so hard*, Keera thought, watching. The rowers had to take it in shifts, the work was so taxing.

A sen'night later, though, they were enjoying tranquil seas again, and favorable breezes. The sun was warm again.

Keera felt a lot better. She felt worlds better.

She joined Gwyl at the top strake of Dragon Wind.

He put his arm around her and leaned down for a kiss. "They say ladies about to be mothers go through a bad patch, and then it's over, and then they feel pretty fine until the babies are born," said Gwyl. "I heard my mother talking about it once."

Keera nodded. "I haven't practiced midwifery, only watched while my mother did, but I do know that much." She was a little worried, though. Gwyl almost never talked about his own mother. It was too painful.

"Let's hope you're past the bad patch," he said. "Those high seas couldn't have helped."

She relaxed. He sounded perfectly ordinary. The thought of his mother hadn't bothered him, or not much. He wasn't acting like a man sad or tormented or brooding about anything under the sun. He was acting like a happy man, in fact.

And she was a happy woman.

They stood together in the sun as the wind poured into the big scoop that Gwyl's black sail made, and she stole her hand into his. The wind sang in their rigging and the seas ran in a joyous rush past Dragon Wind's hull as she cut through the swells.

But then Keera shivered as a strange feeling shook her body. She snatched her hand back from Gwyl and stood puzzled.

"What is it, my darling?"

"I—" she began. Then she realized. She lifted her tunic and eased her hand into the band of her trousers. She felt around. When she brought her hand out again, it was sticky with blood. She stepped quietly away and drew a noggin of water from the butt at the mast. "I think I'll lie down for a little while," she told Gwyl.

He nodded. He didn't turn around.

She made her way to her sealskin pouch and lined it with her extra tunic. Then she got in. Pretty soon the cramping started in earnest. She tried her best not to cry out. She was losing the baby, but Gwyl didn't have to know. She'd tell him when it was all over. Tears leaked from beneath her eyelids.

Somehow he did know. At least he knew something was wrong. He knew her so well. He crouched beside her, touching her shoulder. "Keera. What is it." His voice was tense.

She opened her eyes and gazed into his, the gray of the Sea Child, fringed with black lashes. Would the baby have had those eyes? The tears rolled down her cheeks. "I'm losing the baby," she whispered.

His eyes widened in shock.

"There's nothing to be done about it," she said to him, trying to make her voice matter-of-fact. "This happens all the time. We'll have another baby." But that's not how she felt inside.

He waited beside her, brushing the tears from her cheeks and holding her hand, until it was over. Then he waited while she cleaned herself up. She stepped to the leeward side of Dragon Wind. She had rolled up her spare tunic into a small bundle. Praying to Fire Child and Sea Child for her baby's easy passage across that river to the Land of the Dead, she held it to her for a long moment. She didn't want to let go of it. At last she did it. She made herself toss it overboard. She made herself watch while the seas took it and dragged it under in Dragon Wind's wake. Gwyl stood close beside her, his arm about her. Now he led her back to her sealskin pouch and helped her in. She turned her face away, dry-eyed. Now she felt nothing but numb. She tried to sleep.

A while later, in the silvery light of midnight, she woke, shaking with chills. Gwyl was still beside her. He had gotten into his own sealskin pouch and had pulled it close by hers so he could keep a hand on her. She felt dizzy. She looked to him, and he mouthed words, but she didn't hear what they were. Soon she was burning with fever.

The next sen'night passed in a blur. Gwyl knew to give her willow bark for the fever, but neither of them had any idea what to do beyond that. She kept bleeding. Then the bleeding stopped, but the fever got worse.

During a rare lucid period, she marveled at Gwyl. At the height of the storm, he'd been in control and dauntless. Now he looked completely terrified, his face pale, his eyes enormous.

"Don't fear, my darling," she whispered to him.

"I'm afraid. I can't stop being afraid," he whispered back.

"Just—if anything bad happens to me, think that I'll be with our baby."

"I won't think about that," he said, and a sudden anger clouded his eyes. "Fight, Keera. Don't go with the baby. I won't let you go." He held onto her fiercely. But then he dwindled back into the mist that enveloped her, and she couldn't hear him any more.

At another moment, he was shouting something about ravens. Releasing them. Following them.

At another, the ship was bucking like a wild thing again, but she wasn't afraid. It was as if the whole of the chaos, the shouting of the mariners, the hauling on ropes, the billowing and snapping of the sail over her, was happening to someone else. Happening somewhere else, and she was looking down on it from a mountaintop or some other vast height.

And then the strange sensation of being still.

And then Gwyl's voice by her ear. "Can you put your arms about my neck? Try, Keera. Please try."

After that, nothing, just some voice far away, screaming something. "Help me," the voice kept screaming. "Help her. Help my wife. Somebody." Hands grasping at her. The ceiling of some house, as if it were floating by above her. Maybe there was a bed.

The mist rolling in again and claiming her.

She felt herself in a small boat heading out over a tranquil sea, even though, in another part of herself, she knew she was on land instead, and in a bed. She felt, rather than saw, that the shore behind her was growing dimmer and farther away with every breath she took.

There were people she loved, standing on the near shore, people who were begging her to turn the boat around and come back to them, but she couldn't see them any longer.

She knew her voyage led away from them, so she raised her eyes to that far horizon and gave in to it, let the boat take her there.

## Two Selves

Keera." A voice at her ear. She forced herself away from the voice and deeper into the comforting blanket of sleep pulled tight around her.

"Keera." A different voice. "Can you hear me."

A murmur around her. Voices. Maybe three.

She burrowed down into the blanket of sleep. The voices faded away.

A hand lifting her head, spooning something into her mouth. A reassuring voice at her ear. She didn't know what the words meant, but she knew she was to swallow. She did.

Sunlight filtering into a small room through some chinks in a wall. She stared at the wall for a long time. What was it made of. Bark, maybe.

A smoky smell. Maybe something cooking.

Gentle sounds. Rhythmic, gentle sounds. Someone snoring. She moved.

Then there was an arm about her, someone pulling her over on her side, and she was staring into a pair of gray eyes.

A whisper. "Thank the Child."

She smiled. "Gwyl," she whispered back.

"You're here. You're with me. Don't ever leave me like that again."

"Did I go somewhere?"

"I thought you had." Gwyl's gray eyes filled with tears, and the tears spilled over down his cheeks, and he was gently kissing her.

She tried her best to kiss him back, but then she was asleep again.

She was in Gwyl's big sea cloak, and she was in Gwyl's arms, and he was carrying her out of a tiny hut that looked to be made of bark. He was carefully settling her down under a tree in the sun, and he was lowering himself by her and pulling her over to lean against him. "Take it slow," he whispered to her.

The leaves of the tree were glorious yellows and oranges and reds.

"We're on land," she said.

"Yes."

"When did that happen?"

"A while ago."

"I'm glad. I didn't want the baby to be born at sea."

"Keera . . ." He hesitated.

She looked up to him. His eyes were grave.

"Keera, you lost the baby."

"I—What?" A sense of panic rose in her. Where was her baby?

Then someone else was beside her, bending over. "How are you feeling, Keera? You are looking so much better."

"Fiona. You're here."

"I'm here," said Keera's best friend in the world. "Now we're all together."

"You must help me, Fiona. Gwyl says the baby is lost. We must find her."

"Shh, my darling. Shh," said Fiona.

Someone else was there, someone she didn't know. A woman who looked like no woman Keera had ever seen before. Keera put out a finger and touched her. She had brown skin.

The woman laughed and said something, but Keera didn't understand her. She spoke in a language Keera didn't know.

Keera was suddenly afraid. Things were happening, and she didn't understand them. She made the sign of the Fire Child.

The brown woman crouched beside her and smiled and nodded. She made a sign in return.

"That's the sign of the Sky Child," Fiona told her. "That's where we are. Here's where the Sky Child's star landed. Can you believe it? The stories are true."

"Right here?" Keera whispered.

"Well. Not exactly here. This land is vast. I think the Sky Child's portal is far to the south of here."

All in a rush, as they quietly talked together, Keera understood what had happened to her baby. She turned her face into Gwyl's shoulder and wept.

He soothed her.

The brown woman brought her something in a brown bark bowl and helped her eat it. She brought a drink in a bark cup, and helped Keera drink it. Pretty soon, Keera was drowsing against Gwyl, within the circle of his arms.

She felt a hand cupping the side of her face. "I'll be back tomorrow, dear friend," said Fiona's voice at her ear. Then she heard Fiona speaking to Gwyl. "When Keera and I first met, I was near death, and Keera sat by me and held my hand and whispered encouraging words into my ear. Now it's my turn."

Had she really been near death, Keera wondered. That country wasn't so bad. Maybe out here in the harsh world was worse. Maybe she could go back there, to the Land of the Dead.

As if he could hear her thoughts, Gwyl's arms tightened around her. "I need you, Keera. Don't ever leave me. Promise me."

"Everyone dies," she whispered.

"Then we'll go together. Promise."

That roused her. She raised her head and smiled at him. "Silly man," she said.

He put out a fingertip and touched her lips. Then he bent to kiss them, and this time she kissed him back.

"Or I know. We'll live forever," he said. "Just not apart. Promise."

"I promise," she said.

As Keera got stronger, Gwyl was able to leave her for small periods of time, but he never would unless Fiona was there to relieve him.

"We're building a stockade," he told Keera.

As if it were her riddle of old, Keera gradually assembled the pieces of the puzzle of their life here.

She remembered the voyage, up to a point. She dimly remembered the baby leaving her body, dimly remembered consigning the tiny form to the sea. After that, she remembered hardly anything of their sea journey.

She remembered they were coming here to a place called the New Found Land, and that Fiona and Pierrick had come here before them.

Now apparently there was a village that needed a stockade. It must need protection. From what?

And gradually, Fiona and Gwyl left her with the healer woman for short periods, because Keera was beginning to get her strength back. She was beginning to feel whole and well. During that period, Keera began to learn the language of the brown woman who had taken her into her own small bark hut to heal her.

This woman's name was Tigeny. It meant "two."

"Why are you called that, Tigeny?" said Keera to her one day as they were sitting outside, and Keera was helping her remove the tough shells from a bristly type of nut called a beechnut.

"Because I am two," said Tigeny. She explained further, but Keera couldn't make out her rapid flow of language. Something about having two selves, a regular self and a . . . some other kind of self. A ghost self, perhaps? But Keera didn't know what that meant. And there was more. Something about owls. "But south," Tigeny said, gesturing. Then she said, "I am from the south. The owls don't live here. It's too cold."

"Why are you here, then."

"I was brought here," said Tigeny. "Some people caught me and brought me here."

"A captive?" said Keera.

Tigeny nodded.

Keera wondered if Tigeny had been made a kind of bondservant. But she lived alone in her bark hut, and she didn't seem to answer to anyone, so if she had been a servant or a slave, she didn't appear to be one now.

Before the first snows, Tigeny pronounced Keera cured and ready to go to her home in the village. Gwyl came to get her.

"Thank you, Tigeny," Keera said. "You are my friend."

"I am your friend," Tigeny assured her. "Come to me if you ever need me. There are things I see I can help you with."

"I will," Keera promised. But she looked back at Tigeny, puzzled. Tigeny was talking about more than heals and cures. Tigeny seemed to be suggesting she could help Keera with something else. But what?

"I wish I could give her something more than this," Gwyl said, laying game and furs at Tigeny's feet.

Tigeny beamed.

"I think these are wonderful gifts for her," said Keera. "She doesn't hunt, and she lives alone. I doubt if she ever gets meat, unless some hunter brings it to her. But she knows all about the plants around here, which ones are good to eat, which ones are useful for healing."

Keera hugged Tigeny goodbye, forgetting all about Tigeny's puzzling words, and then she followed Gwyl through the trees down a narrow path winding into the forest and eventually out to the shore.

"I'll have to start all over again with herb gathering," said Keera. "All the plants are different here in the New Found Land. I'll visit Tigeny and ask her about them."

They stopped often so Keera could rest. The days had gotten chill, so Keera was draped in the big sea cloak again. Gwyl held her to him and walked slowly with her down the path.

"Look," said Gwyl, pointing. "There's the settlement. Everyone calls it Fishers' Bay, because there is such good fishing here. No one will ever go hungry here, that's for certain."

Keera stepped up beside Gwyl. "And is that the palisade you built?"

"Pierrick and I and some of the others, yes."

"Is there danger?"

"Maybe. Some of the people here, the native people, don't like us much. We take their fishing and hunting grounds. There's been bad blood," said Gwyl.

"Tigeny seems like such a peaceful woman. But then, she's not from around here, she says. Maybe her own native group feels differently."

"Fiona told me all about her," Gwyl said. "Tigeny lives by herself. I think these others, the natives who live a little way up the path from us, respect her for her healing skills and leave her alone." After a moment, he said, "Thank the Child for her. If not for her, you'd be dead, my darling, and then where would I be? I don't know what I would have done."

Keera looked over at him and saw he wasn't just mouthing words. He meant what he was saying. "You mustn't talk like that," said Keera. "You would have gone on. You would have been sad, but you would have found someone else to love, in time."

"Never. You don't understand," said Gwyl.

"Life is so chancy, Gwyl. Haven't we just found that out, you and I? You mustn't think that way."

Gwyl just stubbornly shook his head.

Keera decided not to press it. "I learned a few words of Tigeny's language," she said after a moment. "Enough to talk to her a little. But I'm guessing that might not be the language of these others, the unfriendly natives."

"I wonder. If we treated them with more respect, maybe they wouldn't be unfriendly. Do you know, the people in the settlement call them wretches."

"We're the unfriendly ones, sounds like," said Keera.

"We're at their mercy. If they wanted to, they could destroy us. We are so few. But they might not need to. We don't know much about living on this land. They know everything."

"Like Tigeny knowing all the herbs."

"Yes," said Gwyl, "while we could easily destroy ourselves, out of ignorance." Gwyl looked ahead of them down the path. "Maybe they're thinking they should just let us, and that will solve their problem with us nicely. Well, here we are," he said, guiding Keera to the big doors of the palisade.

A man lounged outside.

"Hello, Einar," said Gwyl to the man.

"Relieving me soon, Gwyl?"

"Yes, but let me get my wife settled first."

This man named Einar turned a curious look on Keera and greeted her politely. "Welcome to Fishers' Bay, goodwife," he said. "I'm glad I see you well. I hear things were hard for a while."

"They were indeed," said Keera. "Thank you, good man."

"We take turns guarding the gate," said Gwyl as he led Keera down a lane to a small sod and stone house.

She ducked under the lintel and followed him in.

"Keera!" Fiona exclaimed, rising from beside the hearth to embrace her. "Here's your home. We're all living here together. And here are my children. You've never met them!" She urged the two forward, a tiny boy of around three, leading his even tinier sister by the hand. The boy was Alan, and the little girl, just beginning to totter around, was Rozenn.

Keera exclaimed over them, suppressing the sad thoughts that threatened to crowd in. She hadn't told Gwyl yet what Tigeny had said: that she probably wouldn't be able to have children of her own now.

Pierrick came in then. He came over to Keera and kissed her. He and Gwyl embraced as if they'd never be able to let go of each other. They stepped apart and grinned. Keera suddenly saw what they must have been like, as boys. Then Pierrick reached down to swing the little child Rozenn up into his arms and kissed her too. "Kisses all around," he said, leaning down to kiss Fiona.

He turned to his son. "No, Papa," said the boy. "No kiss!"

Pierrick laughed and lifted Alan up. "You're a big boy now, are you? Never too old for a kiss." He planted one on the little boy's forehead, and he squealed with delight.

Fiona stepped to Keera, a look of concern on her face. She pulled a long shawl out of a chest and wrapped it around Keera. "It has already grown chill. They tell us there will come a hard freeze soon, and then we won't be able to do much except huddle around the hearth until spring."

"We've laid in a good stock of meat and fish, though," Gwyl told Keera. "Our leader Yann knows his business. No one in Fishers' Bay will starve over the winter."

"Let me show you where you two sleep," said Fiona, taking Keera by the hand. "You look tired, dear friend."

Keera gratefully followed her to the small area toward the back of the sod longhouse and sat down in sudden fatigue on the furs of the bed there. "You're right, Fiona. Thank you for all your care. How would I have pulled through this last season without you?"

"Tush. It was Gwyl. I could hardly get that man to leave your side. He loves you so."

"Those brothers are amazing men, aren't they?" said Keera. She and Fiona shared a smile, remembering the night the two brothers boldly got them out of the hands of Caedan and the villainy he had planned to do them.

Fiona gave her a kiss and stepped back into the main part of the longhouse, drawing a hide curtain across Keera's and Gwyl's section of it.

Keera lay down in the furs, pulling the shawl tight around her, shivering and turning her face to the wall. She tried not to let the tears come.

A soft sound made her turn her head. Gwyl was beside her in the furs. He drew her to him.

"A lot to take in. You need to get your strength back, Keera."

She turned to bury her head in his chest. "I have to tell you something."

"What is it?"

"Pierrick and Fiona have such beautiful children. I hoped we'd have beautiful children of our own. But Tigeny tells me—" She stopped. She couldn't go on.

"Oh, darling. You are all I want in this world. You. Don't you understand that? If we were to have children, that would have been a great gift. But I am happy with only you."

She raised her face to his, and he kissed her tenderly. Then they lay back in the furs and he made gentle love to her, the first since the time he'd somehow wedged himself into her sealskin pouch on the deck of Dragon Wind several seasons earlier.

Afterward, she lay with her head against his shoulder. "I wanted a child," she said.

"I know. I wanted a child, too."

"Now life has dealt us a blow," she said.

"Not as big a blow as I feared it would." He stroked her hair. After a while, he said, "You know, when I was a boy, I knew mostly fear. If not for Pierrick, and for my mother's sister Elene, I wouldn't know what love was at all. Elene cared for both of us, and she loved us. Then she went away, I'm not sure why, and Pierrick and I only had each other. But now I know love in abundance."

"Thank the Child for your brother," said Keera. "Does he hear anything of your parents?"

"If he does, he doesn't tell me about it." Then he stirred. "I'm overdue taking my place at the gate. Do you need anything?"

"No, I'll come out soon and see how I can help Fiona with the children, or the house, or whatever small task I can do." Instead, she slept away the entire day, rousing only to eat a little and get back in the bed.

During the night, she stirred. Gwyl's arms were around her. She smiled into the dark and went back to sleep. In the morning, things were different. She began to take her place in the household and in Fishers' Bay, the small community within the palisades.

But she felt a change in her life, and not just the drastic change of moving to a new and forbidding land. She'd been one self, a self she thought she knew. Now she felt herself another, a different Keera she didn't know at all.

# 2 GWYL: Both

## Wretches

Gwyl could well understand why Pierrick trusted the man who was their leader. This man was from the same rocky peninsula of the Eastern Baronies as themselves. A man named Yann. It was a great stroke of luck Yann had shown up at the Upper Settlement of the Cold Lands when he did. An almost uncanny stroke of luck. Otherwise, Pierrick and Fiona might have been taken by Ansgar's men just as he and Keera almost were.

Ansgar might not know that he, the possessor of Ansgar's stolen property, was Pierrick's brother, but Ansgar surely knew who Fiona was. Fiona, the viceroy's daughter. Fiona, whose father, Caedon's man, secretly went over to Wat's side from Caedon's. Ansgar, of course, was the enemy of them both. The enemy of Wat, Keera's father. And also the enemy of Caedon, usurper king of the Sceptered Isle. But Ansgar had helped Caedon murder the poor viceroy before he and Caedon turned on each other like a pair of quarreling serpents. He knew who Fiona was, all right.

Gwyl shivered as a kind of dread came over him. By now, Ansgar had probably figured out the connection among all of them: Gwyl and Pierrick, the closest of brothers, Fiona and Keera, the closest of friends.

And now that Caedon was dead, Ansgar saw his way clear to sweep up the Sceptered Isle for himself. He'd already seized the little Fire Isle and had driven Keera's parents, Wat and Mirin, out of it. They were hunkered down in their rocky fortress in the middle of the Northern Sea. Gwyl hoped to his Child Ansgar couldn't get to them there.

Wat and Mirin had become almost parents to him. His own parents were—Gwyl stopped himself. It was hard to think of them. His real father had died before he'd even been born. Killed in the Rising. Throughout his entire childhood, his mother Betrys had stood by, watching, while his stepfather, Maro, had beaten him. "He's beating your father out of you, and a good thing, too," she'd told him once. Gwyl couldn't remember a time Maro hadn't seemed to despise him. He thought Maro must have despised him from the moment he was born. But Maro adored Pierrick, his son by Betrys.

The deep attachment Pierrick felt for Gwyl, his older half-brother, seemed to make Maro even angrier. The two boys were so close in age they might as well be twins. Twins who looked so different that no one ever realized they were brothers until they saw the two together, and saw how they acted as one, almost as if they could read each other's minds.

When Gwyl left home, wretched and angry, and threw in his lot with Wat and Mirin, it felt to him as though he'd discovered the parents he'd never had. Pierrick was there, too. Perhaps this was the first division they'd ever felt. Pierrick had known himself loved by his parents; Gwyl had not. So Pierrick respected Wat and Mirin deeply, but Gwyl loved them.

Gwyl remembered how Keera had once tried to explain to him the difference between real parents and true. Her own parents were both real and true, she said. But her mother Mirin had had a wicked father, just as Gwyl had—the only father he'd ever known, that is. And Keera's father Wat had been bastard son to King Ranulf the Fourth, his real father, a man he'd only seen once or twice in his life. The role of Wat's true father, although not the real one, had been jointly borne by his older brother John and their half-brother, Ranulf's legitimately born son the Prince Avery. Both men had loved Wat. When John died, Avery had formally adopted Wat.

"Do you see the difference, real and true?" Gwyl remembered Keera asking him.

*Yes*, he thought. *Yes, I do see it.*

Now, away from Wat and Mirin, Gwyl felt himself a bit adrift. They'd all agreed that this journey was necessary, though.

"We people of the Twelve Realms have another chance, perhaps, in the New Found Land," Wat had told Gwyl, before he and Keera left. "Maybe a chance for a better place where people can live together in harmony. The two of you are our hope—and others, like your brother and Keera's friend Fiona." Despite Wat's reassuring words, Gwyl and Keera knew they might never see Wat and Mirin again. Those who went out to the Cold Lands, and especially beyond them, rarely ever returned to their families. The journey was too far, and too dangerous. So their departure from Wat and Mirin had been bittersweet. But Wat and Mirin had insisted they try not to grieve, even though Gwyl saw how sad they were themselves. "The two of you are young. There's no future for you here," Wat had told him. "We're virtual prisoners on this island, and The Rising is done for."

The reality of the New Found Land was a bit different from Gwyl's hopes for it. Most of the people in Fishers' Bay were people of the Ice-realm. That worried Gwyl a little. Perhaps, deep down, these people's allegiance was to Ansgar. And if Ansgar's men had established a presence in the Cold Lands, how much longer before Ansgar's reach extended here, as far as the New Found Land?

But their leader, Yann, was no vassal of Ansgar's. Like Yann, a good number of the Fishers' Bay residents were from elsewhere, not from the Ice-Realm. Like Yann, Gwyl and Pierrick were from the Baronies. Fiona was from the northern isles of the Sceptered Isle. Keera had been born on the Western Isle, although her true home was on the Fire Isle. They were all from a little bit of everywhere and spoke a little bit of everything: the language of the Sceptered Isle, Baronies speech, the language of the Ice-realm.

Their ways of doing things were beginning to mesh, along with their ways of speaking. That reassured Gwyl. None of them swore ultimate allegiance to anyone back home in their countries of origin.

*This really is a New Found Land*, he told himself. *Wat was right, and Yann feels the same.*

Gwyl was headed to speak to Yann now.

Yann lived in the biggest of all the sod houses in the settlement.

Yann lived alone there. He had no family, none that any of them knew about. But his house acted as a kind of village center for them all. Everyone was always coming and going from it. Yann never barred the door. If you were a newcomer from beyond the Great Sea and had no house, you could sleep at Yann's hearth until you built one for yourself, and Yann would find you the help to do it. If you were hungry, you could eat with Yann from his own kettle.

Gwyl ducked under the lintel and entered Yann's house. He blinked in the dimness.

Yann was sitting at his fire playing on the small harp he always carried. It was an instrument familiar to Gwyl, an instrument from his own part of the Baronies, even though Gwyl had never learned to play one. But he had always loved listening to the harpists as they sang their heroic lays by the hearths of his childhood.

Yann put his harp aside and stood in welcome. "Gwyl. Come to the fire, man. It may be spring out there, but this land doesn't know the meaning of spring."

He was standing on the other side of the hearth ring. Gwyl approached and sat down.

Whenever he encountered Yann, Gwyl got the uneasy feeling he'd met the man somewhere before, but of course he hadn't. The two of them had tried to figure out where they might have met, and they'd given up on it. Maybe they'd encountered each other somewhere, back in the days when Gwyl lived with his family. After all, the villages where they were born lay not twenty leagues apart.

Yann was older than Gwyl, ten or twelve years older, and he wasn't a very tall man. Gwyl was only a bit taller than Yann, although he was nothing like as tall as Keera's father and all her tall uncles. Nothing like as tall as his brother Pierrick.

Still, Yann was a commanding presence, slender and lithe, as skilled at the sword as Gwyl was himself. They'd had a few practice passes with each other and recognized in each other the training they'd received from some of the best arms masters of the Baronies. Maybe that's where they'd met, Gwyl thought now. Maybe Yann had been one of the older boys at Arms Master Estafan's establishment, when he and Pierrick had been small boys just starting out there. He reminded himself to ask Yann about that sometime.

After serving Keera's father Wat, Gwyl had wondered if he'd ever know the same respect for a leader again. Yann came close.

"Tell me, Gwyl," said Yann now, summoning Gwyl to a place beside him at the hearth. "What must we do about these people, these so-called wretches. Many in the settlement are urging me to assemble a party of men to go out hunting them. To kill their leaders and drive them off. What would you do, in my place? Give me some good advice."

"Sir," said Gwyl. "I wouldn't attack them. I'd try to befriend them instead."

"How do you think we'll be able to do that? After all, they're getting more and more hostile. They're destroying our traps in the forest. Last week, they set fire to Oskar's small house. You know, that old trapper who lives out there by himself beyond the palisade."

"I haven't heard about that."

"It wasn't so bad. They didn't kill Oskar. But they could have. And they destroyed everything he has built for himself here."

Gwyl made a promise to himself to pay closer attention to the goings-on about Fishers' Bay. The winter had been harsh. He and Pierrick, Fiona, Keera, the children. They'd all stayed inside and to themselves, the four friends and the children. Staying apart from the rest of the community was dangerous in a land as unforgiving as this.

"But tell me," said Yann. "Why do you think of these wretches as people like us? I see you do think of them this way. That makes you unusual, Gwyl. Most of the Fishers' Bay folk seem to think of them as animals, wild and threatening."

"That makes no sense to me, sir. They are. They are people like us." Gwyl shrugged. "If not for one of them, my wife would be dead. That was a generous act. I wonder why any of them would think of us in kindly ways. We're encroaching on their traditional hunting and fishing grounds. Why wouldn't they feel hostile toward us?"

"So what do you advise? What should we do about it?" said Yann. "After all, we have to eat. We need shelter. We can't pull up stakes and leave, not after we've built all this."

Gwyl thought about it. "Sir," he said. "When I was a boy, I remember well what happened when we on the peninsula began fishing in the waters of the Mid-Isle out in the Narrows. Those islanders took offense. We were encroaching on their traditional fishing grounds. Our villages and the men of the island came to blows. We hated one another, but we never thought of those Mid-Islanders as animals. We never called them wretches."

Yann laughed. "Do you know, I fought in that war. If you can call it a war. It was a sad affair. Good men died on both sides. It was my first experience of combat. An eye-opener. Our baron and the king of the Sceptered Isle labored a season and more on negotiations between the two parties before the matter was settled. And all for nothing. We could have had those negotiations without all the blood and bad feeling." Yann's eyes had turned serious. His strange eyes. "I fought against a good friend in that war. If not for great good luck, we might have killed each other."

Gwyl nodded, trying not to stare at Yann. Something about the man's eyes unnerved him, he realized, and so did something in his tone, as he told his story. Gwyl was thinking who might have been in power during the brief Mid-Island War. "Baron Gilles?" he asked. "Was he baron then, as he was when I was a boy?"

"No, that was before Gilles extended his territory to encompass the peninsula. Baron de Mornay was our overlord, if I recall. An old man. At his death, Baron Gilles saw his opportunity, and then we were his."

"And on the other side, King Caedon of the Sceptered Isle," said Gwyl.

"Indeed. Caedon had styled himself king by then," said Yann. His voice was soft. He set his harp down on the bench beside him, turned aside, and busied himself with some small matter.

Gwyl sat wondering at Yann. It was not lost on him, how Yann had put it. *Styled himself king.* Could Yann perhaps have sympathized with The Rising? But Yann was looking at him again now, expecting an answer. "Don't go to war with these people everyone calls wretches," said Gwyl. "Trade with them, sir. Draw up agreements between them and us."

"That's good advice. It's in line with my own thinking. You and I may be the only ones who think this way." Yann stood and took a turn about the longhouse. He came back to the fire. "Do you know, Gwyl, I must admit this—in my darkest moments, I wonder if it was a good thing we came here. Not just us. All of us of the Twelve Realms, exploring westward, establishing settlements here in the Unknown Lands."

Gwyl looked at Yann, startled. "You think we shouldn't be here?"

"We are here," Yann emphasized. "But I wonder. I do wonder if we should be." He seemed to shake off his strange musings then and returned to the practical. "I'm appointing you, Gwyl, to go to these natives nearby and try to craft an agreement. Perhaps if we create a working arrangement with them at the very outset, and if there is good will on both sides, we can live together peacefully, and both sides will benefit."

"I'll do my best, sir," said Gwyl.

Yann clapped Gwyl on the shoulder. "See it done as soon as you can. Then come to me and tell me."

"Sir, I will," said Gwyl.

The next day, Gwyl told Keera goodbye.

"I don't like this. It's dangerous. Everyone says the wretches are dangerous."

"Darling, you and I already agreed. It's wrong to call them wretches. They're human beings with as much right to take care of themselves and their families as we have." But Gwyl felt his heart stop at the thought of leaving her, if only for a few days. They'd almost been parted forever, at least on this shore of the wide river separating the living from the dead.

"You're right, Gwyl. I'm just afraid for you. I've been hearing some awful stories."

"I'm sure they're telling their womenfolk awful stories about us."

"Their womenfolk," Keera echoed him. "Their womenfolk. And our womenfolk. What foolish women. How much protection they need from their menfolk."

Gwyl inwardly cringed at the tone of her voice and the expression on her face. "Forgive me, darling. I didn't mean to imply—"

"Oh, yes, you did," she said, and left with a scowl, dropping the hide curtain to their alcove behind her as she entered it.

"I'll be back in a few days," he called after her. Later, he was to hate himself, over and over, that he didn't step through the curtain to give her a last kiss.

But now, at the door of their turf house he stopped, because Pierrick was blocking his way. "I'm going with you, brother," he said.

"Everyone is worrying about me. These people are peaceable. I'll be fine."

"I'm going anyway," said Pierrick.

So the two of them headed out into the forest together, with only a small sack of provisions and a sword apiece. They'd be back with their wives soon.

"This is just like old times, brother," said Gwyl. He was glad Pierrick was along. They'd had too little time together these last few years and really, when he thought about it, they'd been inseparable their first two decades of life. It was odd not spending every waking moment with Pierrick. Now, after a time of separation, they were together again. They and their families. It made Gwyl proud that he and his brother stood together in this new land, protecting and providing for their families.

"Why do you have to do everything that misbegotten brother of yours does?" Gwyl remembered Maro demanding of Pierrick one time during their boyhood. "You're already a head taller than he is." But Maro's sour disapproval hadn't stopped Pierrick from following Gwyl around everywhere, and it hadn't stopped him loving Gwyl deeply, or Gwyl loving Pierrick deeply back.

After several leagues of walking down the path that led from Fishers' Bay northward, the brothers could tell by the smell of smoke that they must be nearing the village of the people their own people insisted on calling wretches.

They stopped and looked at each other.

"What now, brother?" said Pierrick, almost in a whisper. "Do we just walk in there?"

"I suppose we do," said Gwyl, nearly whispering back. Why, he wondered, were they lowering their voices in this ridiculous way? It's not as though they were trying to sneak into the village.

Before they could think it through, a fierce yelling erupted around them, and they were swarmed by men of the village and seized, their weapons wrested away from them. Despite being taken by surprise, they both fought hard, but in the end they were dragged to the fire of their attackers' village. It happened so fast and Gwyl was so taken aback that he hadn't thought of drawing his shortsword until too late. *I'm losing my touch*, he thought in desperation.

Their captors stepped away from them, leaving Gwyl and Pierrick in the middle of a ring of bare-chested, bronze-skinned men dressed in hide trousers.

Beside the fire stood a man so imposing Gwyl decided he must be their leader. Gwyl bowed low to him. Beside him, he saw Pierrick do likewise. This tall man exchanged some words with his men in their language. Then he turned his eyes on Gwyl and Pierrick.

"Why come to our village?" he said in the language of the Baronies.

Gwyl answered. "I honor you as the leader of these men. But why have they seized us and taken our weapons? We're here peacefully, a gesture of friendship from our own leader."

The tall man didn't reply. He just smiled. Then he turned to his men and said something else in their language. Some of them grabbed Gwyl and Pierrick and hustled them to a stand of trees beside the village. A man tied Gwyl's wrists together, and when he tried to wrestle away from the man, another one hit him over the head with some kind of club and he slumped to his knees, half-stunned.

When he came fully to himself, he was strung up with his hands tied above his head, the rope slung over a stout branch of the tree above him. He tried calling out, but no words came from his mouth. Out of the corner of his eye, he saw Pierrick had been slung in the same way from another branch of another tree. Pierrick was yelling angrily.

The men of the village ignored the two of them. They gathered around their leader and conferred with each other. Then they set out in a line, their leader at the head of it, back down the path Gwyl and Pierrick had just traveled.

Gwyl looked around him. A bit further up the path, the village of the natives stood seemingly deserted. He was tied so his feet barely reached the ground. It took all his strength to keep his feet and not go sagging down and dislocating his shoulders. Pierrick looked to be in the same fix.

He swiveled around so he could look at Pierrick. "How are you, brother? Did they injure you?"

"No," Pierrick called back. "Just this. What about you? You're bleeding."

"Doesn't seem too bad," said Gwyl, blinking the blood out of his left eye where it dripped down from a gash in his scalp. It stung. "Nine Spheres," he muttered. To be caught flat-footed like this. He felt the disgrace of it bitterly.

"Where are their womenfolk?" Pierrick called after a while.

*Womenfolk.* The word made Gwyl wince.

"Looks like only the men were in the village. That's strange, don't you think?" Pierrick said.

"Looks like they've sent the women and children away," Gwyl called back over his shoulder. *Dark Ones take it*, he thought. *Looks like these men are preparing for war. Looks like they're heading for Fishers' Bay.* Then he knew a moment of stark panic. *They're heading for our own village. Our people don't know. Keera doesn't know.*

He realized Pierrick was struggling desperately against his bonds. Pierrick realized too.

Gwyl tried, himself. He put all his weight on the branch, hoping it would break. Peering above him, though, he saw it was too thick to break, and the rope, while narrow, was unexpectedly sturdy. Pierrick was stronger than he was, stronger and bigger. Maybe Pierrick could somehow break his rope. Gwyl looked around hopefully, but by now Pierrick had lost his footing and was revolving around at the end of his rope.

"Save your strength," he called back to Pierrick. "Try to regain your footing, brother."

They were too far apart to help each other. *Save your strength*, he beamed silently at his brother. They might be here for a long time.

By nightfall, Gwyl had lost his own battle with the rope that bound him. He dangled from it, sure his arms would be torn from their sockets. The pain was intense. He knew he must be moaning. He could hear his brother moaning too. And he felt a black, bottomless fear for Keera.

Toward dawn, he decided later he must have lost consciousness, because he didn't even realize, not for a long time, that he'd been cut down and lay prone in the dirt. Later he half-felt himself screaming as someone dragged him to some kind of hut and left him there. After a long time, he realized he and Pierrick were in the hut together. It looked to be made of bark, the way Tigeny's hut was built—Tigeny, the healer who had saved Keera's life. He put out a hand and felt for his brother.

"Pierrick," he said. His voice was thick.

There was no answer. But he could feel Pierrick warm and alive under his hand. At least they hadn't killed his brother. *Or me,* he thought grimly. *Not yet.*

As the day drew on, Gwyl grew more clear-headed, and Pierrick started coming back to himself, too. Gwyl could hear voices outside. He decided not to call out. The voices were speaking that language of the wretches. Gwyl had started calling them wretches, in his own mind. He burned with an impotent rage. But he knew he needed to think clearly.

"Pierrick," he said softly.

"Brother." A faint voice back.

"We seem to be in their village now, the wretches," said Gwyl.

Pierrick was silent.

"Can you tell how badly you're hurt? I don't think I can sit up and try to see to you. I don't think my arms are working yet," said Gwyl.

"I'm afraid, Gwyl," said Pierrick.

"Me too," Gwyl replied. He knew Pierrick didn't mean for himself. He meant it for Fiona and his children.

There was a lot of loud talk outside their hut. Gwyl realized with a deep sense of foreboding that it sounded like victorious boasting and rejoicing.

Now a burst of late afternoon sunlight near-blinded him as the hide door to their hut was flung aside. Rough hands dragged both of them outside to the hearth fire. Gwyl tried to stop himself screaming and failed.

He and Pierrick were flung down at the feet of the leader.

There was a lot of belligerent debating among the men standing over them, or so it seemed.

Finally the leader's deep voice cut off the arguing. He made several definite-sounding statements. There was a murmur, and then silence.

"Sit up," said the leader in the language of Gwyl's childhood.

"I'm not sure we can," said Gwyl into the dirt.

The leader made an impatient exclamation, and he and Pierrick were dragged to their feet. They both stood swaying before the leader.

"You are our captives," said the leader.

Gwyl stayed silent, just concentrating on not falling down.

Beside him, he heard Pierrick begin to say, "This is outrageous. We are peaceful—"

*No, Pierrick*, thought Gwyl desperately, but too late. There was a thud, a blow from one of their captors' clubs, and his brother went down in a heap at his feet.

Now the men of the wretches came over to Gwyl and began prodding him with their fingers. One of them reached over and grabbed him by the jaw and tried to get his mouth open. Gwyl lashed out at him but men behind him caught him and twisted his arms behind him, which caused him to yell with pain. Others were bent over Pierrick, doing the same. They were stripping his clothes off him and feeling his arms and legs. Pierrick moaned a little.

"I claim this one," said the leader, laying a hand on Gwyl. Then he said which man got Pierrick. For a slave, Gwyl guessed. He had no idea what this other man's name was. It was some unpronounceable thing. Later, it turned out the man who took Pierrick was named something like Porcupine. His own master's name, the leader's name, meant Three Stripe. He didn't know that now, though. Just that the two of them belonged to these men.

This leader reached out and knotted a leather thong around Gwyl's neck. He pushed Gwyl stumbling ahead of him across the beaten earth before the village fire to a big bark dwelling, almost as big as their own sod house in their village, but round, not long and narrow. Gwyl tried to look over his shoulder to see what was happening to Pierrick, but he couldn't tell.

"Rest," said the leader, shoving Gwyl through the hide hanging before the opening of the dwelling and into a corner next to some woven baskets. He bent down and tied Gwyl's hands and ankles together. "Tomorrow you'll work."

Gwyl lay shivering all night, trying to keep warm by rolling himself in his cloak and holding it together with his bound hands. The leader smoked a pipe at his own hearth fire, dipped meat out of a pot and ate it, and then went to his soft bed of furs on a platform raised above the packed dirt floor of the dwelling.

*One of us is a wretch*, thought Gwyl. He lay in squalor, desperately missing Keera, desperately fearing for her, fearing for his brother and what that other man might be doing to him. He peered over at his captor's sleeping form. It's *not this fellow who's wretched*, thought Gwyl. *It's me.*

# A Walk in the Woods

The next morning, Gwyl slitted his eyes open against strong sunlight pouring through the door of the dwelling. A woman was crouched staring directly into his face. A toe prodded him. He started back, yelling with the pain of trying to sit up with his hands bound and his shoulders throbbing.

A man, the leader, leaned down and released Gwyl's bonds. The leader said something to the woman, and she laughed in derision.

"Stand up," said the leader.

Gwyl tried. Finally he succeeded. He hadn't eaten in two days, and he was light-headed.

The leader said something to the woman. She came over with a bowl of some sort of gruel for Gwyl. Gwyl ate it down greedily, scooping it into his mouth with his fingers. He licked them when he had finished.

"Thank you," he said. Then he realized. He said it again in the language of the Baronies.

"What is your name?" said the leader.

"Je m'appelle Gwyl," said Gwyl, pointing to himself. "What do I call you?"

"Master, and you don't address me. I address you."

Gwyl nodded.

"You should never address me standing."

Gwyl knelt, as if to a king. He was trying to think.

"Not like that."

A young girl came into the hut then. The woman spoke to her sharply. Gwyl saw she too wore a leather thong about her neck.

She crouched down before the leader, put both hands on his feet, and touched her forehead to the back of her hands.

"Like that?" said Gwyl to the leader.

"Yes, and don't address me again or I will—" The leader stopped to think. Then he reached over for a whip hanging on the wall and mimed what he would do to Gwyl.

Gwyl nodded. He bent down to the leader's feet, put both hands on the tops of them, and touched his forehead to the backs of his hands.

"Good," the leader grunted. "Come with me."

Gwyl limped out of the dwelling after the leader, who was taller than ordinary, of middle years, strongly made, strongly muscled. Gwyl felt giddy with relief when he saw Pierrick standing on the other side of the fire with the man he'd been given to, a much shorter man with a crooked shoulder and a vicious look about him.

Gwyl, Pierrick, and a few other poor beaten-down men with thongs about their necks were formed up into a line by another man while the leader and Pierrick's owner looked on. After a while, the leader and the one who owned Pierrick went to the hearth fire. The man charged with the line of slaves urged them with shouts and blows out into the forest ahead of him. There he set them to work chopping down trees with stone axes and adzes and then chopping the trees into logs. It was a tedious, difficult effort. Many times before the end of that day, Gwyl cried out to his Child for the tools of the ironmonger.

By the end of the day, Gwyl was crying out a different prayer. He was perishing of hunger and his shoulders were burning. The gash in his head had stopped stinging and bleeding, at least.

But several times during the day he got near enough to Pier-rick to exchange a few low words with him.

"We've got to get away from here," Gwyl said.

"How? This man is watching us and he has his spear and his club. And we're tied like this," said Pierrick.

Each one of them had a long thong tied from one ankle to the other. They could stand and chop, but if they moved too fast, their feet got tangled in the thong, and they fell down. This didn't happen to the other few slaves, but it happened once each to Gwyl and Pierrick until they got the hang of it, and this caused great merriment amongst the others, slaves and minder alike.

"We just have to bide our time," Gwyl murmured back.

"Meanwhile, what has happened to our families?" said Pier-rick. "What has happened to Fishers' Bay?"

The minder yelled at them. They didn't understand his words, but they got the gist.

For at least a sen'night, they marched into the forest behind their minder to do this work. But both of them had gradually overcome the injury the rope had done their shoulders, and they were getting strong again. They were being given enough to eat, if just barely.

Gwyl began noticing things. His own master, Three Stripe, was severe but fair. He had stopped talking to Gwyl in the language of the Baronies. Gwyl knew he knew it, but he chose not to use it now. He looked at Gwyl blankly when Gwyl directed a question to him in that language. And that's if he dared at all. Mostly he didn't dare.

It was clear Three Stripe regarded him as a kind of animal. He felt Gwyl's muscles all over and made a satisfied-sounding comment to his wife. Once Three Stripe's wife reached over and fingered Gwyl's shaggy beard, which was growing in now, as he started back from her. She looked over at Three Stripe and made some half-amused, half-disgusted noise.

But Pierrick's master, Porcupine, was a mean man, his temperament matching his sour expression. He beat Pierrick.

It wrenched at Gwyl to see the marks on Pierrick's back. When they were children, Gwyl was the beaten one, and Pierrick was the comforter. But most of the time, Gwyl wasn't allowed to go to Pierrick to give him any comfort or talk to him at all.

By now, their own clothes had been taken from them and they wore hide trousers like everyone else. They worked like animals throughout the spring and into the summer, and eventually he and Pierrick got the knack of working with the sharp, cleverly devised stone tools. Every night, Gwyl went to sleep praying to his Child that Keera was safe, and he knew Pierrick was sending up similar prayers to his own Child. But a cold place inside Gwyl told him Keera might not be. She too might be a captive. Or— and here his mind shied away from the thought. He tried desperately to keep it away from him, but deep in the night it came anyway. She might be dead.

Every morning, when his eyes met his brother's, he knew the same thoughts were haunting Pierrick.

When the season made a turn into harvest-tide and it began to get cold, Gwyl was astounded. He found himself wondering how so much time had gone by. One day soddenly, sullenly led to the next, and the next, and the next, in a long chain of misery. And now, in the colder weather, the wretched slaves suffered more. They had no cloaks. Finally it got so cold they were allowed ratty fur robes to pull around themselves, but not while they worked. The work was hard, though, and they were dripping with sweat by the end of each day, even in the cold. They had strange, supple buckskin shoes on their feet, like everyone else in the village, so at least they didn't go barefoot.

One day, after Porcupine had given Pierrick an unusually savage beating, Gwyl risked the wrath of Three Stripe by going to Porcupine's dwelling without permission, while Porcupine was off somewhere, and crouching by Pierrick and bathing his back with water and a kind of bear-grease ointment he'd seen Three Stripe's wife Squirrel making and putting into a pot.

A shadow fell across the door of the dwelling. It was Three Stripe himself.

"Come with me," he said to Gwyl. He said this in his own language. By now, Gwyl knew enough of it to understand what Three Stripe was saying.

Gwyl and Pierrick exchanged a long look. "I can't stand much more of this, brother," Pierrick murmured as Gwyl rose to go.

"You," Three Stripe barked.

Gwyl rushed to put his hands on Three Stripe's feet and bend his forehead down.

Three Stripe grabbed him by the neck thong and jerked him to his feet and out of Porcupine's dwelling.

"You want a beating too?" said Three Stripe.

Gwyl knew he shouldn't, but he shrugged.

"Why disobey me like this."

"That man is my brother," said Gwyl.

Three Stripe turned and leaned back into Porcupine's door to stare at Pierrick, then back to Gwyl. His expression was incredulous, skeptical.

"He is," said Gwyl.

Three Stripe did a strange thing then. "Explain," he said.

They were standing by the village fire now. Gwyl picked up a stick and bent down. He drew the crude shapes of man and woman in the dirt. Then he drew a baby in the woman shape's arms. Then he rubbed out the man shape with his stick.

Three Stripe had come over and was staring down while Gwyl drew. Gwyl thought Three Stripe would probably kick him or beat him, but he didn't. He stood quietly, looking.

Gwyl drew another man shape on the other side of the woman, and a second baby in the woman shape's arms. Then he rubbed out the babies and drew two boy shapes. He pointed at one boy shape with the stick and then at himself. He pointed at the second boy-shape and then in the direction of Pierrick.

"Ah," said Three Stripe. "I see." He stood considering. "But that's over now. You belong to me. The Big One belongs to Porcupine." The Big One is what they'd come to call Pierrick. As for Gwyl, he wasn't sure he had a name. If he did, he didn't know what it was. When Three Stripe needed him, he just pointed at Gwyl and said, "You."

Now he said to Gwyl, "Don't go over there again."

Gwyl looked down at his feet. He would, every chance he got.

Now Three Stripe surprised him again. "You don't want to have anything to do with Porcupine. Stay near me." Three Stripe reached out to grasp Gwyl by the shoulder. He turned Gwyl around. With his finger, he traced the scars on Gwyl's back.

Gwyl shivered. Keera had done that once. But she'd done it in love. Not this.

"Why?" said Three Stripe.

Gwyl looked down at the crude figures he'd drawn in the dirt. With the stick, he pointed at the man-figure representing Maro. "He didn't like me," he said.

"There are men like that," said Three Stripe. He turned on his heel and walked back to his own dwelling. Gwyl followed.

From his place crouching against the storage baskets, Gwyl watched Three Stripe closely. Anything he could learn about Three Stripe might lead to an escape. What did he value? Gwyl wondered. What did he love?

One night, something happened that filled Gwyl with a rage so black he nearly rushed Three Stripe to attack him, and consequences to the Dark Ones. Three Stripe had a bundle in front of him at his hearth fire. Gwyl recognized the tatters of his own clothing. Now Three Stripe drew from these tatters a glittering object.

The brooch of the Six Proud Walkers.

The brooch owned by each of the six leaders of The Rising against Audemar and Caedon. Gwyl thought about Avery, the prince, savagely butchered by Caedon as Avery attempted to rescue the princess Diera. About Conal, Avery's best-loved companion, killed in the same action. Both men had owned these brooches. Wat had told Gwyl that these two men had kept their brooches in a niche in a hiding place, and that Wat had found them later. These were the gold pieces that had been reforged into Diera's crown for her coronation as Queen Diera the First.

But there were four more brooches. Drustan's and John's, two more of The Rising murdered by Caedon. Caedon had probably taken their brooches for himself. There was Wat's own brooch, which he wore, always.

And the last was the one Gwyl's mother Betrys had given to him. His own father's brooch. Because his father Rafe had been one of The Rising.

Now this savage wretch, this Three Stripe, had his father's brooch in his dirty hand.

It was almost beyond bearing.

Three Stripe looked over at Gwyl, as if he could sense the rage his slave was directing at him. Then he stood and moved to the other side of the dwelling with Gwyl's father's brooch, and that was the last Gwyl saw of it.

Three Stripe didn't seem to have any children, but he had a wife, the woman named Squirrel who had fed Gwyl that first day. Every night, she and Three Stripe bundled into their furs piled on their bed platform, and Gwyl, from his place huddled on the floor, tried to close the sound of their love-making out of his ears.

He thought of Keera and clenched his teeth so he wouldn't cry out in agony. What might have happened to her, when Fishers' Bay was attacked? The thoughts wouldn't stop haunting him. They came again and again. Again and again, he thought of the moment when she'd let the hide curtain fall between herself and Gwyl, and he saw himself, as if he were looking at another man, not pushing past the curtain and taking her into his arms for a last kiss. He saw himself just walking away. He found himself despising that man.

The material and physical things of life began to get a bit better, if not the despair. At least he had his own moth-eaten fur robe to keep him warm at night now, and his hands and feet weren't tied at night any longer. The minder who took them out logging still used the thongs on their ankles, though.

But Gwyl began thinking hard about how he and Pierrick could get away from the village in the night. All they had to do was lull their masters into a false sense of security, wait for an opportune moment, and sneak out of the village. He began actively planning it. There came a time when he made a decision. They could do it, and he had some ideas about how. He'd let Pierrick know his thinking that very night.

But that night, he wasn't able to get to Pierrick. Porcupine set Pierrick to some demeaning task and stalked around him, threatening him and taunting him, as he did it. Something about making a lot of holes with a bone awl in a leather strap.

Gwyl abandoned his plans for that night, but he kept watching for another chance. Something always happened to forestall it. Porcupine was watching Pierrick too closely, or Three Stripe was watching him. He started realizing Three Stripe was expecting him to try something. Three Stripe was a smart man who guarded his assets carefully. Gwyl, his slave, was one of those assets.

Then the weather turned viciously cold, at least as cold as it was in the Cold Lands. Back home, winter was cold, but nothing like this.

During the winter, the slave team didn't go out into the forest any longer. The snows were too deep. But the men of the village still hunted. They were all equipped with strange platforms made of the thin wood of saplings crisscrossed with buckskin thongs that they wore on their feet to keep themselves from sinking in the snow.

*Thank the Child for these devices*, thought Gwyl. Without the strange platforms on their feet, the village men wouldn't have been able to hunt, and they would all have starved for sure. But Gwyl also knew that without these platforms and the knack of using them, he and Pierrick would have to wait for spring before they could think of escape. There was the path out of the village. The snow was packed down hard on the path. But they couldn't just stroll down it. They'd be seen and hauled back. They'd have to make their way through the woods, where they could hide.

Gwyl still went a short way out into the woods with the other slaves to chop firewood. In such bitter cold, the work painfully numbed his hands and feet. And he spent hours before the fire in Three Stripe's dwelling, meticulously scraping and preparing deerhide so that Three Stripe's wife could make it into the hide clothing and the strange shoes they all wore. She made furs for Three Stripe so that he would be warm when he went hunting. None for Gwyl. It was clear she didn't think Gwyl needed that kind of protection.

Sometimes he huddled in his corner while Three Stripe entertained the men of the village at a feast in his dwelling. There was a lot of camaraderie and joking and tale-telling at these occasions. On other occasions, though, the men of the village formed a tense little group to talk over serious matters in low voices. Gwyl looked on silently. The worst of it was not knowing how Pierrick was faring. During their frozen forays out to chop wood, he saw his brother, though rarely to speak to. During the time inside Three Stripe's dwelling, he never saw Pierrick.

One starlit night he realized with shock that he'd been left alone. Three Stripe and Squirrel had both gone out. Carefully, Gwyl made his way to the hide covering of the doorway and looked outside. The air was clear, deadly cold, but crisp. He went back for his fur robe and tucked it around himself as best he could. He sidled out of the dwelling and looked over at the village main hearth, which stood burnt out and cold in the light of a bright moon. No one was around.

He stilled himself.

From across the expanse of the hearth, he heard a low murmur of voices. With a sinking heart, he realized the voices were coming from Porcupine's dwelling. There would be no way for him to reach Pierrick and let him know his plan, much less spirit him away on the escape. But Gwyl knew he had to try to get away. If he could do it, he'd have to hope he could come back with armed men for Pierrick. Otherwise, he'd lose this chance along with the others. By now, three seasons had come and gone. He had to try.

The beaten snow path out of the village was a hard crust under his buckskin shoes. He wouldn't need the lath and thong platforms on the path. The people of the village were busy. They wouldn't see, and no one was around to watch him walking away. He'd try to get to Fishers' Bay.

He set out, his breath forming in an icy cloud as he walked, trying not very successfully to shove aside the feeling he was betraying Pierrick by leaving him. He walked for an eternity, or so it seemed. He went numb with cold, and then he could barely feel his feet, his hands, his face. But he knew he was close, so he hurried as best he could, stumbling toward Fishers' Bay.

And then he was there. He could hear the wintry beat of the waves against the stones of the shore. Looking out over the water, he saw no vessels. Not Dragon Wind. Nothing. The little bay was empty.

And here were the palisades. He pushed his way into the caved in gateway and stood in the enclosure. Where there had been twenty sod and stone dwellings, now there were only dark ruins. A triangular shape in the snow drew him. It was Yann's harp, smashed, a few strings still attached to the broken frame.

He stood silent in the snow, his head bowed.

Then he was aware someone was standing beside him. He turned. Without surprise, he saw who it was in the bright moonlight. It was Three Stripe.

*Now I suppose he'll beat me, or kill me*, thought Gwyl, but without emotion. He felt stripped to his dead core.

Three Stripe, who was dressed head to toe in his warm furs, including fur boots, took Gwyl by the arm and led him to the center of the broken down palisades that had once been Fishers' Bay. Three Stripe looked around. He bent down. What was he doing? wondered Gwyl, but mostly he didn't care, just watched Three Stripe without curiosity.

Three Stripe built a quick fire and stood Gwyl before it. He chafed Gwyl's hands and made him stamp his feet.

"This is very dangerous, what you've done. You can die out here," he told Gwyl.

Gwyl looked at him bleakly.

"You see?" said Three Stripe. "They're all gone. Now maybe you'll stop trying to find a way to leave the village."

"My wife," said Gwyl.

Three Stripe regarded him silently. Then he nodded in understanding. Once Gwyl had warmed up a bit, Three Stripe stamped out the fire and led Gwyl like a child back to the village. He put him inside the dwelling, making him sit close by the hearth.

"Stay there. I have things to do. Stop thinking about getting away. All of that is over for you."

Squirrel came in after a while, exclaiming in dismay at the sight of Gwyl. She made him a hot drink and then had him lie down close to the fire in his fur robe. Muttering, she went away again.

Gwyl lay by the fire for hours, staring into the flames. When Three Stripe and his wife came in again and went to their bed platform, he pulled his fur back into his own corner and rolled himself in it. But he didn't sleep. The next morning, he let Three Stripe's wife examine him all over.

"Lucky you. You could have lost fingers, toes," she scolded.

He just looked down wordlessly. He was still waiting to be punished, but punishment never came. Eventually Gwyl realized Three Stripe understood his sight of the burnt-out palisade and dwellings were their own punishment.

It was a long time before Gwyl could bring himself to tell Pierrick what he had seen.

# Born To It

Somehow, Gwyl made it through the endless days of the winter. The only thing that kept him from utter despair was fear. Fear for Keera, of course, and for Fiona and her children. But a more immediate fear for Pierrick. Pierrick was looking more and more haggard. Gwyl wondered if Porcupine gave him enough to eat. Porcupine didn't appear to have a wife, but he must be an important man. Other village men's wives brought him food, and he had a whole dwelling to himself. Porcupine looked well-fed and prosperous, but his slave Pierrick looked half-starved. The few times Gwyl could get to him to talk to him, Pierrick wouldn't complain.

"I have other things to think about," he said.

Gwyl worried when he saw evidence Pierrick's back was bleeding afresh. He worried when he saw how down-hearted Pierrick was, especially after Gwyl told him about his night-time excursion to Fishers' Bay.

*I must try not to be so down-hearted myself,* thought Gwyl. *I must encourage my brother.* But that was almost too hard a resolution for him to keep.

When the first signs of spring appeared, Gwyl was strangely glad to have to rush from Three Stripe's dwelling to line up behind the slave minder on the slaves' first day of real work. The winter inactivity had given Gwyl too much time to think and brood.

As he passed Pierrick, he found a way to seem to stumble into him and then he whispered, "How is it with you, brother?"

Pierrick gave him a wry smile.

The minder barked angry orders at them both, and Gwyl took his place and let the minder put the thongs on his ankles. But he felt some kind of relief. Pierrick had been able to summon a smile, at least. They'd all been sent to their dwellings for their fur robes. Now they were about to head out. Looking back over his shoulder, Gwyl saw most of the men in the village gathered before the village central fire, talking something over.

Gwyl and the other slaves were marched into the forest, but deeper than before. Their minder kept stopping and looking around at the trees, shaking his head, and moving deeper still. Finally he stopped before a towering birch and walked all the way around it, examining it closely.

Then he moved to a stand of cedar. He turned to his team of slaves. "Start with these," he said. He called one of the slaves to him. *One of the reliable ones, not us*, thought Gwyl. Gwyl could never decide whether these other slaves were part of the village's own people or maybe, like Tigeny, who was a person from another group native to this country, they were from a group at war with Three Stripe and his men. A different kind of war prisoner. The minder sent that man by himself away through the forest.

Most of the rest of them spent all day chopping down cedar trees. The minder summoned Gwyl and another man over to him, away from the cedar stand. He led them to a different kind of tree and gestured at it, naming it. Gwyl didn't catch the name, but as he examined the tree, he realized it resembled the spruces he was familiar with back in the Baronies and further north, in the Ice-realm.

The minder gave Gwyl and the other man pointed sticks and demonstrated. They were to dig around such trees and pull up their roots, long and thin, not even as big around as Gwyl's finger but, as he could tell, handling them, supple and strong. He realized how familiar he had become with these spruce roots. They were the thongs that had bound him as he first lay in Three Stripe's dwelling. The thongs that had suspended him and Pierrick from their trees when they had first been captured. Whenever Three Stripe decided Gwyl must be tied up—when Three Stripe suspected he might be thinking of escape, or when he needed to punish Gwyl for some infraction—these were the thongs that bound him. Gwyl and the other slave set to work. By the end of the day, they had a large pile of these roots, and the minder had them coil the roots up.

"Easy duty, brother," Pierrick whispered to Gwyl as he passed by with his stone axe on his shoulder. Gwyl gave Pierrick a sidelong smile. Pierrick actually grinned back at him. But an anxious thought settled on Gwyl. These hard days of work were starting to seem ordinary. Was this to be their life now?

As evening drew on, the minder didn't take them back to the village. It looked to Gwyl as if they were all going to bed down in the forest. And so they did. Now he realized why they'd been told to take their fur robes with them.

In the morning, Gwyl woke up shivering under his robe. They were all covered with a light snow that had fallen during the night. "How are you doing, brother?" he said cautiously to Pierrick, underneath the clatter of the others' activities: finding wood, making a fire, using a dried gourd to dip up grain called maize out of a sack, cooking it into gruel in a clay vessel over the fire.

"Every day away from Porcupine is a good day," said Pierrick. His eyes and voice were grim. His smile was gone now. Then they stopped talking, because the minder was casting a threatening look in their direction.

*Oh, well*, thought Gwyl. At least he'd gotten a smile out of his brother the day before. Not that either of them had much to smile about.

They had hardly finished eating when they all straightened from cleaning up. A shout of greeting rang out through the forest.

The slave who had been sent away the day before was returning. He led an older man Gwyl had seen around the village.

This old man and the minder stepped aside to talk earnestly together, and then they went over to the cedar logs some of the slaves had chopped up the day before. The old man spent a long time looking these logs over, prodding them, holding one up and squinting at it, then another.

Finally he nodded. Next the minder took the old man to the massive birch he had found. The newcomer stood examining it. Finally the old man bent over the coiled up spruce roots, feeling them and assessing them for some purpose known only to himself.

Now, instead of setting the slaves to chopping more wood in the forest, the minder gathered them around the big birch. He motioned to one of the slaves and handed him a knife. *Not us*, Gwyl thought. They'd never trust him or Pierrick with a knife.

The slave seemed to know what he was doing. He headed to the coiled up spruce roots, chose a long one, tested its strength, and looped it around the birch trunk. Then, as agile as some of the forest creatures around them, the man hitched himself by means of this rope up the trunk of the birch. Gwyl stood at the foot of the tree, craning his neck to gape at the climber until the minder shoved him away with an exasperated exclamation. Pierrick rolled his eyes at Gwyl behind the minder's back, but he kept glancing up in fascination too.

The man slit the bark of the tree horizontally all the way around, and then carefully made a vertical slit, hitching himself closer and closer back to the ground as he worked his knife.

Gwyl stood dumbfounded as a vast sheet of birchbark peeled away from the tree and fell down to their feet in a roll.

Now they all trooped further into the forest to a second mammoth birch, and a third. By the end of the morning, the agile slave with the knife had made three rolls of birch bark.

Next, the minder set the slaves to hacking some of the bigger cedar logs into four posts, and then driving them into the ground as the old man gestured and explained how far apart the posts should be.

They were building something, Gwyl realized. The posts were a framework for whatever they were building. He squinted, drawing on his shipbuilding experience. Something maybe around twelve ells long.

The minder summoned them around the older man, who explained rapidly what he wanted them to do. He was talking fast in his own language, a bit too fast for Gwyl to follow, but as the man talked and gestured and demonstrated, Gwyl realized with wonder what they were being asked to build.

They were going to build some sort of vessel. No kind Gwyl had ever heard of, or had ever worked on with the master shipwright he'd served as apprentice in his youth, but a ship or boat for sure.

With rising excitement, Gwyl set to work with the others. First they used some of the cedar to frame up the hull, and they hung it from the posts to work on it. They made gunwales, and then cedar ribs attached to them.

During the day, he became aware that the older man directing their work kept coming over to look at him and what he was doing. The man would walk over, take a look, and walk away. But soon he'd be back beside Gwyl again, watching him.

Finally he put out a hand and stopped Gwyl.

"You've built a vessel before," said the man.

"Yes," said Gwyl, wondering if he was supposed to bend down and put his forehead against this man's feet. But the man didn't seem to expect it. "I've built a ship. Not like this," Gwyl added.

"Like the ships of the ones coming across the Great Sea."

"Yes," said Gwyl. "I built my own ship that came across the Great Sea."

"Explain to me how." The man said a few words to the minder, who frowned at them but stepped away from them and let the man take Gwyl aside and sit him down.

So Gwyl explained as best he could how he had built Dragon Wind, and when words failed him, he drew diagrams in the dirt.

The man nodded thoughtfully when Gwyl had finished. "We don't build vessels to go upon the waves. Our vessels go upon the rivers," he said at last. "I'll show you."

By the time the day was over, Gwyl had become this man's assistant, and had found out the man was called Old Canoe. The type of vessel they were building was called by this word, *canoe*, so the man's name made sense.

They toiled for days building the canoe. They attached thin pieces of cedar to the ribs of the canoe. Then they searched out pitch pine and boiled its sap down to make a gummy substance. They sheathed the cedar framework with the birch bark and stitched it together using more of the spruce root fibers, split carefully in half. Now they coated the seams with the pitch pine's sap.

When the hull of the canoe was finished, the minder hurried his team of slaves to down more cedar and dig up more spruce roots, but Gwyl stayed behind with Old Canoe to craft the finishing touches on the first one: the thwarts bracing the canoe from side to side, spacing out the rowers; the refinements to the hull and to the interior of the canoe.

After that, he copied Old Canoe as the older man crafted the paddles the rowers would wield, broader and much shorter than the long thin blade-like oars used on Dragon Wind and ships like her. And these paddles would be carried and wielded freely by the rowers in the canoe, not inserted through oar-holes into the water, as in the ships Gwyl knew. The canoe rode lower in the water and was much more slender. On Dragon Wind, a row of oarsmen sat along either side of the skeid, but only a single staggered line of rowers down the center of the canoe would row the vessel they were building now. Gwyl was interested to see how that would work.

Unlike Dragon Wind, the canoe would have no sail to catch the wind. That made sense, thought Gwyl. Unless the river were very wide, a sail would probably just be an encumbrance. Still, he thought, it would be an asset on a lake.

Old Canoe expressed great curiosity about Dragon Wind's sail. "I know this sail," said Old Canoe. "I have seen it in the bay. Black, with three lines spiraling outwards from a center. Lines ending in fierce bird heads."

"That's my skeid," said Gwyl, not able to subdue a burst of pride. But then, he thought, *Where is my ship now?* It might be destroyed, and if not, someone else must have sailed away on it, maybe took it as his own. All he really knew is that it was no longer riding at anchor in Fishers' Bay.

When one of the slaves came to summon them again, they went further into the forest to the second pile of cedar and built a second canoe with more of the birch bark.

At the end of their toil, which took maybe a fortnight or longer, they journeyed still further into the forest, this time carrying the long, light craft with them on their shoulders. They walked until they heard a mighty rushing. They emerged from the trees on the cliffs above a broad river gleaming beneath them in the sun of early spring.

Now they were many leagues away from the village. Looking around him with despair, Gwyl realized he had no idea where they were. No idea how to get back to the village or, beyond it, Fishers' Bay. By now, of course, he knew Fishers' Bay had been abandoned. But perhaps the ruined palisades held clues about where the settlers could have gone. After his frozen experience in the woods, he'd given up trying to find out. As the sap rose in the spring and the weather warmed, he turned his thoughts again to what might have happened to the settlers. It was possible they were all alive. It was possible Keera, Fiona, and the children were alive. But when he realized how far from Fishers' Bay they'd come, his spirits quailed.

Yet in other ways he felt a sense of exhilaration. These canoes were their own examples of the shipwright's art, light but at the same time incredibly strong.

His emotions tormented him. Along with the pride, he felt a deep pang of shame. He was aiding these people who had enslaved him. He was building boats and enjoying it, not trying to get away.

The portagers took their canoes down the steep path to the river's edge and left them under the cliff. Then they climbed back up again. As Gwyl stood looking out over the river, Pierrick came to stand beside him. "You were born to this, brother," he said. Pierrick was of the Earth Child.

"Sea Child take pity on me," whispered Gwyl.

"Do you know, brother," said Pierrick slowly. "My first and only moments of pleasure since we were taken have been these. Watching you build these boats." He gave Gwyl a quick embrace and hustled away before they were observed and punished.

## Both

The next task of their team was to hack a camp of sorts out of the forest on top of the cliff overlooking the river.

Gwyl's sense of accomplishment dwindled away into day after dreary day of hard work, starvation rations, and the nightly attempt to huddle together and keep warm. The early spring nights were still terribly cold. At least there was a big incentive to erect shelters as fast as they could. And because they all had to stay close to conserve body warmth, Gwyl and Pierrick could edge near each other and find time to talk. Especially they renewed their idea that they might escape their captors. These plans came to nothing. They were watched too carefully, worked too hard, and buried so deep in unknown country far to the westward that they couldn't think how they'd get back to their families even if they had the chance to try.

"But brother," whispered Gwyl. "We know this river must flow to the sea. We can follow the river east."

"We'd have no way of knowing after that, though, whether to go north or south along the coast, once we found it," Pierrick whispered back.

"I'm thinking south," said Gwyl. But he had no reason to suppose Keera and the others would have headed in that direction, if they'd escaped Fishers' Bay. And both of them knew their wives and Pierrick's children might be dead. They never admitted it to each other. Deep inside, they knew. Or if not dead, maybe captured and taken who knows where. Maybe to live a miserable life of servitude, as he and Pierrick were.

Even when he and Pierrick were overheard and shouted at, they felt secure. They spoke only in the language of the Sceptered Isle together. At least some of their captors knew the language of the Baronies. But when they spoke in this language unknown to their captors, the minder and now a few others who had joined them from the village looked on them with extra suspicion. Once the minder whipped them both, but not hard enough to keep them from doing their work the next day.

As for Old Canoe, he lived apart. He didn't talk to Gwyl any longer. He no longer had need of Gwyl.

The season began to deepen. Slowly further signs of spring manifested themselves. The ice on the river broke up; the deep snow began melting. The camp had long been built, so the slaves hadn't had much work to do.

But now, with the melting of the snow, the slaves were set to their ordinary task of chopping wood for the fire of the new crude camp they had built.

Late one afternoon, as their minder led Gwyl, Pierrick, and the other slaves back to the camp through the lengthened twilight, they saw that all the village men had traveled to the camp during their absence that day and were standing around the central fire. None of the women and children, though.

That's when Gwyl understood why they'd built the camp. He remembered the day he and Pierrick were taken, when they'd noticed all of the women and children had left the village. This camp they had just built, he saw now, would serve as a kind of base for a battle force. The village was going to war.

As they came to the fire, their minder stopped them from rushing to warm themselves, as they usually did. The real men of the village had that privilege. The minder began releasing the slaves' ankle thongs.

Gwyl bent down to rub feeling back into his feet and ankles. When he straightened, Three Stripe was standing before him. He hastened to crouch down and put his hands on top of Three Stripe's feet and bend his forehead down to touch them.

Three Stripe guided him to his feet with a hand. He turned Gwyl around, took the robe from his shoulders, and looked at him hard. He said something to the others. Gwyl knew enough of their language now. Three Stripe was saying, "Look at this. Just like us."

Gwyl looked down at himself and back up at Three Stripe, who overtopped him by at least a head. Gwyl realized that wind and sun and exposure had turned his skin almost as dark as Three Stripe's and the others'. His hair was as dark as theirs.

Only the gray of his eyes would probably betray him now as not one of their people. And his beard, of course. Somehow, the men of The People didn't grow beards. That's what they called themselves. The People.

Gwyl glanced aside at Pierrick. Porcupine was shoving him roughly over to one of the shelters they had built. *That must be where Porcupine will live*, Gwyl thought. He took a good look at his brother. Pierrick, with his long blond hair and big beard, still really stood out. And he had the kind of fair skin that burned instead of deeply tanning, as Gwyl's did.

"Here's our shelter," Three Stripe was saying to him, so he turned his attention back to his master and followed him to the largest of the shelters. They went in. Gwyl started making a fire at the hearth ring while Three Stripe sat and watched him. When he had finished lighting it, Three Stripe kicked a bag of provisions to him, and Gwyl looked in. The meal of the plant called maize filled the bag. As he had seen Three Stripe's wife doing, and as he had done at the camp, Gwyl made a gruel out of this maize. First, he left the shelter with one of the buckets they had fashioned, to dip water out of a small stream below their new makeshift village. It ran into the river, and the water was clear and fresh. He brought it back to their dwelling and made the gruel in one of the camp's clay pots. When the gruel had cooked down, he took it off the fire and let it cool. At last, he offered it to Three Stripe.

Three Stripe ate.

Once he had eaten as much of it as he liked, Gwyl ate what was left.

Before he had even finished, he made his way to the stream again with the pot, scooping out the last of the gruel and cramming it into his mouth as he walked. Sometimes the minder and one of the more reliable slaves did some hunting, and then there was meat in the pot.

Now that it was spring, Gwyl thought, and his mouth watered, maybe meat would be easier to come by. At the stream, he washed the pot. By the time he got back to their shelter, it was full dark. Gwyl just wanted to sleep.

At least there was a fire now, and by now, the heat of it had filled the shelter. Gwyl was used to sleeping with the others around the central fire outside. *This is luxury*, he thought. *This night I'll be warm enough.*

Gwyl went to the edge of the dwelling where Three Stripe had thrown his sacks of provisions, and spread out his fur robe.

But Three Stripe called him to the hearth fire.

"Sit here," he said.

Gwyl came to the fire and squatted down on his heels, enjoying the still warmer place near the fire.

"Old Canoe tells me you helped him build the war canoes."

*So*, thought Gwyl. *I'm right. The village is at war.* "Yes," he said.

"Old Canoe tells me you built one of those ships your people used to cross the Great Sea."

"Yes, that's right, I did."

"Not by yourself."

"I had help. But I did a good bit of the work myself."

"Who helped you?"

"My mariners and my wife's father's workers."

"You're a big man, then," said Three Stripe.

Gwyl recognized the danger he was in. "I'm yours, master," he said, doing that thing with his hands and then his forehead on Three Stripe's feet.

Three Stripe grunted. He appeared to be mollified. "You've been to war?"

Gwyl decided he wouldn't say he'd led his own men in battle. "Yes," he said, and left it at that.

"We took a weapon from you. You can use that kind of weapon?"

"Yes," said Gwyl.

"We have traded it away long ago," said Three Stripe.

Gwyl said nothing.

"Can you draw a bow?"

"Yes," said Gwyl. "The kind in my own land."

"Can you wield a spear?"

"I am not as good at that as I am with the sword," said Gwyl.

"A club?"

"We have a similar weapon called a mace. I can use a mace. Again, not as well as I use a sword."

"Tomorrow, you will show me your skill with the bow," said Three Stripe. Then he went to his own side of the hearth, where he had spread his furs, and lay down there.

Gwyl banked the fire and went at last to his own fur robe, rolled himself in it, and fell into a deep sleep. He didn't even dream restlessly of Keera, as he usually did.

In the morning, he made more maize gruel for Three Stripe to eat, and ate some himself. As he stepped to the hide flap of the shelter, he realized the other slaves had already lined up, and he felt a flat anxiety fill him. He was late. He'd be beaten. But Three Stripe, standing just outside, put out a hand.

"Not you," said Three Stripe.

Gwyl stood beside Three Stripe watching the minder march his brother off with the others to chop wood. Part of him wanted to be with them. Part of him was glad he was not. He was beginning to hate himself. He was beginning to think he had become one of these people and was leaving his own people behind.

He watched Pierrick's bright shaggy head disappear into the thick forest away from him.

"Now," said Three Stripe. He motioned Gwyl to follow him. As they left the circle of the camp, Three Stripe bent to a pile of gear and grabbed up a bow and a quiver of arrows. Gwyl followed him a little way into the woods until they came to a clearing.

Three Stripe handed him the bow and the quiver. He indicated a sapling. "Shoot that," he said.

Gwyl felt the tension of the bow and the bowstring. It wasn't like the longbow he knew. It was shorter and lighter, but he thought he'd be able to shoot it accurately. The balance felt good. He picked up one of the arrows and examined how it was fletched. He nocked an arrow and took up a stance. Then he lowered the bow.

He turned to Three Stripe. "Suppose instead of shooting this sapling, I shoot you?" he blurted out.

"You won't," said Three Stripe. He did a most unusual thing, then. He smiled at Gwyl.

*He's right. I won't,* thought Gwyl miserably. *But why not?* He didn't have an answer. Instead, he nocked his arrow again, took aim, drew the bowstring back, released the arrow, and hit the sapling.

"Good," said Three Stripe. "You'll go to war with us."

As they walked back to the camp, Gwyl was already gathering his hair up with one hand, thinking he'd have to bind it off his face to keep it from being tangled in the bowstring. It had grown halfway down his back by now, and the thong he'd used to keep it off his face had long been taken away from him.

"Here," said Three Stripe, handing him a thong, and Gwyl bound his hair with it.

When they got back to the dwelling, Three Stripe pulled his knife from his belt. His knife with the keen edge. "Take this down to the stream," he said, handing it to Gwyl. "Get that hair off your face. You look like an animal."

When Gwyl came back clean-shaven from the stream, Three Stripe grunted. "Better," he said.

Gwyl handed the knife back to Three Stripe.

In the morning, as before, the village men gathered about the fire, while the minder lined up his slaves. As before, Three Stripe motioned Gwyl over with the villagers.

Gwyl cast a despairing look at Pierrick. Pierrick didn't look back, only down at his feet.

Three Stripe was speaking. "We'll divide into two groups. One goes with me in the first canoe. One with Porcupine in the second." Three Stripe tapped each of the men to go with him on the shoulder, thirteen of them. Fourteen, including himself.

He stepped to Gwyl, looking him up and down and fingering a little bundle of bones and feathers tied in a thong at his throat. He reached out and tapped Gwyl on the shoulder. Gwyl was the last man he chose, the fifteenth.

Meanwhile Porcupine, too, was choosing fourteen more men, most of the rest of them.

"Master," said Gwyl.

Three Stripe turned to him in surprise.

Gwyl crouched down to touch his forehead to Three Stripe's feet.

"What is it?" said Three Stripe. His voice was impatient.

Without daring to look up, Gwyl said, "Pierrick knows how to go on the water. Pierrick is strong. Pierrick can use a bow and other weapons."

"Who is this Pierrick?"

Gwyl thought fast. "The Big One. My brother."

"That is for Porcupine to say. Porcupine has chosen. He has not chosen your brother."

Three Stripe moved his feet out from under Gwyl's forehead and began walking away. "Hurry up," he called back over his shoulder.

Gwyl got to his feet. Pierrick was already disappearing with the others away from the camp after the minder, into the forest.

Gwyl ran to the group of men following Three Stripe as he made his way down the rock-strewn path from the camp to the bank below the river bluffs. There the two big war canoes were tied up to saplings at the river's edge.

In spite of himself, Gwyl felt a thrill as he knelt, bracing his knee against a thwart, about three-quarters of the way down the length of the first canoe, one of the two beautiful craft he had helped make. He ran his hand along the smooth bark of the hull. Three Stripe took his place in the front of the canoe. He handed paddles back. Gwyl hefted his own paddle. He had made it himself.

But he realized he didn't know how to use such a paddle. As the canoe headed out into the main channel of the river, he watched the others and did as they did, wielding his paddle in a way that cleaved the water and propelled the boat smoothly forward. At first the others looked over at him with irritation, especially the powerful rowers at mid-craft, but the Sea Child stood his friend.

Of course She did.

He picked up the cadence of the person in the stern, shaped his motion to the others around him, and soon the canoe skimmed up the river against the current without all of the thrashing around that had put their canoe considerably behind Porcupine's. Now they were catching up.

The man in the stern increased the cadence. Gwyl set himself to meet it and to blend his movements with his team's. Three Stripe, at the prow to scout out snags and obstacles, looked back over his shoulder at Gwyl. Gwyl read approval in his glance.

The unaccustomed motions strained his shoulder muscles, but it was a good pain. His whole body rejoiced in it. He felt at one with the river and the team of rowers.

He felt at home.

And he hated himself.

Both.

## Gull

They had landed well above the enemy village, surrounded by a palisade. Thank the Child, it wasn't a village of settlers from across the Great Sea, like Gwyl and Pierrick and their families. He wouldn't be killing his own. It was a village of other . . . well, people who looked like Three Stripe. Who were these new villagers? From their hiding place on the bluffs above, Gwyl squinted against the sun at the busy little community.

"Who are they?" he ventured to whisper to Three Stripe, who had come up to stand beside him.

"They are our enemy." Three Stripe said a word. Then he headed down the line of warriors, murmuring instructions.

Gwyl puzzled over the word Three Stripe used of these enemies. It meant something like, *the people who don't talk the way we talk.*

Gwyl wondered what they had done to make them the enemies of The People. That's what Three Stripe and the others called themselves, simply The People. Gwyl checked his bow, the arrows in his quiver. He checked to make sure his hair was well tied back. He checked the big club tucked into a leather belt encircling his waist. Aside from the belt and the buckskin about his loins, he, like the others, was naked. The others had painted themselves in swirls and daubs, but Gwyl hadn't been allowed to do that.

"You're not a warrior yet," said Three Stripe.

Gwyl looked over at Three Stripe, who had tensed, fingering the amulet of bones and feathers at his throat. He'd give the signal, and then all of them would attack this little village, peacefully going about its business in the morning sunlight. Gwyl felt a bitter taste in the back of his throat. Women walked back and forth from the village hearth fire to their dwellings. Children played in front of the dwellings. How were they any different from Keera and Fiona, Alan and Rozenn, he thought. But he didn't have a chance to dwell on these difficult thoughts of his.

Three Stripe raised his arm. With a scream to curdle the blood, he dropped it. After that, Gwyl didn't think. He was caught up in the mad rush down upon the village. He found his throat was raw from his own yelling.

The village wasn't as defenseless as it looked. Out of the dwellings and up to its palisade swarmed dozens of men, a force equal to or maybe a bit greater than their own. The women and children scattered with squeals of alarm.

Gwyl drew back his bow and poured arrow after arrow into the bodies of the enemy men. He rarely missed. He thanked his Child and the Baronies arms master who had taught him to steady his aim.

But now the fighting was at too close quarters for the bow. A naked man of the foe was coming straight at Gwyl, so he swung his big club at the man's head. It connected in a satisfying thwack of blood and bone. Gwyl kept going. *If I had my sword*, he thought savagely to himself. He didn't. The club would have to do.

But then, as he beat a foeman down, he spotted something truly strange on the man's person. It was long. It was made of metal and glinted. It was a sword.

Gwyl grabbed it up. Now he was unstoppable. He slashed and cut at the enemy. He hefted the sword in his hand, getting a better grip. The balance wasn't quite right, but it was fine.

Men went down before him, and he showed them no mercy.

Over the heads of the enemy, he saw Three Stripe, taller than any of them. He fought his way to Three Stripe's side. Three Stripe looked over his shoulder at Gwyl with a deep intensity. The two of them fought shoulder to shoulder.

Another of The People set fire to the palisade, and it quickly spread to the whole village. The women and children fled wailing away, and some of The People quickly rounded them up. A few of the enemy warriors still fought grimly on. They must have known they'd be slaughtered if they did, but slaughtered if they gave up, too.

At last Gwyl lowered his sword. His right arm was bloody almost to the shoulder with killing. He'd been clubbed in the head, but it only smarted. Maybe later he'd feel the pain. Now he felt only a chilling kind of triumph.

Three Stripe turned to call to his men.

Out of the corner of Gwyl's eye, he caught movement. One of the downed enemy had risen, just at Three Stripe's back. He was hoisting his club high.

Gwyl lunged for the man and cleaved him from the top of the head into the breastbone. Brains and blood splattered Three Stripe as he turned in surprise.

Gwyl stood heaving over the man as he lay in a broken, contorted heap at Three Stripe's feet.

Three Stripe threw back his head and laughed out loud. He clapped Gwyl on the shoulder, and together they made their way to the center of the enemy village to look over the carnage they had made. Piles of the enemy bodies lay inert. They'd lost a few men themselves, but not that many. A few of their own men had rounded up the captive women and children and were connecting them by long thongs.

Now they made their way back to the river and the war canoes. The blood lust was falling away from Gwyl now. He felt a sick knowingness in the pit of his stomach. He had set upon and killed innocent men, and he had taken their wives and children captive. His mind shied away from Keera's fate. He knew if he thought about it, he'd have to turn aside and vomit and scream out, and he knew he couldn't show such emotions before these men of his war party.

Strangely, he knew he could show these feelings to Three Stripe. *Why is that?* he wondered. He had saved Three Stripe's life. That wasn't why, though. Later, he could tell Three Stripe how the aftermath of the battle made him feel.

Just not here. Not now.

At the canoes, Gwyl saw the dilemma they faced. There had been fifteen men in each canoe, and they were down six men. But that still didn't leave enough room for all the captives.

Three Stripe came up to Gwyl, and Gwyl was surprised to see he was leading the man named Old Canoe. He hadn't realized Old Canoe was part of the war party. He must have come in Porcupine's boat. Surely Old Canoe was too old to be a warrior. But he saw the old man's arms were as bloody as his own.

"You and Old Canoe will make a vessel for our captives and bring them back to the village," said Three Stripe to Gwyl. He gave Gwyl a considering stare. "What is your name?" he asked Gwyl.

Gwyl looked at Three Stripe in surprise. In the language of the Baronies, he whispered, as he had a full year earlier, "Je m'appelle Gwyl."

"What kind of name is that?" Three Stripe muttered. He shook his head impatiently. "What god do you worship?"

"The Child of Sea," said Gwyl, making the Sea Child's sign.

Three Stripe looked at him now with recognition. He reached out and took Gwyl's jaw in his hand and turned it and looked closely into Gwyl's eyes. "Yes," he said. "I see that now."

Then he turned to Old Canoe. "Gull will help you with the elm bark canoe," he said to the older man.

"Come with me, Gull," said Old Canoe.

Gwyl stood puzzled for an instant, and then he realized. His name was Gull now. The two war canoes headed out without him, leaving him behind with Old Canoe and one other of their war party. The war canoes were lighter now, but not by much. They bore away the bodies of the six dead, so that their families back in the village could mourn them.

The other left-behind man watched over their little herd of captives while Gwyl and Old Canoe, quicker than Gwyl would ever have believed it, crafted a large vessel from the bark of a single massive elm they found at the verge of the forest. Gwyl climbed it and took its bark. He and Old Canoe folded the sheet of elm bark and stitched it together using roots Gwyl dug up from a nearby stand of spruce. They spent a day doing this, boiling down sap to make a gum to spread on the seams. After a restless night sleeping on the ground, they loaded their captives and themselves in this makeshift elm bark canoe and the three of them paddled it back up the river, all the way toward home, the canoe surprisingly responsive.

*Home,* thought Gwyl. *Is this my home?* As they came into the village with the captives, the whole village turned out to welcome them, Three Stripe at their head.

Three Stripe took Gwyl by the hand and led him to the central village hearth. The others gathered around it. Three Stripe took out his knife and reached for Gwyl's neck thong. He cut it clean. It dropped at Gwyl's feet, and Three Stripe kicked it away.

Three Stripe held his bone and feather amulet high. "These others killed my son Otter. Otter is gone, but now I have my vengeance," Three Stripe cried out. Gwyl was beginning to understand now. Why Three Stripe was childless. Why they attacked the enemy village. But Three Stripe hadn't finished speaking. He seized Gwyl by the arms and thrust him to the hearth fire. "This is Gull, my son," Three Stripe called out to the rest of the village. Porcupine stepped up to Gwyl. Gwyl kept himself from cringing away from the man, his narrow glinting malicious eyes, the cruel mouth. Porcupine had some quills of the creature for which he was named, and a small bowl of paint. Three Stripe held Gwyl's right arm out straight, and Porcupine stabbed into Gwyl's right shoulder with the quills, and carved with them, and daubed the wound with the paint. Gwyl kept still despite the fierce stinging.

*What are they doing to me now*, thought Gwyl in a kind of shock. *And I'm Three Stripe's son now. Not his slave.*

Porcupine stepped back, and Gwyl craned his neck to look at his shoulder. He had a painted mark there now, etched deep into his skin. He'd seen others with these marks. Three Stripe had three lines etched into his own right shoulder, which Gwyl had finally connected with Three Stripe's name.

Now he himself had a mark. It was just a few lines, curving, a gull in flight.

*These people have taken me. Now they've named me and marked me. I really do belong to them now*, he thought. Beyond the heads of the villagers, crowding around him and smiling, he saw Pierrick staring back at him. Gwyl felt his eyelids prick with tears. He blinked them back. He must not shed them.

# INTERLUDE: THE CLOUDS

Mervin was worried about his friend John Dee. John had not been able to get past what he had seen across that river that separates the living underneath the Spheres from the dead.

Caedon. Where he ought not to be. Not if there were any kind of justice.

Mervin smiled to himself. Dee kept saying Caedon belonged with the Dark Ones. A popular misconception. The Dark Ones were simply the gwrgi. One of the many kinds of creatures underneath the Spheres. They were so feared and misunderstood, though, that ordinary folks thought of them as little more than animals, at best, and at worst, confused them with evil and evil doings.

Caedon was one of the gwrgi. Not many people in the Sceptered Isle knew that. Not at court and around the more populated areas. Caedon certainly never talked about his origins.

Mervin explained it all to John one day, as they lounged at their ease on their cloud platform. "Don't say To the Dark Ones with Caedon. He's already a member of that kind. That's why he has those yellow eyes," Mervin explained.

"Well, then," said Dee, dismissively. "Is there a hell on his plane? That's where he belongs."

"No hell. Some kind of bottomless pit."

"A purely academic distinction," said Dee. "Why isn't he in it?"

Mervin could only shake his head.

He hoped Dee would gradually let go of his obsession. But Dee kept watching.

"There he is, under the tree," he'd say. "Look at him there," he'd say. "He's down by the river, staring across it."

"Give it up, Dee," Mervin would say in exasperation. But the next turning of the Spheres, Dee would be at it again.

One day, Mervin found Dee standing at the edge of the platform, transfixed. And not by Caedon, for a change.

"Now what?" said Mervin, suppressing a smile.

"Look there. It's a bit hard to tell, because these are not their physical bodies, after all. But look. Those two. They are always together. The tall one. And the one who is shorter, but just as commanding."

"Yes," said Mervin, looking too. "I see them."

"I know those men. I know who they are."

"Dee—" Mervin began.

"What do you know of The Rising?" said Dee. He had made himself into a kind of specialist of that particular place and time, on that particular plane. The time on the Sceptered Isle when a band of rebels set out to right a wrong: their king and his heir assassinated, a usurper set up in their place.

Mervin knew why Dee was so fascinated. It was the place and time of his young assistant mage, Keera. She didn't think of herself that way, but Dee knew her powers. She was the one who had killed Caedon. Caedon and Gilles, between them, had engineered the assassinations and the coup. Then Gilles had helped Caedon take the throne for himself. Then Keera had blasted Caedon with fire when he had come after her parents.

"Keera is too young to have had much to do with The Rising," Mervin pointed out.

"But her parents were in the thick of it. And there's the leader of it, right there. That taller man. The one beside him is the man he loved." Dee leaned further off the platform. "Loves," he amended. "See how tenderly they lean together."

"You think they know love, across that river?" Mervin raised a skeptical eyebrow.

"I know so," said Dee softly.

"Dee, you are a sentimental addlepate."

"What if I am?" said Dee.

Mervin threw up his hands and walked away. He had to see a man about a god.

But later on, when he came back, Dee was still watching.

"Now they've been joined by their friends. Three more of them," he informed Mervin. "In life, they were always together. Keera's father is the sixth of them, but he hasn't crossed that river yet," said Dee.

"I suppose every man needs a hobby," said Mervin with a sigh. "I'll bet you had a stamp collection, when you were a boy."

"That one, that's Prince Avery. And beside him leans his lover, Conal. See the tallest one, the man who walks with a limp? That's John."

In spite of himself, Mervin stepped to the edge of the platform and looked, too. "John is a mage," he observed.

"I know."

"But Caedon caught him and killed him."

Dee's eyes narrowed to glinting blue steel. "Only because Gilles arranged it." After a moment, he said, "And there. The young Earl Drustan."

Mervin grunted noncommittally.

"You should be interested in him."

"Why's that, Dee?"

"Because your favorite mage is that young man's mother."

"You're my favorite mage, Dee."

"Second favorite. Little Bird. Aderyn. Ok, admit it. That gets your attention, doesn't it. And there's the last of them. That other one. His name is Raoul, although they all call him Rafe."

"Huh. I thought he was one of Gilles' minions."

"Shows how much you know about it, Mervin. He resisted Gilles to the end. In fact, he resisted him past the end."

"Talking in riddles, are we?" said Mervin. "Oh," he said. "I get it now, why you're so interested. That one, Rafe or whoever he is, that man is the father of your own favorite mage's husband."

"Keera is my favorite mage," said Dee with a grin. "Second-favorite. You're the favorite, Mervin."

They punched each other in the arm.

"Really, Dee. You have missions to accomplish. A queen to serve. Give up on your little hobby and get to work. History is depending on that queen."

"Yes, o wise master," said Dee. But he kept watching.

# 3 KEERA: The Owls

## Inland

Keera thought back to that terrible day, the day Fishers'
Bay was attacked. Their own sod long house was built
close against the far side of the palisades. She remembered how she had flung away from Gwyl through the hide
curtain and into their little alcove. If only she had come out to
him for a last kiss. A last embrace.

Almost as soon as he had gone, she realized her mistake. With a deepening dread in the pit of her stomach, she had run quickly to the gates of the palisade. But she had had to run all the way across the settlement to the gates, and by the time she got there, it was too late. Gwyl had already disappeared down the path.

She remembered going back to the little turf house, disconsolate.

Fiona had come in from washing the children's clothes then, the boy Alan by her side and tiny Rozenn held by her chubby hand. "Don't worry, Keera. Pierrick has gone with Gwyl. He didn't think Gwyl should head off alone to the village of the wretches, no matter how peaceable Gwyl and Yann seem to think they are."

Keera had collapsed in relief.

"The two of you!" Fiona had looked at Keera with an amused smile on her face. "Whenever you're apart from each other, you are heartbroken."

Keera brushed a tear from her cheek and tried to smile.

"It's only understandable," said Fiona, coming to her and embracing her. "What you just went through together."

"I never understood it, what my parents felt about each other, not fully," Keera whispered. "Now I do."

She tried to busy herself with some of the endless household tasks—cooking, water hauling, mending, soap-making, herb gathering—so she wouldn't have to think about Gwyl striding toward the village of the wretches.

But later in the day she and Fiona both turned around, surprised. A slight brown figure stood in their doorway.

"Tigeny!" Keera cried. She rushed to make her friend welcome. "I haven't seen you in too long, my good friend."

Tigeny stepped back from the two of them. "You must take the children and leave at once," she said to them.

Her expression frightened Keera.

"The village is about to be attacked. You have to get out. Take the children and follow me."

Keera and Fiona looked at each other in alarm.

"Gwyl—" Keera began.

"No time." Tigeny was firm. "You have to get out now."

She shoved them both to the door. Fiona grabbed up a child in each arm. They all followed Tigeny to the back corner of the palisade, where she coolly pushed a board aside and helped them through. They had barely gotten to the woods before a horrid screaming and yelling burst out behind them.

Keera thought to herself, *Gwyl.*

She turned to Fiona. "I understand, Fiona," she whispered urgently. "You have your children to think of. But I have only Gwyl. I must go to him, try to find him. He may not know what's happened to us. The wretches he was going off to visit might not be the ones who are attacking Fishers' Bay. He may be able to get these friendly wretches to help us. I'll be able to find out what happened to Pierrick, too. I'll find them, tell them where we're hiding." She knew she was babbling, the words tumbling from her mouth too fast for Fiona to make any kind of sense of what she was trying to say, but she couldn't stop. Still talking fast, the words spilling out of her, she started to rise to her feet from where they crouched in the weeds.

Tigeny grabbed her and pushed her down. Fiona helped her. They held Keera while Keera moved straight from reasonable argument to blind panic. She fought to get away from them.

Tigeny hauled her by the arm into the forest. They all cowered there. Alan's eyes were wide. His mother pulled him to her and held him against her, and cradled Rozenn. Keera stood holding her ears so she wouldn't hear the desperate cries of the villagers. She knew they were all being slaughtered. Fiona coaxed her to crouch with them in their hiding place.

*Gwyl*, she thought. *No.* She rose again. She had to get to him. She must.

In the clearing before the palisades, a woman ran shrieking toward them, one of the warriors of the wretches close behind her. Keera stood transfixed. The warrior raised a club dripping with brains and blood high overhead and brought it down on the woman. Her cry abruptly ceased.

Tigeny yanked Keera down. Keera huddled against her in shock. "He hasn't seen us. Quiet. Wait," said Tigeny. The warrior looked around him and strode back to the palisades. "Quickly." Tigeny touched Keera's arm. She looked around at Fiona where she cringed in horror with her children. "While they are busy back there. We need to get to my dwelling." She led them all deeper into the woods, not by the path Keera knew, but in a trackless roundabout stealthy half-run. Keera held Rozenn to her, and Fiona hoisted Alan onto her shoulder. By the time they came out into a clearing, Keera was fearing she'd drop Rozenn, she was so tired, and she could see that Fiona was nearing the limits of her endurance too. But here they were in Tigeny's clearing. There was her little dwelling. "All of you, get in and stay there. The attackers may bring someone to me for healing."

Once inside, Keera and Fiona put the children down on the floor between them and sat down themselves, wiping the sweat from their faces. They stared at each other with white, set faces.

"I endangered us all," Keera whispered. "Can you ever forgive me, Fiona?"

Her friend embraced her, then turned to comfort Rozenn, who by now was wailing and couldn't stop. Alan huddled against his mother, his thumb in his mouth.

They waited all day. Keera leaned into a corner and tried to sleep, but whenever she managed to fall asleep, nightmares came. The woman she saw killed before her very eyes kept rising up and going down again. Somehow, this nightmare woman became Gwyl. His was the blood on the upraised club. The brains. She wasn't the only one with nightmares. The little group of them spent a restless night of it crammed into Tigeny's tiny bark hut.

In the morning, Tigeny fed them all.

Keera could see poor Alan was trying hard not to cry.

"That's my little man," Fiona soothed him.

Rozenn happily played in the dirt before the fire outside the hut. Keera envied the ability of small children to live carefree in the moment.

"Wait here," said Tigeny. "I'm going back to Fishers' Bay to make sure the attackers have all gone. Wait here for me," she said again, slowly, to Fiona.

Keera knew Tigeny's language pretty well by now, but Fiona, not so much.

"There's food in the pot," she told them. As she turned to slip away into the woods, Keera stopped her. "Tigeny," she said.

Tigeny paused.

"I'm sorry. I didn't do what you said. If the man killing that poor woman had looked up and had seen me standing there, he would have killed us too."

"Yes," said Tigeny.

"I thought about Gwyl. I thought about what they must be doing to him."

"And your friend was thinking the same thoughts about her own man. But she had her children to look to."

"I behaved wrongly."

"Thanks to the Children, we're fine," said Tigeny, making the sign of the Sky Child. "But Keera. You must learn about some things. I'll teach you, at least a little. Then you'll be able to master your fears."

"Thank you," said Keera. As Tigeny melted into the forest, Keera went back miserably to the hut.

She put out her hand to Fiona, and Fiona took it.

"I was too afraid," she whispered to her friend. "Forgive me."

"I'm afraid too," said Fiona.

Late in the day, Tigeny came back. She took Keera aside. "They're all dead," she murmured. "All of them, in the village. The People took no captives."

Keera nodded, feeling sick. *The People*, she thought. *Who are they?* Then she realized Tigeny meant the wretches. The wretches that Gwyl and Pierrick had gone to see. Surely they must have killed Gwyl and Pierrick too.

"Your house is burnt and smashed in. There's nothing left."

Keera turned to Fiona, who had come up to them. She saw Fiona did understand. Her eyes were huge.

"Listen," said Tigeny. "There's another settlement of your kind further south and inland. I think the best thing is for me to take you there."

Keera and Fiona nodded, but they looked at each other in despair. Keera knew Fiona was thinking the same thought she was. What about Gwyl? What about Pierrick?

"I can't leave here," she cried out in a panic. "Gwyl won't know where I've gone."

Tigeny regarded her with pity in her eyes. Somewhere in her, she knew Tigeny must think Gwyl was dead. Maybe Tigeny knew he was. And Pierrick as well. But in some other part of herself, Keera couldn't accept it. She wouldn't.

"You must leave," said Tigeny. "You must." She seemed to know what Keera was thinking.

"I know, Keera," said Fiona softly. "I don't want to leave either. But I have to." She looked over at the children, and Keera followed her gaze. Keera nodded.

So they made ready. Keera knew she had to leave, for her friend's sake. And she knew there was probably little she could do for Gwyl, if indeed there was anything anyone on this side of the River of the Dead could do. But her heart tore from her chest at the thought of walking away into the forest. She thought of the place on her shoulder where her firebird had marked her. A birthmark, others believed. But she knew the truth. Love transfixed by love's burning dart.

Before they left, Keera took a piece of bark Tigeny gave her and wrote on it. *We've gone south*, she wrote. How she wished at that moment for Hildr, the merlin Gwyl had given her so long ago. Hildr could maybe have gotten a message to Gwyl. But they'd had to leave Hildr behind at Gwyl's little house on the islet off the coast of the Fire Isle. The boy Avarr would take good care of Hildr there. Before they left on their voyage to the Unknown Lands, Keera had had to be comforted with that thought.

Now she wished fiercely for Hildr.

Tigeny promised to keep the bark message in case Gwyl or Pierrick ever showed up at her hut. It gave Keera little enough comfort to leave it there, but it was something.

They made ready and trekked away through the forest toward the coastline.

It took them three days of walking before they found the mouth of a broad river that led inland.

"This way." Tigeny pointed. The three women began walking up its banks. They all took turns carrying the children. After another sen'night of walking, they found the settlement. If not for Tigeny's skills, they would have all starved to death, but she knew her way through the forests and down the river, and she knew how to eat off the land.

Tigeny stopped them short of the settlement's palisades. "Here I must leave you. These people don't like people who look like me," she said with a small smile.

Keera gave her a hug, and so did the rest of them.

"Once again, Tigeny, I owe you my life," said Keera to her.

"We all do," said Fiona.

Tigeny motioned to Keera to follow her. They walked a little apart together. "I don't know what to say to you, my dear friend," said Tigeny. "You must learn about yourself. But there are higher matters to understand. Your people have come here to drive my people out."

"No," said Keera, horrified. "We thought we'd find a better life here."

"But we—my people—are here already. This is our life. The better life you want to construct will be on the bones of my people."

"That's unjust," whispered Keera.

"A balance must be found. Keera, you're a part of it. I don't know how, exactly, but you are. I beg you, learn about your powers. Use them to help your people understand."

"I don't understand, myself," said Keeera. She was humbled. Tigeny pressed her hand and looked deep into Keera's eyes. Then she turned and melted away into the forest.

Keera went back to stand with Fiona and the children. They watched until Tigeny was lost from sight.

*Don't leave me, Tigeny,* Keera begged, inside herself. *I need to learn some important things, and I can't do it by myself. It's too hard. Gwyl is gone, maybe forever. I'm far from my parents, far from my home. You're my only hope in this strange land I've come to.*

But before them stood the gates of this other settlement's palisades. Practical matters like food and safety and rest took over from Keera's deeper fears and troubles.

"This settlement is much bigger than Fishers' Bay," said Fiona at last. They looked at each other. Keera hung back. She felt herself unworthy. Let Fiona decide what to do next. Let her speak for them. Fiona gathered the children to her, and Keera watched a resolve settle on her. Following her, they all made their way to the gates, ragged and dirty and footsore.

A man of the Baronies stood guard there. His eyes widened in surprise as they approached.

"Our village, Fishers' Bay, was attacked," said Fiona. "All were killed. We're the only survivors." Keera stayed quiet, her eyes down. Fiona should do all the talking. She felt she had let Fiona down. She'd nearly gotten Fiona and her children killed.

The man at the gate called out to his fellows, who escorted them through the gates. A group of kind-seeming women approached them to welcome them into the settlement. These women took charge of the exhausted little party, figuring out matters like food and shelter. Keera was grateful to them and passively allowed herself to be cared for. She was filled with a dull sorrow.

Eventually they found themselves stuffed in the back of a crowded long house built, unlike their old turf one, of timber. At least they had places to sleep. At least they had food. At least the children were safe.

They soon realized that the whole settlement, called Three Rivers, was a colony established by the Baronies on the broad river that flowed from the coast to its meeting with two other smaller rivers. A rough temple to the Lady Goddess stood at the center of the town. Keera decided to keep her Fire Child sentiments to herself.

The grandest house in the village, timbers and stone, was reserved for the settlement's leader, a man prominent back in the Baronies, who went by a title as grand as his house. The Governor General.

*But, really,* thought Keera, looking around her, *he's just the most important person in a very unimportant, cobbled-together little place on the remote edge of the known world.*

Just the same, others told them, this man had the full support of Baron Gilles de Rais and several of the other most powerful barons of the realm.

"We'll take you to His Excellency soon," their hostess promised. "He's eager to meet you and find out what you know about the attacks of the heathens on your settlement." She didn't speak of their attackers as wretches. She called them heathens. She seemed just as fearful of them, though.

It was a full sen'night before this powerful leader, the Governor General of the colony, got around to interviewing them. At first, it looked like he might be too busy for the likes of a few ragged and destitute women. One of his officers did the interviewing, and it was cursory.

But Keera felt she had to try to get some help for Gwyl and Pierrick, however unsuccessful her attempt might be.

"Good sir," she said to the governor's official. "Our husbands were likely taken by the natives. They may be alive. We beg for assistance finding them."

"I'll relay your concerns to His Excellency," said the official with a stiff smile. "The heathens are troublesome foes. A gnat-bite only, compared to our own power, of course. They're naught but animals. But they do a good bit of damage to our settlements. Up north of here," he said. "That's Ansgar's territory."

*That means no one will do anything,* thought Keera in despair. The ruins of Fishers' Bay were a long way off to the north and on the coast. None of these Three Rivers people knew about that territory or cared. Already Ansgar and the barons were staking their separate claims.

Just when she and Fiona were about to be dismissed without meeting this governor of theirs, the man himself came into the front room of his house, where the interview was taking place.

Keera watched him silently as he came up to them both and inclined his head. He made a gracious gesture to them, although his eyes on the two of them unsettled Keera a bit. He was looking them up and down, assessing them. She and Fiona curtsied to him.

He was an older man, his blue eyes sunken into the fleshy features of his face. His graying hair, tied neatly back, had once been fair. He stood heavyset and tall, dressed in Baronies-style clothing of fine quality. Quite a bit of coin must have been spent, Keera thought, to bring these clothes all the way from the Baronies. A scarlet cloak swept off his shoulders.

He welcomed them to Three Rivers and conversed with them for a few moments. Keera stepped back and let Fiona do the talking, as she'd become accustomed to doing. She gazed around her. Then something Fiona said caused the governor to fix her with an astonished stare.

"Lady, pray come with me," he told her, leading her into an inner room.

Keera stood baffled. But whatever may have triggered this burst of interest in their plight was a good thing, she thought. She sat at the governor's fire, looking around her and trying to stifle her disappointment at his official's reaction. Maybe, with the governor's interest, they'd get some help after all.

After a long time, Fiona came back out with a flushed face. "We're all moving here, to the governor's house," she told Keera. "Get the children and our belongings and come back here with them. Be quick about it."

Keera knew her mouth had gaped open.

"Keera," said Fiona, leaning over her to murmur. "Pretend you're my maid. It's important. I'll explain later."

"Yes, my lady," said Keera. She'd play out her role. She wouldn't fail Fiona this time.

By the time she had gotten their few possessions together and had shepherded the children to the governor's house, servants of the governor were waiting to usher them inside to a very comfortable room. Fiona had a big bed of furs to sleep on. Keera had a much smaller bed in the corner. The children had small trundle beds of their own beside their mother.

Keera scrutinized her friend. She saw Fiona was hugely relieved. But she saw that Fiona was distressed, somehow, at the same time, and that she was keeping her distress tightly controlled.

*What's going on here?* Keera wondered.

Fiona turned to Keera once they were alone. Her friend's expression was hard for Keera to read. Excitement and dread, mingled. "The governor. It's Pierrick's father Maro," Fiona said.

# Enemies of Her Light

After the first shock, Keera's life, and Fiona's, settled into a routine. They all settled in. She and Fiona tried to figure out how Maro had come to be there, and in such a prominent position. They failed. Then they tried not to think about it. They had too many other things on their mind for that.

Keera gathered her hair under a headcloth tied tightly in a knot at the nape of her neck, so her red hair was not so noticeable. She and Fiona played out the fiction that she was Fiona's maid.

"Almost like old times," Fiona consoled her, and Keera saw that she was trying to smile. They both remembered their time on the Northmost Isle of the Sceptered Isle, where Keera and her mother lived incognito, and where Keera spent part of her girlhood as Fiona's companion in the big manor house where the viceroy and his family lived.

Fiona had realized Keera might be in danger if she revealed who she was to Maro. "This man doesn't like Gwyl. I could tell when I talked with him. His look was so cold, when I mentioned Gwyl's name."

"Then we're right to pretend I'm your maid," said Keera. "We need this man. He'll help Pierrick, and when he does, surely he'll have to help Gwyl, too."

She and Fiona stared at each other. Keera knew they were both thinking the same thought: if Pierrick were alive, his father Maro would help him. Once Pierrick was safe, maybe he'd help Gwyl too. Maybe. If Gwyl were alive. If.

Keera determined to be patient. This Maro would surely try to find Pierrick, his son. Keera had her doubts about how much help he'd be willing to give his step-son Gwyl. The brothers had no doubt been taken together. *Or killed together*, she told herself with a chill. That didn't mean they had stayed together, if they were captives.

But if there was something the man might do, Keera would work to the utmost of her powers to make sure it happened, even if only Pierrick benefited. She owed Fiona that much, surely.

It looked for a while as if nothing would come of their efforts. Fiona, as the wife of Maro's beloved son, was treated with every courtesy but mostly ignored. She, Keera, and Rozenn formed a small community of their own, unimportant females who lived a comfortable life away from any affairs of the settlement.

Maro lavished all his attention on Alan, his grandson. More and more often, Maro took the little boy into his own quarters, away from his mother. "Maro puzzles me, Keera," said Fiona, coming back from a meeting with Maro at which she had hoped to persuade him to return her son after an absence of several days. "He says Alan must grow up learning every grace and skill of a warrior of his class. I don't understand that. For one thing, Alan is much too young for that. He hasn't even reached his fourth year. But for another—what could Maro mean by that, a warrior of his class."

"I don't understand it, either," said Keera. She thought of the stories Gwyl had told her of his childhood. Wasn't Maro just some peasant? Where had he gotten his grand ideas, she wondered. How had he advanced so far that Gilles de Rais, the most powerful of the barons, had given him this post in the New Found Land?

It was ironic, thought Keera. She, the daughter of royalty—exiled royalty, but royalty just the same, and Fiona, the daughter of nobility, a high court official, had married brothers who didn't even come of gentle origins, although their fortunes associated with Keera's father had led them to rise in the world. Now here was their low-born father, giving himself airs.

Of course, Keera reminded herself quickly, what did she care about any of that? She and her mother had spent her childhood years in poverty. Her father had spent most of his life as the ignored bastard of a king, relegated to poverty as well, or near enough. All of these notions about rank were foreign to her.

Nothing Fiona said could change Maro's mind about Alan, and nothing could apparently shake the man's sense of his own importance. In the end, Maro brought Alan to live apart from his mother with a few other gently-born boys. Just as if they were at home in the Baronies, these boys had their own minder who tutored them.

"It consoles him, at least, to be with other boys and to play," said Fiona, looking after Alan wistfully during one of the days the minder brought Alan to her for a brief visit. "He has been so frightened and sad. I know he remembers his father. I know he misses him. At least he has friends now, and something to occupy him."

"Do you think Maro will form a party to go after Pierrick and Gwyl?"

"I think he will. The only person he seems to adore more than Alan is Pierrick. If there's a chance Pierrick is alive, Maro will send out a party. And there's a chance. There is."

Keera took Fiona's hand in hers and squeezed it hard. There was a chance. They'd both have to hold on to that possibility. It was that, or run mad with grief.

Maro frightened Keera, especially when he turned a certain hungry gaze on her that she had seen in the eyes of other men. She remembered the days she and her mother spent in the tavern on the Northmost Isle.

*He just thinks I'm the maid,* Keera told herself. She knew some men thought maidservants were fair game for their urges. *I need to keep myself out of his notice. I'm so unimportant. It will be easy to do,* she told herself.

But Maro gave her a bit of hope, too. If he sent a party to find Pierrick, and if Gwyl were with him, surely the party would bring Gwyl back too. She kept telling herself this, over and over, as if saying it, even in the privacy of her mind, would bring it to pass.

She and Fiona carefully never mentioned Gwyl, though. They were especially careful not to let Maro know Keera was Gwyl's wife. Keera knew from Gwyl that Maro had hated her parents. She came more and more to understand that if Maro had anything to do with it, and if their two husbands were still alive, Maro was likely to leave Gwyl to his fate while expending every effort to rescue Pierrick. He blamed Gwyl for convincing Pierrick to settle in the New Found Land. Yet here was Maro himself.

Mostly, though, Maro was an enigma to them both. "He talks about rearing Alan as a gentle," said Keera to Fiona again. She kept trying to figure Maro out. "Yet from everything Gwyl has told me, Maro just lived in some little village with his lowborn wife. They were poor folk. Or close to."

"I know," said Fiona. "Pierrick has told me the same. But I think we're all wrong. Watch Maro, really watch him, Keera. Listen to how he speaks. If you do, you'll notice something astonishing. I've seen him at close quarters now. It's clear he himself was gently born. He has a strange accent, too, as if he were not of Baronies origins. Whatever he was doing in that little village where Pierrick and Gwyl were born, whatever identity he was taking on there and for whatever reason, it was not the real Maro. And have you noticed something about the people here? Many of them aren't Baronies people at all, although this is a Baronies-controlled town. Many of them come from the Sceptered Isle."

"You're right," said Keera, marveling. Ever since they had come to the New Found Land, she had gotten used to a polyglot of languages and people of many different origins. But here— Nine Spheres—there were as many people from the Sceptered Isle as from the Baronies. More, maybe.

Now that they knew Maro better, they could see that while yes, he was healthy, he was not the vigorous man they first took him for. He was indolent. He had a fleet of officials who did all of his governing for him, while he took his ease and enjoyed the good things of life.

There were a lot of good things at the settlement. It was a thriving concern, with its brewers and bakers and distillers. Traders brought sumptuous furs there to exchange for gold. The situation of the settlement at the confluence of the rivers had turned it into the trading center for the entire region.

"This place is a good thing for Maro," Fiona observed. "He'll get rich here."

"After he enriches himself, I wonder if he'll go back home," said Keera.

Maro unnerved Fiona, but he unnerved Keera more.

She doubted he knew anything about who she was. She didn't even bother using a false name with him. How would a man like Maro know much about the politics of the Twelve Realms? How would he know anything about the Fire Isle and her parents? He had no idea Gwyl served her father, or Keera didn't think he did. If he had known, he would have been enraged. Hating Gwyl. Hating her father. The two things, combined. Gwyl would have no chance with Maro, if Maro knew such a thing.

Luckily, or so Keera thought, Maro knew only that Pierrick had lived in the Ice-realm after his departure from home. He doubtless didn't care what Gwyl had been doing.

The Baronies and Ansgar were at odds. Keera knew Maro must be anxious to get his son back into Baronies-controlled territory, especially if, as rumor around Three Rivers had it, Ansgar had taken over the coastal settlements to the north, where Fishers' Bay used to stand. But suppose Maro had decided Pierrick was dead. He might never send a search party.

"You know," said Fiona. "Maybe he does think that. And the more I know him, the more I think he loves himself and his own ease above all. But if he loves anyone else, anyone else at all, it's his son. I don't think he'll give up. I think he'll send an expedition."

Day after day went by, sen'night after sen'night, and he did not.

Keera began to lose heart, and she saw Fiona had begun to lose heart, too. Keera began wondering whether Maro had begun seeing little Alan as a kind of substitute for his son. Maybe it was enough for Maro that he had Alan.

She could see how Maro's control of Alan ate at Fiona.

"But I can't do anything about it," Fiona whispered miserably to Keera. "If I lose Maro's sympathy, he may keep my son away from me entirely. He may never send out an expedition. I have to keep on Maro's good side. I have to."

As for Keera, her heart was riven with anxiety, almost beyond bearing. She feared for Gwyl and missed him fiercely.

And now she had a new fear, based on the rumors she kept hearing of the fighting back in the world they'd come from, fighting between Ansgar and the forces of Gilles de Rais, the powerful noble who had forged the Baronies from a group of warring, jealous warlords into a single force.

Before they left for the New Found Land, Ansgar had driven her parents out of the Fire Isle, and they were in their rocky island fortress. Suppose now he came after them? Suppose Gilles de Rais did?

"But why would they?" said Fiona, reasonably. "Your parents aren't a threat to Ansgar, not any longer. Surely they'll be left in peace now. As for Gilles, how would he know much about your parents at all, or care enough to attack them?"

Keera knew Fiona's words were sensible, but she still feared. Ansgar was a spiteful, vengeful man. She knew this. She knew that if he saw an opportunity to crush her parents, he'd take it, simply because they had stood up to him and thwarted him, at least for a time.

As for Gilles. When she thought of Gilles de Rais, an involuntary shudder racked her body. She couldn't put her finger on exactly why he made her feel so anxious, but he did. She thought back to the time, in her childhood, when Old Dee had seemed to ward him away from her, as if he were a threat to her.

She knew that somehow Gilles had been a threat to her mother's sister, Jillian, although she could never be sure how. She didn't think her mother even realized. Only she, Keera, realized.

And the attack she had made on Caedon continued to haunt her. Sometimes she relived the triumphant moment when she rode her firebird from the skies and destroyed him. At first, she didn't think she'd be able to defeat Caedon, not even with the help of the Fire Child and her firebird. He was too powerful. Something, some force, protected him. Then that force had stepped away from him and allowed him to be destroyed. Deep inside her, she knew that the force protecting Caedon had something to do with Gilles de Rais. She just didn't know what. And she didn't know why Gilles had suddenly withdrawn his protection.

Keera tried to shake off these vague fears. What, after all, did they have to do with her life here in the New Found Land, with all its difficulties? Nothing.

On the other hand. She had to remind herself that Maro was this Gilles's man. And Caedon had been Gilles's man, in ways she didn't understand. There was a connection. What was it?

She didn't spend a lot of time on these worries. She had too many other worries to occupy her. Her main worry, of course, was Gwyl. What might have become of him, and whether he were alive or dead, and—if he were even alive—what she could ever do to find him. Those were the worries that preyed on her.

And if he were dead.

And if she knew he were dead.

Well, then. That would open up a vastly different landscape of difficulty. In that case, how could she possibly move on with her life?

With a bitter smile, she remembered the words she had spoken to Gwyl when she was recovering from her illness after losing the baby.

She remembered how Gwyl had said to her, when he thought she might have died, *I don't know what I would have done.* And she had replied, *You mustn't talk like that. You would have gone on. You would have found someone else to love, in time.* And he had said to her, *Never. You don't understand.*

Now she did.

And so, preoccupied with that thought, she hadn't been prepared for the blow life was about to deal her.

She couldn't do much about her own situation in the community of Three Rivers, but there was one thing she could do. She could keep her ears open around the governor's house.

Keera, as a lowly member of the governor's household, was commandeered into service to cook and clean and see to all of the emissaries, and all of their entourages, as they came and went, bringing the news from the Baronies to Maro and taking the news of the New Found Land back to Gilles.

"How I hate this masquerade we have to maintain," Fiona whispered to her on one of these occasions, as Keera whisked out of their rooms to see to the laundry.

"I don't," said Keera. "You forget, in my girlhood I once ran a tavern almost single-handedly. And as a mere servant, I can get close to these emissaries and their people. I can find out a lot this way."

"But Keera," said Fiona, looking a bit frightened. "Your work takes you far too close to Maro. You know how he looks at you."

"It's a risk I have to take. Some chance remark he might let slip could help us find Gwyl and Pierrick."

Fiona had to nod unwillingly at that.

In her own situation, Fiona couldn't find out very much about the political gossip of the settlement and its relationship to the politics back home. She'd be trotted out for some state dinner but then expected to go back to her rooms and stay there.

*You'd think it would be the reverse,* Keera thought to herself. *I'm the lowly servant, and Fiona is the wife of the governor's son.* But in fact, Fiona's role hampered her.

On the other hand, Fiona was in the perfect position to observe Maro up close.

"So we make a great team," Keera told her.

Meanwhile, Keera was everywhere, her ears open.

Whenever an emissary from Baron Gilles arrived, all the way from the Baronies, Keera made sure she overheard as much of their news as she could. If she thought very hard about it, she would have wondered why she cared. If she'd probed deeper, she would have realized it was Baron Gilles who fascinated her, in a horrifying kind of way. And then she wouldn't have known what to make of that feeling. Why it was important at all.

She and Fiona had been in Three Rivers for several seasons, both of them frustrated and as nervous as the town's many cats, because Maro continued to put Fiona off whenever she tried asking or even gently hinting about his plans to search for Pierrick.

On a particular occasion, Keera was called on to help with Maro's own household matters. An emissary from Gilles was arriving. Everything in the Governor-General's dwelling must be perfect, his head servant told Keera, assigning her to go to Maro's own room to air out his bedding. There was some shrewd, calculating look in the servant's eye that Keera didn't care for.

Gingerly, she cracked open the door of Maro's personal quarters. She'd been all over the Governor-General's residence, but never in here.

She approached Maro's bed and began gathering the bedclothes from it. She'd get the help of one of the serving lads to drag the mattress into the courtyard and then upend it and shake all the old rushes out of it. She already had a pile of fresh new rushes in a corner of the courtyard. She and the serving lad would stuff them in the mattress cover and carry it back inside.

"Ready, mistress?" The serving lad stuck his head in the door.

"Not quite, lad. If you will, go to the courtyard and make sure the new rushes are in a tidy pile ready for us to stuff in the mattress. Then come back and help me with these heavy furs so we can air them out," she told him.

The furs were heavy indeed. Keera struggled to haul them off the bed platform. She was beginning to feel a bit sorry that she hadn't made the lad stay and help her with them, when she heard a step at the doorway. *Here he is back*, she thought. *Good*.

But it wasn't the lad. As she bent over the furs, gathering them up, someone grabbed her from behind and fell heavily on top of her, crushing her down into the bed. Before she could cry out, a big hand covered her mouth.

As Keera struggled and kicked, she heard this man say, "Get out of here, lad."

*Stay!* Keera cried out in her mind. *Don't leave me with this man!* But the hand over her mouth pressed down heavily. She tried to bite it, but couldn't.

The man, she knew, was Maro. "Easy, mistress," he breathed in her ear. She felt him fumbling with himself, and with her skirts. She twisted and then did manage to bite his hand, but he just bore down on her, his heaviness pressing her into the bed so she could scarcely breathe.

"My lord." A voice from somewhere. Not the lad.

"Aye?" Maro eased up on her, and Keera scrambled to get away from him. "What is it, man? You see I'm occupied here."

"Sorry to interrupt your—" The man paused for a tiny moment. "—your pleasure, my lord, but the baron's emissary has just arrived."

"Ah," said Maro. "I'll be out directly."

Now he turned to Keera, who had flipped on her back and was inching away from him across the bed.

"A pity," Maro said, giving her a quick looking over. "We'll have to resume our play later on, mistress."

"Keep your hands off me," Keera cried.

"Hoity-toity, you're naught but a maid servant. Isn't that right?" Maro gave her a strange knowing kind of smile. "So you'll do as I say, mistress." Maro set his clothing to rights. He strode from the room.

Keera crouched on the bed, breathing hard. As soon as she calmed down a bit, she grabbed up the furs off the bed and lugged them to the courtyard.

"You. Boy," she said to the serving lad, who was watching her with big eyes. "Spread these out to air them. Then stuff the fresh rushes into the mattress case. I'm going to the housekeeper. I'll do nothing more for this churl."

"Careful you're not beaten, mistress," said the lad in a voice squeaking with fright.

"I'm the Lady Fiona's maid, not the Governor-General's. He can't compel me," said Keera, her eyes snapping. She stalked away from the courtyard.

In spite of her bold words, the housekeeper sent her back. "I'll speak to the Lady Fiona, mistress," said the housekeeper, her keys jingling at her belt. "You'll do as you're told."

"But he—"

"I'll hear no complaints about His Excellency," said the housekeeper with a cold look. "If maids go flaunting their bodies about the place, no wonder a man might think to ease his hunger. Look to your own self, mistress, if you think of yourself as a modest maid."

Keera fumed with suppressed fury.

"I'll have no answering back, mistress," said the housekeeper, as she bustled away. "Or I'll have you beaten, Lady Fiona or no. She should understand she can't have a shrew of a maid about her, without that shrew being properly disciplined."

Keera quieted herself. The more attention she drew to herself, the worse her situation would get and the harder it would be to help Gwyl.

*But what if no effort under the Spheres can help him?* she thought in despair. *What if, long since, he has already made that journey across the river, and Pierrick with him?*

She went carefully back to Maro's rooms. The man was off seeing to his guests, she thought. He wouldn't be back, not so fast.

She returned to the work of righting Maro's chamber.

The housekeeper stuck her head in the door. "After you finish up there, see to His Excellency's sitting room," she directed. "He will be meeting with his guests there shortly. See the fire is poked up and cushions are on the benches." She gave Keera a dangerous look.

"Yes, goodwife," Keera made herself say meekly.

She went to the sitting room and began working there. At least, if Maro came in, he'd be with others, important emissaries from Gilles. He could hardly try to tumble her in front of them. She was safe from him, at least for a while.

And to him, she argued to herself, one serving girl is as like any other. *It's likely that after this day, he'll forget I even exist, and go after some other hapless woman.*

Then she felt ashamed of herself, for the thought. She told herself she'd warn all the others, so they could protect themselves from Maro if they found themselves alone with him.

She was bending over the hearth with a poker when voices outside the room told her that people were coming. One of the voices was Maro's.

Her heart sped up. She tried to hurry, her sensible arguments with herself forgotten.

The men who came into the room, Maro and two grandly clothed others, the emissaries, Keera supposed, acted as though she were invisible. She continued quietly about her work.

One of the emissaries, the older and, Keera supposed, giving him a quick sidelong look, the more important of the two officials, came to stand before the hearth ring, holding out his hands to the warmth.

"Your Excellency, these lands of yours are cold," he said. "I suppose you must get used to it. I never should."

Maro returned some noncommittal remark. Keera carefully kept her head down. She carefully didn't look in his direction.

"Shall I tell His Excellency the news?" said this emissary to the other one.

"You'll be overjoyed to hear it, Governor-General," said the other man.

"I supposed you had to be bringing me news of substance," said Maro. "It's a long trip."

The first one made a self-important little cough. "My news has notable implications for you and your position at home, back in the Sceptered Isle."

The Sceptered Isle? Keera wondered. Surely Maro came from the Baronies. Then she thought again of what Fiona had noticed, his unusual accent.

The voice of the emissary broke into her speculations.

"The traitor and that so-called queen of his have finally been brought low," he said.

Keera stood stock-still in the act of picking up a cushion.

"Could it be true?" said Maro, a thrill of triumph underlying his voice. "Fine news indeed. They've both been executed?"

"Not exactly. This part won't give you as much pleasure, I'm afraid. Our baron's general led the attack against them. The traitor and his queen fought on that fortress isle of theirs down to the last man. The two of them, those two tinpot monarchs, fought ferociously. One of them died outright, I forget which one, and the other died of his wounds shortly after. Or her wounds. Whichever," said the emissary carelessly.

Keera felt the blood drain from her face. She felt as if she were about to faint. The dead traitor and his queen. It was clear to her. They were her parents.

She suppressed a moan and ran from the room. The emissaries and Maro, absorbed in their news, paid her no heed. She dropped the cushion in the corridor and ran sobbing through the main hall of the dwelling and out into the daylight.

"What's that all about?" she heard someone say behind her.

"What now? Stupid girl." The housekeeper's voice. "These frippery sluts of young women. More trouble than they're worth, I'm sure."

Keera ignored these voices following her out of the residence. She was desperate to be alone. She couldn't just run out of the gates of the palisades and into the forest. That housekeeper would send someone after her to make her come back.

The temple of the Lady Goddess loomed before her. She thrust its doors open and rushed to a seat at the front, where a statue of the Lady gazed out through compassionate blank eyes over the interior.

A startled priest regarded her.

"I have many sins," she choked out. "I must pray." No one could follow her in here. No one would dare violate the quiet and sanctity of the temple.

The priest nodded to her and left her there.

Keera dropped to the stones of the floor in a heap and cried until she had no more tears to cry.

Her parents were dead. One had had to watch while the other was cut down. Then the Children in their mercy had taken that one, too, across the boundary to the Land of the Dead. She remembered what Gwyl had said to her. *Don't ever leave me. Promise me.* She remembered what she had whispered back. *Everyone dies.* But he had said to her, *Then we'll go together.* That's how her parents had felt about each other, too. And one of them had had to watch.

Was Gwyl even alive? she wondered again, for the thousandth time. Suppose he had died, alone and away from her. If he were alive, she vowed to herself she'd make him promise. *Don't ever leave me. Promise,* she'd insist to him. And if death had to come, *Then we'll go together.*

How hard such a promise was to keep.

She moaned in agony at the idea of Gwyl alone and in pain. She moaned in agony at the thought of her parents and what they'd been made to endure.

She would have lain on the stones all day, lain there until the priest made her leave the place, if not for the birds.

A flurry overhead. Two owls, swooping through the open doors to the temple and up to the rafters. The priest came scolding in, brandishing a stick at them.

Keera picked herself up and tried to put herself to rights.

"Nasty birds," said the priest, his face turning red. "Do you know," he said, half-turning to Keera as she stood there wiping her face with her sleeve, "These birds will drink the Lady's holy oil, if you don't keep them out. They are birds of darkness. Enemies of Her light."

Keera blinked up at them. Their bodies were buff, but their faces were stark white. She'd seen them before, birds like these. Back home, she'd seen them. And here, they swooped at twilight over the marshy sedges that stretched between the rivers, hunting. Why were they here in the daylight, she wondered.

"Ghost birds," spat the priest.

Keera realized she probably needed to get out of the temple. She'd take the roundabout way back to Fiona's rooms so the housekeeper couldn't grab her and make her go back to Maro's quarters. She got up off the stones and rose to her feet. But she stopped at the door to the temple to peer back up into the rafters, where the pair of owls perched now, oblivious to the priest's rage, and his brandishing stick.

A voice, crystal clear, came to her, although no one was near, only the muttering priest.

*Gwyl is alive*, this voice said in her ear. *And Tigeny has given you a task to perform.*

Keera looked around her wildly. No one was there.

Words of Tigeny came back to her. "I have two selves," Tigeny had said, then something about owls. And other words Tigeny had spoken. "Keera. You must learn about some things. I'll teach you about yourself. I'll teach you to master your fears."

*Teach me.* She found she was saying this to the owls, out of the depths of her grief. There was no one else to say it to. She whispered these words aloud, to the rafters where the owls perched, watching her. And she didn't understand why.

## Owl Flight

It took Keera a while to tell Fiona what had happened to her parents. She didn't want to talk about what Maro had almost done to her, either. After that first day, she harbored the illusion that if she never talked about either one, she could convince herself she'd dreamed them. She knew she had not. They lay on her heart, especially what she had learned of her parents, a fierce ache that never went away.

Possibly, she thought much later, the shock of learning about her parents' deaths blinded her to some disturbing things she had sensed in Maro.

But knowing her parents were dead sent her into a terrible grief. She had known there was a good chance she'd never see her parents again, when she and Gwyl had sailed away from them. She remembered leaning over the top strake of Dragon Wind to watch them as long as her eyes could still see them.

To know they weren't there any longer, sending their love to her somehow over the distance. That was a bitter thing to her. To know they died a horrifying and brutal death made her cry out in her sleep with the anguish of it.

There was another thing, though. The voice that had told her Gwyl was alive. The thrill of hope that roused in her was powerful; the grief was powerful, too, and so also the outrage over what Maro had done. For a time, Keera felt herself helpless in the grip of contradictory emotions that gave her no rest.

One morning after an evening dinner where Fiona had been present, Fiona took her friend aside. "Keera, I know something is preying on your mind. I know it has been for some time. Something terrible haunting your dreams. And last night, as I listened at Maro's board, I think I overheard what it might be. Your parents, Keera. Your dear parents."

Keera threw herself sobbing into Fiona's arms. Little Rozenn toddled over and began to sob too. Fiona picked her up and they all just huddled together until they could wipe their tears away.

"I couldn't speak of it," whispered Keera. Now that she was able to talk about at least one of the overwhelming feelings that roiled her, a burden lifted from her. She stopped feeling so paralyzed. She started thinking again about how she would act.

Even though Keera didn't tell Fiona about Maro's attack on her, Fiona somehow picked up on her feelings anyway. She connected them with the deaths of Keera's parents. She never realized what Keera had had to endure from Maro. "Maro is acting strangely triumphant over this ill news," said Fiona. "Wonder why he cares. Better never tell him you're Wat's and Mirin's daughter. No telling what he'd do."

"I'm too lowly for him to pay me much mind," said Keera, wiping her eyes, hoping it was the case; fearing it wasn't.

Keera wondered, though. As she went about her tasks at the governor's residence, deftly keeping for the most part out of

Maro's way and out of his notice, she caught his eye on her a few times, shrewd and assessing. Suppose he had his suspicions about her identity? No point in sharing these fears with Fiona. There was nothing Fiona could do about it.

Keera at least summoned up the resolve to talk to the other young women who served about the residence. "Keep away from the Governor-General. He has wandering hands," she whispered to one or two. But they just stared at her in amazement. "Of course he does," said one, the boldest. "Comes with the job." And she winked. So then, although it made her feel guilty, Keera kept quiet about what Maro had tried to do to her.

She was too caught up in the larger matter, acting on what the voice had told her. Bringing Gwyl out of the wilderness to safety. Pierrick too. If either brother had had any choice in the matter, she knew, he wouldn't have left the other.

She didn't tell Fiona some mysterious voice had told her Gwyl was alive. Fiona would think her addlepated.

From time to time, Fiona became downhearted. "I may insist and fret and demand all I like, and finally Maro may decide to send an expedition. But what if it's all for nothing? What if—" She'd never be able to say her next thought aloud. What if Pierrick and Gwyl were long dead. At those times, Keera sat with Fiona, stroking her hand. Trying to communicate her own confidence through touch and sympathetic listening. Hesitating to tell Fiona about the voice and the message. *Suppose it was just a product of my grief and not real?* thought Keera. *I'll give Fiona false hope if I talk about it. Or maybe fresh worries about how balanced I am.*

Most of the time, though, Fiona was enraged. "Why doesn't Maro act?" she cried. "His son is in the hands of the wretches, and he does nothing."

On one such occasion, they were sitting together quietly, both in a state of near-despair.

*Say this mysterious voice of mine is right?* Keera was thinking. *Say Gwyl lived through that day of the attack, and Pierrick too. What happens if seasons, years go by, and no one does anything? How long will they be able to keep themselves alive, especially if they're in hostile hands?*

Keera went to Rozenn and soothed her. The little girl was so sensitive, always picking up on the emotions of her mother and the woman she knew as Auntie. She had burst into tears, and now she couldn't stop her crying.

Keera jiggled Rozenn on her knee.

Her sorrow abruptly dropping away from her, the little girl leapt off and went careening about the room. She found her poppet made of the cobs of the maize plant and began singing it a little song.

"To be so young and innocent," said Keera with a sigh. "She doesn't know yet how cruel the world can be." She and Fiona sat watching Rozenn's play. "She's getting big," said Keera.

"Yes, indeed," said Fiona, looking after her daughter with a fond smile. Her smile faded. "What will it be like for her, growing up in this desolate land? What will it be like for Alan?"

"But Fiona, this settlement is pretty comfortable," said Keera. "Most people have stopped saying *settlement*. They're saying *town*."

Fiona nodded agreement. "And really, when I think of the Cold Lands, what could be more desolate than that?" After a moment, she said slowly, "Last night, a man paid me court."

"That's a hard one," said Keera.

"I'll never marry, not as long as I think Pierrick might be alive. Maybe not even then. Although the Child knows Alan and Rozenn need a father out here." She hesitated. "Maro acts as though he thinks he's Alan's father. I don't like that. I don't like him."

Keera thought once more of his vile attack on her. She thought of the scars on Gwyl's back. "I hate him, myself," she said. "Wonder what has happened to our husbands' mother."

Fiona shrugged. "As near as I can tell, left behind in the Baronies."

"Maybe she refused to come out here with him. Maybe she can't stand Maro either," said Keera.

"Maybe," said Fiona. "But I think Maro just abandoned her there."

"Abandoned her. That would be a hard fate."

"I hear he sends coin back for her keep," said Fiona. "So not abandoned in the way you're thinking."

"The best of all possible worlds, then," said Keera with the ghost of a smile. "She doesn't have to have him around, but he pays her keep." What a difference, Gwyl's parents and her own. And now her own were gone.

"I must dance attendance on the man himself," said Fiona with a sigh. "There's something Maro says he needs to speak to me about. Probably something about Alan's upbringing."

"I'll watch Rozenn," said Keera.

Fiona rose to her feet and made ready to leave. Then she turned. "I'm bringing Rozenn with me. She's this man's granddaughter, after all. He needs to see about her upbringing, too," she said.

So Fiona and Keera set about brushing and primping the squirming Rozenn, and the little girl and Fiona disappeared together out the door into the main part of the dwelling.

Keera sat on her own bed for a long time, looking at her hands. Part of her wanted to get back into the bed and pull the furs over her.

But now that it was full spring again, she had gotten into the habit of going out into the marshes between the rivers to enjoy the fresh air. By now, the guards at the gate knew her. She made sure to come back with her arms full of sedges and rushes so they'd think she'd been sent out on an errand to renew the rushes on the floor of the governor's main hall, or to bring back sweet-smelling grasses for the mattresses.

But really, by now, the guards hardly cared. She was a fixture about the town now.

Once out on the marshes, Keera rambled the river banks trying to think of nothing but the beauty of the day and the useful plants she might identify.

This day, as Fiona left the room with Rozenn, Keera's heart ached with the reopened wound of her parents' deaths. She needed to get out to the marshes, and out from under the eye of the housekeeper, who might send her somewhere Maro could corner her again. *Lucky I'm not directly under her thumb*, Keera thought.

She needed to stay out there in the marshes all day and wait. There was something she needed out there. Late in the day, she'd gotten into the habit of settling under a tree to watch. To watch for the owls.

At twilight, out on the marsh, if she were lucky, she saw them. She couldn't be certain it was the same two, but in her fancy, she always thought it was the pair who had burst into her grief at the Lady Goddess's temple. The same pair that she watched sen' night after sen'night, flitting about in the twilight, calling to each other, down at the marshes. She loved to watch them hunt, watch the silent way they swooped down on their prey. And she loved to watch them all the way back to their roost in a big gnarled hollow tree at the edge of the marsh, the biggest tree at the edge of the forest.

In her fancy, they had a loving home there. Maybe they raised owlets together there. She made time to go out to watch them as often as she could, especially now that the evenings had turned mild.

She kept remembering what Tigeny had said to her. Two selves, not one. And one of these selves was an owl. She kept remembering the voice she had heard, as she had stared up at the owls in the temple.

Birds of evil, ghost birds, enemies of the Lady Goddess's light? Drinking the Lady Goddess's oil out of Her lamps? *Go ahead,* thought Keera, watching the owls out on the marshes in the mild early evenings of spring. *Go over there and drink it. Drink it all up.*

Today, after Fiona and Rozenn had left their rooms and the ringing silence came back in on her, bringing her fears and grief with it, she was resolved. She needed the solace of the owls.

She gathered her things together and headed out of the palisade gates to spend the day wandering the river banks. Until twilight, she occupied herself trying to identify some of the herbs and plants Tigeny had shown her on their trek from the coast south and inland to this place. Often, this activity helped still the ache inside her—the ache for her parents, the ache for Gwyl. She wasn't exactly happy, but at least for the best part of the day she'd feel content, her troubles held far from her.

Today was harder. She was thinking too sadly of her parents, and of Gwyl. Even the marsh couldn't distract her. But she did find some of the herbs she needed, and slowly she found herself absorbed in the work. She collected a few of the herbs, planning to dry them and grind them up. She might be able to make potions of them. Best of all, she found a stand of willow and was able to gather a good bit of their bark to make into a syrup for reducing fever, and to cut osiers from the willows, too. She could use them to weave baskets.

The day passed into late afternoon. Twilight would be upon her soon. She made her way back to the edge of the forest and settled down with her back to a big tree, to wait. This tree was situated so she could easily see the hollow where she knew the owls roosted. Her owls. That's how she had started thinking of them.

As she waited, she began drifting back to her childhood, to the love of her mother. To the time they rediscovered her father, taken from them by Caedon, and the happiness they knew when they were reunited. And she began to think of the powers she had once wielded. Powers to read minds. With a smile, she thought of how angry she had been when the farwydd of the Fire Child had removed her powers. And then, her quest at an end, the farwydd had asked her to choose.

"One of these hands, the left, encloses your powers. Choose my left hand, and you will have them back," she had told Keera. "The other hand, the right, encloses love. Choose my right hand, and you will have the gifts of love—love of parent. Love of kin. Love of friend. Love between flesh and flesh, heart and heart, soul and soul. In time, love of child. Which do you choose?"

Keera hadn't hesitated. Keera had chosen love.

The farwydd hadn't played her false. Keera had rejoiced in all the promised gifts. All but one, perhaps. *In time, love of child*, the farwydd had promised. That hadn't happened. Or had it? When Keera had consigned the tiny remains of her unborn, unknown child to the waves, she had felt such piercing grief she hadn't thought she could stand it. Can great grief even exist without great love? Maybe that's what the farwydd had meant. *Cruel promise*, thought Keera.

And she thought then of her father and mother. *Cultivate your gifts*, her mother had told her. *You may have lost your powers, but you have other gifts inside, other powers.* She remembered what her father had said. *My sight may have been taken, but the Children are generous. They have given me great gifts. They've given your mother back to me. I'd be ungrateful to ask for more.*

Now Keera, thinking of the voice she had heard in the temple, made a promise to her parents, watching over her from beyond that boundary in the Land of the Dead. *I'll cultivate these inward gifts*, she promised. *I've neglected them too long. I haven't acted on the voice that spoke to me. Now I'll act.*

As the twilight deepened, the owls burst from their roosting place, making ecstatic circles in the air.

Keera drew in her breath, praising her Child for this glimpse of their joy.

One of the owls spiraled up, then arrowed straight for Keera. Keera didn't dare to breathe. The owl dipped overhead, just grazing Keera's cheek with the tip of a wing, a touch so light she wondered if she were imagining it, and was away again with its mate, leaving Keera exclaiming under her tree.

She made her way thoughtfully back to the palisades, slipped within, and stepped into her room in the governor's dwelling.

Fiona was already there, sitting on her bed, her eyes sparkling. Rozenn was fast asleep in her own small bed.

"Keera," said Fiona as Keera came in. "Maro is funding an expedition to find Pierrick. The searchers leave in three days," she said.

"How wonderful!" said Keera. But inside, she said, *And I'm going with them.*

## Expedition

*Three days*, thought Keera. She had work to do. She had made her promise to the owls, and they had answered her.

She knew she'd take action at last. She'd follow the expedition. She knew she couldn't tell Fiona, because she knew what she planned to do was madness. Fiona, always loving, never mentioned Keera's rash act as they fled Fishers' Bay. But Fiona knew Keera was rash, and Keera knew her friend thought Keera should control those impulses of hers.

Even if Fiona had been as mad as she, Fiona would never think to do what Keera was planning to do. Fiona had her children to consider. She'd never leave them. It's not that she loved them more than Pierrick. The children were the anchor of their love. The children were the sign and the reality of her love for Pierrick. Pierrick would have had to do the same, if they had changed places.

But Keera was going on the expedition to find her husband. She was all the more determined because she knew, from Gwyl, what Maro was like. If they found Pierrick and Gwyl alive, Maro's men would be told to rescue Pierrick. But they wouldn't be told a thing about Gwyl. Or if they were, they'd be told to leave him. Her fantasy that they'd bring Gwyl back with them was a lie. She had realized it now. Ever since Maro's attack on her, she had realized what Maro was, and she had understood what he'd do if Gwyl were found.

It was up to Keera to get Gwyl out. And she knew that made her a bit crazy. Especially since she didn't have the skill to do such a hard thing as trek through a wilderness.

*I'm going to do it anyway*, she told herself.

She planned to trail the expedition, keep herself hidden, and get to the same destination. Then she'd see what she needed to do. Somehow, whatever it turned out to be, she'd find a way to do it.

During her three days of preparation, she secured men's hide trousers and tunic. It was easy for her to find these things. As a maid at the governor's dwelling, she had occasion to rummage through all his chests. One chest held clothing for his servants. She knew where it was, went straight to it, and found herself clothing that was probably meant for a half-grown lad. She found herself a cloak, too. Dun-colored, so she wouldn't stand out amongst the trees.

The weather was her friend. It was summer now. She didn't need protection from the cold. And the trees were all leafed out. She'd be hard to spot as she trailed after the expedition.

She filled a cloth bag with the meal of the maize plant, cultivated everywhere in the New Found Land, and she took a small wooden bowl she could use to eat from and also to dip up water. She wouldn't carry much. She wouldn't really be able to cook anything. But during the fortnight of their flight with Tigeny to Three Rivers, she had studied Tigeny's knowledge of plants. She knew which were edible. She told herself she'd be able to feed herself. Somehow she'd do it.

She found herself a knife for protection. She looked at it in despair. Not for the first time, she hated her lack of training in the arts of war. But at least she'd have this knife with her.

She already wore the hide shoes everyone wore in Three Rivers, the shoes the natives themselves wore. The heathens, those in Three Rivers called them, and the settlers talked about rounding these heathen people up someday and forcing them all to worship the Lady Goddess.

As the sun peeped over the horizon on the day appointed for the expedition to head out, Keera slipped out of bed. Fiona roused a little. Keera muttered something about going to the jakes. In her mind, she begged Fiona to forgive her and not to worry too much when she turned up missing.

She made her way swiftly to the storage shed where she'd hidden her things, and put on the clothes she had hidden. Her last act was to switch her white headcloth for a length of dun-colored flaxen material. She wound the cloth about her head. It would blend in with the forest, hide her hair, and not signal her presence by any flash of white.

Now she made her way to the gates of the palisade. She waited.

The expedition's men marched up to the gate. Keera sidled up to them. In the half-light of dawn, she straggled after them through the gate, and the guard didn't call out. She must have looked like a lad, maybe a servant, following after the expedition to bring them some forgotten piece of gear. Maybe the guard even thought this slight figure of a lad was part of the expedition.

After making it through the gates without incident, Keera faded back and off the path. She got herself into the woods and followed along with the expedition, trying her best to make her movements silent. She wasn't trained in the skills of stealth and hunting, as her mother was. But the expedition, numbering about ten men, was making enough noise for twenty. Under cover of this noise, she followed along.

The first day wasn't too hard. If she lagged behind, all she had to do was stand silent and listen. Soon she'd hear which direction to go.

Besides, the men of the expedition weren't marching very fast.

The first night, they bedded down just off the path, and she bedded down a little further into the forest.

By the third day, she was pretty hungry. She kept having to stop to forage for food, and she was beginning to feel weak. She needed meat. When she got close enough to the expedition to smell the cooking of some animal flesh at the end of that third day, she almost cried out for hunger.

She wondered how she could steal some. But that was too risky to try. She spent a miserable night of it wrapped in her cloak on the hard ground.

The next morning, the noisy preparations of the expedition for departure roused her. She waited until she heard them leave. Then she rushed to their camp site. She was lucky. The men of the expedition proved very careless. They hadn't completely stamped out their fire.

She knew she needed to keep up with them, but she also knew she needed nourishment. She'd have to let them go on away from her and stay here by their camp site to see what she could devise. She pulled a flat stone to the fire and blew on the flames so they flared up. Then she fed the flames until the fire was hot. On the flat stone, she made a kind of cake with the meal of the maize plant and cooked it there. It was half-raw and burnt her fingers and tongue, but she greedily ate it anyway.

Then she praised her Child. She came upon some meat scraps where the men of the expedition had kicked them aside off the edge of the path. No animal had scavenged them yet. She grabbed them up and forced herself not to cram them into her mouth. All this time, the expedition had been following the broad river eastward toward the coast. She made her way to the riverside and washed the scraps free of dirt and grit. Then she ate them all, and gnawed on the cast-off bones.

It wasn't enough, but it was something. She felt she could go on.

But now, as she headed away from the rushing of the river and back to the path, and as she stood listening, she could hear nothing at all, just the sounds the forest makes, the birds, the creaking of trees as the wind soughs by, the pattering of some small animal's feet.

It was clear to her, though. The expedition's men were heading down the track in the forest that paralleled the river. They were heading for the coast. So she hurried down the track herself. Late in the day, she was rewarded with the sounds of voices ahead, and the noises of men setting up a camp. She had caught up with the expedition again.

The next day, a torrent of rain drenched her to the skin. She squelched her way through the forest, hoping she wasn't making enough noise to get herself noticed. When the sun came out, she gradually dried off, and that night, she spread her sodden cloak out in hopes it would dry completely. But the ground was wet. It was the most miserable of a string of miserable nights she'd spent following the men.

Now they were climbing. The track got steadily steeper. Keera put one weary foot in front of the next. She was so intent on climbing that she nearly came upon the expedition as they stood in a clearing discussing what to do. She crouched, listening.

"From here," the expedition's leader was saying, "it's not too much further to the coast. Then we just follow the coastline until we reach Fishers' Bay."

His voice came to her clearly through the trees. He was a man she knew slightly from her time at Three Rivers.

"What then?" asked someone else.

"Then, I'm not sure," the leader admitted. "All our information says the attackers came from a heathen village just up the coast from Fishers' Bay. That's what that woman thought."

Keera nodded quietly to herself. Fiona was the woman they meant.

"Women," said one of the men. "They're unreliable. Who knows what really happened."

"Indeed," the leader agreed. "We don't know for sure that these heathens are the ones who attacked Fishers' Bay, but they are our best hope of finding out what happened to the governor's son. We'll go to the village, establish friendly relations with the heathens, and ask them."

Another voice. "We don't even know if the governor's son is alive. If he is, and these heathens aren't the ones who took him, we won't even know where to look for him."

"That's true," said the leader.

"What if they're not friendly?" said someone else.

"We'll be more than a match for them, the poor naked creatures," said the leader. "After all, they're little more than animals."

Keera had to suppress a snort of derision at that.

"Whether they're friendly or not, we may have come on a fool's errand," grumbled another voice.

"Not at all," said the leader. "We hope to find this man, the governor's son, but that's not all we're after." After a pause, he continued. "These villagers of Fishers' Bay were led by a man named Yann. He is an enemy of our good Baron Gilles. The governor is eager to find out whether he was killed during the attack on Fishers' Bay, and if not, where he might have gone. The Baron Gilles wants this man taken, if he's alive. In fact," and here the leader's voice dropped, and Keera found herself leaning forward to hear, "That's why our governor is here. The Baron Gilles has sent him here as his representative in the Unknown Lands especially to find this man Yann."

"An important man," said another voice.

"He doesn't seem so, particularly. Those who have met him don't seem to think so. Apparently he is. That's what the governor has told me. Our governor hopes to send this man Yann back to the Baronies for punishment, or, if not, to send back the evidence of his death."

The leader was quiet for so long that Keera thought the men might be finished talking. But the leader resumed. "This Yann is not the only reason for our governor's presence in these lands. As you know, lads, this whole part of the coast has been settled by men of Ansgar. They are our enemies as well. The Baron's enemies. We are to scout their settlements and bring back word. How many. How strong. We'll probably move against these settlements soon. Our governor has been sent here with the express task, straight from the Baron, to crush Ansgar's settlements and remove his influence from these lands. Baron Gilles means for it all to belong to him, and Governor-General Maro is his expressly chosen agent."

A murmur of voices.

The leader again. "So you see, our expedition is quite important to the governor, and the governor is quite important to

Baron Gilles. We'll be well-rewarded when we return with our news, whether we find His Excellency's son or not."

During the last few difficult days, Keera had toyed with the idea of catching up to the expedition and turning herself in to them. Surely they wouldn't leave her out in the woods. Surely they'd allow her to come along with them. But now she realized she had to stay hidden. Gwyl had trusted the Fishers' Bay leader, Yann. Keera realized she didn't know what Maro was up to, not at all. And now she saw he did indeed have some mysterious connection with Gilles. Yann did too, somehow, although of course the poor man had no doubt died with the others during the attack on Fisher's Bay.

She didn't dare reveal herself to the men of the expedition. They'd think her a spy. When they dragged her before Maro, he'd do something dire to her. He already wanted to, and this would give him the perfect excuse.

Keera hung back until the expedition was well ahead of her. Then she trudged on. The man's words had solved one mystery— why Maro was here—but it had raised two or three more, so she was just as baffled as she had ever been. She continued toiling along in the expedition's wake, eating its leavings when she could, foraging for edible plants when she couldn't.

Until one day, she emerged onto a high cliff pounded by the mighty waves of the Great Sea.

By now, she had lost the expedition entirely. All she could do was follow the coastline. A trail worn deeply into the forest led her north, saving her many detours along the indented coast. She kept following the trail, trying hard not to stray away from it when the markings turned faint.

And by now, she was starving.

She moved ahead doggedly, sleeping when her strength failed her, eating what she could, whenever she could find anything.

She lost track of how many days she'd been traveling.

One day, the trail took her close to the sea. She decided to head for the coast, not far off, because she could hear the sea from where she stood.

At noontide, as she looked out over the little bay that spread before her, she realized she recognized some landmarks. That massive boulder over there. The headland she could glimpse from where she stood. Fishers' Bay. It had to be.

She picked her way down to the shore and stood gazing over the water. Then she sucked in her breath.

The timbers of a wrecked ship lay along the shoreline. She bent to touch them. A dark shape in the sand poked up in a rippled ridge of some half-buried unraveling material. She went to it and tugged at it. Cloth. Black woven wool. She scrabbled at the cloth with her fingers until they were raw and bleeding. The more of the black material she uncovered, the more dread she felt. When she came to the white shape of a fierce bird head woven into the cloth, she stopped and fell weeping to the sand. It was Dragon Wind's sail, and the timbers were all that were left of her.

Inside herself, she well knew that if Gwyl were dead, he hadn't died of shipwreck. But here lay his beautiful vessel, ruined and destroyed. It was if the ruined ship signaled his death. She herself felt ruined and destroyed.

She wondered if she'd ever get up. She wondered if she had the strength to do it even if she decided she would. Her parents, gone out of the world. And maybe Gwyl too. No. Certainly Gwyl too. How could he have survived? She remembered the warrior of the wretches, his club lifted high, brought down on the village woman again and again.

If not for Tigeny, she realized, her own bones, and the bones of Fiona and the children, would be lying strewn around the ruins of Fishers' Bay the way that woman's bones were surely lying there.

Keera must have stayed crumpled on the beach for a candle measure and longer. As she lay there, the voice came back. The mysterious voice from the temple. Maybe it actually spoke. Maybe it was her imagination, taunting her. *Gwyl is not dead. And you have a task to perform.*

Somehow she pulled herself to her knees and then to her feet.

Somehow she found herself moving back into the woods. At least she knew where she was now. She didn't try to go to the broken down palisades of the burnt-out village. Instead, she headed deeper into the forest.

By afternoon, she stepped into a small clearing. A figure rushed at her from a bark dwelling. Keera staggered into the arms of Tigeny, who led her inside, spooned broth into her, and put her to bed.

# 4 GWYL: Promises

### *Some of Us Are Luckier*

Gwyl came into the village from hunting deer with the other young men of The People. He had shot one himself, a clean shot that brought the animal right down, and he was flush with his victory. All the villagers gathered around to prepare the feast of game the young men had brought in.

Three Stripe stood looking down at the dead deer. "Nice work, son," he said.

"Thank you, Father," said Gwyl.

By now, it didn't even seem strange to him, that he was saying words like these to a man like this. He found himself meaning them. He found himself wanting to prove himself in Three Stripe's eyes.

He looked around for Pierrick but didn't see him. They'd all feast tonight, but that terrible man, Porcupine, was likely to keep his part of the meat entirely for himself and not let Pierrick have any of it. Gwyl planned to save a portion out for Pierrick. He'd sneak it to his brother later.

"Let's go to our hearth fire, son. I need to talk to you about something," said Three Stripe.

Gwyl followed him to their dwelling.

Three Stripe's wife Squirrel was never that motherly toward Gwyl, not even now, but she treated him kindly. She gave him a smile as she hurried from the dwelling to help prepare the feast.

Gwyl sat down by the hearth ring with Three Stripe.

"You are of the Sea Child, Gull," said Three Stripe.

Gwyl nodded.

"But we do not worship the Children. Many do, especially to the south."

"The Sky Child," said Gwyl.

"Yes. But here, we worship the old gods. And the Sun God is the greatest of these."

Gwyl was beginning to get uneasy. He was beginning to think Three Stripe wasn't just giving him religious instruction. He was edging into some disturbing topic.

"The Sun God admonishes us to revenge ourselves upon our enemies. You have seen this."

"Yes," said Gwyl.

"Especially if our enemies have taken our sons and sent them to the Land of the Dead. Then, we kill our enemies in revenge.

But from time to time, we take captives. If a man has been deprived of a son by his enemies, two things may happen. The man may adopt a captive in place of his dead son."

"As you have adopted me, Father," said Gwyl.

"Yes, exactly. But there is another way, equally honorable. A man might choose instead to sacrifice a captive to the Sun God in the name of his dead son. Then the son will have an easier time in the Land of the Dead, and the bereaved father will gain great honor, because he has honored the Sun God in this way."

Gwyl nodded that he understood.

"I lost my son Otter. That caused me immense grief, but now, because of you, Gull, my grief has eased."

Three Stripe looked into the fire, then back up at Gwyl. "Porcupine too has lost a son. He lost a son to your kind. A son and a wife, too. He too wants vengeance, and it is a matter of honor for him."

Gwyl was beginning to feel a flicker of outright fear now. Porcupine, too, had lost a son. Had lost a son to a settler from Fishers' Bay or some similar place. And a wife.

"Porcupine has decided not to adopt a captive in place of his lost son. He will sacrifice a captive to the Sun God instead."

It became suddenly clear to Gwyl what Three Stripe was talking about. He found he was shaking his head. "No," he heard himself saying. "No. Not my brother."

"My dear son," said Three Stripe. "This is not up to us. It's up to Porcupine what happens to the Big One."

"This is my brother we're talking about," said Gwyl. Surely Three Stripe would be able to understand this and stop it.

"You must bear it, son."

"No," said Gwyl.

"You must," said Three Stripe. "If I have to tie you up in here while they do it, I will."

Gwyl felt the flat taste of horror in his mouth. "Why would you tie me up? I thought I was your son. I thought I wasn't your slave any longer."

"You're not. Don't you understand? If you interfere, Porcupine can demand your life too."

"Porcupine can have my life," Gwyl burst out. "Not my brother. Not Pierrick. You're the leader of The People. Can't you do anything to stop him?"

"I'm the leader of The People in all areas but one. Porcupine is the religious leader of The People. What Porcupine says about matters involving the Sun God stands. I have nothing to say about it."

"I'm begging you to help my brother," said Gwyl. He put his hands on Three Stripe's feet and bent his head down to them.

"Never beg, son." Three Stripe thrust him angrily away. "This is unworthy."

"What would you do, to prevent your brother from being killed by a brutal man?" Gwyl demanded. "How far would you go? A brother you love more than your own life?"

Three Stripe stood. "You may not sacrifice yourself for the Big One, Gull. I forbid it. I'm telling you this long before the event, so you can steel yourself."

Gwyl leaped to his feet and rushed from their dwelling. In three steps he was at Porcupine's door. Without asking permission to enter, he slammed through the hide door, looking around wildly for Pierrick.

Porcupine was sitting at his own hearth fire. Now he rose. "Why are you here, Gull?"

"I want to see my brother," said Gwyl.

"You have no brother," said Porcupine.

"Where are you keeping him?" said Gwyl, and he advanced on Porcupine.

But before he could do anything to the sneering little man, Three Stripe and four other village men swept Porcupine's hide door covering aside and grabbed Gwyl. They dragged him out. Gwyl was shouting and struggling. He saw and heard himself doing this, as if he were standing outside himself, watching.

Past him, he heard Porcupine say, "You see, brother? This is what comes of adopting a fully grown captive. This never works out."

And he heard Three Stripe say, "Gull is my son. Don't speak to me of him in this disrespectful way."

But that's all Gwyl heard, because then the other men had thrust him back into Three Stripe's dwelling, and they had tied him up tight with spruce thongs.

All night, Gwyl struggled in vain against the thongs. All night, he tried to think where Porcupine could have put Pierrick. And all night, one thought kept intruding itself. The thing he'd overheard. *You see, brother?* Porcupine had said.

*Porcupine is Three Stripe's brother. How could this be. How could this be.*

In the morning, he came out of a dull kind of sleep to find Three Stripe bending down beside him.

"How are you, Gull, my dear son," said Three Stripe softly.

"Porcupine is your brother. Explain how in the name of my Child such a thing can be," whispered Gwyl.

"If I untie you, will you listen? Or will you run over to Porcupine's dwelling like a crazy person and threaten him again?"

"Untie me. I'll listen," said Gwyl.

Three Stripe undid the thongs binding Gwyl and helped him sit up. He gave him gruel to eat. Squirrel hovered around anxiously.

"Look," said Three Stripe. With a stick, he started to draw in the hard packed dirt of their dwelling's floor. Three Stripe drew a man figure and a woman figure. The woman figure held a baby.

Three Stripe scrubbed out the man figure and drew another man figure on the other side of the woman figure. He drew another baby in the arms of the woman figure. He scrubbed out both babies and drew boys instead.

He pointed to one. "Me," he said. He pointed to the other. "Porcupine."

Gwyl looked at Three Stripe, astounded. And then he and Three Stripe began to laugh. Gwyl couldn't help himself.

"These situations. Many find themselves in these situations," said Three Stripe. "Only, some of us are luckier in our brothers than others."

"But Father," said Gwyl, when he could speak again. "What must I do?"

"You must endure it, son," said Three Stripe.

Gwyl's laughter died in his mouth. He felt his heart turning to stone in his chest. He could not endure it. He would not.

"You must endure it," Three Stripe said again.

"You must eat," said Squirrel firmly, shoving Three Stripe aside and squatting down with a bowl of something hot for Gwyl.

## Promises

Day after day went by. Every day, Gwyl scanned the village for Pierrick. Twice, when Porcupine was away, he sneaked into Porcupine's dwelling to look. Pierrick was gone. But one day, as he headed for the little river below the village to check on a vessel he and Old Canoe were building together, he glimpsed a knot of village men against the river bank, talking among themselves. As he came near, they stopped talking and stared at him. After he went by, he heard them resume their low talk.

*Something's going on back there*, he thought, with a prickling at his neck. Later in the day, as he came back up the path with Old Canoe, he glanced over to the bank where the men had stood.

On impulse, he said to the old man, "I left my adze. Go on ahead, Old Canoe. I'll go back for it."

Old Canoe nodded at him. "Good work today, Gull," he said, and continued up the path.

Gwyl retraced his steps, but as soon as he was sure Old Canoe was far enough up the path, he returned to the bank and started poking along it with a stick.

There it was. A hole. The entrance to a cave in the overhanging bank.

Gwyl pushed his way in. "Nine Spheres," he muttered, flinging himself on Pierrick, bound and lying on the dirt of the cave floor. With his knife, he released his brother and they huddled together, embracing.

When Gwyl could speak again, he said, low, "I've been looking for you everywhere."

"You know what they're planning to do to me," said Pierrick.

"I know." Gwyl looked his brother up and down. "Dark Ones take them, they may not get around to it if they keep starving you like this."

"Why waste food on a dead man," whispered Pierrick.

"Can you walk, do you think?"

"I'm not sure."

"Will they come back today? How often do they come down here?"

"Seems like only once a day, and they've already done that," said Pierrick. "They gave me a little water and a little gruel. Then they left."

"Thank the Child. We'll wait for dark. Then I'm getting you out of here. I can promise you that."

"What about Three Stripe?" said Pierrick.

"What about him?" said Gwyl.

They gave each other a long look. Then they fell on each other, embracing again.

"Eat this," said Gwyl, digging around in a pouch at his belt and producing a piece of dried meat. "I've got to get back before I'm missed. Three Stripe is watching me all the time. He knows I'll try to get to you if I can."

"He knows this," Pierrick said, his voice soft.

"Of course he knows it. No one is going to hurt my brother, I don't care who they are or who they think they are or—" Gwyl stopped. "Or however highly I may regard them. No one."

"Should I try to get out of this hole?" said Pierrick.

"I'm thinking the safest place for you now is in the hole," said Gwyl. "As long as you're sure they won't be back before tonight. If you come out, and anyone spots you, they'll all be on you, and then—"

"Yes," said Pierrick. "You're right."

"But take this," said Gwyl, easing the club from his belt. "If anyone does come down here, use this on them." He cautiously stuck his head out of the cave and looked around. Pierrick had come to the cave mouth and stooped to look out too. Gwyl turned and put his arms around Pierrick. "Child keep you, brother. I promise I'll be back."

Gwyl tried hard to still his breathing as he came back up the path. He must school himself to act completely ordinary. He must give no hint of what he'd seen and done.

As he came into the village, Old Canoe looked up from the fire. "Find it?"

Gwyl had a sick moment of blankness. Then he remembered. The adze.

"No. I must have dropped it. I'll look again in the morning," he said, and made his way toward Three Stripe's dwelling. But as he passed the central fire and headed that way, he heard a strange hammering sound. He looked over in the direction of Porcupine's dwelling.

The little man was standing with a group of others. These others were erecting a sort of scaffolding of poles.

Gwyl stopped still to watch.

Porcupine turned to him. His eyes glinted. "Go on about your business, Gull," said Porcupine.

The other men looked over at Gwyl and down at their shoes. Then they resumed their hammering with their mallets and adzes.

Three Stripe was standing in the door to their own dwelling. Gwyl strode to him. "What is Porcupine doing?"

"Son," said Three Stripe.

"Tell me," said Gwyl.

"Let's discuss it inside," said Three Stripe. "Not here in front of the entire village."

As soon as Gwyl stepped through the hide curtain, he saw his mistake. Five of the village men lay hands on him and wrestled him to the dirt floor. They bound him with spruce roots and left him there.

"Father," said Gwyl. "Why."

"You know why, Gull. Tomorrow is the day."

"No," said Gwyl.

But Three Stripe stood up and left the dwelling, and as twilight darkened its interior, he didn't come back.

Gwyl cursed himself bitterly. If only he had told Pierrick to get out of the cave and hide somewhere. They'd be coming for him, and they'd be too many for Pierrick, especially in his weakened state.

Tears leaked from Gwyl's eyes. What a fool he'd been.

The night darkened around him. Three Stripe didn't return, and Squirrel was somewhere else, too. No one came to see about him.

*They have me safely stashed away. Then they'll deal with Pierrick, I won't be able to stop them, and when it's all over, they'll let me out,* he thought.

His imagination left him no rest. He imagined them tying Pierrick to the scaffolding they'd built. He imagined Porcupine with his sharp knife.

Gwyl groaned aloud.

Out of the darkness came a voice. "Keep it quiet, brother."

Pierrick was slashing the bindings with a knife he laid hands on at Three Stripe's hearth. He was helping Gwyl sit up, and, befuddled, Gwyl was trying to make him out in the darkness.

"How?" said Gwyl, feeling spectacularly stupid.

"I had an assistant," said Pierrick, laughing a little in the dark. He was pushing someone into Gwyl's arms, and this someone was exclaiming softly and crying and touching and fiercely hugging.

"Keera."

"Don't ever leave me again, Gwyl. I need you. Promise me. If you leave again, we'll go together. Promise?"

"I promise," said Gwyl, burying his head in the sweetness of her. "I promise."

## A Scaffold

They had to move fast. They had no idea how much time they had, or whether anyone would come to check on Gwyl or Pierrick.

"Is the moon up?" Gwyl whispered.

"It's just edging up now," said Pierrick.

"Stay back, then, and let me look out of the doorway." He could feel rather than see the others' confusion. "It's that white-blond hair of yours, brother. You're covered with it. You'll shine in the moonlight like a hairy beacon. Let me do it."

The feeling was coming back into Gwyl's limbs now. He clambered to his feet.

"I see," breathed Keera. "With your dark hair, you—"

"Brother," said Gwyl to Pierrick. "When my wife sees me in the daylight, will she even want me any more?"

Pierrick chuckled a little.

"What?" said Keera in alarm.

"I look like one of The People," said Gwyl.

"The People?" she said blankly.

"Never mind. You'll see," said Gwyl, giving her a kiss in the dark.

"Your hair is so long," she whispered, stroking it.

"Enough lovey stuff," said Pierrick. "We need to go."

Gwyl edged to the hide covering in the doorway and eased it open a crack. No one was about. The scaffolding gleamed in the moonlight, and he shuddered.

"We're good," he whispered back to them. "Let's get going." He took Keera by the arm, and the three of them got themselves to the doorway.

But then the covering was thrust aside.

Outlined in the moonlight stood Three Stripe.

He looked from Pierrick to Keera, then at Gwyl. "Son," he said. "Gull."

"Father," said Gwyl. He shoved the other two aside and bent down to put his hands on Three Stripe's feet. He bent his forehead low.

Three Stripe lifted him. Tears streaked his face. "My son," he said.

"I must get my brother out of here, Father," said Gwyl. "I must do this."

"I know, son," said Three Stripe.

"What are they saying?" Keera murmured behind Gwyl.

He held up a warning hand to them. He knew Pierrick probably had his club out by now.

"Father," said Gwyl. "I promise you this. Once my brother is safe, I'll come back. Then you will do with me whatever you think fitting. I promise this on my honor as a warrior. I promise this on my Child."

"No," said Pierrick, low, behind him.

"No talking," said Gwyl. "Let's go."

Three Stripe stepped silently aside.

*Drop the club, Pierrick,* thought Gwyl. *Raise it to strike, and Three Stripe will gut you sooner than you can blink.*

So he had to act fast before Pierrick did something stupid. Child knew there was enough stupidity to go around this night.

Gwyl took Keera's hand and guided her out into the night. Pierrick followed close behind him. As he looked sidelong at Pierrick, he saw Pierrick was without the club.

*Only one stupid man here,* thought Gwyl, *and it's not you, brother.*

Involuntarily, the three of them turned to look back over their shoulders at the scaffold, the white raw peeled wood of it stark in the moonlight. They moved swiftly then through the village into the woods, and they didn't take the path.

## Some of Us Are Luckier

They were holed up in Tigeny's hut, and Keera couldn't stop stroking Gwyl and exclaiming over him, and Pierrick couldn't stop smiling. He couldn't stop asking Keera, over and over, how Fiona did, and how the children did. Keera talked and talked to him about them, and Pierrick drank up every word.

"What's this?" said Keera, fingering Gwyl's shoulder.

"That? It's a gull."

"Why a gull?"

"Because—" Gwyl stopped. "It's too hard to explain."

"It's not," said Pierrick. "You know that man? The one who let us go? That's Gwyl's father."

"His father?" Keera looked at them both blankly.

"Yes, see, and when Three Stripe—the man who let us go—realized Gwyl was his son Gull, he did that to Gwyl."

"I don't understand," said Keera.

"Never mind," said Gwyl, and tried to smile. He should be feeling glad, and he was, but then there was a place inside him that was not glad.

"Your actual father, Maro, sent an expedition to save you two," said Keera.

"He's not my father." Gwyl's voice was sharp. Then he was contrite. "Don't cry, Keera, my darling Keera," he said. He hugged her to him. "But anyway, we all know it. He's not. So tell me." He knew his smile was thin. "Maro sent an expedition to rescue Pierrick, and. . . me?"

Keera looked back at him, her eyes wide.

"You don't have to pretend, Keera, not with me. Not with Pierrick either. He might have sent an expedition to rescue Pierrick, but if he'd known I was around too, he'd have told them to leave me there."

"And you would have been just fine," murmured Pierrick.

Gwyl cast a quick look at him. "Only if they'd gotten you out, brother."

"Aren't you forgetting someone?" said Keera.

"Yes. Foolish man that I am. If they'd left me, and I couldn't have been with you, I would have—"

"Hush, then," she said, and kissed him. Then she said, slowly, "But what Pierrick really means is that you do think of that man as your father."

Gwyl squeezed his eyes shut. He didn't want to acknowledge it. But it was true. And it was also true that Wat was his father. "Keera, your father—"

"Gwyl, my mother and father are dead."

Gwyl went cold at her words. He looked searchingly into her eyes and saw she was telling him the truth. He felt as though some great force were tearing him apart, cleaving him from the top of the skull to the breastbone and spilling his life onto the ground. He found he had leaped to his feet. He found himself running into the forest. What was happening to him, he wondered. The world seemed to be tilting dangerously upside down.

Keera found him wandering around under the trees.

"Darling," she said. "Come back to Tigeny's house now."

"They're dead. It's not possible."

"I know, Gwyl. It's hard. But it's the truth. Gilles de Rais's forces caught them and killed them."

"The grief of this news is almost more than I can bear. You know I thought of them as my true parents."

"I know when you married me, you really married them."

"Don't tease me."

"I'm sorry." She gathered him into her arms. "I know you loved them. They thought of you as a son, too. They loved your father. My father loved yours deeply. My mother hardly knew your father, your real father, Rafe, but Father knew him well. They had some experiences together that chill me to the bone, and I only know a little about what they went through. When people undergo such moments together—"

Gwyl stood under the trees with Keera and pulled her to him. "If not for your father, I would be lost in my own anger. I owe him everything. But Keera, let me tell you something. You'll probably hate me."

"I'll never hate you," she said.

"I do think of that man you saw last night as my father. To get Pierrick out, I had to make him a promise."

Keera raised her eyes to his. "You made me a promise."

"I know I did."

"So what are you going to do about that?"

"Keep them both," Gwyl whispered. "But how can I? You understand, once I get Pierrick to safety, I have to go back there. I have to."

"Then I'm coming with you."

"You can't."

"I can," said Keera.

They had to leave it at that, because the shadows were lengthening. Leaning into each other, they walked slowly back to Tigeny's hut.

After they'd eaten, they talked quietly.

"Where is this expedition now, Keera?" said Gwyl.

Keera was exclaiming over Pierrick. He was bleeding into his tunic. "What did they do to you? They are savages."

"Only some of them," said Pierrick. "Like any of us."

"Come here to me," said Tigeny. "Let me see to your back." She set to work on Pierrick.

"The expedition?" prompted Gwyl. Darkness had fallen now, and they sat around Tigeny's little fire eating and staring around them into the velvety night.

"The men of the expedition were following the path," said Keera, "and I was following them."

Gwyl found himself shaking his head and smiling at her.

"And I think they are camped out near the place where Fishers' Bay was destroyed."

"In the morning, Pierrick, you and Keera must go to them," said Gwyl. "They'll take you to this place—what is it? Three Rivers? And Maro will be overjoyed to see you."

"He won't be overjoyed if I'm with them," said Keera. "He'll be suspicious and angry."

"Keera, stay here with me," said Tigeny. "I'll get you back to Three Rivers when it's safe."

"She will, too," said Keera to Gwyl. "She got me, Fiona, and the children to Three Rivers. She warned us to get out of Fishers' Bay. Otherwise, we'd be dead."

"Thank the Child for you," said Pierrick over his shoulder to Tigeny, trying to sit still on his stone. He was fidgeting under Tigeny's hands, and she gave him a little shake. "That stings," he said. "But brother. You can stay here with Tigeny too. I'll have to go with the expedition. You're right, my father will be overjoyed." He looked over at Gwyl with a wry smile. "Some of us are luckier in our fathers than others. I'm not going there for him."

"I know, brother," said Gwyl, reaching out a hand to him and gripping him by the arm. "It's Fiona and your children."

"I'm on fire to see them. But brother. You can't go back there, to The People. Something bad will happen if you do." Pierrick regarded him soberly.

"Three Stripe loves me. He won't let anything bad happen to me."

"That's not how I read the situation, Gwyl," said Pierrick. "The love part. Yes. He does love you. I hadn't quite seen that, before. I see that now. But protecting you? I don't think you should count on it."

Gwyl exchanged a look with him. Pierrick might not have gotten himself adopted by the leader of The People. He might have only remained a wretched slave. Yet he knew as much about the ways of The People as Gwyl did. In certain awful ways, he knew more. Until recently, Gwyl hadn't realized what Porcupine's role in the village was. But now he saw.

Pierrick knew. Pierrick had known for a long time. Gwyl might have been trying his best to protect Pierrick, but in many ways, Pierrick had been trying to protect Gwyl.

That's how it had always been between them, and always would be.

"I see it clearly now," said Keera, looking from one of them to the other. "You can't go back there, Gwyl."

"I have to," he said.

"What about me?"

"You have to go with the expedition or stay here with Tigeny. It's too dangerous for you to go with me."

"Some of us, I see, are luckier in our promises than others," said Keera.

"No, Keera. You don't understand. It's extremely dangerous. You can't go there," said Pierrick.

"I just did, and nothing bad happened to me."

"That's because you were incredibly lucky. That won't happen twice," said Pierrick. They all sat thinking about Keera and her unlikely exploits. How, as she sneaked up river, she had seen some stealthy dark native come out of a hole in the river bank and a tall gaunt man with white-blond hair stand at the mouth of this hole, bidding him farewell. How she had waited until the native had gone away, and then sneaked to the hole herself. And all the rest of it.

Gwyl stayed silent. Pierrick was right. Keera had her spooky qualities. But they could protect her only so much. And how could he ever explain? To keep one promise, he had to break the other.

"Suppose," said Tigeny softly, "there were a way you could do both."

The three of them turned to her in surprise.

"Suppose Keera and I could go together to the village of The People. In a spiritual sense, I mean," she said. "And then, Gull, you'll keep your promise to Three Stripe. And Keera will be there with you too."

"Gull?" said Keera. "Oh," she said. "Gull."

# INTERLUDE: THE CLOUDS

D ee was inconsolable. Mervin felt helpless. There was nothing he could do for his friend except let Dee talk it out.

"I watched it all, Mervin. Gilles sent his men in ships across from the northern reaches of the Sceptered Isle."

"How did he manage that, Dee? Caedon is dead. So how does Gilles have any control over the affairs of the Sceptered Isle? Any access to ports and ships?"

"Ailys," said Dee.

"Oh," said Mervin. "Right." The tangled political affairs of the Sceptered Isle were too much for him to keep up with. They were like the weather. They changed so rapidly.

"Ailys is queen now."

"Ah," said Mervin, remembering. "And Gilles controls Ailys."

"Yes. So Gilles's plans advance. He is the real monarch of the Sceptered Isle, and Ailys is his figurehead."

"Nothing new there. He had the same arrangement with Caedon."

"I doubt Gilles would have withdrawn his wards from Caedon, when Keera went after him, if he hadn't had an understudy waiting in the wings."

"Good point," said Mervin.

"And so, with Ailys's help, Gilles sent men to destroy Wat and Mirrin on their island fortress."

"Keera's parents. I see why you are so distressed."

"Keera's parents, the last of The Rising." Dee stood with his hands shoved in the pockets of his robe. He insisted that his robes have pockets, even though it wasn't traditional. But when had Dee ever been traditional?

Dee heaved a sigh. "I watched it. The two of them fought til their last breath. Gilles's men landed in the dark of the moon and overran the island, killing most in their sleep. Mirrin fought with her knives. Wat had his sword, and he's good with it, Mervin. In spite of being one-armed." Dee shook himself. "Was good," he corrected himself. "His eyesight is not perfect. I tried my best with it, and Jillian tried, too, and he does have sight in that remaining eye of his. Did. Not perfect, though. Someone came up on his blind side, while he was fighting off several of them, and they killed him. Then they killed her. I think she was glad of it. When she saw—" He gave a little gulp. Mervin wanted to put his arms around his friend and console him like a child. He waited.

When Dee didn't or couldn't go on, Mervin finished for him. "And now they are across that river."

"Umm," said Dee.

Mervin looked at him sharply. "John. What have you done."

Dee waved a vague hand at something going on below and turned and walked away, wiping at his eyes.

Mervin leaned far over to look. Not across the river. Down on the land. Two owls, winging their way improbably across a forest, following a young woman with wild curling red hair and a determined air about her.

"Oh, John." Mervin sighed. "You're so predictable."

# 5 KEERA: Bird Magic

## Ornithomancer

"Do you trust me, Keera?" said Tigeny

"Yes," Keera whispered, but she was deeply unhappy. That morning Pierrick had left to meet up with the expedition, which filled her with joy. But Gwyl had headed back up the path to the village of The People, as he called them, and that filled her with dread. Especially because she wasn't with him.

After a night of reunion when she thought no force under the Spheres could pry her from his arms, he had kissed her and slipped from the furs of their bed in a corner of Tigeny's hut.

"It's time for me to go, my darling. You and Tigeny will do what we discussed," he had whispered to her. Then he had stood outside in the first light of dawn, talking things over with Pierrick. She could tell Pierrick, too, was reluctant to leave Gwyl's side. She could tell Pierrick knew too well the dangers Gwyl would be going back to face.

"You've been lucky with The People so far, Gwyl," Keera heard him murmur. "But now things have changed."

And Gwyl's voice. "I'm Three Stripe's son."

Keera didn't know what he meant by that. *I'm Three Stripe's son, so I'll be protected?* Or maybe, *I'm Three Stripe's son, so I have a standard to uphold no matter what price I have to pay.*

Now both brothers were gone. Keera stood hugging her arms around herself in the chill morning light, trying to warm herself at Tigeny's fire. She knew something the brothers didn't know, and she suspected Tigeny knew it too. She hadn't stumbled on Pierrick by accident in that cave. The owls had led her to it. And she didn't even know how they could have done it. It was too far north for the owls.

"Shall I tell you about yourself?" Tigeny said to her now.

"Yes, please," Keera whispered.

"When you were young, you had unusual powers."

"Yes, and then the Fire Child's farwydd took them away."

"She took some of them away," Tigeny corrected.

"My mother, Mirin, always told me I had other, softer powers to draw on, if I would only cultivate them, but I never have. Not really."

"Yet birds are your friends. I'm guessing you've had some experiences with birds, getting close to them."

Keera thought of Hildr. "Yes," she said.

"And the ghost birds are your friends."

Keera looked at her carefully. "You know, don't you. You know they led me to Pierrick, and so to Gwyl."

"They're my friends, too. They told me how they've been visiting you."

"I don't understand something. I thought it was too cold for them this far north."

"Maybe they weren't here with you in the physical sense. Maybe in another sense. The ghost birds are a deep part of your abilities, Keera."

"What do you mean by that? When I was a child, our neighbors accused me of witchcraft. Do you mean something like that?"

"Witchcraft is a very different thing. You're not a witch, Keera. You are a mage."

"Like Old Dee?"

Tigeny laughed. "Yes, if you want to use as your example one of the most powerful mages under the Nine Spheres. Most of us aren't so powerful. You're not."

"I know Old Dee. He had to have a lot of help to cure my father's blindness." Keera couldn't keep herself from looking skeptical. "Not that I'm not grateful. I love Old Dee. Or did. I think he dwindled away."

Tigeny laughed harder. "No, you can be assured he did not. He may have left your plane, but he's still out there."

Keera felt a burst of joy. "I love Old Dee!" she said again.

"And he speaks most highly of you, Keera."

"So you're a mage, too?"

"Yes, with rather minor powers."

"The farwydd took my powers."

"Only some of them," Tigeny repeated. "She was doing it for your own good, you know."

"I'm grateful for what she did for me and my family. I hated her at first, but now I don't."

"That's good, Keera. But you must know, you have other powers, and not just the soft powers of your mother. At one time, your mother was granted other powers by agreement between her Child and the Child of Earth. The granting of powers under unusual circumstances. That can happen. And cooperation among the Children happens all the time. Otherwise, there'd be no balance."

Keera started to raise an objection. Then she decided maybe she'd better just listen.

"Most mages don't even know they're mages. Their powers are hidden from them. Your father's brother John, for example. He had certain powers, and his Child allowed him to use them. It's possible he could have developed them further, but he wasn't willing to pay the price."

"There's a price to be paid for witchcraft. My mother told me that."

"This is different. Maybe in time you'll learn more about your own powers, Keera. For now, you and I should focus on some very simple abilities of yours. Your connection with owls, for example. You can channel what they know and see. You're a certain type of mage, Keera, and so was your mother. And so too was your uncle, John. The kind called *ornithomancer*. I myself am an ornithomancer. That means you and I understand the language of birds and see through their eyes. It means we can make predictions based on the movement and behavior of birds. It means we can call birds to us and draw their power into ourselves."

"My best friend back on the Fire Isle was a falcon. And my spirit animal is the firebird," said Keera.

Tigeny nodded. "You are the Fire Child's, inscribed as her own." She reached out to touch Keera where her firebird had marked her shoulder. "I am the Sky Child's," Tigney continued, "so I have special connections to the Sky Child's own birds, the ghost birds. The owls. But the Sky Child has allowed me to grant you some of my powers."

"Do you mean that the birds I kept seeing in Three Rivers came because of you?"

"I sent them to comfort you. I had the permission of a mighty one to do so."

"Thank you for this gift, Tigeny. They did comfort me. My parents were dead, but in a way. . ."

"Yes," said Tigeny. "In a way, they were still with you. They still are. And now they'll help you again."

"There was a voice," said Keera, "a voice that told me Gwyl was not dead."

"You were right to trust that voice," said Tigeny.

"I can tell Gwyl didn't believe you, when you said you and I would be with him in the village of The People. I think he just nodded along, as you explained, so I wouldn't try to follow him."

Tigeny laughed. "You're right, Keera. That's exactly what he thinks. But you'll follow him just the same. You will."

"How will I do that?"

"All the birds of the sky are connected. Did you know that? They are connected in a vast network. I can call on my birds, the owls, to let us see through the eyes of birds here in the north. Which bird shall we choose?"

Keera thought hard. Her answer would determine a great deal. "I choose," she said. She thought harder. "I choose the gull."

"And that, my dear Keera, is why you are an ornithomancer. You chose exactly right. You haven't had much training, but you have a strong natural ability. It has come to you from both sides of your family, too. Why the gull, do you think."

"The firebird is my spirit animal. The gull is the spirit animal of Gwyl. Even though he doesn't believe."

"In a way, he does. Why would he go back to his father Three Stripe? It's because of his sense of honor, true. But because Three Stripe saw something in Gwyl, and gave him that channel, and so the two of them have a deep connection that nothing will ever put aside."

"Is Three Stripe a mage, too?"

"No, he just instinctively knew something about Gull. Let us call him by his name. When I call your man *Gull*, my dear friend, I'm calling him by his true name, son of the Child of Sea. You and I are mages, Keera. We are ornithomancers. We will follow Gull by connecting with the birds and what they see and know. That knowledge of theirs will become our knowledge."

All this time, Tigeny had been stirring something in her pot. Now she dipped up a bark cup of its contents for Keera, and a cup for herself.

"First we'll join ourselves with my own spirit animal, the owl, through the grace of my Child, the Child of Sky. After that, we'll beg the owls to join us further to the bird of the northern coast, the gull. And then we'll see what we see. Have courage, Keera. We won't see with human eye. We must not allow ourselves to fear as humans do. Are you ready?"

Keera nodded. She drank her cup. It was bitter.

She saw that Tigeny was drinking hers.

Tigeny began singing a hypnotic song. Keera recognized it. Her mother had sung a few verses of it to her once. But she'd never heard the whole thing, and she'd never heard it in this form.

> One for sorrow,
> Two for mirth,
> Three for death,
> Four for birth,
> Five for silver,
> Six for gold,
> Seven for secrets never told.
> Eight for Ghost Bird, eight for Owl
> underneath the Nine Spheres' bowl.

As soon as Tigeny finished the song, she began it again. The song cycled around and around until Keera felt herself getting impossibly sleepy. She felt herself moving into a mist of sleep. Then she felt herself rising into the air. The owls were there, one on either side of her, and she was flying with them, supported by their love. The mist deepened. She no longer saw the owls, or any bird at all. She herself had become a bird, and she felt the sweep of the ocean wind underneath her wings.

She flew over the sea to the cliffs at the edge of the sea. She flew high above, so that she could look down to the land beneath.

Far below, there was a village. She swerved and spiraled closer, always looking.

A young man was walking the path that led to the village. She followed this young man, dark, hard-muscled, intent. He stopped short of the common area of the village. Ranged to meet him were many other men, all with weapons in their hands. The young man showed them his own hands, empty. A tall older man stepped out to him and took him by the arm, leading him through these grim other men to a dwelling. The two went inside.

A voice somewhere was insisting. *Blend with the smoke, Keera. Filter with the smoke of the hearth fire into the dwelling.*

And so Keera did. And so what the gull saw, she saw.

## Fathers and Sons

"Gull. Son. You have kept faith with me," Keera heard Three Stripe say to Gwyl.

"I always will, Father," said Gwyl.

"Do you know how this fills me with joy, son?" said Three Stripe. Keera heard his voice choke with emotion. "But it fills me with terror, too."

"Porcupine demands his sacrifice," Keera heard Gwyl say.

"Yes," said Three Stripe.

"If he can't have my brother, he'll have another of my kind," said Gwyl.

"Yes," said Three Stripe.

"He'll have me," said Gwyl.

"Yes."

"Then tell him, Father. I'm ready," said Gwyl. "I'll pay the price for my brother."

*No no no no no* thought Keera.

*Have courage, Keera,* came a voice, the voice of Tigeny. *If your courage fails you now, Gull is lost. The two of us are lending our courage to the two of them.*

Keera watched the hide curtain of Three Stripe's dwelling pushed aside. The men of the village came in, then parted as one man shoved to the front of the crowd of them. It was Porcupine.

"Give me Gull, brother," said Porcupine, his voice low and menacing. "It is my right."

Keera felt her courage flow into Gwyl and into Three Stripe. "Don't speak to my father in this disrespectful way, old man," said Gwyl, stepping forward. "He doesn't have to give me to you. Here I am. Take me."

Porcupine nodded to the others, who stepped to Gwyl and quickly bound him. They hauled him out of the dwelling and toward the scaffolding of poles.

Keera soared up through the smoke hole and followed. She hovered over the scaffolding as the village men tied Gwyl to it.

Porcupine turned to them all. "In the morning, when the first light of the sun strikes this platform, I will make sacrifice to the Sun God in the name of my dead son, as is my right."

The village men dispersed, each to his dwelling, leaving only Three Stripe standing before Gwyl.

As soon as they were all gone, Three Stripe stepped up onto the platform. He drew his knife.

"Will you cheat the Sun God out of his sacrifice, Father?" Keera heard Gwyl whisper to Three Stripe. "I'd rather it be you who kills me."

"The god won't get my son," said Three Stripe, not bothering to whisper. "Porcupine won't take my son." Swiftly, he cut Gwyl free of the scaffolding, and hauled him bodily off the platform.

"You've done what you said you would do, Gull. You have made your father proud. Now go into the world, my dearest son. Find your wife. Have children. May your Child keep you always." Three Stripe hustled Gwyl to the path out of the village. He and Gwyl stood for a long time, embracing. Then Three Stripe stepped back, fingering the amulet of feather and bone at the cord around his neck. "Go, son, and I'll stay to do what I need to do. Do not be troubled," he said, when Gwyl hesitated. "There is a way to make this right. I've consulted with those who know the ways of the god, and I know how to get that done." He embraced Gwyl. "Trust me, son. I have gained understanding. If only I had before—but all is well, and I have that knowledge now."

Gwyl turned his face away from the village and strode down the path, his back straight. Keera swooped to him, and then somehow she was walking beside him. He looked over at her but said nothing. She saw he couldn't speak. He put his arm around her shoulders. They walked together down the path underneath the stars hanging by their golden chains from the spheres. The silver moon shone over them. A snatch of her mother's song came to her. Tigeny's song, she realized. *Five for silver, six for gold.* . .

They walked arm in arm all the way to Tigeny's hut, and then they tumbled into bed together and slept until the morning made them squint and blink.

"Nine Spheres," Gwyl whispered. "Here's that unruly old sun. Calling on us and waking us up. Why us? Must our lovers' seasons run to his motions, the busy old fool?"

"You belong to me," said Keera. "Doesn't the Sun God know that?" She put up a hand to ward off a beam shining in from a chink in the hut. "His beams are so strong."

"Foolish sun, to take pride in that. I could eclipse them just by closing my eyes, except that I don't want to lose the sight of you that long."

They reached out to each other. She twined her body into his and in some deep place marveled at how her pale creamy self connected so seamlessly into the reaches of his dark polished body. The whole world lay here in her arms. *From the Forgotten Kingdom far to the east, to this place, the Unknown Lands in the west, with all their spices and all their mines of precious gems and gold, the sun shining on us shines on the whole world. The whole world is right here with us. Right here in this bed*, thought Keera. Mostly, though, she didn't think at all. Just savored. Looked. Breathed him in. Listened to his breathing, as it hoarsened and came faster, and as hers did. Touched. And touched. And touched.

Much later, Gwyl looked over at Keera, a dangerous glint in his eye. He pulled her closer to him under the furs. "So tell me, darling wife. What were you doing there in the village. I thought you had agreed to stay here with Tigeny and think mystical thoughts about me."

"I did," Keera assured him.

"Where is Tigeny now?"

"She hasn't come back yet, looks like."

"Come back from where?"

"Up there," said Keera, vaguely gesturing upward.

"Two spooky women," said Gwyl, and shivered.

"We were right there with you the whole time," Keera told him.

"What would you have done if Porcupine had tried to, you know—"

Keera put her hand over his mouth. "Don't say it," she said. "I don't want to hear it. I want to leave this place and never come back."

"I think we will come back," said Gwyl. "Some day." He got a faraway look in his eye.

"Who's the spooky one now?" demanded Keera.

Later that morning, when they came out of the hut, they found Tigeny calmly cooking up a pot of something that smelled very good. She dipped out bowls for them both, and they sat at her fire and ate it.

"I'll guide you to Three Rivers, if you wish it," she said, when they'd finished.

"What do you think, Gwyl," said Keera. "Maro doesn't know me there. He just thinks I'm Fiona's servant." Keera hoped to her Child she was right about that. She wasn't as sure as she made herself sound.

"He'll know me, though," said Gwyl. "But I don't see where else we can go. Everyone at Fishers' Bay is dead. I suppose that means Yann is dead. All the settlements on this coast are Ansgar's, so we can't seek out any of them. I suppose I may as well go to Three

Rivers. Maro doesn't know I've been serving your father. What can he do to me? Kick me out? Maybe that. Or maybe he'll just ignore me. Once I'm at Three Rivers, I'll talk it over with Pierrick and figure out the best place for us to live, and then we'll go there. While I'm at Three Rivers, we'll pretend you don't know me."

"I suppose that's as good a plan as any," said Keera.

So the next day, with Tigeny as their guide, they headed out on their journey to Three Rivers. When they got there, over a sen'night later, Tigeny gave Keera a quick embrace and melted back into the trees.

"I felt something leave us, when Tigeny left. Some extra layer of protection," said Gwyl. They stood under the shadow of trees at the edge of the forest, looking toward the palisades of Three Rivers.

"You felt something leave us because it did, Gwyl."

"But I still have you," said Gwyl. "It's strange. Deep inside, I feel like I have Three Stripe too. Deep inside, we're still keeping faith with each other."

"You're a man in search of a father," said Keera.

"I suppose I am. I've lost the only thing I've ever owned of my real father. I've lost the brooch of the Six Proud Walkers."

"Maybe it's the inner feeling that counts," said Keera.

"I suppose you'd better go into the town and find Fiona," said Gwyl. "I'll wait a few days so it won't look like we have any connection. I'll camp outside the town. Then I'll show up. I wonder what Maro will have to say to me."

Keera looked him over. "Will he even recognize you?"

"I still look like one of The People?"

"Yes, you do," said Keera. "Anyone will think it, until they notice your eyes." She examined him carefully. The deeply bronzed skin, the silken black fall of hair over the hard muscles of his shoulders and back.

"Maybe I should cut this all off," he said, gesturing to his hair, "and let my beard grow. Then I'll blend in more." It was a practical country they'd come to. Every man of the settlers went about with cropped hair, not the long hair of the lords and gentles back home.

"No!" she heard herself blurting out. In her mind, she said, *It suits you, Gull.*

He sighed. "I think I'd better," he told her. "And put on a tunic that covers this." He tapped the gull tattoo on his shoulder.

"Well," she said. "Yes. I suppose so. My man has prettier hair than mine. That's just wrong."

Her heart broke, though. His eyes had filled with tears.

"Before we go away separately, let's at least eat something together. I can't stand the thought of parting with you. Let's stay together just a little longer," he said at last.

*Thank the Child*, Keera thought. *He had a momentary pang, but he's fine now.* She wondered then about Gwyl's life with The People. She saw how deep his feelings ran.

Gwyl reached into the pouch slung over his shoulder and pulled out the haunch of a roasted rabbit. The two of them sat down together in a little clearing, leaning together underneath the trees, enjoying the meat but enjoying more the way they sat touching each other. Every so often, one reached out a hand to stroke the other as if neither one of them could believe their great good fortune.

Gradually, though, Keera realized that underneath Gwyl's joy lay a grief maybe beyond healing.

"Something happened, back there. I'm beginning to see it now. Three Stripe sent me away so I wouldn't try to stop it."

"But he said—" Keera began.

Gwyl looked brooding up into the trees and shook his head. "I should go back." He stopped then and looked over at her with the quick smile she loved. "Too late for that, and it would be ungracious to walk away from the biggest gift the Children have ever granted me. You, Keera." He brought her hand to his mouth and kissed it.

But soon turned somber again.

"Whatever did happen back there at the village, I've lost that life. That part of myself. One life ending. My other one beginning again. You're right, Keera. I'm a man always looking for a father. And I keep losing them."

## A Stacked Deck

Keera had no trouble slipping back into Three Rivers. The guards gave her a strange look, as she came in through the gates in her trousers and tunic, but by then she'd removed the head cloth and her red hair fell free in ringlets about her shoulders. She smiled at them as if her odd clothes were the most ordinary thing in the world, and they shrugged and slouched back blinking against the wood of the palisades.

As soon as she got to Fiona's room, which was deserted, she changed into her regular servant's long cloth dress of gray homespun, not really a kirtle, more of a very long shapeless kind of tunic with sleeves. Everyone except the womenfolk of the gentles wore clothes like these. Fiona had beautiful fancy clothes she could have worn to court, if she were back home. Not Keera.

She tied her hair up again in a snowy white cloth, and tied another white cloth at her waist for an apron. Everyone used the supple hide shoes of the natives, but her own were worn out from all the walking she'd done. She burrowed around in the servants' chest of clothing to find herself a new pair.

Then she went into the kitchen to help set up for the evening meal. A few of the other servants cast startled glances at her. The rest just nodded at her and handed her platters of meat to carry into the governor's great hall. She'd made herself so quiet and inconspicuous that most of them hadn't even realized she'd been gone.

Fiona caught sight of her in the corridor to the main hall and rushed to her for a discreet hug. "Is Gwyl—"

"He's fine," said Keera. "He's waiting a little while before he comes into the town."

"Pierrick told his father that Gwyl was out hunting when the expedition came. He has told Maro that Gwyl will be at Three Rivers soon."

"What did Maro make of that?"

Fiona shrugged. "Pierrick said he didn't say much about it at all."

"But Maro is glad to get Pierrick back."

"Oh, yes. If I didn't already know how much I dislike that man, I could almost think I do like him. He dotes on Pierrick. That's clear to see. He's overjoyed to have Pierrick with him." Then she turned a misty-eyed smile on Keera. "And Alan. Wait until you see Alan. He just glows. Rozenn is happy too, of course, but she's too little to realize how long he has been gone. She just knows he's here and loves her."

Keera hugged Fiona tight. Then they parted, because people were beginning to arrive at the hall now, and they didn't want to attract undue attention.

For close to a sen'night, nothing happened. Keera found herself getting nervous. Where was Gwyl? Why hadn't he appeared in Three Rivers? Suppose he had headed back to Three Stripe? That thought above all tormented her, because she knew how tormented Gwyl was at what might have happened once they left the village.

She took to hovering around the town gates.

And then one day, around mid-morning, she saw a man enter through the gates, and the guards stepping to him, to question him. A slender young man with shaggy chopped off dark hair and the hint of a new beard on his deeply tanned cheeks, dressed in hide trousers but a faded cloth tunic and patched cloak.

He and two of the guards headed for the main hall as Keera hung back in the shadow of the town granaries.

She knew she shouldn't call out, even though she mightily wanted to rush to Gwyl. But she didn't like it, the way each of the guards had a hand on him. She didn't like it at all.

She followed at a discreet distance.

They walked Gwyl into the main hall. One of them stood with him there as Keera watched from the doorway. The other guard made away into the depths of the house.

An interior door crashed against the wall and a man strode through into the hall. It was Maro. He stood glowering. "Gwyl," he bit out.

"Maro," said Gwyl. Gwyl did not bow to his step-father, or make any gesture of respect toward him.

Keera noticed Gwyl didn't call him father, either. She wondered if he ever had. She knew he never would.

"Pierrick told you I was coming," said Gwyl.

"He did. You are a renegade."

"A renegade?"

"You've gone over to the heathen."

Gwyl shrugged. "Pierrick and I lived with them for a while. That hardly makes me a renegade."

"They beat my son."

"We had some hard times." Gwyl's voice was perfectly even.

"You didn't fare so badly, I hear."

Keera put her hand to her mouth. Maro was twisting what had happened to Gwyl and Pierrick. Keera knew this couldn't be what Pierrick had told his father.

"I got Pierrick out," said Gwyl.

"My men got Pierrick out," Maro snarled. "You, I hear, ingratiated yourself with his torturers."

"That's not true," said Gwyl.

*We have all made a terrible mistake,* thought Keera now. *We have all misunderstood Maro and his vindictive ways.* Then she couldn't help thinking, *Ha. I was the one who got Pierrick out.* In some part of her, she wanted to stride up to Maro and tell him so.

"Lock this man up," said Maro to the guards and turned on his heel. The door slammed closed behind him.

The guards put hands on Gwyl. He looked from one to the other of them and shrugged. As they hustled him out the door past Keera, he flicked his eyes in her direction and managed a wry smile.

*Nine Spheres*, thought Keera. *How many times will I have to go about rescuing this man? And how will I do it?*

As she stood there stunned, Pierrick rushed past her to the doorway. He hardly looked like the same person. He looked prosperous, well-dressed, clean, his cheeks shaven, his beard gone, his hair neatly cropped. He gazed out after the guards, his shoulders slumped.

He swore under his breath. Then he turned to her. "Keera," he said, skipping over the niceties. "Go tell Fiona what has happened. I'll come to you in Fiona's rooms after board this evening, and we'll figure out what to do."

Keera nodded and sped to the rooms. Oddly, Maro had been keeping Pierrick with him and had not allowed him to move into Fiona's rooms with her.

Fiona hadn't been worried.

"He doesn't want to let Pierrick out of his sight just yet. But I'm his wife, and Maro has always treated me well. In a day or two, Pierrick will move in here, or Maro will find us some place else to live. We'll all be together. And Alan will be back where he belongs, with us."

Keera wondered about that. Maro snatching Alan away from Fiona. Now Pierrick.

That night, they all crowded into Fiona's room. Pierrick and Fiona sat close together on Fiona's bed, Pierrick's arm about her, Fiona leaning against his broad chest. Even hollow-cheeked from near-starvation, Pierrick was a large man. Rozenn played at her parents' feet. Keera perched on her own small bed.

"Keera, you have to believe me. I told my father none of the things you heard him say to Gwyl," said Pierrick after Keera had made sure no one was lurking about in the corridor outside the room.

"I do believe you," said Keera. Keera had told Pierrick every word she could remember of Maro's accusations.

"If not for you and Gwyl, I'd be dead," said Pierrick. "If not for Gwyl, I'd be long dead, because sometime during those terrible seasons with that terrible man, I would have given up, and I would have—"

"Shhh," said Fiona, putting a finger to his lips. "None of that now."

"None of you know the half of what he did to me. Gwyl doesn't know." Pierrick looked haunted

"Shh, now," said Fiona.

Keera wondered if Pierrick knew Gwyl had gone back to die in his place. She decided not to tell him that. Pierrick knew only that Gwyl had gone back to say a last goodbye to his father Three Stripe.

Truly, no one else would have gone back at all.

But Pierrick knew too well what Gwyl's feelings were about fathers. So it made a kind of crazy sense to Pierrick, and Keera decided he didn't have to know anything further than that. Otherwise, Pierrick really might have seen that, in a way, Maro's accusation was right. In a way, Gwyl was a kind of renegade. He had taken on The People's sense of honor as his own. He'd gone back to make things right, whatever the consequences. But he had known Pierrick had not taken on The People's values. It wasn't for Pierrick to pay the price. It was for Gwyl, if a price had to be paid.

Pierrick knew his brother better than Keera gave him credit for. "Gwyl became a part of them. He became that man's son. He gave it all up for me," he whispered.

Keera wanted to shout at him, *What about me?* But she kept quiet.

She suddenly thought of the spiral on Dragon Wind's sail. The three birds of prey, each spiraling outward in a different direction. It was as if Gwyl stood at the center, and those fierce birds were pulling him apart.

She shook the thought off. They needed to attend to practical matters. "What do we do now? How do we get Gwyl out of Maro's hands?"

"There will be a trial. I heard Father talking of it at the evening board," said Pierrick. "I'll speak at the trial. I'll make Father understand. I'll say it in public, so he can't twist my words."

*But Pierrick,* thought Keera, and then a phrase of Old Dee's came to mind. *The deck is stacked.*

"Husband," said Fiona. Her voice was gentle. "I know your father loves you, and I know you can't help loving him. He's your father. But you must know—"

Pierrick raised a hand, forestalling her. "I know. I do know. I'm always hoping, I suppose. But from the moment Gwyl and I walked away from him, and from our mother, when we were still just boys, I've known what he is."

"It's a hard thing," murmured Fiona. "But you do know that no matter what you say at the trial, your father is going to condemn Gwyl."

Pierrick stared hard at the floor.

"Well," he said, looking up at them. "There's only one way. We must bust Gwyl out of there. Too bad he's in a barred room, and not some earth cave."

"With vines for bonds," said Keera.

"You'd be surprised. Those vines, as you call them, are tough."

"So how do we get him out of there?" said Keera.

They all sat and thought about it.

"Fiona, you'll take the children and wait with Keera down at the river." Pierrick turned to Keera now. "Keera. You're in danger too. I got the oddest impression the other day. I got the feeling Maro knows who you are, somehow."

Fiona exclaimed, but Keera just nodded.

"I think you're right," she whispered.

"I got the impression he's just biding his time, with you. After he deals with Gwyl, you're next. You and Fiona must both get out of here. Take the children. Hide somewhere down by the river. I'll sneak up on the guard who stands before the room where they're keeping Gwyl, and I'll overpower him and take the key. I can do it. Hard living has made me strong, and now I'm strong and well-fed. The guard won't be suspecting anything from

Maro's son. As soon as I spring Gwyl out, he and I will join you two."

They all nodded.

Then Fiona looked stricken. "You're forgetting something."

Pierrick realized at almost the same time. "Alan," he said. "Can't a father and son go off on an expedition together? A father-son walk in the woods?" he said after a moment. "The rest of you will sneak out. Then I'll circle around and—"

"He'll never let Alan go off alone with you." Fiona's tone was grim.

"His own father? Maro's own son?" said Pierrick.

"He won't," said Fiona. "At the least, he'll send someone with you. Probably several someones."

"He'll say he can't risk it. I've been a captive so long," said Pierrick, looking gloomy. "He'll say he would be riven with fear the entire time we were gone. He'll say for the sake of my old father, I need to allow his men to accompany us."

"Yes," said Fiona. "That's exactly what he'll say."

"Do you think he'll suspect? That I'm trying to get to Gwyl?"

"After you two walked away from him like that, in your boyhood? You know he will," said Fiona.

"He's jealous of Gwyl," said Keera with sudden insight. "That's the half of it, right there. It's not that he hates Gwyl so much, because his father was in The Rising and he hates The Rising. Well, that too. But he's afraid you love Gwyl more than you love him. And he can't stand that."

Pierrick looked at her silently. Finally he nodded. "And he is right," he said softly.

"Alan," said Fiona. "Maro's little hostage. He'll keep him close, and that way, he'll keep you close."

"So," said Keera. "Two rescues. Alan and Gwyl."

"It will be a while, before this trial Father plans to hold," said Pierrick. "Let's think it over. In the meantime, we need to sleep."

Keera gave Fiona and Pierrick a quick smile. "Do you know, I sometimes get restless, and I've found an unused room, an empty storeroom where I can pace without disturbing Fiona until I fall asleep. I even have a bed set up there. Rozenn," she said to the little girl and held out her hand. "Come with me, darling. We'll see your parents in the morning."

She and Rozenn left the room. As she softly pulled the door closed behind her, she saw Pierrick reach out a loving hand to Fiona. Then, chattering brightly to the little girl, Keera led Rozenn down the corridor.

## A Scaffold

It was clear to them all, as the days drew on, that Maro was never going to let Alan go, and in that way, he could control his son.

A fortnight later, something chilling happened.

The trial was to start in two days, and out in the courtyard, a kind of square made by the governor's house and its outbuildings, some men were building a scaffold.

Fiona, Pierrick, and Keera met to strategize.

Pierrick sat staring at the floor. "If I see one more scaffold, I am going to run mad and tear it down with my teeth and hands," said Pierrick, low.

Fiona put out a hand to Pierrick and kept it on him. How Keera wished she had Gwyl beside her, his comforting presence.

Fiona looked at them both. "This is what I think," she began. "I think we're out of time. I think we need to get Gwyl out. It's clear to me what's about to happen to him. This trial your father is going to hold. It will be a sham," she said to Pierrick.

He nodded.

"Maro is actually going to kill Gwyl," said Keera, feeling a horror grip her.

"Yes," said Fiona calmly. "Looks like he is. So we'll get Gwyl out. Then you and he will go far away from here, Keera. And Pierrick and the children and I will have to stay behind," Fiona concluded. "That's the only thing we can do."

"You're right, Fiona. We'll have to work to get ourselves out later," said Pierrick. "Get Gwyl and Keera out first."

"But how?" said Keera. "Me, I'm the easy part. I can just walk out of the gates. No one will stop me. Maro may have his suspicions about me, but I'm guessing he doesn't think I'll try to get away from him as long as he has Gwyl, and the men at the gates will just think I'm headed out to gather herbs." She thought for a moment. "But how will you get Gwyl out of that locked room?"

"The way I said before. I'll walk up to the guard, knock him down, take his key, and get Gwyl out," said Pierrick.

"Meanwhile, your father will be doing what?" Fiona's voice was gentle.

"I don't care what he will be doing. I just know what I'll be doing," said Pierrick.

"That's a good way to get yourself locked up too, Pierrick," said Keera.

"My father will never hurt me. So I don't care."

"But Pierrick. Remember back in the village of The People? When Three Stripe realized what Gwyl was about to do, Three Stripe had some men tie him up so he couldn't get to you," said Keera.

"I'll kill every one of them," said Pierrick. His big hands clenched and unclenched.

"Your father won't let that happen," said Keera.

The three of them sat together in a state of despair.

There came a knock on the door. Fiona rose to get it.

Three men stood shuffling awkwardly on the doorsill. "Sorry for the interruption, my lady Fiona," said one of them. "But the Governor-General needs Sir Pierrick, and we're to take him to His Excellency." They looked apologetically around at Pierrick. Their hands hovered over the thick clubs at their belts.

Pierrick darted a quick look at his sword, hanging from its baldric on the other side of the room. The three men stepped in and stood between him and the sword. "Please come with us, sir," said the one doing all the talking.

Fiona turned to Pierrick. "You have to go with them," she said.

He rose to his feet and turned a look of despair on Fiona and Keera. Then he went out into the corridor with the men.

Fiona rushed to Keera and was about to put her arms about Keera when they heard a banging and scuffling from the corridor.

Pierrick was thwacking one of the men over the head with his fists, kicking at another, and it looked to Keera as though he'd grabbed the club from the third.

"Pierrick's winning," said Fiona.

And he would have, if two more men hadn't rounded the corner to subdue him.

Keera pulled Fiona with her back into the room, yanked the door to, and tried to bar it, but before she could, another of Maro's men thrust into their room and pushed her aside. "Lady Fiona," he said. "The governor wishes to see you, too."

He stood to let her pass out into the corridor. She glanced over at Keera as she went. "We'll talk later," said Fiona. "In the meantime, see to the laundry and mend my best dress."

"Yes, my lady," said Keera, with a deep curtsey.

As soon as Fiona had been led away, Keera dropped to her bed and burst into tears.

*What now?* she thought. *Where are the owls now?*

Since arriving back at Three Rivers, she'd gone out to the marshes every evening, but the owls were gone.

She tried to steady her mind and send a message to Tigeny, but she despaired. *I'm too untutored,* she thought. *If I have power to do this thing, I don't know how to tap into that power.*

She wandered out to the gates, thinking maybe she could try one more time to find the owls, but what they could do to help her, or any of them, she failed to understand. As she went through the courtyard, she tried to turn her face away so she wouldn't see the scaffold Maro's men were building, but the pounding and tapping of their hammers followed her mockingly all the way to the gates.

As she neared the gates, one of the guards straightened up.

"Goodwife Keera," he greeted her politely.

"Good day to you," she said, trying to make her voice pleasant and ordinary. She clutched her hands underneath her apron to stop their trembling. Suppose this man had orders to seize her.

"Going out to the marsh?"

"It's a fine day. I thought I might look for herbs along the river." By now, she had become known throughout the town as the woman you'd come to if your stomach ached or your head, or you had an embarrassing flux, or an enflamed sore.

"Goodwife, I have a message for you," said the guard, pulling a bit of parchment from his cloak.

"A message?" Keera looked at him, startled. Almost no one in Three Rivers knew their letters, not outside the governor's house.

"This," said the guard. "One of them dirty heathen brought it this morning, said to give it to Lady Fiona's servant." The man chuckled. "He said he'd give me a shiny thing if I'd get it to you." The guard held up a coin. "I don't think the poor naked fellow knew what it was he was giving me." The guard bit the coin. "But it's good silver, mistress."

Trying her best to keep her hand steady, Keera reached out for the little parchment the guard held.

"Wonder what it could be?" she said. He was watching her curiously, so she unrolled it. "I don't know my letters. It must be for her ladyship, or maybe for Sir Pierrick. I'll take it to them later," she told the guard. "You have my thanks." And she gave the guard a coin, too. Then she forced herself to walk calmly through the gates, calmly down the path.

As soon as she was out of sight of the gates, though, she broke into a run. She ran all the way to the marsh, and to the trees beyond, and into Gwyl's arms.

*If I see one more scaffold, I think I will run mad*, the parchment had read. *Meet me by the big hollow tree down at the marsh.*

# 6 GWYL: The Journey

## Where and Why

As they made their way through the forest away from the town, Gwyl kept his hand on Keera, to guide her. But that really wasn't it. He had to keep a hand on her. He had to keep touching her. He had to touch her or die.

"I hate leaving Pierrick and Fiona behind," said Keera.

"We have no choice," said Gwyl.

"They can't leave their children, and Maro has Alan."

"At least we know he'll never hurt either one of them, Alan or Pierrick," said Gwyl. "If there's anything good about Maro, anything at all, that's it."

"I fear for Fiona, though."

"I doubt Maro will connect her to any plotting. He thinks women are empty-headed and silly. He's just had her taken as another way to control Pierrick." Gwyl stopped and looked around. "This is a good place. We'll camp here. It's getting on twilight."

"Will Maro send men after you?"

"Maybe, but they won't know where to look. This land is vast," said Gwyl. He regarded with satisfaction the little clearing where they stopped. "I'll make a fire here," he said.

Keera began to gather up downed limbs of trees. She brought them to the clearing, and Gwyl began to make a fire.

"How did you get flint and steel?"

"I was busy that sen'night when you went into the town and I stayed outside. I can make a fire without these implements. I've learned how. It's just easier and quicker with flint and steel."

"But where did you get any coin?"

"Trapping. Selling the meat and furs to Maro's factor."

"Right under his nose."

"Right under it." Gwyl grinned at Keera. "I'm near-invisible to all these townspeople, like this." He wondered if his appearance frightened her, or maybe repelled her. His hair hadn't grown out, but he was clean-shaven again and nearly naked. Just a hide about his loins, and his skin was almost as dark as a native's despite being locked away in Maro's squalid little jail for over a fortnight.

Keera moved close to him as the flames rose and began making a satisfying crackle. She put a finger out and traced the gull on his shoulder. "I love this," she whispered.

He pulled her to him and kissed her. They tumbled down before the fire. He helped her wriggle out of her dress, and he unwrapped her headcloth so he could bury his hands in her curls and run his hands through them and bury his head in them. He turned her face to his and kissed her more deeply. She was kissing him back, meeting him kiss for kiss. Their hands were on each other, and then they were entwined as if they were one being.

They lay together in the firelight, gleaming with sweat. He slept a little, his head on her breasts, and she was stroking him and murmuring words of love in his ear.

But at last they rolled apart, and Gwyl sat up. "It's a warm night, and the fire is warm, but we'll get a chill," he told her. He pulled their few bits of clothing over them both, and they lay back again.

"I can hear the river," she said.

"In the morning, we'll go in, and then we'll be as clean as newborn babes," he said.

They slept little. They kept reaching for each other and murmuring to each other in the firelight. Before dawn, they made love to each other again.

Then they did go to the river. The cold river water was clear and delightful on his body, and she was exclaiming and splashing like a girl.

When they clambered out onto the bank again, he took her in his arms. "Look at you. Look how beautiful."

"And you are beautiful, Gwyl," she said, running her hands down his flanks.

"But we'd better put our clothes back on. We have a lot to do," he said. "I need to find some trousers, at least."

"And I'll be an encumbrance in this stupid dress," she said.

"Trousers for both of us."

"I can rip the bottom of this dress off and make myself a tunic out of it," she said. "But where are we going to get any trousers?"

"There's a village a bit downriver." He stopped and turned to her. Her eyes were huge. "Don't fear, my darling. They're friendly people."

"How do you know?"

"I've visited them already. They know my father." At her startled look, he said, "Well, they really don't know him. They've heard about him. He's a famous warrior. I'm just now finding out how famous. They've heard stories about him. I'm lucky to be the son of such a man." Now he did worry. Would she understand?

She seemed to.

He kicked out the smoldering remains of their fire. Arm in arm, they walked down the bank of the river until they could glimpse, through the trees, signs of a little village.

"Stay here. You'll raise a lot of questions if you come with me," he told her. He melted into the trees away from her, and when he came back to her, he had a pair of trousers for her and was wearing a pair himself. He handed her the knife from his belt, and she hacked off her dress to make herself a tunic, belting it with the sawn-off hem of the dress.

He had food for them, too. She held out her apron, and he put it in. She tied the apron around it into a bundle.

"This is the best thing I got back there," he told her. He took the bow from his shoulder and handed it to her. "Now we'll eat like kings."

"Do you have arrows?"

"A few," he said, showing her. "But I got arrowheads back there, and I can fletch."

"Where do we go now?"

"I'm not sure." He had to admit this to her. The land was vast indeed, but the two of them were adrift on it as surely as if they were out on the wide expanse of the Great Sea.

Where did they belong? They belonged nowhere.

They sat down together under a tree, and she leaned against him.

"That's unusual," he said.

"What?"

"Owls in the daytime."

He was astonished when she leapt to her feet. She saw them. She stretched up her hands to them. And then.

He didn't know how to explain to himself what happened then.

The owls came to her. First they hovered about her, two of them. Then they lit on her outstretched arms. Then they flew away.

"What was that." He stared at her. She had folded herself back down beside him.

"Owls are Tigeny's friends, and now they're mine."

He shook himself, hard.

"And these two owls are—" She stopped. He saw she didn't know how to talk about it with him. "The two of them watch over me," she said at last.

He sat quietly holding her.

"Do you know how I got to you, when you had to go back to the village to fulfill your promise to your father?"

"I'm not sure I want to know how you did it," he whispered.

"Then let's not talk about it," she said. "But now I know where we must go. The owls have told me where."

"They've told you?"

"One for sorrow," she whispered to him. "Two for mirth, three for death, four for birth, five for silver, six for gold.'

He looked over at her, his heart stopped in his mouth.

"Seven for secrets never told," she whispered to him. "It will be my secret why, but I will tell you where."

## How

There may be a why of this, and that I'll never understand," Gwyl was saying to Keera, scrutinizing the forest around them.

"You will. Someday you will."

"Maybe at least the where of it. South, you say."

"Far to the south.

"To the portal of the Sky Child."

"Yes," she said.

"But here's one thing you haven't told me. The why of it, yes, you've hinted you know. You've told me the where of it. Everything but the how of it. You haven't told me the how."

"That's your part," said Keera.

He looked down into her big trusting eyes. The how of it. "Very well. I'm not the Fire Child's or the Earth Child's or the Sky Child's, whoever the Sky Child is and whyever she wants us to visit her portal. But I do know this. I'm the Sea Child's."

He walked over to a big stand of elm and began running his hands over their bark. "We can do this the easy way," he murmured. "But you're telling me we have to go a long way south."

"That's what the owls told me."

He ignored the part about the owls. "Very well. A long way. So we need to do this the right way, not the easy way. Child knows, we have the time." He moved further into the forest. "There," he said, pointing.

A big birch. Not huge. But it didn't have to be huge. *Build me a boat that can carry two.* Was that how it went? Something like that. It was a song echoing in his mind, a song he'd heard somewhere.

"Now I'll give you a task," he said to Keera, smiling down at her. He led her over to another stand of trees, spruce trees. "Dig there," he said.

"Dig?" She looked at him doubtfully.

"Wait." He hunted about for a stout branch downed by the wind, and found one. With his knife, he shaped it quickly into a crude digging stick, a point at its end.

"Use this," he said. He demonstrated. He showed her the roots, how to find them, how to pull them up.

When she saw them, she shuddered.

He realized suddenly why. "These make excellent thongs and ropes. They're very strong."

"I know," she whispered.

"Don't think about that night, my darling. Just think about what good ropes and lacings we'll need, and dig me up a lot of them. I'm going to head into the forest a little way. I saw some cedar back there," he said. He took the stone axe from his belt and hefted it.

"You're going to cut trees down with that?" she said.

"I don't need very much cedar. But yes, I am. Once you know how to use it, an axe like this makes an excellent tool."

By the time he came back with a nice load of cedar, she had grubbed up a good coil of spruce roots.

"One more thing we'll need." He took her over to a pitch pine. "I need a lot of this gummy sap."

Then he thought about it. "That will have to wait," he said. Instead he took a coil of the spruce root rope and went over to the birch. Looping it around the tree, he began hitching himself up the trunk as she exclaimed below him. He took out his knife and girdled the trunk, then came back down as he sliced the bark vertically away.

Breathing hard at the bottom of the tree, he pulled the roll of birch bark away from it. "There now," he told Keera. "We're going to build a boat. A boat that will carry two. They call this kind of boat *canoe*. I've made big ones, but we just need a small one."

"You and your boat-building."

"It saved me. Maybe saved my life, I'm not sure," he told her. He made the sign of the Sea Child.

With a small bit of the birch bark, he fashioned a rough bowl and a scraper. He handed them to her. "Use this to gather the sap from the pine," he told her. Then he turned to the task of pacing out the length they'd need and setting up a cedar frame.

Several days later, he'd made them a canoe and had made two paddles, as well.

"I'm going to teach you how to paddle this canoe. Don't look so worried, child of the Child of Fire. You can do it."

A few days after that, they were on the wide breast of the river heading south.

## Cold

Because Keera had skin fairer than even Pierrick's, and even more prone to burning, Gwyl made her a broad birch bark hat.

She laughed when she saw it. With his knife and her head-cloth, she made two cloth straps to fasten it to her head and tie under her chin.

They spent all day on the river, and each night, they camped under the stars.

But Gwyl was starting to worry. The nights were getting shorter, the air more chill. If they were at home, he knew they'd be seeing the sights and smelling the delightful odors of harvest-tide, the smoke of fires burning the plowed-under fields, the wine of apples. Along the river banks, some of the trees were spruce and pine that never turned, but other trees were the kind that lost their leaves, and the leaves of these trees were beginning to turn from green to brilliant yellows and oranges. Soon the leaves would fall, leaving the bare branches of winter.

Occasionally they spotted a village through the trees, but Gwyl never chanced stopping at one, not even to trade. His father's name may have reached a good way west and a good way down river, but they had come so far west and south that even his father's fame could not have penetrated so far.

As they paddled under the brilliant early harvest-tide sun or huddled beneath their canoe together in the rains sharp-scented of the winter to come, Gwyl started thinking about how they'd shelter during the cold times. He remembered his frozen walk in the woods as he had tried to escape to Fishers' Bay. He couldn't leave them unprotected.

So now he trapped and hunted not just for meat but for furs. He showed Keera how to scrape and dry and stretch these furs. Then, together, using the spruce root lacings, they turned the furs into warm clothing. Soon they found they needed it. Fur boots, mittens, hats. Long fur tunics and fur trousers.

*We can't stay out here on the river,* thought Gwyl. *We must find a place to over-winter.*

Not two days later, the river broadened to flow swiftly around both sides of a point of land. Gwyl wondered if it might be a large island. But soon he stopped wondering. The waves became so rough and terrifying that he knew, even with his skills and the help of the Sea Child, the canoe would upset and they would go under. In these frigid waters, they wouldn't last long. So, reluctantly, he signaled to Keera to angle in to shore.

It took them over a candle's measure to make it safely to a protected bay. They pulled their canoe out onto the shingle.

"Now what?" said Keera.

Gwyl squinted, looking along the river bank. The rapids, or whatever they were, seemed to go on for as far as the eye could see. "Portage around them," he said. He wondered how long the portage might be. If it were too long, they'd have to hide their canoe, make themselves a quick elm-bark vessel for the times they might be able to spend safely on the river, and then, far downriver, make themselves a new birch bark canoe. Or they could just trudge on with their existing canoe, hoping the portage was not so long. It was hard to tell.

"Who are you?"

Gwyl whirled around at the voice, shoving Keera behind him and flipping his knife from his belt scabbard into his hand.

A man stepped from the canopy of trees growing close by the river bank.

Clearly not a native. A settler.

And he spoke. . . Gwyl regarded him silently. A sort of Baronies language, but not quite.

"Je m'appelle Gwyl," he said.

The man began speaking rapidly to them in some other language. Behind him, Gwyl heard Keera's quick intake of breath.

"He's speaking the language of the Fire Isle. I came to know a little of it, when we lived there." She called out something to the man in that language. Gwyl didn't know what she said, because—in spite of living amongst the people of the Fire Isle for several years—he'd been able to get by with the language of the

Sceptered Isle, which he knew well. Now he wished he had learned the islanders' own language.

"These people are whalers, but now they've moved inland for other fishing," she told Gwyl. "They're not from the Fire Isle, though. It's a puzzle. They're speaking a kind of blend of Fire Isle words and Baronies words. It's a bit hard to make out."

The man came down to them now, showing open hands.

Gwyl put his knife away.

He and Gwyl built a fire and Gwyl led Keera before it to warm her up. At least they were in the furs they'd made for themselves.

They all sat down together, and the man offered them some dried fish.

Among them, they pieced out what each was trying to say. But then Gwyl found out an astonishing thing. He could communicate with the man through his Baronies speech, but he could do so much more easily through the language of The People. This man knew some of that, too. It wasn't exactly like the speech of his father's village, but close enough.

"This man and the others here are from a very remote place in the Baronies," he told Keera. "Down by the southern mountains and the great bay south of the Narrows there. They're notable sailors. They've fished the waters of the New Found Land longer than the men of the Ice-realm. And they have a strange speech of their own that no one recognizes, not even others in the Baronies. Over here, they don't use their language with outsiders. They speak in words combined from the Baronies, the Fire Isle, and the natives. They must be very ingenious people."

To the stranger, he said, "My wife and I are headed south, but we'll need a place to over-winter. If you have suggestions, we'll be happy to hear them. We don't know this land. Looks like you do."

The man spoke rapidly. Between them, Keera and Gwyl figured out he was issuing them an invitation.

Gwyl accepted with gratitude. When the snows came, they were warm and dry in the snug dwelling of this man, whose name, he told them, was Etor. A few other dwellings, housing one or two men each, huddled around a small smithy. There were no women.

"We come here to fish," Etor told him. "Some of us have wives back home. The rest of us make do." He gave Keera a wolfish smile.

"I'm keeping you close to me," Gwyl murmured to Keera. "I'm not sure I altogether trust these men."

What Etor meant later became obvious when they saw a few of the men with native women.

"I don't like that either," said Gwyl.

But the winter passed without incident. Gwyl was valued because he could hunt, and he could use the sapling and thong platforms the others called snowshoes. He had learned, back during his time with The People. He brought meat into the village. Every time he headed out to hunt, though, he left his knife behind with Keera, and he spent quite a bit of time teaching her how to use it. In the spring, as the snows melted and the sun shone more warmly, they dug their canoe out again and set her afloat. They waved to Etor and paddled away.

Etor had told them about the rapids and how far they'd have to portage. Shortly after leaving the small community of the fishermen, Gwyl and Keera beached the canoe, hoisted it on their heads, and walked it around the worst of the rough waters.

From there, the traveling became easy. "We're coming to a very large lake, Etor tells me," Gwyl called over his shoulder at Keera. "A lake almost as big as an ocean. I don't know whether to believe that. Anyway, Etor says to hug the south shore."

They spent most of the long, peaceful summer doing so. At the end of the summer, as Etor had explained, they came to a river that would take them further south.

"But this river has a mighty falls," Etor had told Gwyl. "I've never been past them. I don't know what kind of portage you'll face."

When Gwyl and Keera stood at the falls, they stared in awe. The thunder of it shut out every other noise. The waters foamed and boiled over it from an astonishing height.

"We'll never get around this," said Keera at last.

"We will," Gwyl promised. "It may take a while, though. But I'm thinking we'll have to leave our canoe behind. She's served us well," he said, running a hand over her much-patched hull. He thought of hiding her in some brush but, really, he realized, there would be no point. They wouldn't be back for her. They pulled her up on shore and walked away.

He considered what they should do. They could head overland straight south, but if they did, they'd have no idea where they were. Their best chance would be to stay to the river banks and keep forging west, even though he could tell by the sun that they were now heading straight west, not south at all. South, the direction the owls wanted them to go.

"If only I had Old Dee's magic needle," he said to Keera wistfully, as they sat by their fire below the great falls. "The People took it from me. I suppose Three Stripe has it, or maybe he threw it away. I never thought to ask him for it."

"You could have shown him how it works."

"Yes, I could have. But in the early days, I didn't dare speak to him, and he'd taken everything from me."

"Yet you consider him your father. I don't understand."

"He wasn't cruel to me, as his brother was to Pierrick. But I was nobody. A slave. A nothing. An animal, even. I didn't have any possessions beyond the clothes on my back, and those weren't even really mine."

"I would have hated him," said Keera.

"At first, I did hate him. But later I came to love him."

"How did that happen?"

"Little things. Once I tried to escape, but it was winter, and I nearly froze to death. He found me. He made a fire for me, to warm me up, and he took me back. He didn't punish me. I thought he would maybe kill me."

"Wonder why he didn't," said Keera, with a shiver.

"I think he was coming to love me too," said Gwyl slowly. "There were things we had in common, and things we respected about each other, and he was coming to see that." He stared hard into the fire. "So was I. We went to war together. I saved his life. I didn't think, let me save this man's life so he'll treat me better. I saw someone threatening him, and I rushed to defend him. I rushed to defend him because—"

"Because you love him," Keera said.

"Yes." Gwyl felt a chill hand on his heart. "Where is he now? What became of him, when he let me go?"

"You must not torture yourself about that, Gwyl," said Keera.

"But I do," he whispered. He shivered as if he'd never get warm.

## Cold

By the time they got around the falls, Gwyl and Keera found themselves at another large lake, so large they couldn't see across.

"That other lake wasn't the ocean. But maybe this one is," said Keera.

Gwyl laughed. He dipped his finger in the water and let her taste it. "See? Fresh water," he said. "But a very large body of fresh water, another one like the huge lake above the falls."

It was early harvest-tide, and Gwyl was already worried about a second over-wintering. They had lucked out last time. They wouldn't be so lucky this time, he was thinking.

They had to stop for a full sen'night to build themselves a new canoe.

By the time the first snows flew, they had battled their way to the west through high winds and choppy waters. They put in at a big bay and buried their canoe. The waters were getting icy. Already, some of the smaller bays were iced in.

Every time Gwyl thought he could risk it, he found a protected place for Keera and explored the surrounding countryside. If he saw any village of natives, he watched and waited, trying to decide if they were friendly. If he thought they might be, he snowshoed in. By then his hair was long again. Only his eyes gave him away, but if he gained entrance to a village, he made sure they saw his tattoo, and he made sure to speak to them in the language of The People.

Only once or twice had he had to flee. Only once had he had to do violence to one of the natives he met, leaving the man bleeding in the snow.

But no one here had ever seen settlers from across the Great Sea. No one here had ever seen the Great Sea or knew about it. So his eyes were just a strange thing some of them noticed about him every so often.

He could tell by the way they behaved toward him. Many of them thought he must be a witch. Sometimes, that even helped him.

In this way, he found out the big bay was just a massive impediment to their journey toward a river that could take them south. "Many portages along that river," said one man, or Gwyl thought that's what he was trying to say. They had had to use gestures and drawing with their fingers in the snow more than words, which failed them pretty completely. "But it heads south," the man let him understand.

It was too late in the year to do anything about getting to that river. He and Keera would have to find shelter or risk freezing to death. He tried to make the man understand his dilemma. The man reached down and drew him a diagram in the snow. He stabbed a finger into a place in his diagram. He gestured.

*A cave*, thought Gwyl. He studied the crude map the man had drawn him and nodded. Then he set out to find the cave's entrance.

Late in the day, he came upon it. As he descended into it, he realized the air was getting progressively warmer than the frigid air at the mouth of the cave. He made himself a torch and went deeper. The cave was immense. It would do.

He spent the night in it. In the morning, he retraced his steps to Keera.

He found her terrified and miserable. "I thought something bad had happened to you. I thought you weren't coming back," she sobbed into his arms. Then she turned angry. "Remember our promise? You're not keeping it."

"But now I've found shelter for us, my darling girl." Gwyl helped her up. After a frozen walk, they came to the cave entrance, and he hoisted her up and over and into it.

Later he realized the cave probably saved their lives. They were warm there all winter. The air inside was the temperature of a moderately chilly harvest-tide day. Nothing like the temperature at the surface. And a crystal stream of water ran through a lower level. It never froze. It was clear and delicious. He went out to hunt and find wood, and he kept a fire blazing the whole winter.

He and Keera found the remnants of other fires. "People have used this cave for shelter before," he told her. He thought again, gratefully, of the man who had told him of the cave by gestures and crude drawings, and how to get to it. "That man saved our lives," he told Keera.

The days were long. Gwyl taught Keera the language of The People, and she taught him the language of the Fire Isle. "Ha," he said. "I'll probably never use it."

"You don't know. What about those fisher folk."

"But we're far away from them."

"Anyway, the language of The People is pretty useless, too. We're nowhere near their territory and likely never will be again."

They told jokes, talked about their childhoods, invented games, made love, and were secure and snug. "It's probably a good thing I can't have a baby," she said to him once, lying in his arms. "It would be too dangerous to give birth to a baby, out here alone." But he could tell just by looking at her how melancholy it made her feel.

They were content. But it seemed spring would never come, and after a long time, Gwyl saw how anxious Keera was to resume their journey. One day he stepped to the cave mouth and heard a welcome music, the melting of thousands of icicles and the groaning of lake ice breaking up. It was spring at last.

As soon as the air was mild enough and the lake was open enough, they set out to find the river of the many portages, and to build themselves a new canoe.

# The Good and the Great

And so they wandered their way southward until they came upon a large river that led to a larger river, a much larger river, in fact, that looked to be a swift waterway south.

"What do you call this river?" Gwyl asked a friendly native through gesture and a few words he had picked up along the way.

"Good river," said the man.

They could never decide whether that was the name of the river or that's what the man thought about it. But that's what they started calling it. They'd started down too many rivers, only to find them dwindling away to creeks and then unnavigable trickles, even in a vessel with as shallow a draft as their canoe.

This river was different. They dashed along, borne south and west by the current. Navigation in the brown waters of the main channel was swift and easy. And the river kept broadening. By summer, they'd traveled so far south that the sun was warm on their bodies, almost too warm. Gwyl had his tunic off most days, he'd made Keera a new bark hat, and they'd long since stored their fur clothing underneath the thwarts of the canoe, where they transformed it into soft bedding whenever the two of them headed to shore for the night. They swam and splashed in the shallows like delighted children.

As they set out one morning, the sun sparkling on the water, they came to a place where, or so it seemed, a new river poured into theirs. The waters of this great river were much greener. As they paddled southward, Gwyl wondered if this would be their new river highway south. It was mighty. It was the biggest river either of them had ever seen, the old man of rivers. That's how Gwyl began thinking of it, as they paddled along.

But that night, as they stopped to make a fire and cook something to eat, Gwyl stepped back quickly into the shadows. The owls. They were back. He couldn't say why they frightened him. They just did.

Keera wasn't frightened. She cried out in joy as they swooped around her. Just as quickly, they were gone.

Keera sat back down at their fire. She craned her neck to the river bank. "Tomorrow, we have to go back the way we came."

"But that's north," Gwyl objected.

"We need to stay on the Great River, but the Good River merged into it too far south. We need to head back up the Great River a way.

"What you're telling me," Gwyl said slowly. "You're telling me we're almost to our destination."

"I'm not sure," said Keera. In the firelight, he thought she looked troubled. "I just know that's what we're to do."

"Then we'll do it," he said.

In the morning, as they reversed course up the Great River and went even further past the place the Good River met it, Gwyl began to realize how thickly populated its banks were. Glimpsing so many villages worried Gwyl. "I can't stop to check out the friendliness of every one of these villages," he said to Keera. "We'll have to try to outrun any hostile parties that come our way."

By then, Keera was an experienced canoeist.

"You could be the Sea Child's," Gwyl told her, looking back over his shoulder at her with a smile. They were making good time up this huge river, even against the current.

"A person can get used to just about anything," said Keera.

"Just about," said Gwyl, turning around forward again, scanning the river for obstacles. But his mind flicked uneasily back to what his brother had had to endure. By the time they'd walked away from The People together, Gwyl had come to realize that whether Porcupine sacrificed Pierrick to the Sun God or not, Pierrick was at the limits of his endurance. He wondered sometimes. He knew some of what Pierrick had been up against in Porcupine's hands. But he didn't know all.

He was glad he was facing forward in the canoe and Keera couldn't see his expression. He knew it must be grim.

"In a while, we'll change places," he called back to Keera. Usually it was his job to power the canoe from the stern, while Keera looked for snags and floating logs and steered from the front. But then he held up a hand. They stopped paddling and drifted with the current, their paddles resting on the gunwales.

"Look at that," he called back.

Both of them just stared.

"Let's put in," he said. They paddled to the east side of the river and drew the canoe up at a sandy place on the bank.

He held out a hand to her, and they climbed the bank together. They stood and marveled.

"Remember when you and Old Dee got me out of Lunds-fort?" he said at last.

"How could I forget? Nine Spheres, I'm always having to rescue you from some predicament or other." She smiled at him.

He pulled her to him and gave her a quick kiss and a poke in the ribs. "But do you remember? How vast that city was?"

She nodded against him.

"Look at this one."

"It's immense."

"It's the biggest city I've ever seen. Maybe bigger than Lutetia. Bigger than the big city of the Primacy, their city dedicated to the Lady Goddess. Bigger than the Great City of the Lyre Lands."

"Maybe not as big as that."

"The biggest I've ever seen," said Gwyl.

"I have to agree. The biggest I've ever seen," said Keera. "What shall we do?"

"Keera, you have to give me some direction. Where did your owls tell you to go? When the owls visited you last night, did they tell you the portal of the Sky Child was here in this city?"

"I'm not sure," Keera admitted.

"I've asked before, and I've been patient. We've gone south. Now we've turned around to go north. I don't think we should paddle another league until we, you know, actually know where we're going."

"We could go into this city and ask. If we make the sign of the Sky Child, and they recognize it, that could tell us a lot."

"But darling. Suppose they hate outsiders. Suppose it's dangerous."

Keera stood stock still. She got that faraway look she got sometimes, the spooky look. Then she turned to Gwyl. "We should ask here."

"Very well," said Gwyl. Not for the first time, he wondered if he might be crazy, following her crazy instructions.

A broad highway led toward the palisades surrounding the city, but outside the palisades, they passed many houses crowded shoulder to shoulder. The people in these houses came to their doors to stare.

"It's me, isn't it?" whispered Keera. "You look like them, if they don't look too close. But I—" She put up her hand to her fire-red hair.

Gwyl nodded slowly. "And the whiteness of your skin."

They kept walking. At the gates of the palisades stood guards. They were dressed in colorful garb just barely covering them. Mostly they were naked. The sun was so hot. Gwyl wished he had thought to exchange his trousers for the hide loin covering. He would have fit in better. And he noticed that many of the women went about bare-breasted. Keera really stood out.

The guards spotted them and came over, surrounding them. One of them prodded Keera with the butt of a spear he carried. Gwyl thrust her behind him and shoved the man in the chest.

The man looked over at his fellows and laughed. They grabbed Gwyl and Keera and marched them through the gate and into a thatched house and shut and barred the door.

"Not a good sign," Gwyl muttered.

"We'll just wait," said Keera. "Someone will see about us soon, and then we'll explain."

"How will we do that?" said Gwyl.

Before she could answer, the door opened, and the same men came in. They spoke to each other rapidly. Keera made the sign of the Sky Child. They stared at her. That seemed to decide them.

One of them grabbed her and hustled her off, protesting loudly, while the others shoved and hit Gwyl and drove him into a corner of the room as he shouted and tried to fight them off.

Then they left him alone in there.

*Dark Ones take those owls*, Gwyl thought viciously to himself. He had to work himself up into a towering anger, because if he didn't, part of him knew he would collapse on the floor in such fear he wouldn't be able to bear it. Where had they taken Keera? What would they do to her?

# INTERLUDE: THE CLOUDS

Y ou see there? I was right all along," Dee said to Mervin. He gave his fellow mage a superior smile.

"Oh, very well. You were right," said Mervin with a grumpy look. "That doesn't mean I condone it, what you did."

"After all," said Dee, taking a reasonable tone. "The Sky Child is my Child. And I've often served as an emissary between Her and the monarchs underneath the Spheres. How is this any different?"

"You know how. You're too involved. You've gotten yourself too involved. You know it, and I know it. By now, The Three probably know it." Mervin was gratified to see Dee flinch a little, at this piece of information.

But Dee just rambled on.

"Love has its reasons, Mervin."

"I wouldn't know," Mervin muttered. "You have the lovely Mrs. D'Nofrio, but I—" He thought with a shudder of Morgan the Witch. "I haven't fared so well with women."

Dee laid a hand on his shoulder and squeezed it. "Morgan tricked you. She made you think she loved you, and then she stuck you in that rock, like Sylvester."

"It was an oak tree, actually." Mervin broke out into a sweat, remembering. "I thought she loved me. She said she loved me."

He winced at Dee's sympathetic eyes. He made his voice brisk. "Then she stuck me in an oak tree. We all know the story. Old story. Boring. Eventually, I got out. I've put it behind me, Dee."

"Uh huh," said Dee.

"Her sister did something similar, to Ariel."

"Sycorax, yes. But that was a pine. I was the one who got Ariel out, did you know that?" Dee gazed down at the lands beneath their cloud platform. "Is it true that Gilles sent Ailys to Morgan to be tutored?" His voice was careful.

"I don't know," said Mervin. "I want nothing to do with witches."

"There are good witches, you know," said Dee.

"I only know the bad ones."

"Mervin, there is such a thing as true love."

Mervin looked sidelong at Dee. He wondered if Dee knew his parentage. He thought of his poor mother, driven mad. Driven to distraction. He swallowed hard. He thought of how she had done away with herself. For the first time in a while, he thought of his father, and had to tamp down the rage of it. His father the incubus, coming to his mother in the dead of night, a demon lover. *Bah*, he thought. Love. What was it but danger and despair?

"Look there, Mervin," said Dee suddenly, pointing. Pointing across that river. "There are the five friends. Two are lovers. But the other three—"

"Sad, what happened to them," said Mervin briskly. He thought hard about how to divert Dee from his favorite topic, The Rising, and all the dead people it had generated.

"See, the three of them are moving toward that group of three women."

"How can you even tell they're women, Dee? They're dead, is what they all are."

"They are women, and they are lovely. See that one with the dark hair? The young man who intrigues me most is the one she loves. Rafe."

"That's the Princess Diera? Death, the great leveler," said Mervin.

"She is beautiful. And there, that one, with the honey fall of hair. The wife of Earl Drustan. See with what delight she steps into his arms."

"Ah," said Mervin, catching sight of the third, the young mage John, tragically slain by Caedon. Mervin wished John's fate had been otherwise. He wished John had come more fully into his powers as a mage. Then maybe Caedon and Gilles wouldn't have been able to destroy him. He sighed. Of course that wasn't true. He and Dee together could control and thwart Gilles, but only with great effort. A young mage like John? Once he came to Gilles's attention, once he had rejected Gilles's inroads on him? He'd been doomed. "A sad case," said Mervin. "But at least he had no woman to love, and mourn him afterwards."

"Yes, he did," said Dee softly. "He did love a woman. And here she comes, her hair glinting red-gold, hoping he'll sing and play for her."

"You have quite an imagination, Dee. Music in the Land of the Dead."

"There was Sir Orfeo—" Dee began.

Mervin cut him off. "What about those other two, Wat and Mirin? Next, you're going to point them out to me."

"No," said Dee, giving him a nervous look.

"No," said Mervin. "That's right, no." He got up from his golden chair, disgusted. "You've involved them in your crazy schemes. What am I thinking? And I suppose you're going to tell me that all this justifies why you've disguised yourself and gotten yourself into the city of the Sun King."

"What if it does? What if I have?" Dee shrugged and stepped away.

"Dee," said Mervin. "You're not down there. You're up here. Change yourself back. You're pretty darn blue, and you look really odd."

# 7 KEERA: Strife and Love

## Sun and Sky

When Keera tried to fight away from her guards, they kept a good grip on her, but they didn't hit her.

One of them kept reaching out to tousle her hair. She couldn't stand that, tousling.

She and Gwyl had arrived in the morning and were taken early in the day. Now, all day long, as she worried about what might be happening to Gwyl, left back in the house where they'd been secured, Keera found herself passed from one man or group to some other group of men. Each man or group seemed more powerful than the next and dressed more elegantly. Always men.

By the end of the day, she was in the hands of an older man whose neck and arms and even ankles were loaded with gold ornaments. The cloth of his robe was finely woven of some substance she didn't know the name of.

She was weary, by then, and more and more frightened for Gwyl.

"What have you done with my husband?" she said despairingly to this new man. She didn't expect him to answer.

He did answer. His voice was low and courteous. She couldn't understand his words, but she understood his tone. *Patience, young woman. You're almost at the end of the line*. That's what she thought he must be saying to her. She just wasn't very sure what fate the end of the line might hold for her.

She and this richly dressed older man stood alone together in a spacious room of fragrant timbers, planed smooth. The room, except for an imposing throne-like chair, was empty. Tall slits of windows let in light and air. At the beginning, she had been marched to a monumental structure, platform upon platform of earth, sort of in the way the keep of a castle might be built upon its motte. But much, much larger with many more levels.

At the base of this system of earthen platforms, a narrow corridor led deep within. She had been in the interior of this structure all day long. Torches flickered on its walls, but there appeared to be no natural light.

To come out at the very top was strangely freeing. The sun shone into the big airy chamber.

An echoing sound of many feet came to them.

The man with her put out a hand and grasped her on the shoulder.

She turned to him in surprise.

He said an urgent word. Said it again. He pushed her shoulder down. He himself knelt. She realized what she was meant to do, so she knelt too. When the man pressed his forehead to the floor, so did she.

The tramping of feet drew nearer. A massive door swung open, and someone struck a massive pole resoundingly against the stones of the floor. A call reverberated through the chamber. Sneaking a look to either side, she saw many men, all of them bent to the floor as she and her man were. And one big pair of richly embroidered boots.

They were red leather. She gazed at them in fascination.

A man said something in a soft voice, and her own man got to his feet. She wasn't sure what she herself was expected to do, so she stayed down.

Now her man tapped her on the shoulder, and she understood she was to rise.

She found herself eye to eye with a smallish man. But his gaze was as powerful as any she had ever encountered. She dropped her eyes.

Her own man emitted a lengthy, rapid stream of language.

The small powerful man said nothing. At the end of it, her man bowed to the ground again, and she wondered if she were supposed to as well, but the powerful man put out a hand to her and kept it on her.

She stood still. He lifted the ringlets of her hair and examined their color in the light. He rubbed them in his palm and hefted them. He did not tousle.

Then he gazed into her eyes. His own were deep pools of near-black. She realized the green of her own eyes must seem very strange to him. He wore a sort of crown on his head, a crown that appeared to be made of feathers. She looked uneasily away.

He put out a finger to her skin. She made herself stand still while he ran his finger down her cheek, then down her arms. He stepped back and nodded.

Her own man stood up.

The powerful man, their leader, she surmised, said a few words, and her man started undressing her. She tried to squirm away from him, but when she did, he slapped her hard. She stood stunned, blinking tears out of her eyes while he finished his work.

The leader walked all around her, examining her, prodding her with a finger.

She knew she was blushing red. Probably all over, she thought with despair.

The leader stepped back from her and said something to her own man. The leader put his hand out to her cheek again. Keera felt herself burning with shame and fury. The leader said something again. Maybe expressing amazement.

Her own man took a package from under his arm then and unfolded it. It was a length of the same soft, finely woven material as the cloth of his splendid cloak. He wrapped it around her, and she clutched it to herself gratefully.

The leader said something else to her own man, and he stepped back away from her.

Then the leader looked directly at her and said something to her.

She looked back at him dumbly, trying to blink the tears from her eyes.

He put out a finger and wiped them away. He put one of his fingers into his mouth and tasted it.

He said something to her again.

She couldn't think what to say, so she made the sign of the Fire Child and pointed to herself. Then she made the sign of the Sky Child and waved her hand about the room.

He looked at her gravely. He said something definite and hard.

She decided he was saying *No*.

He pointed to the stately chair. Was this his throne, she wondered.

On the back of the chair was a sunburst, painted gold. She looked at it more carefully. No, it was not painted gold.

It was made of gold.

And it was huge.

These people must worship the sun, she thought, and then she shivered. When that horrid man Porcupine decided to sacrifice Pierrick, that was the god he was about to sacrifice him to.

Now she saw the leader, like his man, was covered in golden ornaments, except that his were bigger and shinier. At his neck was a sunburst of gold. She realized something about his crown of feathers then. They were not real feathers. They were feathers of gold.

He now spoke again to her own man. And as he spoke, she saw them exchanging signs of Fire Child and Sky Child.

*So they know the Children,* she decided. *They just don't worship them.*

Her own man left the room and returned with two others, Keera saw out of the corner of her eye. She kept her gaze on the leader.

One of these newcomers hung back. The other cast himself down before the leader, or king, or whoever the powerful man was. He too was decked out in golden emblems of the sun.

After he was beckoned by his monarch to rise, this new man stepped to Keera and scrutinized her. He shook his head disdainfully. He lifted the golden sunburst he too wore, lifted it on high, and the king did likewise. Everyone in the room murmured words then, maybe words of praise.

*They all worship the Sun God, looks like,* thought Keera.

The king turned and mounted the three steps to his throne and seated himself there. It was huge; he was small; yet somehow the chair did not dwarf him. The other man, maybe the Sun God's priest, took up a position at one side of the throne, and her own man resumed his prostration.

But the second man, the one who had come in with the Sun God's priest, if that's what he was, now stepped to the king. He made the sign of the Sky Child.

The king nodded at him.

They too exchanged a stream of language.

Keera looked over curiously at this second man and nearly let out a yelp of surprise.

He was a slender, elderly, bent-over man with a pointy white beard. What made her cry out with surprise was the color of him. He was bright blue. And then she noticed something else that at first she did not, seeing as he was blue all over. He had piercing blue eyes.

Blue eyes she recognized in an instant.

"Old Dee," she breathed. Old Dee, the powerful mage who had been her beloved mentor and teacher on the Fire Isle. The one she had helped with a jailbreak in Lunds-fort. She had thought he was dead, but she knew now he was not. Tigeny had told her so.

"How are you, dear Keera. You've had an ordeal."

"That man undressed me and prodded me all over," she fumed.

"He's never seen anyone like you before. He wasn't sure you were real. You mustn't take offense."

"Hmph," said Keera.

Old Dee gave her one of his benign smiles.

"Looks like these are all Sun worshippers," she told him.

"Yes, indeed. I'd expect no less from you, Keera, that you'd see that right away."

"But Old Dee! They have Gwyl somewhere. And you are very blue."

"Oh, dear," said Old Dee, ignoring the part about being blue. "That's bad news. Where do you think they've put him."

"I don't know. Do you think they've—" she stopped and gulped back tears. "Might they have—"

"I doubt it, dear Keera. Let me ask."

He spoke rapidly to the king in their language. Without taking his eyes off the king, he said sidelong to Keera, "No, they haven't hurt him. They're thinking about it, though. They think he might be a witch."

"Because of his eyes," she said.

"Right. Why don't they realize he's a person of your type, though. That's confusing," he said.

"He doesn't look like a person of our type. Of my type," she said quickly, glancing at Old Dee's odd blue skin. "Not any more. He looks like one of them. Except for his eyes."

"He does?" Old Dee turned to her, baffled.

"It's a long story, Old Dee. But yes, he does. And witchcraft is not involved."

"Well. Let's just convince them he's not a witch, but a mage. Like myself."

"Is that how you explain why you're blue? And your eyes, Old Dee?"

"No explanation needed. The blue. It's self-defining. Perfectly clear I'm something else. Pretty impressive, no?"

He turned to the king and made a lengthy speech. In the end, the king nodded. He stood and made a pronouncement.

"Bow to His Majesty," muttered Old Dee to Keera. They both bowed, although not the face-on-the-floor bowing of the others.

"Here we go," said Old Dee. In a dramatic puff of smoke they went. . .Keera wasn't sure where they went, but they wound up outside the same thatched house where she and Gwyl had started out that morning.

Old Dee drew himself up with dignity. He made some quick motions with his fingers and handed a length of cloth to Keera, which she grabbed and wrapped about herself, and another length for himself. He gabbled at the guards. They hastened to unbar the door, and then Keera rushed inside and clutched Gwyl to her.

Old Dee came in after, tucking his cloth more securely at the waist.

"Old Dee!" said Gwyl in surprise. "But you're—"

"Always having to bust you out of jail, my boy," said Old Dee fondly. Then he did a double-take. "Geez Louise," he said.

"You see what I mean, Old Dee?" said Keera, showing off Gwyl proudly.

"I do. I do indeed." Old Dee walked all around Gwyl, scrutinizing him.

"You're a bit different yourself, Old Dee," said Gwyl.

"Heh, yes," said Old Dee. "If I can't blend in, I try to wow them. I see you're doing a good job blending in."

"Not really, Old Dee," said Gwyl with a smile. "My skin just naturally tans like this if I'm outdoors in the sun and weather. And my hair just grows, if I let it. My eyes don't change, though. That seems to disturb the people around here."

Keera was trying it out softly to herself. "Wow them."

"My, my," said Old Dee. He tapped a thoughtful finger against his teeth. "And all this time you were really Gull. You'd think I would have seen that. I didn't, though."

Keera exchanged a smile with Gwyl.

"Yes. I'm surprised too, Old Dee. But all along, that's who I was. That's who I am," said Gwyl.

"My boy," said Old Dee, putting a hand out to him. Abruptly, he turned away. Keera saw with alarm that his keen blue eyes had filled with tears against the metallic blue of his face. What might that mean, she wondered. But she and Gwyl were together again, and Gwyl was unhurt. That was what mattered.

So the weather changed from sun to darkened sky, from threatening to sunny, and back again, and back again, as it does.

As it will.

## Rapid Transit

Keera stood with Gwyl at the edge of the river. "There's our canoe," she said to Old Dee, pointing it out.

"Do you know how long it will take, if you keep trying to find the portal of the Child of Sky in that?" said Old Dee.

"But the owls told me to go there."

"I suppose She has her reasons, then," said Old Dee. "Who is a mere mage to question that? I'm just thinking you two will be quite old once you get there. If you ever do."

He stood considering. Then he squared his shoulders, as if he had decided something. "We're not to interfere, you know, we mages," he told them. "I do keep interfering." His voice dropped low. "As Merlin keeps reminding me." He looked up with a cheerful smile. "But if the owls led you here, why did they do it if not to connect you with me? I'm going to cast my own small portal. Step through it, and you'll be there. After all, just for the convenience of not having to go down those twelve entire sets of stairs, I cast one for you earlier, Keera." He pointed up to the top of the majestic mound of the king. "Or maybe for myself. My knees, you know. Or maybe to impress His Majesty. Always a good thing, every now and again."

"These people worship the Sun God. Would they have sacrificed us, as that terrible man was about to sacrifice Gwyl's brother?"

"Not you. The king was examining you to see if he wanted to add you to his collection. I'm pretty sure he was about to sacrifice Gull," said Old Dee.

"The Sun God keeps trying to get me," said Gwyl.

"But why are you here, Old Dee?" said Keera.

"I'm an emissary from the Child of Sky. The king has given me a hearing. He won't change his god, though."

"The Children send out emissaries to kings?" said Gwyl.

"Of course they do," said Keera. "Remember my grandfather? Ranulf the Good? The farwydd of the Child of Earth came as an emissary to him, and he did change his god."

"Why kings? Why not ordinary folks?" said Gwyl. Keera saw he had that stubborn, skeptical set to his mouth.

"They send emissaries to ordinary folk as well," said Old Dee, with a glint in his eye. "Save them from jail fever, and bloodthirsty Sun-worshipers, and such."

Keera glanced over at Gwyl, amused. He looked down at his shoes.

"And now one is about to send you straight to the Sky Child's farwydd. Ready?"

"Ready," said Keera.

"Wait—" said Gwyl. "My canoe—"

But too late.

"There," said Keera. "That was easy."

Gwyl stood looking up at the tall pyramid before them in dismay. This one was built of stone, though, not platforms of earth.

"Another one," he muttered.

"A person who has just paddled thousands of leagues down a mighty river? And then another? And then another? This daunts you? Really?" said Keera.

"Okay," said Gwyl.

*Old Dee is rubbing off on you*, thought Keera. She was busy knotting a piece of cloth around her. Old Dee had handed it to her as they came out of the portal. "Clothes don't make the trip through," he told her apologetically, handing a pair of ragged trousers made out of some kind of bark to Gwyl. "And now I must get back." He was gone again.

Gwyl pulled on his trousers and looked up again at the pyramid. "Let's do it," he said.

He put a foot on the first step.

Guards came bursting at them from everywhere. They looked angry. They were shouting in some strange language Keera could not understand.

Surrounded by those fierce faces, she did the only thing she could do. She made the sign of the Sky Child.

The angry guards stepped back, their eyes narrowed. They turned to each other and talked in their language. One approached her and took her arm. He smiled at them both. Keera regarded him uneasily. He gestured. He walked her over to the base of the pyramid, where a narrow door led inside.

"This must be it, I think," said Keera over her shoulder to Gwyl. He rushed to catch up.

The guard gestured, smiling broadly. His eyes glittered, his teeth glinted. He pointed again to the doorway. Keera took Gwyl's hand, and the two of them went in.

The interior was dank. A dim green light filtered down on them from somewhere far above. Behind them, they heard the hollow clang as a door settled into its frame.

Keera turned in alarm.

"We're in here now," Gwyl whispered. "And I don't think we can get out. Those smiling men just shut us in here. The villains. That one can smile and smile and be a—"

"There's nowhere to go but up, then," she whispered back, interrupting, and they began to climb.

The air was heavy and stifling. The steep narrow stairs were slimy with mold. One misstep would send them both tumbling to the bottom.

Both of them were fit, but the humid atmosphere weighed on them. They both began to gasp, and they weren't even halfway to the top.

*One foot after the other*, Keera thought to herself. *One after the other.*

"Don't stop. If we stop, something bad will happen to us," said Gwyl in her ear.

She looked over at him in shock, then down. In the dim light, it seemed to her that they were climbing steps out of a void. Nothing was below them, and if they fell, they'd fall into nothing.

Echoing through the interior of the pyramid, a shrill cry came from somewhere, reverberating against the close, dripping stone of the walls.

*Up*, she thought, her breath coming hard.

"Keep going, Keera," he whispered. "You have to keep going."
Only a few steps more.

And they were both on top, a platform encased in the larger pyramid looming with its tons of rock just overhead.

Keera seized Gwyl to her, and they stood together, terror-stricken, their hearts beating together in their chests. To their right, a reclining figure smiled its ageless smile, staring at them through serene and sightless eyes. To their left, a blood-red altar with the head and tail of an animal of prey, bulging green eyes of jade that saw into the depths of them both. Sharp white teeth bared to rend them.

Serenity and love on one side of them, the struggle and torment of blood on the other.

A deep hollow booming reverberated through the pyramid. A voice. *Which?*

As they stood transfixed, the stones beneath their feet collapsed, and they fell together in a soundless rush to lie stunned on a platform far beneath.

After a long time, Keera felt herself stirring. She knew she was alive. A blind panic seized her. In the blackness, she put out her hand.

"Keera."

*Thank the Child. Gwyl.*

"What happened to us?"

"I don't know, exactly," he whispered back. "We were standing at those altars, and the floor beneath us collapsed. Now we are here." After a moment, he said out of the dark, "I think it was a trap. When we stepped onto the platform, we triggered it. Back in the village, The People would set out into the forest and dig a pit. They'd cover it with sticks and leaves, and put something enticing in the middle. A piece of meat, maybe. Something an animal would want. Then the animal would happen by, and step onto the platform, and—"

Keera found Gwyl in the dark and burrowed her head into his chest.

He put his hand out, and then he exclaimed. "You're bleeding."

There came a grinding of stone far above them.

Keera looked up. A small square of light opened up, and now it dimly lit the trap they'd fallen into. The walls of their trap were steep-sided, rising to a point above. They lay on a small platform. When Keera craned her neck, she could see they lay on the flat top of a pyramid, a top barely big enough to hold their bodies. A pyramid inside a pyramid inside a pyramid.

"Don't move," Gwyl whispered to her. "If you do—"

"If I do, what?"

"I don't know this," he said carefully, in her ear, "but I think if we move too much, the platform we're lying on now will collapse, just as the one above collapsed."

"We'll fall still further inside?"

"That's just what I think will happen," he said. "I don't know for certain."

"You have an inner voice, Gwyl," she said quietly. "Just as I do. It's telling you things. It told you not to stop, on the stairway. Now it's telling you this."

"Yes," he said.

"Where does the falling end," said Keera.

A voice breathed down on them from above. "It never ends."

The light from the square above them brightened unbearably. Keera flinched away from it, and she felt Gwyl doing the same.

"You have us now, Lady," Gwyl cried out. "How may we serve you and the Sky Child?"

A hollow laugh came filtering down to them.

"Oh, you think I'm the farwydd of the Sky Child, do you?"

Keera looked over at Gwyl with dread.

"You're not?" she whispered. Somehow she knew this presence, so far above them, could hear that whisper.

"Listen," came the voice.

"Four elements, Earth, Sky, Sea, Fire," said the voice. "But two forces. Love. Strife. Without Strife to drive them apart, the elements collapse into themselves. Without Love to bind them together, the elements fly into chaos. This is the Children's balance. This is harmony."

The light dimmed. In spite of the oppression of the heat, Keera felt her teeth chattering.

The voice came again. "What have you come to ask me? You are not my Children."

"I am Keera, child of the Child of Fire. This is Gull, child of the Child of Sea. The owls sent us, and Old Dee helped us get here. We came to seek the farwydd of the Child of Sky."

"We are not of that Child."

"We?" said Keera.

An eerie music filtered down. *What is your seven, oh?*

And then, *Seven for the seven stars in the heavens.*

"You're in our hands now, the Three of us," breathed the voice in a great rushing of wind. A wind that filled the pyramid. Keera and Gwyl clung to each other. The wind intended to push them apart and off the platform.

"Hold onto me, Keera," whispered Gwyl. "No one will come between us. If we fall, we fall together."

Keera had the feeling that, if they did fall, they'd never get out of the trap set by The Three. And who were these Three?

Keera's inward voice told her. The three unknown Children who had fallen to land who knows where. Now she and Gwyl knew where. They had landed here.

The mighty gust blew again. Keera held desperately to Gwyl. She had the feeling that, this time, if they fell, they'd fall to their deaths. Would the fall kill them outright, she wondered, or would they lie broken in the dark until their bones dissolved into the murk.

From far above, a pebble dropped caroming off the walls of the pyramid that encased them. It fell on her face with stinging force. And then a larger rock, which missed them. And then another, and another. One clipped Gwyl on the side of the head and he slumped against her.

Keera cried out in horror. "Why torment us like this, when we come to the Children for help."

The voice again: "You and your people, pushing into places where no one has invited you. You have ruined your own lands. You shall not ruin these."

She thought about Tigeny then. About the magic wielded by the ornithomancer.

*I'm an ornithomancer*, she thought.

She concentrated her mind to a single point. She called upon the owls.

Around them, a faint beating of wings far above grew into a terrible pounding of the air. They were enclosed in a colossal rush of wings that carried them up with eruptive force.

They burst together into the sky and light.

As the nested trap of the pyramids faded away and behind them, the voice called out again. "Tell your people. Warn them before Our wrath drives them from the earth. Not today. Not tomorrow. But believe it. Someday your people will die. They'll die horribly. Of hunger. Of thirst. Terror from the skies. Terror from the depths of the sea. Terror from the depths of the earth. Fire will rain down upon them. Pestilence, unleashed by their heedlessness. They'll bring it upon themselves, through their inattention and their greed, and all under the Nine Spheres will perish with them."

But whatever had borne them up so explosively now wafted them away from the terrible voice of The Three and deposited them as if they were feathers gently down onto a stone floor.

Keera lay cradling Gwyl against her. The space where they lay was dim and vast. She could do nothing. All of her concentration, all of her powers had been sucked out of her. *Please*, she prayed, although she was not quite sure to whom she was praying. *Please don't take Gwyl away from me. Or if you take him, take me too.*

The words of The Three were hideous to her. They spoke of huge and terrifying and important matters. She felt herself dwindled into insignificance.

She found she couldn't care about some huge and unattainable goal. "Forgive me," she whispered to whatever god might hear her. "I am very small."

It was Gwyl she wanted. She could feel him breathing, but she could feel how faint they were, the breaths he took.

## Harmony

All around them, intricately-carved columns stood casting their long shadows in stripes across the vast space.

Keera was weak from lack of food and water. If she didn't have water soon, water especially, she felt she would wither away to a husk on the stone floor and die there. But to go in search of it, she'd have to leave Gwyl.

She couldn't. She wouldn't.

He lay motionless, his head cradled in her lap.

They sat together that way as the shadows crept across the floor and, outside, the burning sun sank to the horizon.

*The Three*, she thought. Strife and Love. Bitter and sweet. The conflict of strife pushing all outward and away into the cold void, love drawing all inward to the warm core. Two forces that, in their opposing, kept the world in tension. Without them, the Nine Spheres of the world would collapse. The spheres would not be able to stand and revolve in their harmony. The twelve realms and all their people would be crushed underneath their weight as they flattened into an undifferentiated lens of matter, everything in a soup of all the elements together. Strife and Love together, though. Those opposing forces created Harmony. The Spheres rose, the beings crawled beneath them, the sun and moon and stars hung shining from the glittering undersides of them, and the Spheres made their crystalline music as they revolved, nested one inside the other inside the other, all Nine.

*One for sorrow, two for mirth.* The song echoed in her mind. *Three for death. Four for birth.*

*Strange*, she thought. For most people, harmony described only the gentle and kindly strains of the Spheres' music. That's what she'd always thought. But now, *That's not what harmony actually is*, she said to herself.

What did any of that matter to two of the helpless creatures that crawled ant-like across the surface of the realms? The Three had told her something. Given her a task. It was too big.

Let the Spheres do what the Spheres did. Just let Gwyl be alive. Just let him come back to her.

She thought it more likely they'd realize their opposite wish. By morning, they'd both be lying there dead, twined in each other's arms. If she had been further along in her training as an ornithomancer, perhaps now she'd have the strength to save them both. Instead, she was drained completely.

She wondered about her parents, dying almost together. She hoped they knew peace and were able to help each other across that river to the Land of the Dead.

Darkness fell in a deep blanket over the land. It crept with its fingers into the place where she and Gwyl lay.

With darkness came the owls.

The pair of them swooped in through the broad high doors and under the roof far above where Keera lay looking up at them. She was glad they had come. She was glad they'd be there with her when the end made itself known.

But as she watched them, they spiraled down. They seemed to call to her, *Follow us.*

She doubted she had the strength.

*Follow us*, they called.

She laid Gwyl aside from her gently, cradling his head so it wouldn't fall back against the stones of the floor. She rolled to a sitting position. After long moments of trying, she tottered to her feet. The owls swooped around her. *This way*, they called.

She half-staggered, half-crawled out of the big doors underneath the stars.

Reflecting back their light, a small rectangle gleamed ahead of her.

A pool of water.

She fell to her knees beside it, lay out full length alongside the lip of it, cupped her hands, and drank.

The water infused every particle of her body. She felt the parched shell of herself twitching and uncreasing where every minim of herself had shriveled. Now, piece by piece, she felt herself returning to life.

After a while, she could sit. She could stand. On the lip of the pool stood a vessel made of some thin translucent shell-like material. She made her way over to it, dipped water into it, and returned to the building where Gwyl lay.

She went to him and pulled him to her, trickling water from her fingertip into his mouth, moistening his lips with it. She leaned down and kissed him. With the water, she bathed his face, coated in a sheen of sweat and dust.

The moon rose, and cast its shafts directly through the doors to the place where they lay.

"Gwyl," she whispered.

His eyelids fluttered.

He looked up into her face and smiled.

All night, she went back and forth between the pool and Gwyl, pouring the water of his life back into his body.

In the morning, she wondered about going outside the building. What was it, anyway, she wondered. A temple, maybe. The people out there had not seemed friendly. They'd shut the two of them up inside the inner pyramid and left them to the wrath of The Three.

She wondered if she and Gwyl had survived the night together only to be killed as unwelcome outsiders by the people on the grounds of this city of temples.

As dawn touched the interior of the building, she examined the carvings of the pillars. They were carvings of owls.

The owls protected them here.

When footsteps sounded outside, she wasn't even alarmed.

A file of women entered the building of the owls. The women were dressed in long cloaks of feathers.

They didn't seem surprised to see Keera and Gwyl there.

One of them approached with food, sticky balls of maize. She bent down and put a ball of it in Keera's mouth, and a ball of it in Gwyl's. Throughout the day, one or the other of these women came into the owl temple to feed them and bring them a sweetened drink.

Once Keera made her way to the big doors to try to find a way out. One of the women came to her and led her gently back to the center. Keera understood they couldn't leave the sanctuary and protection of the owls.

"We're safe here, but we're prisoners," said Gwyl, when she returned to him.

"All we can do is wait here," said Keera.

"Tell me something, Keera," said Gwyl. "How did we get out of the trap we were in? Back in that pyramid?"

"The owls helped us."

"How."

"I don't think I can explain."

"It was like the time you came to get me in the village of The People."

"Something like that," she said. "Last time, I had Tigeny to help me. This time, I was on my own."

"Why would your owls lead us into the trap and then get us out?"

"I don't think they did," Keera said, thinking about it. "Those people out there did. The smiling people. They took us to the pyramid of The Three, not the Sky Child's portal."

"This Three you speak of. It. . .They. . .meant us ill. They thought of us as a threat."

"We're not welcome in this land," said Keera with a shiver.

"We seem to be far from the sea, or from any river. My Child can't help us."

"I doubt the Fire Child can help us, either."

"But Old Dee helped us. Do you think he will again?"

"I know he means us well. I know he's a powerful mage. Beyond that, I don't know how far his powers extend."

"You, Keera. You're a mage."

"Tigeny says so," Keera whispered.

They were quiet then, because one of the women came to them with healing herbs. She examined Gwyl and gave him a potion that made him sleep all that night and all the next day.

When he woke, Keera rejoiced to see he looked well.

At night, the brilliance of the moon shone in on them again. Gwyl got to his feet and walked to the big doors leading to the courtyard of the pool. He looked out. "At night, this place is empty," he said.

Keera followed him and stood looking out too.

They had walked out under the moon, its light making sharp, angled shadows in the courtyard. A voice breathed on them, "This. This is the Sky Child's portal."

"Why are we here?" Keera cried.

Gwyl looked over at her. "You told me you knew the where and I knew the how. But I thought you knew the why as well."

Keera bit her lip. "No," she whispered. "Not the deeper reason. I only know my owls told me I must seek the portal and hear the Sky Child's message."

Gwyl just shook his head.

"If you come to this land, you must respect it," said the voice. "You didn't discover it. It's not the New Found Land. It's been here a long time. If you don't respect this land, it will destroy you."

"So we came here for a warning. We already got the warning, from The Three," Keera called.

"And you survived. You did well, child of the Child of Fire. Child of the Child of Sea. And now you must take this warning back to others like yourselves. This is My charge to you."

"I promise," Keera called. She nudged Gwyl.

He looked startled. "I promise," he called, too.

"And now you must leave this place. You've been here two days. This is the third. If you are still here at dawn. . ." The voice dwindled away, leaving only a heavy sense of menace behind.

A silence descended.

Keera and Gwyl rushed to the end of the courtyard, but the gates out of the temple were shut fast.

"What do we do?" Keera said to Gwyl.

"You don't know?" His voice held an edge of panic. "From the sound of that voice, I got the distinct impression that if we can't find a way out of here, something bad will happen to us."

They retreated to the temple and gazed out together across the courtyard, where the rectangular pool of dark water reflected the wavering moon back up into the sky.

"Perhaps if I asked the owls, we could fly over these gates," said Keera after awhile. But the owls had left her. She felt it.

Gwyl began to prowl restlessly around the courtyard. He came up to the gates again and beat on them with his fists. They echoed back massively, hollowly, but they didn't budge. The moon was going down. The moon's reflection had begun edging to the far side of the pool.

Keera started to tell Gwyl not to waste his strength, but she stopped herself. Maybe this would be where it ended for them. Maybe they just needed to wait. Then they'd never be parted again.

Gwyl stepped to the pool and stared into its depths. He moved back to her.

"Darling, if I asked you to—"

"No. You may not leave me. No."

"It won't be for long. I need to test something. I'll be right back." Before she could object, he was shedding his bark trousers and dropping them on the stones of the floor. His body gleamed in the moonlight. He took a few running steps to the pool and, over her shriek of protest, he arched up and arrowed down into the pool.

*No,* she cried out from deep inside her.

But just as he had promised, he came back up almost immediately, hoisting himself out of the pool and shaking droplets off him like some water creature.

He stepped to her, smiling. "I know a way out of here," he said, "and it doesn't involve any spooky stuff. Just the skills of a child of the Child of Sea."

Keera stared at him, open-mouthed.

"We've been in one trap, a deadly one we weren't meant to get out of. Thanks to you and your owls, we did. We flew out of it. Now we're in another. But there's a way out of this one, too, and the Sky Child is waiting to see if we find it. I'm going to get us out of this trap. Will you wait quietly again while I explore and test my idea?"

Keera nodded, feeling numb. There was no stopping the man when he got around a body of water, no matter how unpromising it seemed.

"This is no pool. It's more like the receptacle for a spring."

She shook her head in disbelief. Not that he wasn't right about the spring. He probably was. But just the sheer Gwyl-ness of him. That's what always astounded her.

"Wait here." He stepped to the side of the pool and dove again. He was gone longer this time.

When he came up again, she was clasping and unclasping her hands in terror.

"We can do this," he told her. "You just have to trust me and summon up all your courage."

"You're going to make me go into that pool, aren't you? You're going to make me go under water."

"Yes," he said, giving her a kiss. "And it will be fine. The first part, I'm really going to enjoy. I want you to take your clothes off."

Keera decided not to tell him about the sun king and his examination. She untied the cloth she had knotted around her and let it puddle at her feet.

Gwyl put out a hand and caressed her. "This nearly defeats my resolve, Keera. But we'll have to act on that later. First things first. I want you to jump onto my back and put your hands about my neck." He turned his back to her. "Go ahead," he said. "I'm ready."

"No," she said, seized by fear.

"Yes," he said. "Go ahead."

She made an awkward little leap at him, and he pulled her up onto his back.

"There. Now twine your legs about my waist, and your arms about my neck. I'm going to swim us out of here."

"No," she said, burying her face in his neck.

"Yes," he said. Without giving her a chance to object further, he jumped into the pool.

She couldn't help herself. She shrieked.

"Now, then. How is this any different from all the times we swam around in the river on the way here?"

"It's different because you're about to do something very frightening," she said into his neck.

"When I give the word, I want you to take the deepest breath you can. And I want you to hold it. When you don't think you can hold it any longer, don't let it out in a gasp. Let it out in a long string of bubbles. Ready?"

"No," she said.

"Here goes. Hold your breath." He dove under.

Terrified, she clung to him, squeezed her eyes shut, and held her breath until she thought she would die. She felt his body moving powerfully under her. She thought she would die. He arrowed through the water. She was sure she would die. She was so panicked that she forgot and let all her breath out in a gasp. But it didn't matter. They had surfaced.

They had swum down some kind of tunnel or channel into a completely different space. Everything around them was dark, except for an eerie green glow in the water.

"How are you, my darling girl?" he rasped, carefully prying her fingers, one by one, off his windpipe.

"You just about scared me into the next world."

"You of the Fire Child are timid creatures," said Gwyl.

"You of the Sea Child are out of your minds," said Keera.

"We're swimming down an underground river. Remember the cave where we wintered? Remember the stream that ran through it? This river is like that."

"Suppose it just keeps going along under the ground?" she asked. "Suppose we're just as trapped here as we were before."

"It will have to come out somewhere," he said.

"You don't know that," she said.

"It will be fine."

"We are completely naked."

"Hmm," he said.

## Crazy

"We are completely naked," said Keera to Gwyl.

"Not sure what we can do about that. I don't have anything I can hunt or trap with, to get furs for us, and we wouldn't want to wear furs anyway. Not in this heat."

"Maybe I can somehow put these big leaves together into kind of aprons for us," said Keera, wandering over to examine a tree. She stood there lifting her arms into the shade of it. She felt herself melting away into the landscape, stepping out of herself, becoming one with it. A green thought in a green shade.

"Come back to me, Keera," said Gwyl.

She turned to him, startled. His eyes were anxious.

"Where did you go?" he said, putting his arms around her. "At least we're warm," he murmured into her ear.

"At least that," she agreed, coming solidly back into the moment. "I like being warm."

They'd risen from the underground river into a big lake surrounded by thick greenery.

"We could just stay here," said Keera.

"Keera. This place might look like a nice safe garden. But I'm sure it's not. I'm sure it's dangerous. Maybe dangerous serpents. Wicked ones."

"Everything is dangerous," said Keera. "The whole world underneath the Spheres is dangerous." She wanted to stay.

"But look," said Gwyl. "There's a man over there, fishing."

Keera made a little cry and hid herself behind the tree.

"This is a good thing. We need food."

"How are you going to persuade him to give us some," she said from behind the tree trunk.

"I can only try," he said. He strode over to the man, who turned without, as far as Keera could tell from her post behind the tree, any surprise at all and seemed to greet him warmly. She saw them both starting to amble in her direction, talking animatedly. She didn't like it, some other person in their garden.

When Gwyl and the other man got closer, she peeked around.

In outrage, she exclaimed, "Old Dee!"

"I'm here to bring you clothing," he said. His skin was no longer blue. He looked more or less like himself.

"How did you know we were here?"

"The owls told me."

"Did you know Gwyl would be able to get us out?"

"I hoped he would," said Old Dee, handing her a new length of cloth that she wrapped and tucked around herself before stepping from behind the tree. She was beginning to like dressing in long oblongs of silken-smooth cloth.

Gwyl was winding another piece of cloth around his hips.

"If you knew where we were, why—" she began.

"Dear Keera. I am not allowed in that holy precinct."

"No?"

"No. It's expressly forbidden me. Even though my Child is the Sky Child."

"She's not very friendly." Keera stopped and thought about it. "But She fed us. And She gave us a chance. The most frightening of all were The Three."

Old Dee looked at her in amazement. "You went in there?"

"Yes, some natives led us to Their pyramid."

"Jesus, Mary, and Joseph," Old Dee said quietly.

"We nearly died," Keera burst out.

"Why didn't you," Old Dee muttered to himself. Then his voice turned practical. "I'm going to give you a lift back to your canoe, Gull."

Gwyl praised his Child.

"But Keera. You need to come with me for a little while."

"Why?" said Keera, feeling a sudden suspicion. "Where?"

"It's hard to explain."

"We'll be parted," said Gwyl. An anxious look was settling on him.

"Just for a little while. This is what I want you to do for me, Gull. Will you do it?"

Keera looked over at Gwyl, whose mouth was starting to shape the word *No*, and she had to laugh.

Gwyl drew a ragged breath. "Very well, Old Dee."

"I want you to get in your canoe and head up river the way you came."

"Without Keera."

"Just for a little while. I'll get her back to you."

Gwyl nodded. He looked deeply reluctant.

"Every time we've been parted, something bad has happened to us, Old Dee," said Keera. "It's not that we don't trust you."

"I understand. But Gwyl needs to get far away from here so the sun king doesn't catch him. They like to take people's hearts out while they're still alive, up that way. Here too, in fact." Old Dee stepped over to what looked like a mound of creeper and brushed it aside. A tall carving had been hidden in the lush vegetation. Old Dee pointed.

A man lay on a jaguar altar. Keera recognized that altar. It was the one at the top of the pyramid of The Three. In the carving, two people held this man's feet. A person at the other end held his head back. Others held his arms and shoulders. A figure that might have been a priest stood over him. This priest had cut deep into the victim's chest. With one hand, he held the knife. With the other, he held the victim's heart aloft.

Keera shuddered. Maybe not such a safe little garden after all.

"Why would they do that?" Gwyl asked.

"It's the life and courage of their enemy. They're taking it for their own. And the enemy courageously gives these up to his tormentors, because in defeat, he realizes his life and courage have become theirs," said Old Dee.

Keera turned to Gwyl. His eyes were haunted. She wondered if he, like she, was remembering how the scaffold in the village of The People gleamed white in the moonlight.

Old Dee broke into their thoughts. "Keera, you and I have a task to perform."

"What task."

"We need to look into your ornithomancy, so you'll be able to use it when you need it and not practically kill yourself depleting your life force. Or wandering into the wrong place."

"Those people back there misled us," Keera said. She knew her expression was sullen.

Gwyl glanced from the carving back to them both. He'd put out his hand to touch the carving. Touch the heart. Now his hand dropped to his side. "Her ornith—"

"It just means that I have a special connection with birds, Gwyl. You already knew that. Not just the owls. Remember Hildr?" But she schooled herself not to sound exasperated. It wasn't his fault they'd been tricked into that pyramid. If it was anyone's fault, it was probably hers.

So it was decided.

"At least we had a lovely day or two naked together," Gwyl whispered to her. Then he stood ready.

Old Dee cast a portal for Gwyl. Keera didn't want him to go. She saw how hard the dark thoughts assailed him, multitudes, vicious birds of prey that tore at his vitals. He glanced back at the carving and looked quickly, uneasily away. But he squared his shoulders and walked through Old Dee's portal.

"Now it's our turn, Keera. Ready? We're going some place strange. Strange to you, anyhow."

Keera squeezed her eyes shut. "Okay, Old Dee," she said, using his favorite word. "I'm ready."

She and Old Dee stepped through the next portal together.

She stood dazzled. She was in an odd little room. Old Dee handed her a strange white garment with strings that kept it closed, and she put it on, turning her back for modesty's sake.

"The strings go in the back," Old Dee told her helpfully.

There were windows in the little room, and they had that kind of glass the worshippers of the Lady used in their temples. Only this glass was clear. She walked up to one of these windows and rapped on it with her knuckles. It was thin, but it was strong. Both, somehow.

What she saw outside the window made her jump back with an exclamation.

The things she saw outside that window. She couldn't describe them. They rushed and swerved. She backed away until she came up against a high sort of bed, and sat down on it abruptly.

The bed. She stared at it. The posts of it weren't wood. They were some sort of metal, painted white. She reached out a finger and touched this metal. Maybe iron. And the bed was soft and springy. It was made of a padded material. Not furs. Not sheepskin. Cloth covering something firm and soft at the same time.

Old Dee had stepped away for a moment through a narrow door into an even smaller room attached to this main room. Now he was back. She turned to him. His skin had stayed white, the way it had been in the garden, almost as white as hers. He had the same piercing blue Old Dee eyes. Thank the Child. If not for those, she might not know him in all his transformations.

He was dressed very strangely. His trousers, poking out from under a long white coat, looked strange and shiny. His shoes were shiny.

He had an odd object perched on his face, and he looked at her through two pieces of glass attached to this object.

Her eyes darted from one marvel to the next and the next and the next.

Everything was completely strange.

"Feeling a bit faint?" said Old Dee.

She nodded.

"That's understandable. Everything is going to seem very un-usual to you for a while, until you get used to it."

"Where am I?"

"Well," he said. "That's a bit hard to explain. Where isn't too hard, but the rest of it is. *Where* is across that big river from the huge city of the sun king. Except it's on a different plane."

Keera thought about her Aunt Jillian, and how Jillie seemed to inhabit another plane that only she and Old Dee could peer into, through the thin barrier that separates one plane from another. "I see," she said.

"This city we're in is much, much larger than the sun king's city, and it's very different."

"There are strange whizzing things outside that window," she whispered. She stepped to it again and fingered two straight pieces of fine cloth that fell down on either side of it. The weav-ing of it was like nothing she'd ever seen.

"The whizzing things are vehicles. Kind of like wagons."

"Where are their horses? Or their oxen?"

"Do you know, when these wagon things were first invented, people called them horseless carriages. So you've got exactly the right idea. They go very fast, and they're not pulled by animals at all."

"By magic," she breathed.

"By a machine," he said. "Each one has a little machine inside that makes it go."

Keera thought hard about machines she had seen. The big winches that allowed towns and forts to pull their drawbridges up, for example. She couldn't imagine how such a device would allow a wagon to whizz around without a horse, especially not that fast.

"And this," he said, moving to an odd small rectangle on the odd wall. He flipped a little protrusion on it.

The room was flooded with light.

Keera screamed.

Old Dee hastily flipped the protrusion again, and the light went away.

A woman pushed open another very odd door set into the wall and stuck her head into the room. "Everything all right in here, Dr. D?" she said.

"Just fine, thanks, Mrs. Winston. I'm getting our patient comfortable."

This woman named Mrs. Winston pulled the door to again.

"Winston is dark like the natives. Darker than the natives," said Keera. She figured the "Mrs." part must be like "mistress" or "goodwife" on her own plane.

"Have you ever met a person of the Burnt Lands?" said Old Dee.

"No, but I have read about them in books."

"Winston's ancestors came from a place in that region," said Old Dee. "Mrs. Winston."

"How did she get here?" said Keera, dumbfounded.

"How did you and I get here?" said Old Dee.

"Oh," said Keera. "By boat."

"Exactly. You came recently. Mrs. Winston's ancestors came later. Mine came a lot later."

"I hope her boat was as nice as Dragon Wind," said Keera.

"It was not. You can trust me on that. Now, Keera. You're in a place called a hospital."

Keera nodded, trying to follow along.

"It's a special hospital for people with troubles in the head."

*I'm not following any of this*, she thought.

"People who see and hear things that aren't there. People who cry all day long. People who go around telling other people they come from a different plane and time. People who talk to owls."

"Crazy people," said Keera.

"We don't call them that here. I wouldn't call them that while you're here."

"Why am I in a place for crazy people?"

"It's the best way to keep you safe. It's the best way for people not to notice how odd you are, because they'll just think you're—er. . . troubled."

"I'm hiding out here."

"Exactly," said Old Dee, beaming at her. "As you know, I'm a neurologist. I have many patients here, and I also have a psychiatrist buddy who works here and knows about me, because he's a mage himself, so we thought this would be a good place to stash you."

"What's a patient?"

"A person a healer tries to heal."

"Okay," said Keera. "I understand. A person a healer is trying to heal must be very patient."

"Exactly," said Old Dee.

"So," said Keera. "Why do you need to stash me anywhere?"

"We mages are about to have our annual meeting at the Doubletree down on New Ballas. I'm going there to confer, converse, and otherwise hobnob with my brother and sister wizards, mages, sorcerers, galdrmasters, and—"

"Neurologists," Keera put in.

"Yes, and also to take you to the conference with me so you can see what being a mage involves. And I'm going to ask advice from my other mage friends about your ornithomancy. I'm sure they can give you many tips. Ornithomancy is not a specialty of my own," he added.

"I see," said Keera.

The woman named Winston pushed the door open again and knocked to get their attention. "Here are all the immunizations you ordered, Dr. D," she said.

"Come right in, Mrs. Winston," said Old Dee. "Now, Keera. Roll up your sleeve, please. This won't hurt a bit."

She looked at him suspiciously, then at Winston, who was advancing on her with what looked to be a glittery weapon in hand.

"Just a little stick," said Old Dee. "My goodness, look over there. A chicken."

"Where?" said Keera, startled. Then she howled in outrage. Old Dee grabbed her before she could rush after Winston and give her the drubbing she deserved.

She sat on the edge of the bed, sobbing in rage.

"Now, now, Keera. That wasn't so bad."

"Yes, Old Dee. Yes, it was."

"You're fine now." He handed her a very strange sort of cloth, or maybe the very thin parchment she was now hearing people call paper, or maybe a cross between the two of them. Old Dee popped it up out of a flimsy kind of box with a slot.

Keera took it and blew her nose. Then she couldn't help herself. She reached over to the box and popped one of the cloths or papers out herself. And another.

"Keera, remember the dis-ease you and your mother cured? And remember the jail fever that nearly killed Gull?"

"Gwyl," said Keera.

"You can call him Gwyl if you like. But Gull is really his name, you know."

"Hmpf," said Keera.

"On this plane, in this time, people mostly don't get dis-eases like that any more. If we inject them with a vaccine. . ." He stopped. He could probably see how frightened those words of power always made her. "Mrs. Winston just stuck some magic juice into you. Now you won't get those dis-eases."

"That's amazing, Old Dee. Can I bring some of the magic juice back to Gwyl?"

"No, I'm sorry, you can't."

"But suppose he dies of a dis-ease and I don't? I will be heart-broken, Old Dee."

"It doesn't work for everything that can kill you, just some things. You could probably both die together of something else, like your poor parents."

Keera nodded reluctantly. She rubbed her arm. It stung where that woman had attacked her.

"Keera, something worries me a lot. May I talk to you about it? It's kind of private, but I'm a doctor, so you can talk to me about it."

"A doctor?" said Keera doubtfully. *After all,* she thought, *that woman Winston keeps calling him Doctor Dee.* "Like the doctors in the great university at Lutetia?"

"Sort of. At that university, 'doctor' just means 'professor.' At many it does. I guess I should say I'm a healer."

Keera thought about how Old Dee had cured her father Wat's blindness. She nodded.

"So here's my worry. You and Gull are out in the wilderness for months, years at a time. Aren't you worried you'll have a baby? What will you do if you have one when you're all alone in the wilderness? I could give you some pills that—"

"Oh, Old Dee," cried Keera, burying her face in her hands and ignoring all the strange words he was using. *Months. Pills.* "I can't have babies."

"No?" He sounded shocked.

"No. On the voyage from the Cold Lands, I lost my baby. Then I almost died. If not for Tigeny, I would have died. She told me I'd probably never have a baby, after that."

Old Dee murmured sympathetically. Then he brightened. "With modern medicine, there's a good chance we can fix that for you."

"Really?"

"Really. No promises. We'll have to take a look. But there's a good chance."

"Oh, Old Dee!"

# Doubletree

Where are the trees, Old Dee?" said Keera as they walked through a big bright room he called the lobby.

"Huh? Look, Keera, don't be alarmed by all the strange people."

"I've seen a lot of strange people in the last few years," said Keera. She thought of the sun king. The People in their village. The crusty fisherman who spoke a mélange of three different languages.

But she herself was wearing some very strange clothing, and so was everyone around her.

"Let's put you in something not totally strange to you," Old Dee had murmured as they started to get ready for the gathering of mages. He laid out some clothes on her bed in her room at the crazy place. He gave her some small-clothes that, frankly, resembled torture devices. And a pair of trousers that felt so soft she couldn't quite believe them.

"Tencel," said Old Dee.

And an equally soft and smooth tunic-type thing.

"I thought buttons and zippers might be a bit much," said Old Dee. "This is a pullover."

And shoes that were as shiny as his were. She held one up and examined it. It seemed to be made of leather, but maybe not.

She looked over at the chair in her room, covered with similar stuff. She'd asked him once about what sort of animal that skin came from.

"Many naugas died to make the hides for that chair," he assured her.

Winston came in and shooed him out then.

By then, she trusted Winston.

"I'm going to show you how to wear this bra," said Winston. She meant the odder of the small-clothes, a contraption with straps and bits of metal on it. The other piece was odd too, so tiny as not to be necessary, but it was nowhere near as odd as this one.

"I don't like it," said Keera, once Winston had wrestled her into it.

"But it holds up the girls, sweetie," said Winston. "You're going to wonder what you ever did without one."

Once, she overheard Winston say to one of the others (some person she called *the head nurse*, except that there were no babies about the place crying to be fed, so Keera couldn't imagine what this nurse did with her time), "Think she must'a been raised by hippies."

When Keera was all dressed up, though, she loved herself. The trousers were black, but the pullover, as Old Dee called it, was a beautiful bright blue.

There were parts she didn't like. The only items she hated worse than the bra were the shoes. They pinched.

Winston had shown her about something she called make-up, though, and that made up for all the other discomforts. *That must be why they call it make-up*, she thought. "Thank you, Winston," she had told the woman, and she meant it.

"You're very welcome," said Winston. "Any time."

So now, as Keera walked across the lobby of the building that promised to have an extra supply of trees but didn't have any, she felt proud and happy. She had a little purse a bit like the pouches that dangled by chains from some women's belts, except that here you held it by a tiny useless chain in your hand. The make-up was tucked inside it in case she wanted to put more of it on her face. And a cloth-paper thing from the pop-up box.

Old Dee hustled her along. "Mervin!" he called out to a big man standing behind a long table stacked with odd looking parchments folded in odd ways.

This man came out from behind the table to greet them. He was tall. His skin was like beautiful polished mahogany. She knew about mahogany now, because the table in the day room of the crazy place was made out of it.

"Well, hello, little lady," he said to her in a basso profundo voice. He held out an oversized hand.

She curtsied and bent over his hand to kiss it.

Mervin laughed.

"Ornithomancy, huh?" he said to her.

"Yes, my lord," she said.

"Just like old times," Mervin said over her head to Old Dee.

Old Dee said, "Mervin, here, drives a truck on this plane. But on your plane, you have heard of him by some other name."

Keera looked at Mervin curiously. She knew by now that a truck was one of the whizzing things.

"Merlin," he told her.

"Myrddin," she corrected.

"That too," said Mervin, smiling at her agreeably. But then he frowned.

Old Dee stepped quickly forward and nudged Keera behind him.

Another man had come up to the table. A thin, saturnine man, close-shaved.

"Hello, Gilles," said Mervin softly.

This man named Gilles nodded at them with an affable smile. "Mervin," he said. "John."

Old Dee turned to Keera and steered her by an elbow away.

"What?" said Keera.

"That man. You don't want to have anything to do with that man."

"Who is he?" said Keera, craning her neck to look.

"He's a man named Gilles de Rais, and he is very dangerous."

"Gilles de Rais?" Keera looked up startled into Old Dee's face. "But he's the most powerful man in the Baronies."

"I know," said Old Dee, and he looked uneasy. "On your plane, he is. On ours he has the same name, but he lives rather differently. Well," said Old Dee, almost to himself. "Not so differently at that." He looked down at Keera, and his eyes were grim. "Promise me you'll stay away from him."

"I promise, Old Dee," said Keera. *I don't trust him either*, she thought, remembering her forebodings about Gilles de Rais.

After that, though, she forgot about Gilles and his menace, because everything was so new and astounding. She, Old Dee, and the rest crowded into a big uncomfortable room with many other people and sat on hard little uncomfortable chairs.

Mervin stepped behind a box-like structure. He tapped his finger against a bulbous object in front of him. "This thing on?" he said. Everyone chuckled.

Keera jumped. Mervin was all the way across a large room from her, but his voice boomed in her ears.

Old Dee put a reassuring hand on her arm.

Mervin began talking. Not much of what he was saying made sense to Keera, but she tried to listen.

Afterward, they all milled around in the room called the lobby again, and Keera got to drink a cold brown liquid that tickled her nose. It was her favorite. Diet Dr. Pepper. Winston told her a few days earlier she might have to lay in a case of the stuff, the way Keera was going through it.

"You should avoid that stuff," Winston had warned her. "One day you'll glow in the dark."

"Great keynote," said Old Dee to Mervin as they passed in the hall. He turned to Keera. "Now the break-out sessions."

Old Dee walked Keera down to a smaller room, but actually it looked like the very same big room, or one just like it, divided into smaller rooms by some kind of stiff material that felt nubby and shiny at the same time when she ran her fingers over its surface.

The session was called "Ornithomancy For Beginners." Old Dee was right. The leader of their session gave her many important tips she determined to try out on the nearest birds as soon as she got home.

At the end of the day, Old Dee ushered her into yet another of the cold, mammoth rooms—really cold, and she wasn't sure how or why, because outside, the air was sweltering. This room was outfitted with a long board to rival a king's. The board was covered by a snowy cloth. Keera peeked under the cloth to see what the trestles were like, but there weren't any trestles. Just complicated-looking metal struts. And there were no dogs under there, either, quarreling over the bones, and no rushes on the floor.

During the entire conference, she kept running her feet over the floor, which was covered in a soft patterned substance that was not fur. It actually seemed as if it might be wool. But who in the Nine Spheres would think to cover a floor with wool?

This wool floor was very different from the floor in the crazy place, which was also patterned, swirls of color somehow embedded in it. But that floor was hard. It wasn't stone or wood. She knew that much. She didn't know what it was made of.

She did know it was easy to mop. Workers mopped it every day, and they didn't have to go down on their hands and knees to do it. They stood up and guided the mop around on a long stick.

She decided to make herself one of those once she got home. She studied them, every chance she got, to see how they were made.

They were labor-saving devices. She'd heard someone in the crazy place use that phrase, although he had used it of a mysterious shaking metal box the purpose of which Keera had no inkling. Through a little window, she could see cloth swirling around in it. The mop, though. That was without doubt a labor-saving device, and Keera was impressed.

By now, she knew to expect strange and exotic food. This food at the mage conference was even better than the amazing food in the crazy place. She would hardly have credited it.

The food in the crazy place was the best food she had ever eaten. You got it by standing in a long line and holding out a hard flat disc, not a trencher. This disc was made of something she couldn't identify, run through with ridges dividing the disc into sections, and colored either a sick green or a sick pink.

Somehow, the food was kept hot in open metal boxes until a kindly person spooned it onto your disc. A raised edge around the rim of the disc kept the food from sliding off.

And there was a shivery substance known as Jello. It came in different colors, like the colors of rich jewels. Sometimes, little bits of fruit were embedded in it. Once, small white puffy delectable things were in there.

This food of the conference, if it could be believed, was even better than hospital food.

Dessert was especially fine, a triangular slice of yellow gum resembling the gummy substance she and Gwyl had used to seal the canoe, topped with a very high shelf of white, fluffier gum. But they were both very sweet, so Keera liked them anyhow.

"Mrs. Winston taught you how to brush your teeth, didn't she?" Old Dee leaned over to murmur.

"Oh, yes," she said. "I like that. It tickles. I like the toothpaste, too. It's not as good as this, though," she said, accepting his own slice of the two gummy layers and digging in. "But easier," she said between mouthfuls, "because you can squeeze some out whenever you get a hankering for it."

"Hmm," said Old Dee.

After dessert, she, Old Dee, and Mervin went into a dark little room they had almost to themselves. They sat at a round table. She slid into a bench behind it, which was slick with the hides of the naugas. The two men sat on chairs pulled up to the other side of the table.

"What do you think, Mervin?" said Old Dee.

"Honestly?" said Mervin, kicking back his chair and scrutinizing her. "John. You're doing what you always do. Getting too involved."

"I know it, but she's just so smart."

Keera looked from one to the other of them. She didn't like it when people talked about her as if she weren't even there. It made her mad.

"Hands off, man," Mervin continued. "You've got your mission. Stick to it."

"I suppose," said Old Dee.

A woman in a very, very short skirt came by to set down before the two men tall cups made out of the same clear glass as the windows.

Each cup was filled with some kind of amber liquid. Maybe mead, Keera decided. And some bobbing, clinking small cylinders of ice. Actual ice. Where they got it in this weather was a mystery, and where it was to be found in cylinders, each one with a hole in its center, was another.

"Take your order?" said this woman to Keera.

"The young lady will have a Diet Dr. Pepper," said Old Dee.

"Gotcha," said the woman and whisked away.

"But listen, Mervin," Old Dee continued. "It's hard to do that, stay hands off, concentrate on my mission, when Gilles is . . . you know. Being Gilles."

"I understand," said Mervin. To Keera, he said, "Young lady. How do you like ornithomancy."

"It's fine," said Keera, with enthusiasm. "I picked up some good tips."

"Excellent," said Mervin. In an undertone he said to Old Dee, "She shouldn't even be here, you know. Not at this stage."

"How is she supposed to learn, then? Tell me that. How is she supposed to practice her art without hurting herself? Inadvertently killing herself, even."

"Most of them don't learn. You know that, John."

Keera felt her face flushing and her eyes narrowing. "Would you prefer to talk about me while I go elsewhere?" she said.

Mervin guffawed.

Old Dee turned to Keera. His eyes were serious. "You have a talent, Keera. It concerns us. It would be best for you to know how to use it. But as Mervin says, most mages don't even realize they're mages."

"What will it mean, if I learn how to control my. . .whatever you call it. Talent."

"It means that eventually you might travel the planes. Eventually you might get an important assignment. You'd have to work hard, though."

"Would it mean I'd be parted from Gwyl?"

"Yes," said Old Dee.

"Then I don't want to do it," said Keera.

"But Keera—" Old Dee began.

"That's entirely your choice," Mervin interrupted. "Child knows, it doesn't make you any happier, doing this stuff. The reverse, in fact." He sucked in a breath. "Especially with the likes of him roaming the earth." He said this last thing softly.

Keera looked up. Gilles de Rais had come into the room. He strolled over to their table with a smile.

"What do you want, Gilles," said Old Dee in a flat sort of voice.

Ignoring him, Gilles leaned across the table to Keera. "Did you know I'm your monarch?"

"You're no monarch of mine."

"Oh, I believe I am, now that I've rid myself of your troublesome parents."

Keera felt her blood begin to boil. She found she was standing up. She found she had thrown an entire glass of Diet Dr. Pepper into Gilles de Rais's face.

"Better leave the lady alone," said Mervin to Gilles.

He cast his malevolent eyes on all of them. "Mind your own business, Mervin, and let me mind mine. Or you'll find yourself back in that rock."

"Oak tree," said Keera and Mervin almost simultaneously.

Keera sat back down, shaking, as Gilles stalked away, wiping off his face with one of the big swaths of cloth they called a napkin.

"You sure do know a lot about me," said Mervin, grinning at Keera.

"Gull, her husband, you know? He's Breton," explained Old Dee.

"Breizh," said Mervin, smiling nostalgically.

"Huh?" said Keera.

"Another Diet Dr. Pepper for the lady," said Mervin to the woman in the very, very short skirt.

# 8 GWYL: Fathers and Sons

## Never Say Die

They were together again, and that was fine. The sun shone, the paddling was good, the canoe was a worthy craft that made Gwyl proud.

"I'm thinking we should retrace our journey, so that means we have to head south on the Great River until we get to the Good River again. Then we can head north and east," said Gwyl.

Keera had nodded along. Now that her mission to the Sky Child's portal was complete, she seemed to be leaving the technicalities of their journey up to him.

But where should they go? The worst part was not knowing.

They had many long talks about it at night, in the firelight.

"We can't go back to Three Rivers," Keera would say. They'd agree. They'd start to imagine other places, other towns. Then they'd stare into the flames in silence.

The second thing they knew they couldn't do was live in the wilderness by themselves. For one, Keera had promised Old Dee.

"Besides, it's not safe, even if Old Dee hadn't done that thing to you," said Gwyl.

They were lying by the fire together on their fur in the aftermath of their lovemaking. Gwyl reached down to run his fingers over the two small scars on Keera's abdomen. They were the only evidence to show Keera had had what Old Dee had called "keyhole surgery."

"What did Old Dee mean by that, *keyhole?*" Gwyl asked Keera.

"Silly, a hole for a key."

"Well, I knew that, but I've never heard of putting a keyhole in a person. Why did he make these keyholes in you, Keera?" He felt unsettled. Was it some spooky mage thing, maybe? Did those mages now have keys that would enable them to somehow open Keera up and . . .He gulped. Do things to her? What things?

"No, he told me these holes are just in the shape of keyholes, and that's why the surgery is called that."

"Surgery meaning someone cuts a hole in you."

"Yes."

"Like the priest in that carving." He couldn't get the carving out of his mind. Someone cutting a hole in someone else to pull their heart out of their body. Is that what Porcupine intended to do to Pierrick? And then to him?

"Not like that. Remember, we talked about this. When I got so sick after losing the baby, I damaged something inside me, the place where the baby is carried. That's why I can't have another one. Couldn't," she corrected herself. "But now I can, because one of Old Dee's friends cut these holes in me and fixed the damage, and now I can."

He lay looking at her in the firelight and twining one of her curls about his finger. "We could have a child," he said. He tried to push aside the unsettling image of men actually looking inside Keera, rummaging around inside her.

"Yes. So Old Dee made me promise. No living out somewhere all by ourselves. He told me women who are having babies need help. He told me it's risky if we try to have a baby all on our own."

"You could die," he whispered.

"Yes."

"You could die anyway."

"I suppose so. Life is risky, Gwyl."

"I don't want you to die. Maybe I liked it better before Old Dee cut holes in you."

"You could die, too, you know. Some animal you're hunting could turn on you. Or some enemy."

"Or some dis-ease," said Gwyl. Saying that seemed to unsettle Keera. He looked harder at her. "What?"

"Nothing. I don't want you to get a dis-ease."

"So," he said. "We need to find somewhere to live. Somewhere with people. But where. Not Three Rivers."

"No, that horrible stepfather of yours would try to kill you."

"At least he wouldn't cut my heart out of me."

"You'd be just as dead. Don't let's talk about that. I don't want to think about it."

"Where, then. Yann is dead. I wish we could find someone we trusted as well as Yann, someone organizing a new settlement. There must be others."

"But how will we find them?"

"That's the question, isn't it. There were those fishermen we met."

"I was grateful to them for their shelter, but I was happy to see the last of them. I didn't really trust them," she said.

"Nor I. You know, the happiest I've ever been since I left your father and mother was the time I lived in the village of The People. Except for one thing."

"Porcupine."

"Him too. But I was thinking of no Keera," he said, smiling at her. "That was the fly in my ointment."

She nodded. "Dead flies cause the ointment of the apothecary to send forth a stinking savor."

"You smell delicious," he said, moving closer to her and gathering her into his arms. "And as for your savor . . ." He moved in closer still for a kiss.

"I'm thinking we both need a swim in the river tomorrow," she replied.

Much later, as the fire burned lower, they resumed their talk.

"Wonder if we could find a village of friendly natives, and live with them," he said.

"After what the scary things in the pyramid told us? They all want us gone," Keera whispered.

"Three Stripe didn't want me gone. He wanted me to stay."

"And you wanted to stay with him."

"Part of me did," Gwyl admitted.

"I want to be home with my mother and father," Keera cried out suddenly.

He held her and soothed her. "Would you like us to go far to the north, where we know there are trading vessels, and try to go back there, even though your parents are gone?"

"No," she said after a while. "That life is over for us. And this life, has it even begun? I feel caught in the middle. In a trap." Then she sat up. "But maybe we should find a place to stay that's warm. Like that beautiful green place. Thinking about all the freezing and the snows. That does make me want to be somewhere else."

"It's no different in the Cold Lands. No different in the Icerealm. Even some of the places you lived in your childhood were pretty cold. Mine too."

"But now that I've gotten really warm," she began.

"It's warm and pleasant here," he agreed. "We don't even need clothes. Let's stay here forever. We can have a baby here, the two of us. Let's stay here by ourselves, and we'll make a compact between us. Let's never die."

"Let's never die," she echoed, and they were in each other's arms again.

# Owl-cry

**K**eera," said Gwyl, low. "There they are, your owls." They'd just beached the boat in the twilight and hadn't even yet thought about making a fire, although they had stopped along the banks earlier to trap something to eat.

He sat on the bank of the Good River, pulling her close to him. They were already on their way north and east. They watched quietly.

Two owls, flying in and out of a hollow tree. They were making soft, wavering, purring sounds at each other.

"They must be getting a place ready for their young," said Keera. Her voice sounded odd. She put out her hand to him. He took it in his own. Then he got a strange feeling, part fear, part excitement. "Keera."

She looked over at him, and he saw it was true.

Their brave words of only a fortnight or so earlier came back to him. Now he was afraid. "We need to get further up-river. We need to find a place with people. People who will be there with you and help you when the baby comes."

Her eyes were huge in the twilight, and she nodded now. But she said, "Friendly people. Suppose they're not?"

"We're not just going to go strolling into some village or city or temple we know nothing about, I don't care what your owls tell you." He looked over to the birds again. "I'm going to check everything out thoroughly first." He thought back to the bad time, on Dragon Wind, when he was sure she would die. "How are you feeling? Sick?"

"Not even a bit sick," she said.

"Is that a good sign or a bad one?"

"I'm not sure," she said.

"But you're sure about the baby."

"Pretty sure." She shivered, and he led her to the place they'd spread their furs out. "I don't want to put a iunx on it by saying I am," she said.

It was still very warm, but he settled her onto the furs. "You lie here. I'm going to build us a fire, and then I'm going to cook something good for us."

"You should have seen the food they have, on that other plane. You wouldn't believe it. There was a delicious herb-tasting gruel that came out of a little tube. Like that mint patch we passed. Exactly like that. It was so good. But Old Dee told me the tube wouldn't come back with me through the portal, so I had to leave it."

Gwyl tried and failed to imagine this little tube. "What about that mint patch ?" he asked instead. "Did you gather any?"

"Yes, it's in the pouch."

"I'm going to see how it goes with the roast badger."

"Mmm," she said. "That does sound good."

That night, after she had fallen asleep in the crook of his arm, Gwyl looked up at the stars hanging by their golden chains from the underside of their Sphere. "Take care of this baby," he pled to his Child. "Take care of Keera."

The trip down the green waters of the mammoth river away from the sun city had been fast. The going now was not as easy up the other river, the brown one, the Good River.

But Gwyl was pretty confident of his way now. They'd canoe up the Good River, and then, once they got far enough to the north, they'd see how to get to the big lakes. Surely there had to be an easier way than the meandering small streams down which they had come.

In the morning, Gwyl took the stern and Keera steered. From time to time, they had to stop to shelter from storms, but except for one gusty, drenching, two-day ordeal, their progress up the Good River was satisfying, even though it was not as easy as their rapid westward journey had been. Keera insisted she felt well. She insisted that paddling the canoe would not hurt the baby.

"In fact, it's keeping me strong for her," said Keera.

"That boy had better not give you trouble the way the last one did," said Gwyl. But then he wished he hadn't said anything. Keera looked so sad at the memory.

The leaves had fully turned, and they had headed so far north that they now needed their warmer clothing, when they came upon another confluence of rivers. This place wasn't as dramatic as the landscape where the Good had poured into the Great, but the three rivers where they now stood were big enough. He scrutinized all three. *The Good River*, he thought, glancing behind them at its waters, then looking up to examine the sky and the signs he saw there, orienting himself. His gaze moved back to the two other rivers forking before them. *Here's a river cutting away . . . hmm*, he thought. He glanced at the horizon. *Looks like it's heading south from us, and the other appears to be cutting northeast.*

Keera turned her eyes trustingly on Gwyl as he steered them into the northeastern river. And up it. The owls weren't telling her anything now, and she looked to him to tell them where they'd go. "You're the Sea Child's, after all. Not me."

Gwyl reflected, as they paddled up this northeastern river in the brilliant harvest-tide sun, that he wasn't as certain of his own reasoning as he led Keera to believe. Not as confident as he had been just a fortnight ago. Going northeast, he thought, would be the surest way to put them in contact with settlers like themselves. But these settlers, as they both knew to their dismay, might or might not prove friendly. They were as chancy as the natives. Chancier, because they'd see exactly where Gwyl and Keera belonged. Or didn't.

Meanwhile, the weather was going to get cold once more. Maybe so cold they'd have to over-winter again before they found any settlers. If they ever did.

Gwyl tried to push this idea away, but it would keep coming back to torment him. Suppose they never found any settlers. Suppose the settlers were beholden to Maro, or to the henchmen of Ansgar. Suppose the baby came, like it or not, and they were in the hands of unfriendly people. Suppose, Gwyl thought with a shiver of fear, he came too early into the world, the way the other one had.

Gwyl decided that as they paddled further upstream, he'd perform two tasks. First, he'd carefully scout any native villages they came upon, when they went ashore to hunt or repair the canoe or portage around rough water. Second, he'd look for natural shelters, such as the cave where they'd stayed the winter on their way down.

None of the native villages he came across seemed that promising. The people were suspicious. Once they were outright hostile, but he'd left Keera safe on the river bank, and he'd gotten himself out of the range of their bows and back to her side before the hostile natives could catch up with him. Then they'd paddled their canoe out of danger.

There were no caves. There were no settlers. And the weather was getting cold enough so that the two of them began wearing their furs.

At last, out hunting while he made Keera stay warm and dry in a brush shelter he'd thrown together with the up-ended canoe serving as one side, he came upon a tiny village where the natives seemed friendly. They didn't understand the language of The People, of course. But he could communicate with them using gestures. They were a little afraid of his eyes, he saw. And now his tan was fading. But he soon reassured them with gifts of meat and fish. Most were women and children. He wondered if he'd happened upon a village that had undergone some crisis or disaster.

*Where are your men?* he tried to gesture, pointing to the one or two older men and half-grown boys and shrugging and making himself look puzzled.

*War.* That was the answer he got back, or seemed to.

*War*, he thought to himself sadly. *What is it good for?* In the end, he brought Keera with him to the village, and the villagers made them both welcome. By now, it was clear Keera was with child. Some of the women surrounded her, smiling at her and patting her belly. They also realized the two of them were others. Not like themselves.

*Others*, one of the natives said to Gwyl, pointing to him, then to Keera.

*Us*, the native man said, pointing to himself and then pointing, pointing, pointing to the rest of the villagers.

Gwyl nodded. *Others*, he said, mimicking their word and pointing to himself and Keera.

He turned to Keera. "It may be we should over-winter here. When will we find people this friendly? But the weather is still fine. I hate to stop. I want to get us further north."

"To find communities of settlers," she said.

"Yes. I think that might be safest."

"I'm sure these women know about babies," she said, looking around at all the children.

But later that first day, he found an older man who pushed one of the boys toward him and said something to him, and something to the boy.

*People who look like you. North of here.* The old man said that word, *Others*, and pointed at Gwyl.

That was the message, as far as he could make it out.

The boy drew a diagram. A little river. An overland trek. Another little river. Then a lake. Finally, a big river that could lead them north.

The next day, their supplies replenished through the generosity of the villagers, Gwyl, Keera, the old man, and the boy went down to the river and the canoe.

The old man ran his hand along the hull. He looked up at Gwyl and said something.

"I think he's admiring the canoe," said Keera.

"Looks like it." Gwyl turned to the man and tapped his chest. Then he drew a quick diagram showing the making of the canoe.

The man smiled broadly. He tapped his own chest and drew a similar diagram. The two of them stood looking from diagram to diagram and pointing various features out to each other, and nodding, and smiling.

"A man I respect very much taught me how to make this canoe," Gwyl said to the old man. He knew the old man couldn't understand his words. But in a deeper way, the man did understand. He made a sign of blessing over Gwyl and Keera.

"I'm not sure what god he means. Not one of the Children."

"The sun god?" said Keera. He heard the dread in her voice.

"I don't think so," he reassured her. "Some other god. But I don't know which. Maybe the rain."

Then the old man pushed the boy forward. By gestures, the boy told them he'd lead them. So they put the boy in the canoe between them and headed out.

A few days later, after a portage that was long but not too strenuous, they reached the lake the boy and the old man had told them of. Drawing yet another diagram with a stick in the dirt, the boy showed them the outlet into the river that would take them north. He made a water gesture. They nodded. Then a rushing of water, dropping off some vast height.

"A falls. We're to go to a falls."

"That huge falls, the one we walked many leagues to get around?" said Keera.

"I don't know," Gwyl admitted.

After giving the boy gifts—a fur robe, some game—they said goodbye to him and watched him walk away from them.

That night, they bedded down on the shores of the lake. It was not one of the huge ones they'd traversed with so much difficulty. "Those are still to the north, I'm thinking," said Gwyl. "So I suppose the falls we're meant to find aren't those falls. We'll see, once we leave the lake and head up the river." It was a pleasant lake, and the night air was not too severely cold yet.

As they huddled together before the fire, they heard a cry, a harsh, long kind of scream. Then, ghostly silent, two shapes cutting the air.

"The owls," said Keera, pointing. "Now I'm easy, Gwyl. We're heading in the right direction."

## Fathers

They heard the falls long before they came to them. And they felt them. The river started to roughen and boil up into rapids.

"Let's get the canoe to shore," said Gwyl. They had a struggle getting her up on the bank. "I don't want you portaging. It looks like we have a steep climb ahead of us. We'll leave the canoe here." He looked at the little vessel and gave it a reluctant nudge with his toe.

"I know you hate to leave her," Keera said.

"I do. But we'll be over-wintering near here anyhow. We'd have to leave her. And if we need to build something quick—" He looked around them. "Plenty of elm," he said. "Big stand of spruce for rope and twine. Lots of pines for caulking the seams."

*I just hope to the Child we find people here,* he thought. *I'd welcome anyone, at this point. Natives. Settlers. Anyone.* He knew by the time winter was over, the baby would be here. His heart misgave him now. Maybe they should have stayed back in the village with the friendly natives after all.

"The owls say we're doing the right thing," said Keera.

"I'm glad to hear it," he said, trying to keep the skepticism out of his voice. Of course she heard it anyway.

"You'll see. Something good is about to happen to us."

"When the owls led us to that pyramid, nothing good happened."

"It wasn't the owls. Those people tricked us, that led us to it. And remember, the owls saved us."

"I'm glad they saved us. Make sure they know that."

"They do," she said with a smile.

"Here we go, then. Ready for a hard climb?"

"Yes, I'm ready."

"But promise me. The instant you get tired, we'll stop and rest. Do you promise?"

"I do."

"No, really," said Gwyl, taking her face in his hands and looking down seriously into her green eyes. "I mean it."

"I mean it too. I don't want to hurt the baby either."

Gwyl had to let her go then, but it was hard. He could stare down into those eyes forever. They were like bottomless pools. He wondered if the baby would have eyes like that. A little son with green eyes and red hair, the Fire Child's own.

She reached up and caressed his cheek. "Do you know, I dream about the baby. And when I do, I see she has eyes just like yours, gray Sea Child eyes."

"What will we name him?" he was asking, but they had to laugh, because at the very same time, she was saying, "What will we name her?"

"Let's wait and see. My mother said when I was born, she hadn't thought of a name for me. When the midwife put me into her arms, she knew whatever she named me should mean *Fire*."

"My mother told me once I didn't have a name, not for close on a year. Then my aunt came to us to help care for me and Pierrick. She started calling me Gwyllie, and it stuck, and then it became Gwyl. It might have been a pet name for her favorite brother."

"Now I see it," she said quietly. "Your real name really is Gull, because a father who loved you named you that. The same thing happened with my mother. Her true father Drustan named her, because her real father couldn't be bothered. Old Dee is right."

"Keera. Promise me something?"

"Anything. No, stop. Stop. Don't say it. Anything except, *Stay right here, Keera, while I go off somewhere and leave you to wait.*"

"It's not that." He kissed her. "It's this. Promise we will take the baby to the village of The People to show him to Three Stripe?"

"That's a long journey. But yes. I promise we'll take her to see him."

As Gwyl feared, the climb was long and steep. He made Keera stop many times to rest, even when she didn't say she needed it. Near the top, though, they were rewarded.

"These falls aren't as huge as the others, the ones we saw further north," he said. "But how beautiful they are." They gazed out over three mighty cascades stretching off before them into the misty green of wooded cliffs.

"In the Fire Isle, there were falls as mighty as these," Keera said. "It makes me a bit homesick."

"I know the falls you mean," he said. "I know that feeling. Will we ever see them again?"

"I doubt it," Keera said. "We're so far away, and getting back there will be very hard."

But as they were gazing in awe, a voice above them cried out, in the language of the Baronies, "Identify yourselves, strangers."

Gwyl moved to put his body between Keera and the man who had shouted, standing above them on the very top of the cliffs. Keera gently pulled Gwyl back. She stepped forward. She knew the Baronies language from her time in Lunds-fort. "We're travelers," she called up to the man. "My name is Keera. This is my husband Gwyl."

The man bounded down a small steep path to stop a little way from them. He had his hand on the hilt of his sword, and Gwyl had his hand on his bow, ready to swing it off his shoulder.

Keera stepped between them. "We're peaceable folks," she told the man.

"I took you for a native," said the man to Gwyl. "My apologies, goodwife," he said hesitantly to Keera. "I took your man for a native."

"Many do," said Gwyl, warily.

"You're travelers?"

"Yes, and my wife is with child. We're seeking shelter for the winter, a place she can deliver the babe in safety."

The man peered at them both. "I see. Come with me, then. Our leader will question you."

Gwyl hesitated. He didn't want to walk into yet another trap. These people were Baronies folk. Were they beholden to Maro?

"Gwyl," said Keera. "It's fine. No trap. These people mean us well."

So Gwyl nodded to the man, took his hand off his bow, and he and Keera went with him back up the steep little path and by a winding trail into the forest. After a walk of a few leagues, Gwyl could see the palisades of a village ahead.

They walked through the gates, which stood wide open. A single guard nodded at them as they came in.

"We have friendly relations with the natives around here," said their guide. "But I had to make sure of you." He took them to a small longhouse of timbers. A woman there made them welcome and hurried to find Keera a comfortable place to lie down.

Although Gwyl didn't like seeing her move into the dwelling away from him, he knew she needed rest.

He turned abruptly to their guide. "I must ask you something. Are you ruled here by Maro?"

The man looked startled. Then it was his turn to look wary. "Are you a man of Maro?" he countered.

"I am not," said Gwyl, hoping that didn't get him seized and hauled away.

"Good," said the other man. "We don't like him here."

Gwyl drew a breath. *Thank the Child*, he thought. "I had to be certain," he told the man. "Otherwise I wouldn't want my wife in your hands. No offense."

"None in the least taken," said the man with a smile. "I think we understand one another. Our leader will be out to see you shortly." He turned and left Gwyl to himself.

Gwyl stood examining the walls of the dwelling. They were well-built. Implements for farming and for defense hung on the walls. *I haven't had a sword in my hands for too long*, thought Gwyl. He remembered the sword he had used to defend Three Stripe. That was the last time he'd held one. The People had traded it for things they needed more, after that battle. Steel was valuable.

Footsteps behind him warned him someone was approaching. The leader, maybe.

Gwyl turned to face this leader, hoping he'd be able to explain who they were to the man's satisfaction. The village looked like it might be a safe place for Keera to have their child.

The man stood and stared at him. "Gwyl."

Gwyl looked up in surprise. He looked into this man's strange eyes. "Nine Spheres," he said quietly. "Yann. I thought you were dead."

Then the two were embracing. Gwyl found he had tears running down his cheeks. He wiped them away and smiled at Yann. "I saw your harp, broken in the ruins of Fishers' Bay."

"I was bereft without it. Now I have a new one," said Yann. "I had to send all the way across the water to get one." He stood shaking his head. "For a long time I thought you were dead, too, until I learned your brother had survived. Everyone told me you were dead, Gwyl. Otherwise, believe me, I would have gone back to Fishers' Bay and—" He stopped himself. "But by the time I realized, we were far away from there, the few of us who made it out. And your brother was with Maro."

"Is he well? Did you see him?" Gwyl tried to keep the edge of panic out of his voice. He knew Maro wouldn't hurt Pierrick, but still he worried. And about Fiona and the children, too.

"No, I didn't see him. I don't know how he does there," said Yann. "I don't go to Three Rivers, or any place controlled by Maro."

"My brother isn't with Maro by choice," said Gwyl. "Did you know Maro is his father?"

Yann nodded slowly.

"Did you know Maro is mine?" He stopped himself. "No. He's not my father. I suppose he's my step-father, but in reality, he's not that either. Not in any way that makes any sense. He married my mother. But actually, he's nothing to do with me, because she has let me know I'm nothing to do with her. Just some unhappy accident." Gwyl looked down at the packed earth of the floor and smiled. He knew his smile was bitter. "While I was in Three Rivers, Maro imprisoned me. I think he was about to sentence me to death. When I see Maro again, I'll kill him." He looked up at Yann. "If he gets to me first, he'll try to kill me. But he's old. I'm thinking I'll win."

Yann gave him a long look. "We'll talk about that, Gwyl. I don't think Maro fights his enemies man to man. I hear he gets others to do that for him. Unlike some opponents you've faced. But now, I need to find you a place to stay and something to eat. Fathers," he said softly. "Some of them can be difficult. Some, inscrutable."

"I have a father. A true father. It's not Maro," said Gwyl. Yann looked at him in surprise. Before Yann could ask the question that stood in his eyes, Gwyl rushed on, because he didn't want to talk about Three Stripe. "My wife is with child. A kind woman took her off somewhere so she could rest. We've had a long journey."

"I want to hear all about it," said Yann. "But first, food, and a place to live."

## Sons

At the settlement, Falls Village, Gwyl and Keera were beginning to feel secure. But Gwyl wasn't feeling very secure just at the moment. Keera was crying in pain, and they weren't letting him see her.

"Tush, man," said one of the women at the door. "You'll just be in the way. Stay out there. Occupy yourself. We need to bring this child safely into the world."

*Suppose something bad happens*, he thought desperately. He remembered the time on the ship when he thought Keera would die in his arms. He remembered trying to steel himself for the worst. He remembered not being able to do that, thinking instead that he'd be shattered into a thousand pieces. If something happened to Keera now and he was not there with her—

He put his ear to the door. The women in there were murmuring encouragements. Keera's cries were getting louder.

Keera shrieked.

He jittered before the door. Barge his way in there? They weren't going to keep him from her. He wouldn't allow it.

But before he could try something, the door suddenly opened.

The midwife stood there, looking at him and shaking her head in pity.

"How is she? Tell me she's all right. Tell me nothing bad—"

"You poor man," she said. Behind her, a lusty squall. "Come in here and see your son. Come in here and see your brave wife."

Gwyl rushed past. He flung himself on Keera.

"Ow," she said. "I'm fine, Gwyl. Look at your lovely baby."

He slid into the furs next to her and looked into her arms. There was a red-faced infant snug against her, and he was furious.

"I need to feed him." She put him to her breast, and he soothed. "This world is too cold and cruel for him, after being in a nice warm place for nine turnings of the moon."

Gwyl was speechless.

The baby opened his eyes and gazed up into his mother's.

"That's a child of the Child of Sea if ever there was one," he breathed.

"Indeed he is. Just look at those eyes."

"I'll teach him to build a canoe. I'll teach him to build a skeid bigger and better than Dragon Wind."

"First let's just get him fed, darling man," said Keera.

He leaned over to kiss her, and he put out a finger and touched the tiny nose of his son.

"So now," said Keera. "What do we name him? I have an idea."

"I have an idea too."

"I want to name him John, after my uncle and also Old Dee," she said. "I never knew my uncle. I've just heard stories about him my whole life."

Gwyl was silent. "John is a wonderful name. Wat's older brother. Wat told me once that John was the heart of The Rising. Avery was its leader, but John was the heart of it," he said at last.

"But you had a name in mind, too. What is it?"

"I wanted to name him for my father."

"For Rafe?"

"No," he said, with a smile. "I know my real father was a fine man. So if we did name him Rafe, that would be a good thing. But that wasn't my thought."

Keera took his hand and brought it to her lips. "You want to name him for Three Stripe," she said.

"I do. But we'll go with what you want. Names are different, for The People. Each person has his own name. Three Stripe's is only his own."

"We'll think of some other way to honor Three Stripe."

Gwyl kissed the top of Keera's head.

The midwife shooed him away then. "Your wife needs to rest. She has worked hard. Get out of here now."

Gwyl didn't want to leave her and little John. But he knew the midwife was right.

Outside the room, he leaned against the wall in relief. Keera was fine. The baby was fine. It was good to name him John, because if not for Old Dee, the baby wouldn't be here at all. But *someday*, he told himself, *I'll take my son to show to Three Stripe.*

He went over to the main house of the settlement, Yann's house, to tell Yann. He wanted to tell the world, but first, he wanted to tell Yann.

"Well?" said Yann, laying his harp aside when Gwyl came in "I can tell everything is fine, because you are positively glowing."

"Keera is fine. The baby is fine. I have a son," said Gwyl. He was smiling so wide his face hurt.

One of the other men standing around Yann's hearth clapped a hand on Gwyl's shoulder in congratulations. "What have you named the lad?"

"We're calling him John."

"Good name," said Yann, and laughed.

Gwyl looked over at Yann in surprise. "Oh," he said. "Just like your name." Yann. John. They were the same name. One was just the more usual spelling in the peninsula of the Baronies where they were both from; the other, more like the spelling across the Narrows. "We've named him for Keera's uncle," he explained. "Her father's older brother. He was a musician, like you."

Yann's smile faded. "Yes," he said, and he practically whispered it. "Yes, I see that now."

"Did you know Keera's uncle?" Gwyl asked. He didn't see how that could be, but Yann was looking so odd.

"No, I was only a small child when he died," said Yann.

"You know about all that," said Gwyl. "That surprises me."

"I do know."

"You know about my father," said Gwyl, suddenly realizing. He thought back to the conversation he and Yann had had, when Gwyl and Keera had first arrived. Gwyl had meant to ask why Yann knew so much about The Rising. But then, somehow, he never had. "My real father, Rafe. You've always known."

"Yes, I always have."

"But when I asked where I might have seen you—." Gwyl hesitated. "Yann. What you're telling me is a bit strange. Why wouldn't you have told me from the beginning that you knew my background? And Pierrick's?"

"There are complicated reasons," said Yann. "I wish all those complicated reasons could stay across the Great Sea, where they caused so much trouble and sorrow. I wish our lives here could become a fresh start for us all. My goal is to make it so."

"Then I won't ask to know those reasons," said Gwyl. "Some day, maybe you'll tell me."

"Some day, I promise I will."

"That's good enough for me, then," said Gwyl.

"All of you in The Rising, you're very brave. And so few of you are left," said Yann. "John, I've always heard, was one of the finest and bravest. Your father was another. I know it well. I can tell you that. And Wat. John's brother. Your father Rafe's best friend in this world. All gone now." He picked up his harp, abruptly left the room and closed the door behind him.

Gwyl stood looking thoughtfully into the fire at Yann's hearth. He saw how moved Yann had been. How was it Yann knew so much about these men of The Rising, he wondered. He hadn't thought of himself as a member of The Rising in some time. In fact, when he'd learned the news of Wat's and Mirin's death, he'd buried The Rising with them in some deep compartment of his heart and hadn't opened it since. Yann was right. Only a few were left. He was left. And Pierrick, although Pierrick had been more on the fringes. Fiona's father had been involved, before Caedon caught him and executed him. Fiona herself, a little.

And Keera. He thought of the remarkable role she'd played. If not for her, Caedon would still be out there somewhere. Other opponents were still there. Ansgar was, a scavenger hoping to gobble up the pieces. And the barons opposing him, hoping instead to gobble up the Sceptered Isle for their own. They'd fight a war with Ansgar over it, if they weren't already fighting it. Maro was the toady the barons had sent out to these lands, to make sure Ansgar's toadies didn't grab them for Ansgar.

As if these lands belonged to either.

That must enrage Yann, he thought. Yann wanted a fresh start. Men like Maro were trying to drag the same old conflicts across the sea and plant them here.

*You have ruined your own lands. You shall not ruin these.* With a chill, Gwyl recalled the angry words of The Three.

Gwyl knew he wanted what Yann wanted. He wanted a fresh new world for his son. But the world here didn't belong to him, or to any of them. It belonged to the people who had been here for eons before the settlers arrived. How that would be resolved, Gwyl didn't know. If The Three had their way, the newcomers would all be driven out. The Sky Child seemed to think the same. Driven back to the sea they came from.

What was the just solution? He told himself he'd ask Yann his thoughts about that. He remembered their conversation before disaster struck Fishers' Bay. He and Yann had agreed on some important matters, ways the settlers and the natives could live together peacefully. Yet disaster had still befallen them.

Maybe it would be up to his son, and to his son's sons, to find an answer. Maybe the balance of the Children would help them find one.

# INTERLUDE: THE CLOUDS

**M**ervin had long given up the fight as more trouble than it was worth. Dee was going to do what Dee was going to do. Dee was going to interfere, and there was no stopping him.

In spite of himself, Mervin had gotten interested, too, especially after his own encounter with Keera.

Now, from one turning of the Spheres to the next, he sat beside Dee and watched the changing configurations of the little groups of the dead across that river. Especially, they watched the five of The Rising and those they loved. The two men who loved each other, and the three men who loved the three women ever by their side.

As for Wat and Mirin. Mervin gave a resigned sigh.

Dee turned to him. "Don't you send Aderyn out from the Land of the Dead on missions? Doesn't she practice ornithomancy, the way Mirin does? The way Keera does?"

"What are you, a mind reader?" Mervin growled. "There's no need to send Mirin on a mission. Little Bird is special."

"Mirin is special."

"What about Wat? He's no mage. He shouldn't be flapping around out there."

"Where Mirin goes, Wat goes."

Mervin grunted.

"Hsst," Dee interrupted, raising a hand and pointing. "Look at that. Two of the friends. No, I'm wrong. Just one of them. Rafe. And another one. I'm not sure who that other one is. Take a look and tell me if you recognize that man."

Two shapes of men, arm in arm, stood in the dusk watching from the banks across that river. One was definitely Rafe, Mervin thought. But the other was a strongly-made man in midlife. What were they watching so intently, Mervin wondered.

*Gwyl*, he thought. *It's Gwyl they're watching.*

"Look at that, Dee. I know why Rafe watches Gwyl. Gwyl is his son. But why is that other man watching him so intently?"

Dee looked hard at this other, older man. "Ahh," he said. Then, carefully, "Mervin, did you know that Gwyl's name is actually Gull?"

"Gull?" said Mervin blankly. "If you say so. What does that have to do with anything?"

Dee did not answer.

# 9 KEERA: Discoveries

## Baby Love

Keera would always remember the first year of little John's life as one of the happiest periods of her own. He was a healthy child, and the other mothers in the settlement, kindly and knowledgeable, helped her with her many questions. Fretfulness. Teething. Sleeping through the night.

How she wished Fiona were nearby. How she wished her parents could have lived to see John. She imagined her mother holding John in her arms. She imagined her father smiling at him, a proud grandfather. If they had lived, though, maybe they never would have seen him. They would have been too far across the Great Sea. She shooed these bittersweet thoughts out of her head.

The life of the village was tranquil.

Gwyl wasn't much of a farmer, but he was easily the settlement's best hunter and fisher. Yann was a fair-minded and organized leader, and he'd made sure the settlement enjoyed good relations with its native neighbors, whose fruitful plantings served as a model for their own.

Gwyl made friends with the natives, too. They were not connected in any way with The People, but he recognized some shared values. And they recognized what the gull sign on his shoulder must mean, and grew to trust him. Gwyl had taken to going out on hunting parties with their men.

But he was no renegade, as Maro put it. Gwyl was loyal to Yann. Gwyl thought Yann was a fine leader.

Keera herself was leery of Yann.

"Why do you say that, Keera," said Gwyl once, as they talked about him, "that you find him unnerving?"

"There's something about him I can't figure out. I think that's what makes me uneasy."

"Well," said Gwyl. "You're right. Do you know, all this time he has known my parentage, and Pierrick's? He told me he honored The Rising and its bravery. He knows a lot about where we come from and what we faced, back there."

"But if he knew, why didn't he say anything?"

"I'm not sure. He's a man with secrets. I wouldn't want to press him. He's a great leader. I think I'll leave it at that."

"Oh, Gwyl," said Keera, smiling at him. "You're always in search of a father."

"No, I just think he's a good leader. I have a father. I don't need another one."

She steered the conversation to another subject then, because when Gwyl thought about Three Stripe, he got a tense look about him she wanted to soothe away and didn't know how. She knew he wished he could take the baby to Three Stripe. She wondered if they made that journey, whether Gwyl would ever be able to bring himself to leave The People.

As for herself, she liked it here in their settlement, Falls Village. Although most of the settlers were from the Baronies, Yann got them all together to explain he wasn't beholden to Baron Gilles or anyone from the Baronies.

"Gilles's governor, a man named Maro, is the person trying to force all Baronies settlers to pay a tax to Gilles and live in settlements Maro controls. We're never going to do that here. If you feel you want to be connected to the Baronies in that way, go to one of the settlements paying tax to Maro. I'm from the Baronies myself. I know Gwyl Hunter, over there—" and here he pointed Gwyl out—"is from the Baronies too. Many others. But we have other people with us here. People from the Ice-realm. The Fire Isle." Here he had looked over at Keera with a smile. "Other places. A man from the fishing communities in the south of the Baronies."

"That's me," said the man in his fractured Baronies language. "We don't hold with barons and such, where I'm from."

Keera remembered their winter stay with such people.

A woman stood up. "Yann Harper, they say those settlements controlled by Maro are getting closer to us."

"Yes, that's right. His base is at Three Rivers, on the Inland River. But now their settlements have spread to the big isle below the rapids, and along the shores of both big lakes that flow into the Inland River. Even past the Great Falls."

"And what about Ansgar?" said another.

"His settlements seem concentrated on the New Found Land shores," said Yann. "I haven't heard of Ansgar settling any of his people south and west of there. But Maro's settlements there and Ansgar's are in conflict. So I hear. Anyone in Falls Village from the Ice-realm who would rather be under Ansgar's control, you may leave with our blessing. We stop no one leaving. Leaving to be on your own, leaving to join Maro or Ansgar. We'll even help you. But those monarchs and governors don't control us here and never will."

After that, a few families did leave, mostly Baronies folks. Keera heard their muttering. Usually it was about the natives and how Yann acted like they were human beings when it was clear they were savages who would someday murder the Falls Village people in their beds. "Those heathens are just biding their time," she overheard one man say darkly. "And that Gwyl, he's practically one of them. A renegade."

Keera tried to ignore this man. She was glad to see the last of him, when he took his family and left for the nearest Baronies-controlled settlement.

Keera participated in the Falls Village community as best she could. She aided the others with her knowledge of herbs and healing.

On fine days, as she walked out into the surrounding meadows and forests in search of herbs, she thought about the owls. She had John with her in his sling. But she knew Gwyl would worry if she and the baby were still outside the palisades at dusk, so she always went back before the owls were likely to be about.

"I'm not worried about the natives," Gwyl told her. "Just the usual things. Bears. Falling down and breaking your leg. Rattlers. Those big cats."

"I have my knife," said Keera.

"That won't help you much. Wonder if I should teach you how to use a bow?" he fretted.

"I'm sure I wouldn't have the strength to pull one of those bows you trained to use."

"No, look, Keera." They were in their little dwelling, and he stepped over to the pegs above the door where he hung his bow. "Look at this," he said, taking it down. "It's nowhere near as long and heavy. Doesn't need such a big draw. Those bows I trained on as a young man were made so we could pierce through armor if we needed to. And to use one, you had to stand at range. But these are for more close-in work. They don't need to have the big draw. They just need to take down an animal."

Keera shook her head. "I'll leave the bows to you, Gwyl," she said.

"Promise me you'll be careful," he told her.

"I will," she said, giving him a kiss.

"Look at this baby," he said, reaching for his son, who had begun to fuss. He held John up high as he squealed with delight, and brought him down gently and nuzzled him. John began to whimper. "He's getting so big." Gwyl jiggled him until he stopped crying.

"He looks like you, Gwyl, with those eyes," she said.

Gwyl examined John. "You know, I think he looks like your mother. That's what I think."

*But mostly*, thought Keera, *he looks like a baby*. Time would tell what he'd actually look like, as he grew older.

Now, though, little John was starting to howl.

"We know what he really wants," said Gwyl, handing him back.

Keera sat down to feed him.

"I don't blame you, son," said Gwyl, stroking the top of John's head and giving Keera a kiss on top of hers. "That's what I'd want if I were you."

So one day succeeded the next, and by summer, John was a happy child rolling over; grabbing at things and putting them in his mouth, no matter how unsuitable; screaming while he teethed; drooling; spitting up on Keera's shoulder; babbling. And eating and eating and eating.

Keera felt tears come to her eyes at the thought of weaning him, but she did know she must start giving him some solid food.

"If you were home in the palace, your mother would have arranged for John to be sent out to a wet nurse," said Gwyl as she was debating how soon to begin this monumental act.

"Never," said Keera, shocked. "I would never have allowed myself to be parted from him." She looked down at him, wriggling in her arms, and he gave her back his mostly toothless smile. "And my mother had no wet nurse for me. We were poor folks."

"Mine sent me out. To a neighbor woman."

"So then, right away your mother had Pierrick."

"Are they connected?"

"Silly, yes," said Keera. "As long as I'm nursing John, it's unlikely I'll have another babe so soon."

"My mother was glad to be rid of me."

"Knowing Maro, and what he is," Keera said slowly. "Your mother might have had some bad experiences of her own."

Gwyl looked unconvinced. Then he left to meet with Yann and some of the others about village matters.

*But really,* Keera said to herself. *I think I hate that woman.*

## Separation

When he brought her the news, Keera looked at Gwyl in a kind of despair. "You have to do it," she said. She had put little John in his cradle for a nap, and now she was sitting on the bench before their hearth, twisting her hands in her apron.

"Yes, I do."

"This reminds me of the last time Yann sent you off on some errand without me."

"I know, but I'm the best person to lead this expedition, and you know it too, Keera." Gwyl looked troubled just the same.

Keera did know Gwyl was the best person for the job. She couldn't pretend she didn't. Yann needed a person to lead a scouting party north.

Rumors had filtered down to them. Maro, they'd heard, was organizing some kind of campaign to eradicate the Falls Village people or bring them into his fold.

"We have to go now so we can get back here well before the weather turns," said Gwyl.

"For the first time, I know—really know—what Fiona was up against. Pierrick would go off somewhere dangerous, but she had to be there for her children."

"I can stay here with John and you can lead the scouting party," he teased. "After all, who tracked that expedition to rescue me and Pierrick? For over a sen'night, alone, through the woods?"

"We know you have to go and I have to stay," said Keera, dully.

"If you went, what would little John eat?" He flung himself down beside her in their nest of furs. John had stirred and had begun to squall. Now she picked him up and began feeding him. Gwyl stroked her hair. "I'll have a hard time leaving you. As always," he whispered.

Then he reached over to touch little John on his nose. "Think we might try for another one of these?" he said.

"A daughter!"

"A brother for John! Brothers are important, Keera."

"Daughters are important," said Keera, indignant.

He grinned at her.

"How far do you have to go?" said Keera, turning from indignation to worry.

"Three Rivers." He lay toying with her hair.

"That's a long way."

"Yes. But that's where we'll find Maro."

"You won't let him take you."

"Certainly not. But I will try to get to Pierrick and find out what their lives are like now. Yann heard some things about them, but not much. I'll want to see for myself. Are they well? Do they want to stay there? Do they want to get out? Things like that."

"Fiona and Pierrick may have made a life for themselves there. It might not be too bad for them. After all, Maro loves Pierrick."

"We'll have to be ready for that, and not think badly of them if that's what they want to do," said Gwyl. Then he said, low, "I miss my brother."

"I see how much you do. You know, Gwyl. Maro is getting old. The situation Fiona and Pierrick are in can't last forever." After a moment, she said, "I know what else you'll do, once you get up there."

"I'll be so close to the village of The People. Even though I won't have John to show him, I'll have to try to find Three Stripe."

"Promise me to be careful. The situation in the village may have changed. It wasn't safe for you before. It may be even more dangerous now."

"I'll be careful. You know I will. There are two people right here I need to be careful for."

That had to be enough. The next day, Gwyl and a party of three or four others left for the trek north.

# Yann and John

While Gwyl and the others of the scouting party were gone, Yann mobilized the community. The settlers checked and rechecked the palisades for vulnerable points. New defenses were devised. A group of the settlers dug a deep ditch around the entire perimeter of the little town. Yann refused to speak ill of the settlers who had left for one of Maro's towns, but some of the others were not so gentle.

"Those rascals will tell the men of Maro where the palisades are weak," one man said, encouraging his group to work harder. "They'll kill us all, if they can."

Because, through Gwyl, Keera had come to know some of the natives, Yann assigned her to lead a party of settlers to the native village to buy maize from them.

"We need enough supplies if the men of Maro decide to besiege us," he said.

When Keera and a few of the others got to the native village to dicker over the maize, one woman pulled her aside.

"You're preparing for war," she told Keera. By now, Keera could understand their language fairly well.

"Yes," she said.

"Against us?"

Keera's hand flew to her mouth. "No! Not you. You and your people have been nothing but kind to us."

"Who, then?"

"Bad people to the north, *Others* like us." These people in the nearby settlement were part of the same group that had led Keera and Gwyl through the territory to the south of them and had showed them how to find the falls and Yann's settlement, Falls Village. Keera knew these natives all used the word *Others* to speak of the settlers.

"I've heard of these bad *Others*," said the woman. "Very dangerous. Not like you and your friends. Not like Gull. Although Gull—" she stopped, looking puzzled. "He's not one of you *Others*, but then again, he's not us, either." The woman stopped. She put her hand out to Keera. "I'm sorry, Keera. Gull is your husband. I hope you don't think I speak ill of him. We here in our village think highly of Gull."

Keera shook her head at the woman and gave her hand a friendly squeeze. But she thought, *This woman is right. Where does Gwyl belong? Not here. Not there. Somewhere uncomfortable in between.* And then she thought, thinking of Gwyl's upbringing, *Will there ever be a place where he is comfortable? Or will he always stand in the middle, betwixt and between?* To the woman, she said only, "You're right that these bad *Others* are dangerous. We want to be ready if they attack us."

"You want us to help you," said the woman slowly. "We're happy to sell you this maize. If we help you fight, though. Some in our village say that will put us all in danger."

"You're helping us greatly by selling us this maize. But—" Keera wasn't sure what prompted her to say what she said next. Maybe her experience far to the south, in the grip of the Sky Child, and in the even more frightening grip of The Three. "Don't endanger yourself and your children for us. We'll fight them ourselves. If you fight them too, and we lose, this man Maro, their leader, will come after you next."

The woman nodded soberly. "Wise advice."

*What have I just done?* Keera thought. *We might very well need these people.* Somehow, she had had to say it. She decided Yann and the rest of the settlers wouldn't understand. She'd keep her words to herself.

It took the whole day to walk to the natives' village, negotiate with them for the maize, see it loaded in packs and contrive a way to get it back to the settlement. The natives showed them an ingenious dragging device for heavy loads, so they bought a few of those, too, and set out for the return trip to Falls Village.

By that time, Keera was missing John, and she was hurting, too. She needed to nurse him. A good neighbor was watching him, a neighbor with a baby of her own. "I'll feed him, never fear," she told Keera. "There's enough for two here."

Keera wanted to feed her little child herself. She hurried back up the trail, a bit ahead of the other villagers.

It was twilight. The owls came.

Keera stepped quietly off the path, letting the rest of her party go past. In the near-darkness, they didn't see her stopped there.

She stood watching the owls, a pair. They seemed to have a hollow tree nearby, to roost in. She saw them silently swooping toward a big tree a little further into the forest and then back again. *That must be the tree*, she thought. They kept coming back to hover near her.

*What must I do?* she asked them. *I fear for Gwyl.*

*Don't fear.* That was the answer she somehow received, and she knew this message came from them.

*I worry*, she said to them. *That man Yann troubles me somehow.*

*Don't be troubled.*

Then the owls were gone.

She made her way back to the village and to her child. The next day, she went to Yann to tell him about their success.

"Welcome, Keera," he said, when she entered his dwelling. "Sit here by the hearth and tell me what you discovered in the native village."

Keera settled herself on one of the stones around his hearth, and pulled John to her, trying to settle him, too. He was restless, though. He wanted to wriggle out of her arms and get to the floor.

"Put him down," said Yann, laughing. "Let him explore."

He was a crawler now, and he fussed to be let down. Keera smiled and released him to roam around on the floor.

"He's a fine child," said Yann.

"You have no children of your own, Yann Harper," Keera blurted out. Then she felt appalled by her rudeness.

"No, and I'm not likely to have any," he said.

"No wife?" Now she was curious and couldn't stop herself.

"No."

*Stop prying*, she scolded herself. Perhaps he didn't like women in that way.

But he continued to talk, looking into the fire. "Some of us are lucky in our parents. Some not so lucky. Some say that a child will take something of its parents into the world with it. In some cases, a person might not want that legacy to continue, in the world. And some," he said, and stopped. "Some are unlucky in love."

*What could he mean by this?* thought Keera. His words were mysterious to her. The part about being unlucky in love was pretty clear. He must have known heartbreak. The part about parents, though. She wasn't sure what he meant about that, so she just nodded. But then she couldn't help saying, "My mother was unfortunate in her real father, but fortunate that her mother gave her a true father. What was inside her counted more than what her real father might have given her. And Gwyl. I know you know his history."

"Well. Yes. You're right about that. And I do know your husband's history. His step-father, as we both know, is a villain. His real father, though, was a very brave, very unusual man who fought an overwhelming force. Some people fight when such a force is ranged against them. Some can't. Or don't." He sighed. "Or won't." He looked deep into the flames of the hearth. "Or don't even want to," he murmured.

Keera looked at him, puzzled. She knew Gwyl's father had fought with The Rising. He had been one of the Six, the leadership. They did face an overwhelming force, even though they were defeated and knew they probably would be. Maybe Yann's own father had been a coward during those hard times. Maybe— she looked at him through narrowed eyes. Maybe he himself avoided the conflict. Gwyl fought for The Rising. She had fought, too. This man was at least ten years older than Gwyl, so he could have fought.

Then Keera was ashamed. She was judging Yann, thinking he might not have fought for The Rising. But why would he? What was Ranulf's dynasty to him? Gwyl's father, a Baronies man himself, had been sent to Ranulf's court as a young man. Otherwise, he'd never have gotten involved.

Yann was staring down at John, crawling his floor. Yann didn't meet her eyes. "When I look at your husband, I see a brave son of a brave father. And now here is little John. He'll grow up to be a brave man, too. He's named for a brave man."

Keera thought to herself, *This man knows a lot about The Rising.* Deep inside her, she realized she knew something about Yann. *No, this man is not a coward*, this inner voice said to her.

Keera couldn't help herself. She couldn't keep quiet. "But Yann. You're brave. Why wouldn't you think, no matter who your father was, that any child of yours—" *Just stop, Keera*, she said to herself. "I'm sorry, sir. I presume far too much. I'd just hate to think you torment yourself over something like this.

"Thank you for that, Keera. And now, let me hear your news." Yann's voice had turned impersonal.

*What a fopdoodle I am*, Keera thought. *What an addlepate. What an intermeddler. Let the poor man alone.* She hurried to tell him about the supplies they were able to buy from the natives. "And they have an ingenious device for carrying loads over long distances, so we bought a few of those, too." She counted into his hands the remainder of the coin he had given her to make the purchases. By that time, the natives had learned these small shiny objects were valuable tokens for trade with the settlers, even though they had their own tokens and ways of trading among themselves.

She thought of her words to the native women, and she thought about the owls' message. So she summoned up her courage. "And, sir, I said something to one of the native people that maybe you won't like," she told Yann.

"What's that, Keera?"

"A native woman told me she was worried she and her people would get drawn into our conflict with Maro. I told her it was our fight, not theirs."

"You were right to say that, Keera. That was exactly the right thing to say. We have to be careful here. This land's not our own."

So then, as Keera left Yann's dwelling with John in her arms, she felt much better about the man. She felt better about herself, too. Yann hadn't treated her as if he thought she were a fopdoodle or an addlepate, and even though she knew herself for an intermeddler, he had graciously not pointed this out. He'd treated her as if she were a valuable member of the community with some valuable information and insights to bring to him. She could see why Gwyl regarded him so highly.

But when she thought about him and his obvious distress, she couldn't help worrying for him. *Anguish*. That's what she'd call it, what she'd glimpsed in him. Yet he was perfectly calm as he talked to her, so why would she think so? In that regard, Keera found him just as unsettling as she always had. He must, she decided, have lost the one he loved. *Unlucky in love*, he had said. That might explain a lot.

## Eyes

Tensions ran high in those next few weeks of preparation. Everyone knew that if Maro was going to move on them, he'd attack before winter set in. Yet the scouting party had not returned.

The party was overdue.

Keera felt a sick fear gripping her heart. She couldn't let it show. She had to be calm and cheerful for John. He picked up on her feelings right away. *He's spooky that way,* she thought.

Then she thought, *Oh no!*

But, she thought, it's only a natural thing, the close connection between mother and baby. Nothing spooky about it.

She continued her daily round, feeding him, cleaning him, clothing him, playing with him. Soothing him to sleep with a few remembered lullabies of her mother's, although singing them sometimes made her cry out of loneliness for her mother.

John was pulling up on things by now, a table leg, the bed platform, the door frame of their dwelling. He was dangling from her hand and thinking hard about something. She could see the determination in his gray Sea-Child eyes. His eyes. She knew his eyes so well.

"I know that look, little John. You can't fool me. I know someone else who has that same look about him. And I know what you're thinking. You're thinking about breaking away from your mother and heading out on your own," she whispered to him. "Heading out into the unknown, like someone else I know very well."

Pretty soon, John would be toddling around. Keera longed for Gwyl to be back, so he could see his son take his first steps.

Meanwhile the tension kept rising. All day long, she and everyone else in Falls Village could hear the hammering. Men up on the palisades, making them stronger and better.

The men of the smithy were working overtime, turning from farm implements like scythes and hoes and plowshares to forging the pikes and other weapons of defense that they might soon need more.

Some of the men, like Yann and Gwyl, had their own swords and were skilled in their use. Others could draw a bow. Most of the villagers didn't know much about weapons, though, so Yann and some of the others drilled the rest of the villagers in how to use the pikes. Keera took her place with the rest of them, learning how to stay in a tight defensive formation. And she practiced with her knife. Keera's muscles were still hard from a thousand leagues and more of canoeing, even after having a child.

"If Maro and his villainous crew think they'll march in here and take helpless women, they're wrong," said Keera's neighbor to her. She hefted her pike. She was a hefty woman, and she looked like she'd be able to do formidable damage to whatever unfortunate enemy came across her path.

But would they really be able to stop trained, armed men? Keera thought. And while the massed pike wielders could do a lot of damage, what would happen to them when Maro set his bowmen on them?

She knew from her time in Three Rivers that Maro was assembling an army. By the standards of the Sceptered Isle or the Baronies, it wasn't a large army. But it was larger and better prepared and equipped than anything the Falls Village settlers could summon up. By now, it must have grown much larger.

Late one day, Keera looked up from the endless task of washing out little John's cloughs to hear a commotion at the gates of the palisades.

With a glad cry, she sprang up, nearly overturning her washtub. She grabbed John to her and ran for the gates.

The scouting party was back.

Gwyl was through the gates first and to Keera and John, pulling them into his arms and covering them with kisses.

"I've missed you so much," he murmured in her ear. Then, looking around her at John, his eyes widened. "He's huge."

"He's going to be a tall man, like his uncles, I think," said Keera fondly. "Like my father." She put John on the ground. He grabbed onto one of his father's legs and pulled himself up. "I was worried you'd miss his first steps, but you're just in time."

"I have to go to Yann with the others. I'll be back soon," he told her.

"Tell me everything."

"Soon."

As he strode away from her, she looked after him uncertainly. What had she seen, haunting those Sea-Child eyes of his?

She took John back to their dwelling and fed him. John was eating real food too, now. He was growing. Every time she turned around, she swore he was a measure bigger.

She bedded him down in his small pallet next to her own bed and sang to him. "Five for silver... six for gold," she sang. His big eyes grew heavy-lidded. He put his thumb to his mouth and fell asleep without a fuss. She stroked the soft curve of his cheek, the down of his hair.

She heard the muted closing of the door, and Gwyl was there beside her. They couldn't talk, not then. He flung his bow aside and they tumbled together into their bed, making sure to be quiet about it, and made urgent love to each other.

"I missed you," he said, nuzzling into her neck.

"And I missed you. And I worried, when you were late coming home."

"We had a bit of trouble. Not much, but it slowed us down."

"Trouble?" She was trying to whisper.

"We ran across some men of Maro, who began tracking us as we left Three Rivers. They didn't go back to tell anyone what they'd seen, though. We made sure of that."

She shuddered in his arms.

"It's fine, my darling. We're all fine. We were more than a match for them."

*Yes, but you're the best we have,* thought Keera. *And they have so many more.* "What did you find out?" she said instead.

"Just as we thought. Maro is preparing to move against us."

"What about Pierrick."

"Here's the strange part. Pierrick is no longer there. But Fiona and the children are. I tried to find out why, but I never could. It scares me, what that might mean, Keera. I tried to get to Fiona, but I couldn't."

"Did she seem well? And the children?"

"From everything I could see, yes, they seemed well. So that at least is a comfort."

"Maro would never have hurt Pierrick."

"No, I don't think so. But then why? Where was he?"

Gwyl lay in Keera's arms. Then he turned his face into her shoulder, and suddenly his body heaved. With alarm, she realized he was sobbing.

"Gwyl, what is it?" Keera half-sat up, but she glanced over at John, to make sure he was still sleeping, and she slid down to cradle Gwyl. She realized she knew. "It's Three Stripe, isn't it."

Gwyl nodded. When he could speak, he said, "Three Stripe is dead. Almost all of them are dead, and the village of The People is burned to the ground."

"One of their enemies?"

"Ansgar," said Gwyl. His voice was grim. "Men of Ansgar took them by surprise and destroyed them all."

"Ansgar isn't here, is he? He himself is not in the New Found Land."

"No, he'd never undergo the discomfort of such a long and dangerous voyage. Just his men."

"How do you know it was Ansgar's men?"

"There were a few survivors. Squirrel survived. She was in a neighboring village. I went there to see what they knew, and I found her there, and she told me."

"Squirrel is Three Stripe's wife."

Gwyl nodded against Keera's shoulder. He turned over and wiped his eyes.

"They would never have taken the village like that if Three Stripe had been alive."

"Wait. Three Stripe was dead before the attack?"

Gwyl looked away from Keera. "Yes," he whispered.

"When did he die? How?" Keera exclaimed, then made herself lie back. *Don't wake John*, she thought.

But she felt a kind of horror now. Gwyl was having to make himself say the words. She could see the struggle he was waging with himself.

"He died the morning after he let us walk out of the village."

"Oh, Gwyl."

"Someone had to be sacrificed to that terrible god of theirs," he said.

"Child keep him. His own brother did this to him?"

"I did it to him."

"Darling, no."

"How could I not have known? How could I not have understood?" Then he said, which broke Keera's heart entirely, "How can I be a good father to our son? Look what kind of son I was to my father."

"You were a son he loved so much he was ready to die for you," she whispered.

"But it should have been the other way around."

"No. I'm thinking he knew what we all know. The children carry on when the parents no longer can. And here's his son, right here with me. And there's his grandson. His true son, his true grandson."

"If only he could see our boy," said Gwyl. "I went back to the village and poked around our old dwelling. It had been burned pretty badly, but not entirely burned down. There was a place dug into the dirt of the floor where Three Stripe kept his most precious things. I never saw what they were. It was a place private only to him. I would never have looked. But now I did."

"And you found something there?"

Gwyl leaned over the bed platform and rummaged through his cast-aside clothing. "Here." He unfolded a little bundle. Out of it he took a thong with an amulet and a few feathers. "This was the most important thing my father owned. He wore it always. He must have taken it off when Porcupine came to—" Gwyl stopped. He was silent. "I'm not sure about the amulet, but these are eagle feathers."

"His spirit animal? Like your gull and my firebird?"

"Yes, because his tattoo, on his shoulder, represented the eagle. I hadn't known that. Squirrel told me. Three stripes, a pale one for the eagle's white head, the top one. The middle one was yellow, for the eye and the beak of the eagle. The bottom stripe was dark, for the eagle's dark body. I never knew that's what his name meant."

"Will you wear it now, in his honor?"

"Never. It's his. Besides, I'm not worthy to wear it."

"Don't say that, Gwyl. You're torturing yourself over something you couldn't have known."

"I should have known it."

"But you didn't. Let it rest." *Besides*, thought Keera, *if you hadn't walked away from that village when Three Stripe allowed you to go, what would I have done?* She tried to put that thought far away from her.

"But look what else I found in that niche," he said, after a long moment. He held it up to her, something heavy and gold.

"The brooch of the Six Proud Walkers."

"He'd kept it always. It was valuable, and he must have seen that. He traded away my sword, but he didn't trade or sell this. He must have known it was like my own amulet. This I will wear, in honor of both fathers of mine, the real and the true."

"I think you may have had two true fathers, Gwyl," said Keera. "Lucky man that you are."

"My real father never even knew I existed."

"Really? Do you believe, then, that Three Stripe somehow, somewhere doesn't know John exists?"

"Maybe I do believe that," said Gwyl, leaning over to look at John, his chubby arms flung wide, his lashes thick on his little cheek. "Maybe," he said, giving her a skeptical look.

"You're impossible, Gwyl."

He tried to smile. "And look what else," he said. He drew a final object from the little bundle.

"Old Dee's magic needle!"

"Here it is. And it still works. It always works."

"So how can you be such an infuriating skeptic? This magic doesn't fade."

"Is it magic?" he said, cupping the needle in his palm and staring down on it. "Suppose it's not magic at all. Suppose what it does is a natural thing."

"Silly man," said Keera fondly.

He put the objects back in the bundle and laid it carefully aside.

"So you told Yann everything you found out?" said Keera, after a moment.

"Yes, we talked it over. We have a plan for defense. One thing troubles me, and I told him about it."

"What's that."

"It's very troubling."

"Tell me."

"We think we saw evidence that Maro has joined forces with Ansgar's men to bring us down. We think Maro has made some kind of deal with Ansgar."

"Then we're done," said Keera flatly. "We'll never survive that."

"Yann is trying to decide what to do. We can surrender. If we do, most of us will survive, just have to swear allegiance to—well, I don't know who we'll have to swear allegiance to. Maro or Ansgar. It really doesn't matter. I suppose the two of them have decided that, between them."

Keera lay back with a chill. She saw it clearly. Yes, maybe most of them would survive. Yann and Gwyl and a few of the others, though—they'd pay the price.

As if he could read her mind, Gwyl reached out to her. "Don't worry, Keera. If it comes to that, it does, and no one can stop it. There's no point in worrying about it now."

"Yann may be able to garner some kind of respect from them. Maybe walk away with his life. Once Maro gets you in his hands, you know he'll kill you. Yes, I'm going to say it. You can't stop me saying it. It's just the truth."

"I got away from him before," said Gwyl.

"I'm guessing you won't be so lucky twice. I'm guessing he won't be that careless twice."

They lay thinking about the rusted bar in the window of Maro's room where he'd jailed Gwyl, and how easily Gwyl had been able to pull it aside, and how easily he'd been able to get out of that window, using a few tricks he knew and a coil of spruce roots he had wound about his waist for convenience. No one had thought to take the coil away from him. "They thought it was some kind of heathen belt," Gwyl told her with a grin. "How can we lose, going up against people that thick-headed?"

"What is Yann going to do about this," said Keera at last. "Tell me, Gwyl. This is no time for joking."

"I know it," Gwyl said with a sigh. "He's going to call a meeting of the entire settlement and ask them to decide it. He knew he shouldn't be the one. Say he and I decide we should fight to the last man. Our hides are on the line, whichever way it goes. So it's not fair for us and some of the others to decide it. We'll leave it to the village."

"We've been training and preparing."

"So I hear."

They couldn't talk further about it, because little John began to stir beside them and fuss. Keera leaned over to pull him into bed with them. She began nursing him.

"Look at him. What a perfect little boy," said Gwyl, marveling. "When the fighting starts, you two need to get out. You and John could go somewhere, Keera. I know you can do it. I'll make you a canoe, and you can just paddle out of here with him. You won't have to surrender to Maro or Ansgar's men, either one of them. Find a friendly village. You can speak the language of the natives around here now, I hear."

"You've been talking to Yann about me. But no. I'm staying with you, Gwyl. Whatever happens."

"We have our son to think about now, Keera. The owls will tell you what to do, where to go. They'll protect you. The owls haven't told you anything about the situation we're in right now, have they?"

"No," she said. She was thinking hard about the dilemma they were soon to face, and what she really did need to do. "Look at John," she whispered to Gwyl instead of answering him. "Look at those eyes. They're your eyes, Gwyl."

"I need to get back to Yann now," he said, moving off the bed and grabbing up his clothes. "I'll be back soon."

As he was heading for the door, though, Keera had a thought so startling that she exclaimed.

Gwyl hadn't heard. The door closed behind him.

Eyes. Yann's eyes. How could she have been so stupid. Now she saw the thing that had unsettled her about Yann since the moment she'd met him. It was his eyes. *Maybe it's a coincidence,* she thought.

The conversation she and Yann had had ran through her mind.

*Not a coincidence,* she thought. *It's his eyes, and I'm right.*

# 10 GWYL: Secrets

## Enough Mystery

Something was bothering Keera. Gwyl knew he should stay with her and tenderly question her to find out what it was, but things had taken a bad turn around the settlement. People were panicked. They'd had the meeting to decide what to do, but nothing had been decided. A vocal minority wanted to leave, and Yann assured them they could.

"We'll help you, the way we've helped anyone who wanted to leave Falls Village. It might be better for you to get out now than wait to surrender. You might get more kindly treatment that way, from Maro or from Ansgar's men," he told them. Little by little, the families had trickled away into the forest, some going due north to Maro, some to Ansgar's settlements on the northern coast to the east.

The rest wanted to stay and fight. They met again the morning after the meeting.

"You understand, it's likely we'll lose," Yann said to them.

They nodded.

"Some of us will lose our lives," said a woman, clutching at her husband.

"But we'll give those people what-for," said another woman, and her husband joined her in arguing that they should all stay and fight.

"I don't know what we should do, Gwyl," said Yann at his fire after the meeting was over. "I know some of these people are so stubbornly independent, they're prepared to fight until they can't fight any longer. Some of them are outcasts from Maro's or Ansgar's settlements and can't go back. But what about the families? A few are left. What about their children? We're going to lose."

"With Ansgar's men and Maro's against us, I believe you're right, sir," said Gwyl. "And I'm one of those people with a wife and child here. But sir," he said, thinking over the battle on the Fire Isle, and how hopeless it had seemed, and the remarkable thing Keera had done to change its outcome utterly. "I've seen stranger things happen on a battlefield, and in a war."

"You have, have you," said Yann. He gave Gwyl a bleak smile. "But we can't count on anything like that happening again, can we." It wasn't a question. It was a statement.

Gwyl looked over at him, startled. What did Yann know, he wondered. What did he know about Keera. Gwyl's statement was pure bravado. Keera's owls had told her nothing good. They'd told her nothing at all. He didn't even believe in such a thing, that magical forces could change the outcome of a battle. He said this firmly to himself. On the other hand, he thought with a shiver, he couldn't deny what his own eyes had seen on the Fire Isle. And he couldn't deny Old Dee.

"Keera is up against something she won't be able to fight, this time," said Yann.

"You must explain to me, Yann. You know things about us. What things? How?"

"Keera had help on the Fire Isle," said Yann. "The help of a powerful mage."

"Old Dee," said Gwyl.

"Yes, and her farwydd. But now Old Dee's opponent in the Magisterial High Council sees what he's up to, siding with Keera, and he's not going to let it go by. In fact, Old Dee is on thin ice with the entire Council, interfering at all."

"Old Dee's opponent, you say. Who is Old Dee's opponent."

"A man named Gilles de Rais."

"I know about Baron Gilles. Of course I do. The most powerful man in the Baronies. I suppose he's the one who has sent Maro here. Although how that happened, I couldn't tell you. It's a complete mystery to me."

"You might think you know who Baron Gilles is, but you don't know who he actually is," said Yann. "You don't know what he's capable of. As for Maro—"

"How do you know about any of this?" Gwyl demanded. "I don't know what you mean by the Magisterial High Council, all the things you're telling me. And what do you know about Maro? I need answers now, Yann."

But before Yann could provide them, a clamor broke out at the palisades.

"We'll have to talk about it later, I suppose," murmured Yann. "Here they are, those two armies. They've taken our decision out of our hands."

At first, Gwyl made his mind up to die defending his home, his wife, his baby. It was too late to get them out now. He tried not to let himself give in to despair. Two armies coming against them. It was impossible.

But as the ragged little group of settlers mounted their defense and he moved from group to group, encouraging and exhorting, and as he watched Yann doing likewise at the other end of the palisades, he grew a bit more hopeful.

He and Yann dashed past each other in the thick of it. "Looks like one army only," said Gwyl, "and if I had to guess, I'd say Ansgar's."

"My thinking exactly," said Yann. "They're far from their villages in the north. They've over-extended themselves."

He and Yann moved apart then, helping out at different parts of the palisades.

At one moment, Gwyl's heart practically stopped. On the very top of the palisades, Keera was wielding her pike with ruthless efficiency. She was horribly exposed up there. But then he saw some others calling her back down, and she was in a safer place.

They all kept fighting, and valiantly.

Still, even one army opposed to so few, so ill-equipped, was too much.

As noontide waned into mid-afternoon, the few remaining settlers, bloodied and filthy, were gathered in a grim knot before the gates of the palisades. A relentless pounding came at them from outside. The army was battering its way in.

"Good people," Yann yelled out above the uproar. "We've fought well. We've lost. Let me surrender the town now. They'll let many of you go, I'm thinking. It's the only way."

The fighters stood looking at their feet, their pikes trailing in the dust. Gwyl saw many heads wearily nodding. It was over.

Yann strode to the big doors of the palisade and climbed up the inside, to the sentry box at the top. They could hear him from where they stood.

"We surrender. We ask mercy for our families."

A quiet settled over the town and the attackers outside it.

Yann climbed down and opened the doors. Men of Ansgar burst through. They rounded everyone up. By then, Keera had John in her arms, and Gwyl stood close beside her.

The men of Ansgar marched the settlers out of Falls Village and into the big field at the side of the village, the place they planted the crops. The settlers looked around them at the field. Gwyl could see how down-hearted many of them were. Ansgar's army had trampled the crops into the mud.

Everything they worked for lay ruined.

Gwyl found himself standing near Yann. He shouldered over to the leader. "I don't know who you are or why you know some of the things you know," he said. "But it was an honor fighting by your side."

Yann clasped his arm warmly. "Your father would have been proud to see you in action this day," he said.

Gwyl wanted to ask, *What do you know about my father? And which father do you mean?* But Ansgar's men were prodding them into a tighter group with the flats of their swords. He rushed back to Keera and put his arms around her.

"I'm frightened," she said. "Frightened for us, but more frightened for John."

"The owls are telling you nothing?"

"Nothing," she said.

The settlers were left to themselves with a cordon of Ansgar's men around them, guarding them. The rest were gathered about their army's leader on the other side of the field. Gwyl supposed they were deciding what to do with the settlers. Was it possible these men knew Keera was somehow Ansgar's property, as those men in the Cold Lands thought? Gwyl decided that if he possibly could, he'd make Ansgar's men understand about Keera, if they didn't already. Then perhaps Keera and John would be safe. These men would take Keera to Ansgar, and John with her. He supposed that meant they'd be Ansgar's bondservants, but they'd be alive.

Before he could think it through, though, the men over by the leader of Ansgar's forces started throwing up their hands and screaming and going down. Gwyl squinted to try to see what was attacking them. His hands tightened on Keera. "Whatever happens, stay by me," he murmured in her ear. The men guarding the settlers dashed across the field to help their fellows. Gwyl saw the leader cut down. The men of Ansgar were being swarmed by other men. These men encircled Ansgar's army and were slashing it to pieces with their swords.

Yann saw it too. "Everyone, to me. Let's make our way to the forest," he called out.

But as they headed toward the edge of the field, armed men stood up to bar their way. They were encircled as surely as Ansgar's army was.

Yann laughed.

Gwyl suddenly realized. "It's Maro, isn't it."

"That's what he does. Lets others do the dirty work. Then he moves in," said Yann.

"Who is Maro, really?" Gwyl demanded. "How is it he's in authority here? I've never understood that."

"You don't know?" said Yann, looking at him sidelong. He started laughing again.

"Stop laughing. Dark Ones take you. Enough mystery. Tell me." Gwyl was beginning to feel a growing rage.

"Gwyl, that man—there he is, your stepfather," said Yann, pointing him out as some of these newcomer soldiers escorted him out onto the field.

*Yes,* thought Gwyl grimly. *There he is. Look at him, him and his scarlet cloak.*

"You've known that man your whole life. Maro, your stepfather," said Yann with a small smile. "And you're right. "And you're right. I did see you, when you were just a small boy. I knew your family. I should have told you. I was remiss. I don't—I don't like to think of those days." He faltered to a stop. "Maro made sure to keep all but a few ignorant of who he really is. He hid out for years in the Baronies, with his family, after Caedon defeated him. He worked out a deal with Caedon, and he lay low. Now, with Caedon dead, here he comes again, with the support of Gilles. Gilles has thrown him a bone, to keep him tame. A little king here in the New Found Land."

"Maro is—" Gwyl began. He felt his eyes opening wide in surprise, the breath practically leaving his body.

"Audemar, deposed usurper king of the Sceptered Isle."

## Winning

Gwyl was reeling as the men of Maro surrounded him and bound his wrists. Maro. Audemar. It all made sense now. His mother knew. Of course she knew. He was pretty sure Pierrick had no idea. Or hadn't when Gwyl saw him last. He wondered if Pierrick knew by now, and what he was doing with that knowledge. To creep back into power, Maro had become Gilles de Rais's toady.

Maro stalked across the field toward Gwyl and stood at a little distance, directing his soldiers in tying Gwyl up. Gwyl stared at him with amazement and hatred, but Maro looked past him as if he were ignoring some piece of offal in the road.

Maro pointed to Keera. "Her too," he said. He came up close to Keera and looked her up and down. "I know about you," he said. "I've known about you all along. Too bad you didn't enjoy my attentions and give in to my wishes." He put out a hand and ran a curl of her hair through his fingers as she drew back from him with a cry. "It's all a waste now, isn't it? Pity."

Gwyl looked over at them, suddenly realizing what Maro meant. A fury boiled up in him.

"Bring that baby to me," Maro directed his men.

Gwyl struggled with the men trying to bind him, and beside him, Keera was struggling too, and screaming. Little John was screaming as the men bore him off. Keera huddled against Gwyl. Her wrists were bound as well.

Maro pointed at Yann. "And him. Bind him too." He turned on his heel and swept away.

Gwyl, Keera, and Yann were herded to the side of the field, where some men were putting up a tent. The men shoved the three of them inside, then came in after them and tied them to some kind of frame they'd erected in there.

"John," sobbed Keera.

Gwyl maneuvered over to Keera so he could touch her.

"I doubt we can get out of these," said Yann, examining his bonds. Then, to Keera, he said, "I don't think anyone will hurt little John."

Keera, as she always did, Gwyl saw, moved from grief to rage in an instant. "If Maro knows John is the last of his line, then yes. He'll hurt John. Whatever you may pretend, I know you know my history, my parentage. What did Maro do to his nephews? Tell me that. What did he do to all of them, every time he could?" She turned a cold look on Yann. "Although Caedon carried out most of those orders," she said. "Until he couldn't. Did you know I was the one who made sure of that?"

Yann looked away. "Yes, I do know that," he said softly.

Gwyl looked from Keera to Yann in despair. The three of them needed to be united. They needed that strength, if only to get through the last hours of their lives. He had no illusions about what Maro had in mind for them. Yet he saw Keera was somehow blaming Yann.

His thoughts swiveled to Keera. Suppose he could convince Maro to keep Keera safe, as a counter to use with Ansgar. Gwyl thought of Maro's words to Keera, and now he forced himself to consider them. If Maro regarded Keera as an object of his desire, maybe... But Gwyl had to drive down the bile rising in his gorge at the thought. *Whatever it takes*, Gwyl told himself after a bleak moment of recognition, *whatever it takes to strike a deal with Maro, or convince him somehow, so that Keera will be safe.*

Keera turned her eyes on him. "You're forgetting our promise. I'll never let that vile man put his hands on me."

"Nine Spheres," he muttered. "You always know what I'm thinking."

"And I don't need my lost powers to do it," she said.

"Listen, Keera. It's a chance. I don't have one. You do. And there aren't the two of us any longer. There are the three of us."

"A good chance," Yann said.

"You keep out of this," Keera practically hissed at him.

Yann looked down at his feet and was silent. He moved away from the two of them as far as his tether would let him, and stood turned aside.

"Keera—" Gwyl began.

"But anyway, forget Maro. Gwyl, let me ask you something." Keera fixed him with her green eyes, huge and intense and angry. "Remember on the Northmost Isle, when you and Pierrick rescued me and Fiona from Caedon? Remember fighting Caedon."

"Yes," said Gwyl.

"Was that the only time you'd ever seen Caedon."

Gwyl nodded. Then he looked troubled. "But in childhood—" he began.

Keera talked over him. "You fought Caedon. And it was pretty dark in that room. Just rushlights. But Gwyl. Over the course of my life, I came face to face with Caedon a number of times."

Gwyl turned slowly to look at Yann.

"Do you remember Caedon's eyes? How strange they were?"

Yann faced them. Gwyl didn't think he'd ever seen a man as tormented as Yann was now. "I was about to tell you. I didn't have time."

"You're Caedon's son," said Gwyl in slow realization. "You must be."

"Somewhere in Caedon's dark, twisted heart, he knew this moment would come," said Keera, staring at Yann. "Maybe this man in front of us"—she stabbed a finger at Yann—"is about to cut his own deal with Maro. Do you know what I overheard in the woods? That Gilles de Rais wants this man alive. Maybe Yann is about to remind Maro of that, and maybe we're a nice good-faith offering he can give Maro, so that Maro will keep him safe."

Gwyl found he was having a hard time catching his breath.

"But maybe not," Keera went on. "Maybe he has only misled us to our deaths, Gwyl, instead of actively conspiring for it. Just the same, think, Gwyl. Who sent you off to that village of The People, alone? Who sent you off again on a dangerous mission just a sen'night ago? Who maybe thought you wouldn't be coming back? Who survived The People's attack on Fisher's Bay, when almost everyone else was slaughtered?"

Gwyl found himself shaking his head. He couldn't believe that Yann was some villain. But Keera believed it.

In the waning light, Keera looked into Gwyl's eyes. "Whatever the truth turns out to be, one thing is clear to me," she said. "We thought we'd defeated Caedon. But look at this." She turned to Yann again, and her very gaze was made of fire. "Will you look at this, Gwyl. Caedon has won, after all."

## Field of Battle

Gwyl spent an uncomfortable night with Keera, helping to steady her as they tried to sleep standing up. The bonds were too short to let them lie down or even sit.

*I've done this before*, thought Gwyl, remembering the bad times with The People. *But Keera never has. Here's a last way I can help her.* His love for her almost brought him down, but he knew he needed to stay strong.

If they slept at all, they didn't sleep much.

Yann kept to his own side of the tent, as much as he could. Gwyl was glad to see it. He didn't know what he'd do if his hands were free. But they were at close enough quarters that Gwyl thought he could hurt Yann, if he tried.

This situation they found themselves in was so baffling, though, that he wasn't sure what to make of it. He saw Keera was sure. Keera thought Yann had deceived them. And he had, hadn't he? Just maybe not for the reasons Keera was thinking.

Gwyl tried to set his mind on Keera, and on John. He didn't have time to think about revenging himself on Yann, if that's what was called for, or figuring out the mystery that was Yann. Gwyl was pretty sure Maro was going to have them all killed outright. Him, anyway. He wanted his last hours to be with Keera, and her alone. He determined to shut Yann out of his mind and his line of sight. He concentrated on Keera.

He'd have to forestall Maro, if Maro looked to be about to hurt Keera. He'd have to try. If Yann thought that was possible, too, and if Yann was able to save his own life, maybe he'd help Keera. But after Keera had angrily accused him and unmasked him, maybe he wouldn't care to.

*No*, Gwyl thought. *Don't think of that man. Only Keera. Only her.*

But other thoughts came crowding in. Little John, of course. Ensuring Keera's safety could maybe ensure their child's. But Keera's words about John terrified him. Maro surely realized John was the last of his line, if he knew who Keera was. Looks like he did know.

And Keera was right. Whenever Maro had been confronted with any threat, even the slightest, to his place in the succession, he had snuffed it out. Suppose he killed their son. Could he be that heartless? Thinking of how Maro had killed Artur's sons, how young they were when he did it, Gwyl knew he was as heartless as that.

As the night drew on, the night he thought would be the last of his life, Gwyl thought about others. He thought about the dead he was soon to join. Three Stripe. And the father he'd never known.

"I want to give something to you," Yann said, breaking the silence of hours. It was deep into the darkest part of the night, and no moon shone.

"Give something to me." Gwyl was incredulous.

"Yes, they're really for Keera, but I know she won't take them from me. So here."

Yann had moved closer. He thrust a small bundle into Gwyl's hands with his own bound hands. Then he went back to the furthest side of the frame.

Gwyl could make out his figure in the dark.

As Gwyl opened the bundle, he knew what they were. The brooches.

"I don't want anything that man has to give me," said Keera, low.

"You'll want these, Keera," said Gwyl, passing them into her hands. After a moment, he felt her silently crying against his shoulder.

"The more damaged one was John's," said Yann, out of the dark. "It's for the baby. And the other one was Keera's grandfather's. Drustan's.

Gwyl didn't answer. He wondered what would happen to his own father's brooch in the morning. Would Maro rip it from his cloak, once he was dead, and destroy it?

Yann had saved these other two brooches, which Caedon had surely taken, for Keera. *Yann thinks Keera may live. But he doesn't think he will.* In spite of not wanting to mull that over, Gwyl did. *Yann isn't going to try to cut a deal with Maro,* he kept thinking.

Pretty soon, dawn turned the inside of the tent to gray.

Soldiers shouldered into the tent and untethered them from the frame. They marched the three of them outside, where another tent was erected. A magnificent embroidered affair, it looked incongruous against the backdrop of the forests of the New Found Land.

Keera stumbled against Gwyl, and he steadied her as best he could.

The soldiers chivvied them to stand in front of the tent.

There Maro sat in a carved chair.

*Audemar,* Gwyl corrected himself.

His scarlet cape was swept off his shoulders, and Gwyl saw to his rage that it was fastened with another brooch of the Six Proud Walkers.

"That must be my father's," Keera murmured beside him.

"He's wearing it to taunt us," said Gwyl. Then he looked aside at her in amazement. To her own cloak, she had somehow managed to affix one of the ones Yann had passed to her in the night.

"Drustan's. My true grandfather's," she said, trying to smile.

Underneath his tunic, Gwyl was wearing Three Stripe's amulet on a thong. He'd told himself he'd never wear it. But then, the day before, when he thought he might be dying in battle, he had put it on. Now he'd die with it today. He was glad. If anyone from Maro's army had found it, after, they might have thrown it aside as a piece of trash. Whether he had done the right thing to wear it or not, he was glad it was close to his heart.

Maro stood up and stepped forward. Gwyl realized with a catch in his throat that Fiona stood beside Maro, with her children, the boy Alan and little Rozenn. This would hurt Keera deeply, he knew. He looked aside to her.

Instead, Keera was smiling.

"Your Majesty," said Fiona in a clear voice that carried to them. "I have a request." She knelt to Maro.

"What is this request, my daughter?" said Maro.

"I lost my last babe, your grandchild. I request I be given this baby, the son of the traitor Keera, to raise as my own."

"Your request is granted," said Maro. A soldier stepped forward now and handed the squalling John to Fiona.

Gwyl watched as Fiona and Keera exchanged a long look. *Fiona will always be Keera's friend. And mine. She is doing this for us, so we won't worry,* he realized.

But then, with despair, he knew it meant Keera had no chance to escape death.

He had to try to advocate for her. But how in the Nine Spheres would he address this man, when Keera's life might hang in the balance. He couldn't call him *father*. He wouldn't, and besides, he never had. He wouldn't call him *Your Majesty*. He wouldn't call him *Audemar*.

"Maro, I too have a request," he called out. "My lord," he made himself choke out.

"No request of yours will be heard," said Maro in a loud voice. "The prisoners will kneel."

The soldiers forced them down in the mud. Keera put her bound hands out as if to steady herself against Gwyl. "You tried," she whispered. "But John will be safe with Fiona. And you and I will be together."

They knelt for a long time in the mud. The sun had edged up over the trees and was shining weakly over the field before Maro finished dictating some elaborate document to a scribe under the shade of his tent, conferring with his officials.

At last Maro stepped out of his tent and stood before the place where Gwyl and Keera knelt.

"These are the charges." Maro's voice rang across the field. Looking around him, Gwyl could see the assembled army ringing the field and, off to one side, the miserable little clump of surviving villagers.

An official called for quiet, and the people on the field settled down. Maro stepped forward to speak, his voice reaching the farthest corners of the field.

"Keera, daughter of Walter the Bastard and his wife Mirin, False Queen of the Fire Isle. You have treacherously insinuated yourself into my household and have spied for the remnants of the Rising there. For this crime of treason, you will die," he proclaimed. A man came to stand behind Keera and looped a thong of leather about her throat. Keera stared ahead, dry-eyed.

*The scum*, thought Gwyl. Instead of executing them by sword, as was the custom with an honorable opponent, this vile excuse of a man was going to kill them as if they were common criminals, by garotte.

Now came his own charges. "Gwyl the Bastard, taken into my own household after your father treacherously opposed me, ungrateful child, traitor yourself in going over to fight with The Rising. You're a lucky man. My son Pierrick is missing. If I knew for a certainty you had foully done away with him, as I suspect you have, I would have devised brave tortures for you first. But even your crimes as I know them now are unforgivable. For these crimes of treason and ingratitude, you will die."

"Nine Spheres, ingratitude too," Gwyl couldn't help whispering sidelong to Keera as the garotte was placed over his own head and tightened around his neck.

"Must you always make light of everything?" she whispered back.

"Seems so," he said to her, wincing as the thong bit into his neck.

The man behind him grunted and kneed him in the back, so he decided he'd better live his last moments in peace. But Pierrick. *Thank the Child*, he thought. Maro's words meant Pierrick had gotten away from his father's grasp.

"Yann, called the Harper, son of Caedon," Maro cried out now. At the charges against Keera and Gwyl, a buzz of talk had risen from the assemblage. Now a hush fell on the field. "Yann, son of Caedon." Maro's voice rang out again. "You are the son of a traitor, the most treacherous of all. Your father, a man I elevated from nothing to the most powerful position in the realm short of my own. A man who treasonously attacked me and drove me from the realm. Like father, like son. You fled your father's keeping and joined his enemies, a spy for Walter the Bastard."

Gwyl felt his mouth gaping open. He looked sidelong at Keera and saw how astonished she was, as well.

An official standing at Maro's shoulder tugged at his arm. Maro bent over while this man whispered some urgent words in his ear. "No," he said aside to this man. "That won't be the way of it." Gwyl was near enough to hear him. Gwyl found himself breathing hard. He and Keera were wrong, what they'd thought about Yann. Yann was as much a part of The Rising as they had been. As anyone.

"Now that I'm about to return to the Sceptered Isle and take my rightful place as monarch, no traitor spawn of Caedon must be allowed to live. No, the baron must be content with the news of his death. Consequences to the Dark Ones," Gwyl heard Maro say to the man at his shoulder, and the man shrugged and stepped back.

Maro's voice rang out over the field again. "Yann. For this crime of high treason, you will be disemboweled."

Before Maro had finished passing sentence on Yann, before the soldiers had finished yanking him away from the two of them and over to a stake beside the field, Gwyl felt Keera stiffening in distress beside him.

"I was wrong! It's too late to tell him I'm sorry for the hurtful things I said," she burst out.

Her own minder whacked her on the head, and she fell against Gwyl.

Gwyl was glad. She wouldn't know the pain, when it came.

But her eyes opened, and they were filled with tears.

"He knows, darling. He knew. Don't grieve."

Their minders shoved them apart.

"And now I'll see the first two sentences carried out," Maro called over the field. He swiveled and returned to his tent, looking out at Gwyl and Keera with an implacable small smile.

Gwyl wished desperately he were standing close enough to Keera to let her feel he was there. Let her feel his support and love to the very end.

"No," came a shout, splitting the silence of the field, where the amassed army stood breathless to watch the executions.

Gwyl risked a quick look over his shoulder.

A man came striding over the field, a man dressed entirely in black, barefoot, bareheaded.

"I challenge this sentence. Under the laws of the Baronies, I challenge you to trial by combat, Audemar the Usurper," cried the man. "Here. I'm dressed in cloth. I'm barefoot, bareheaded, as the rules bid me. I have my sword only. Come out to meet me if you're a man." His voice rang like a gong in the early sunlight burning the dawn mists from the verges of the forest.

Gwyl just shook his head, but Keera was smiling.

"Pierrick," she whispered.

"That brother of mine," he whispered back.

Maro sank back into his chair. He looked shattered. Now he stood and came out of his tent. "Carry out those sentences," he muttered to Gwyl's and Keera's minders as he stalked past them.

But Gwyl saw his chance. His hands might be bound, but his minder was looking startled over his shoulder, and so was Keera's. He knocked the man off balance, and the man let go of the thong. Gwyl rolled sideways into Keera's minder and bowled him off his feet.

With an angry roar, his own minder came at him.

Gwyl rocked back on his heels, his bound hands dropped between his knees. He regarded the man calmly. "My good man," he said. "As you see, my stepfather, your leader, is quite old. He won't live much longer. That man challenging him is his son, my brother. My best friend in this world. What do you think is going to happen to you if you and this fellow carry out Maro's sentences? Maybe not today, but next year?"

The man stopped and stared at Gwyl. Doubt was written all over his red beefy face.

"My advice?" Gwyl said to him. "At least let's see what comes of this challenge, before you and your fellow do anything rash. We can't get away from you. Our hands are bound."

So their two minders sat down beside them in the muck to watch what was playing out in the field.

"I'm your father," Maro cried out to Pierrick, drawing nearer to him. "I'm old. How can you do this to me, I who always loved you and provided for you, even in my own troubles."

"Father, I know what you are. Meet my challenge," cried Pierrick in a voice carrying across the entire field.

"No. I won't," said Maro. He was making his way out to the middle of the field, holding his hands out desperately to his son.

"Then appoint a champion in your stead."

"No. I won't," said Maro, coming nearer.

"What in the Nine is about to happen?" Keera murmured to Gwyl.

"Shh," said her minder, looking over at her, irritated. He leaned forward, intent on the scene before them.

Gwyl's minder pulled a little leather sack from his belt, shook a few parched cracked maize nuggets out of it, and popped one into his mouth. He passed one to Keera's minder.

Pierrick raised his sword high.

The two minders' mouths gaped open. All around the verges of the field, people settled down to watch

Suddenly they stood and exclaimed. Or cringed back.

Out of the forest came a silent swooping of owls.

"Hundreds of them," Keera breathed to Gwyl.

"Did you call them?"

"Not I," she said. "I couldn't have if I tried. I did try," she added.

People who worshipped the Lady Goddess began making their warding sign against evil. Many flung themselves on the ground, Keera's and Gwyl's own minders included. Gwyl leaned awkwardly over and eased his minder's knife out of its sheath. He cut his wrist thongs apart, then Keera's.

Fiona was there beside them. "Give me the knife," she told Gwyl. He handed it over. She darted to Yann at his stake, shoved the startled minder out of the way, and cut him free, too. She led Yann back toward Keera and Gwyl.

There was no time for words among them. Their eyes were riveted on Maro and Pierrick.

Beside him, the hairs on the back of Gwyl's neck prickled. Keera began singing a strange sort of song in a strange sort of monotone.

*One for sorrow,*
*Two for mirth,*
*Three for death,*
*Four for birth,*
*Five for silver,*
*Six for gold,*
*Seven for secrets never told.*
*Eight for Ghost Bird, eight for Owl*
*underneath the Nine Spheres' bowl.*

In a wedge of pale whirring, the owls floated to the middle of the field between Pierrick and Maro. The wedge swerved on Pierrick, overwhelming him, driving him flailing back, putting themselves between him and his father.

"Are they protecting Maro?" said Gwyl.

"They're— It's—" began Keera, but then she stopped. She wasn't sure what she was seeing.

Maro stood isolated at the center of the field.

The skies opened.

Dark clouds had been massing that morning. Now they parted. A voice resounded over the field. *You have ruined your own lands. You will not ruin these.*

A thunderclap brought all still standing to their knees. Out of the skies, a jagged stripe of lightning forked down on Maro. Knocked back across the furrows, his body jerked, then crumpled over, a hissing, steaming dark knot of twitching limbs in the middle of the field.

Gwyl jumped to his feet, but Keera pulled him back.

"Stay down," she warned him.

On one side of the field came stalking a mighty presence, a towering figure with a pointed beard and piercing blue eyes. "Gilles de Rais," this figure's voice boomed out. "Stay away from this place. Go back where you came from. Gilles de Rais, I adjure you."

From the other side of the field, a still more imposing figure walked out. "John Dee. Stupid man. My powers are greater than yours, and you know it. John Dee, I adjure you."

Something mightier than the lightning met between them. Gwyl squeezed his eyes shut. When he could force them open, the two figures stretched to the sky.

Before they could do to each other what they seemed to have come there to do, a man ambled out to the center of the field and stood looking up from one of them to the other. Even from where he crouched, Gwyl could see this newcomer to the field was a big man. Compared to the two menacing figures in the sky, though, he was a puny stick of a man.

"I won't allow this. You know I won't," he called out to them in a booming basso profundo voice.

"Myrddin," said Keera, startled.

"Merlin?"

She gave him the most conciliatory look he'd ever received from her. "He goes by both."

"Get back to your planes, the both of you. Next time, don't make me come down here," cried the man in the middle of the field. "And I don't mean maybe." Even from where Gwyl watched, he could see the man's eyes blaze up into twin gimlet points of light.

The two towering figures began to shrink and dwindle. Wisps of them began to blow off the field, back the way they had come. The owls had disappeared.

"My Ladies, forgive us," the man in the middle of the field called to the sky. "It won't happen again."

"See that it doesn't," the voice of some mighty presence boomed down. "And quit sending red-headed silly girls into my pyramid. Or you'll find yourself back in that rock."

"Oak tree," Gwyl found himself whispering.

The clouds drifted away, the sun shone out, and by the time everyone came to their senses and began looking around, the big man in the middle of the field was nowhere to be seen. As for the owls, who had so unaccountably appeared at mid-day, they were gone.

Gwyl could see Keera was fuming.

"Red-headed silly girls," she was muttering.

But he ended her fuming with a kiss.

Fiona rushed up to her then with little John, who stopped his screaming and the drumming of his feet against Fiona's restraining arms, put his little hands up to his mother's face, and began to say *Momma Momma Momma*.

So there were miracles all around. A pause in mid-tantrum by a small upset child was not the least of them.

## Seven for Secrets

L ater that day, Pierrick was firmly in command of his father's army.

Kierra's minder walked angrily away.

"That man actually wanted to strangle me," she said, looking after him dumbfounded. "He actually wanted to do it, and now he's disappointed."

"Fancy that," said Gwyl. "No, really, Keera. It was a serious occasion, and you wouldn't stop talking."

"That was you," she grumbled, and he saw she was angrier still after his own minder had sidled up to him to apologize and to thank him for the timely warning.

"Otherwise, this new man would have had my head, he would," said the man.

But now Gwyl whispered in her ear what he hoped she'd do with him once she had him helpless in bed, and she had to stop fuming and smile.

Yann stood quietly apart from all the commotion.

"I need to speak to him," said Keera, looking over at him.

"We both do." Gwyl took her hand and they went to him.

He turned to them with a mild look in the strange amber of his eyes. "I take it all back, Gwyl," he said. "Wherever Keera is, especially on a battlefield, something surprising does always happen."

"I didn't have anything to do with it," said Keera. "Not if you mean those two huge figures. I think you might have had more to do with it than I did."

"I?" He looked genuinely surprised.

"There's something I can't quite figure out," said Keera. "Something about your father and Gilles de Rais. I know why Old Dee was here. He can't stop interfering, and he really likes me. But why should Gilles care? I don't mean the baron. I suppose the baron might have cared whether Maro won or lost, since Maro was his bootlicker. I mean the real Gilles. The mage whose powers rival Myrdinn's."

"Myrdinn—" Yann began doubtfully.

"Never mind him. Listen, Yann. I believe the real Gilles, the powerful mage, had some kind of hold on Caedon. Some kind of deep connection with your father. Maybe he thought he owned your father. Maybe he thinks that you, the son of your father, belong to him. And just now he saw his chance to stake his claim on you. He saw Maro was about to do away with you, and maybe he didn't want that. He was about to pluck you away and take you for himself."

"Maybe he was," said Yann. He stood looking thoughtfully at the ground. "But maybe there are some fathers of some sons who have it in them to resist Gilles. Maybe that's the model I looked to, when I thought of the father I might have had, instead of the one I did." He addressed this to Gwyl.

*What do I know of my father, really?* thought Gwyl. That father. That man named Rafe.

"We're talking about mages and magic," said Keera, "and about true fathers and real fathers, and those subjects are both important, Child knows. But I'm just avoiding what I really came over here to say, because I'm so ashamed. I came to say I'm sorry I said hurtful words to you, Yann. I'm sorry I judged you on who your father was and not on what I knew about you for myself."

Yann looked at her with his haunted eyes. "My father Caedon hurt you and your family more than anyone else could possibly have hurt them, and in many ways. It tears at me, what he did. It tears at me, that I have those same impulses somewhere inside me. I must. I'm his son."

Keera was shaking her head no.

"And I'm sorry, too, for my own words," said Gwyl.

"My father killed your father. His men did, anyhow, and at his direction," Yann said to Gwyl. "And my father damaged yours in other ways, too. Terrible ways I don't even know how to describe.

Your father told me a little about it, once." At the question in Gwyl's eyes, he nodded. "I knew your father. Knew him well. He was the best friend I ever had." He looked to Keera. "And yours was a close second."

To Yann, Keera blurted out, "I killed your father with my own firebird. I burned him to a cinder."

"What a muddle. How will we ever get past it?" said Yann with a smile, and he walked away from them, his shoulders hunched.

Gwyl watched him go with concern. He knew himself to be tormented by his own past. But Yann's past seemed an impossible burden for him to bear.

Keera stole her hand into his and squeezed hard. He saw how she was trying to get a grip on herself and failing. He kissed her gently and led her into the shade of Maro's fancy tent.

In the early evening, Pierrick gathered them all together under that tent. He'd already sent the villagers back inside the palisades to see what they could salvage of their lives, and he had promised them help doing that.

He had sent out a team of men to scrape up what remained of his father, and to bury it.

"Later, I'll find out where. I'll go there and mourn him in my own way," he said to Gwyl. He and Gwyl had rushed to each other and embraced as if no force underneath the Spheres could stop them.

"But let's agree the damage ends here. No more rescuing each other from garotting, or sun sacrifice, or whatever it might be," murmured Gwyl in Pierrick's ear. "Let's just raise our children to be honest people, and get these crops growing again." Gwyl looked around him at the trampled maize.

Of course, thought Gwyl, it wasn't going to be that simple.

Emissaries from Ansgar had appeared almost immediately to demand satisfaction for Maro's cowardly attack and betrayal, since they were supposed to be allied in the crushing of Falls Village, and to suggest a truce and a treaty.

"You must be your father's heir," said this emissary to Pierrick politely. "If you would be so kind, please sit down with me tomorrow so we can work out fair terms. King Ansgar will abide by these terms, and he will be honored to meet with you personally, later, as you will now no doubt return to the Sceptered Isle to assume your throne."

Pierrick turned the fellow away with some noncommittal polite words of his own. When the man had gone, Pierrick shook his head at the few at the board Maro's servants had set up under the tent. "We have much to talk over. Let's do that after everything settles down a bit. I don't know about the rest of you, but I am churned up inside. Too much has happened too fast, all of it too disturbing and too hard to understand."

The servants went about setting rushlights in their holders and bringing food out from a cart Ansgar's army had brought with it.

Pierrick and Fiona sat down at the board, with Alan beside them. They had sent Rozenn to bed under protest, with the nurse who was to look after John as well.

"You're treating me like a baby," cried Rozenn.

"She's grown so big," Keera marveled.

And Yann was there with them, but he sat apart from them, brooding. He had his harp, and he was playing it softly, not looking at anyone, just bent over his music.

Gwyl was worried Yann's inner wounds might never heal. He worried his own actions had unfairly added to them.

Outside the tent, at makeshift tables, ranged the men of Maro's army, now Pierrick's. The villagers sat with them.

How must they feel, eating shoulder to shoulder with men who had just been trying to kill them, wondered Gwyl.

After those at board underneath the tent had pushed the remaining scraps of food away, Pierrick looked around at them all. "That emissary from Ansgar assumes I'm king," he said to them. "He assumes it because my father was Audemar, of Ranulf's line, in the succession behind Artur, his older brother, and Artur's two sons. By line of succession, when Artur and his sons died, Audemar became king. As his only heir, now I become king at Audemar's death." Pierrick dropped his head and absently took up Fiona's hand. "You see how straightforward it all is. How straightforward it looks. But we all know it's not straightforward. We all know Artur and his sons died because my father murdered them. I was ready to kill my own father, if the Children hadn't intervened." He looked hard at his trencher and Gwyl saw him shiver. "If that's who They were," he heard his brother murmur. "If that's who sent those owls."

Pierrick abruptly swung off the bench and went to stand in front of the tent, before the fires that blazed for warmth and light here and there over the field.

"Men of Audemar. You're mine now," he called out to the assemblage of people. With a rustling, they all turned to listen to him, hundreds upon hundreds of faces gleaming in the firelight. The murmuring of their talk dwindled. The field went silent. "I'm my father's heir. Does that mean I'm a king? I'm not sure it does.

We're beholden to the Baronies now, to Baron Gilles de Rais in particular, even though many of us are from the Sceptered Isle. I'm not. I was born in the Baronies. Now, though, I've found my heritage and inheritance are from the Sceptered Isle. But if I've somehow become king of that realm, I'm a minor king. I serve at the pleasure of Gilles."

He looked around at them. "Some of you who are older may remember how it was in Ranulf's day. And after his time, many of you remember the civil war between my father and Caedon. Many of you remember when the Sceptered Isle was in Caedon's hands. Those days are over. Ansgar is looking to pluck that realm for his own from the north, Gilles is there to oppose Ansgar on the east."

He took a breath. "That's reality. But it's not our reality. It's reality for people back on the Sceptered Isle. In the Baronies. In the Ice-realm. We're not there. We're here. We're so far away from there, those realms and their conflicts, that most of us, when we said goodbye to our parents across the Great Sea, knew we'd likely never see them again. So let me propose another reality for you, right here where we sit."

He turned and motioned Keera to come to him.

Keera looked over at Gwyl. Gwyl shrugged. She got up off the bench and went to stand beside Pierrick.

"Here's yet another reality," he called out to them all. "Yes, I inherited in the Sceptered Isle after Audemar. But was Audemar the true king there? How many of you know he murdered the real heir, Artur, and his sons?"

Gwyl heard a muttering from the throngs sitting at the long tables before them.

"By now, every one of you knows that's the truth, especially those of you who come from that realm. Yet no one is ever willing to speak it. I'm speaking it now. In the past, there were men brave enough to stand up and say what they knew. They were led by my father's younger brother Avery. They called themselves The Rising, and they committed themselves to bringing justice to the Sceptered Isle. One by one, they died for their beliefs. Avery died. By his decree, the realm passed to Diera, Artur's daughter. Caedon executed her. Until recently, the one remaining member of Ranulf's line was this woman's father. Walter, if you don't count my own father, the usurper." Pierrick pulled Keera into the firelight. "Here she is. Walter's heir. Many thought Walter was the true king of the realm. My own father hid himself away and stayed safe, while Caedon the Traitor seized the throne. One usurper taking the throne away from another usurper. But this woman's father fought on."

From his place at the board, Gwyl saw how uncomfortably the people stirred. He saw how no one wanted to be reminded of those foul times. Probably most of those from the Sceptered Isle, the majority of Maro's army, had looked away, over there in their homes across the water, as events played themselves violently out, and just tried as best they could to live their ordinary lives. And if not them, then their mothers and fathers. Let the powerful savage each other, commit any vile injustice, as long as they themselves were left alone.

"Now Walter is dead. Gilles de Rais had him killed, and his wife Mirin." Pierrick pointed to Keera. "There's your monarch. Walter's daughter, the last of Ranulf's sacred line."

The people at the long tables were getting to their feet, turning to each other, whispering, staring over at Keera in shock.

"I don't want to be queen," Gwyl heard Keera saying to Pierrick as Gwyl moved to her side.

Then she said something strange. "I'm not queen. I'm not the rightful monarch."

"But I'm surely not," said Pierrick. "So you must be."

Keera began to speak her strange little rhyme.

> *One for sorrow,*
> *Two for mirth,*
> *Three for death,*
> *Four for birth,*
> *Five for silver,*
> *Six for gold,*
> *Seven for secrets never told.*

"There's a secret here," she whispered. "A secret that has never been told."

The people ranged outside the tent began cringing away. "The owls!" they cried. "The owls are back!"

But only two of them. They swooped to Keera. She held up her hands to them. Then they flew into the dark again, and no one saw where they went.

> *Eight for Ghost Bird, eight for Owl*
> *underneath the Nine Spheres' bowl.*

she chanted. She stood silent.

"I'm not the true heir to Ranulf's line, but I know who is," she called out to the people. "The owls have told me the secret, but it's not mine to tell."

She looked over her shoulder at Yann, where he stood underneath the tent, hanging back into the corner.

"Come here, Yann. You have to tell these people what you know," she said to him.

Slowly he moved to her side.

"This man knows who the true heir to Ranulf's line really is. It's not I," she called out to the assemblage.

"No," Gwyl heard Yann say to her, low and fast. "I can't tell them."

"You must. It's the only way to end this. Otherwise, it might go on forever."

"But I'm a misbegotten thing," he whispered.

Gwyl said to him, urgently, "No. You are you, you're not Caedon."

Yann was able to give Gwyl a smile. "She's not talking about my father, man. She's talking about my mother."

"Yann," said Keera. "It wasn't her fault. She was forced to it. And that means it isn't your fault either. You must say what you know. If this were a private matter, it could stay private. But the security of these people depends on their knowing the truth."

The people were buzzing now, restless, getting a bit angry.

Yann stepped before them. Gwyl saw Yann steel himself to speak.

"I'm the true heir," he said, after a long moment when Gwyl feared he wouldn't be able to. "Yes, you all heard Maro—Audemar—accuse me for who I am. My father was Caedon. Caedon the Usurper. He's right. And that, I've always thought, would be the best reason never to tell you my story. Caedon has nothing to do with my claim. And yet—"

Gwyl thought to himself Yann might not be able to bring himself to say it. Because now he thought he knew what Yann was about to say.

"—And yet he has, in a twisted way, everything to do with my claim." Yann took a deep breath. "My mother was Diera the First. My father forced himself upon her, and I was the result. He hoped to legitimize his reign that way, but he only demeaned himself with the act of a base villain. He was a sham of a monarch. My mother, whom he executed when he saw she was a threat to him, was the true monarch, daughter of the assassinated Crown Prince Artur, the true heir to King Ranulf the Fourth. Her rule as monarch was ratified by Prince Avery when, for less than a day, he assumed the throne. I am Diera's heir and true son."

"Hail, King Yann," said Pierrick, dropping to a knee.

"Hail," repeated Gwyl, and he heard Keera saying it beside him.

"No," said Yann, as he saw them all about to go down on their knees. "Stop. I have told you truly what I know. Yes, I am Diera's heir, if succession proceeds by blood. But we are not in the Sceptered Isle, my dear friends. We're not controlled by that realm and its rules."

He spread his arms wide to include all the people assembled on the field. "We are here, in the New Found Land. We come from many realms, the Sceptered Isle only one of them. I'll lead you, or not, just as you choose. But I'm not a king, and I won't be a king. My life is here. This land doesn't belong to us. It belongs to the people who already live here. If they allow us to live among them, I will go down on my knees in thanks to them. We may have ruined our own lands. Let's try not to ruin these."

The firelight flickered across his face. He looked around at Keera and Pierrick with the strange amber eyes he got from his father. "So if, after that, either of you want to claim the throne, go ahead. As for me, I say, let's have no king."

He turned, shouldered the bag with his harp in it, and, like the owls, went away into the darkness.

# EPILOGUE

Matters in Falls Village, and in Three Rivers, and in all the settlements between, took a long time getting sorted out. Some wanted the old verities. Pierrick agreed to govern Three Rivers after a lot of talking it over with Fiona, Keera, Gwyl, and most of all, Yann.

"But not as a king," Pierrick told them as they sat together one afternoon. "And not as a person beholden to a king. I've come to take Yann's view on that matter. We need a leader, though. I foresee war coming with the settlements of Ansgar." He had a parchment with him. "And this. This tells me something strange. The Sceptered Isle has a new monarch, a queen. My father's first wife, and before that, the wife of Artur. Everything we've learned makes me think this woman had as much to do with the disruption of the succession as my father, or Caedon."

"What is the name of this woman?" asked Keera, wondering if her parents had ever talked about her.

Pierrick looked down at the parchment and back up. "This message is sea-stained. I can't quite make it out." He squinted at it. "Agnes. Alyce. Something like that."

"Whoever she is, I'm thinking she won't be queen long. Ansgar or Gilles, whichever one of them gets to her first, will do for her," said Gwyl.

Pierrick put the parchment down on the table before them, and then, caught up in practical matters, they all forgot it and the tangled affairs of the Sceptered Isle.

More important issues demanded their attention. Crops. The coming winter. Good relations with their neighbors in the native villages. Yann helped re-establish Falls Village as one of the settlements under Pierrick's protection. Sorting out these matters was the work of years.

A hard, pinched winter followed the harvest-tide battle that had destroyed Falls Village's crops. Then a springtide of planting, a summer, another harvest-tide, another winter. And so the rebuilding proceeded, season after season, some of them difficult, some of them easier. There were failures the settlers learned from; successes they celebrated.

"As for me," Yann told Gwyl and Keera one evening some years later, "now the work of repairing Falls Village is over, I'm heading west." He had been playing his harp. It seemed to comfort him. He set it aside.

"We'll go with you," Gwyl and Keera said at almost the same time. "And John and Miri," said Gwyl, looking over fondly at his son where he sat learning his letters with his mother before the fire in their small dwelling, and at his little daughter Miri, playing with her toys at his feet.

"You'll teach me the bow, father," said John, looking up at Gwyl.

"You're old enough, son. Yes, and how to make one, too."

"What about me?" said Miri.

"You too," Gwyl promised, reaching down to tousle her hair. "You're too small to pull one yet, but I'll make you a little one and you can practice."

"But Father," said Miri, and she looked over at Yann shyly. "I want to learn how to do that."

"Do what?" said Gwyl, puzzled.

"That," she said. She pointed at Yann's harp.

"I promise to teach you," said Yann, his eyes soft. He looked over at little John, not so little any longer. "Your son and I were named for the same brave man. Did you know that?" he murmured to Gwyl. He stepped to the door to scan the spring-tide sky for the weather. "If we're going, we'll need to get started so the cold, when it comes, won't catch us in an inconvenient place," he told Gwyl and Keera, pushing the hide of the door aside.

Gwyl and Keera looked at each other. "Will he never be at peace?" Gwyl whispered.

Keera shook her head. "I don't know. But Gwyl. Are you certain about this? It will mean leaving Pierrick."

"He and I have had many long talks about that, of late," said Gwyl. "I've gotten restless, Keera. My work here is done. But Pierrick still has his obligations here. Even before Yann made his decision, Pierrick and I decided I should head west. Maybe found a new settlement. Pierrick and I will stay in contact. Once we've established a new settlement, and Pierrick is sure of the stability of Three Rivers, he and Fiona and the children will follow us there."

Keera tried not to look skeptical. "Did anyone think to consult me about that?" she said instead.

"It was an unformed idea. But now that Yann has made his decision, I see that in going with him, we can turn the dream into reality together. So," he said slowly, "I suppose I'm consulting you now. What do you think?"

"We'll go," said Keera, with sudden decision.

From outside the dwelling, Yann exclaimed in amazement. Keera and Gwyl looked at each other and rushed to the door of the dwelling to look out. A brilliant light rode in the sky. It was not as bright as the moon but brighter than Venus, the planet Old Dee had described to Keera so long ago. A long tail streamed across the sky away from it.

"Is this a good sign from the Sky Child for our journey, or a warning?" said Yann, looking to Keera.

"Could it be both?" she said, peering up into the sky. "After all, you know, she's a duplicitous old Child."

From the higher vantage of his cloud platform, Merlin, or Myrddin, or Mervin, whatever you may wish to call him, was watching the bright light, too, its tail flaming behind it, the hairy star that had come before and would come again. The bright streaker across the skies of the Sceptered Isle, portending change.

And down below him, too, he watched it flame across the skies of the Unknown Lands.

"You've come!" Mervin, or whatever his name might be, cried out to this traveler in the skies. "Many a mother will cry bitter tears over your coming. I've seen you before, but this time you're much more terrible to me, threatening to hurl destruction on this land."

"Mervin, you're so pessimistic," his friend John Dee said, standing alongside. "These people, and their children, and their children's children might bring it off in the end. They're good, at the core."

"No, they're not," said Gilles de Rais, with a hollow laugh. He had come up stealthily behind the other two mages. "They're the most pernicious race of little odious vermin the Children ever suffered to crawl across the face of the earth."

"Who asked you, Gilles?" said Dee.

"Oh, stop your endless squabbling," said the arch-mage, Mervin, or whatever his name might be. He waved them to their seats. "In the end, it doesn't matter. Let's agree to take the long view. To the elements it came from, everything will someday return. Our bodies to earth, our blood to water, heat to fire, breath to air. In the meantime, strife and love endlessly contend. The result is harmony. That bright contention, the force that holds up the Spheres."

And so the soothed mages smiled at one another. They inched a little forward in their golden chairs to peer down through the layers of crystal at the hapless humans ant-like underneath the Spheres.

"It's been a long winter," observed Dee.

"But look," said Mervin, pointing to the horizon where the Spheres revolved and clicked into place. "Here's the sun," he said, rising.

Gilles cringed away.

The other two mages stood arm in arm and watched. And smiled.

When they heard Gilles's cynical laughter behind them, they did not turn around.

"There she goes," said Dee. From the height at which they stood, he looked down fondly on the little figures heading west. "And that man of hers, and their children, and their friend."

"And there goes the comet with them," hissed Gilles, looking on too over their shoulders. The three of them watched that hairy star as it rode on, its tail licking down to parch the land the small beings toiled across.

"Enough," said Mervin. The Spheres had clicked continually on, from morning, to afternoon, to twilight. "High time we got some rest."

But Dee had seen something the other two of them hadn't, and he still stood looking, his hands in his pockets, a secret smile on his face. Following the little group of travelers, two owls on silent wing.

*There goes Keera,* he thought, and laughed to himself. More than one ornithomancer in that family. *And there go her Watchers, the two who love her. Always have. Always will.*

Behind him, he heard Gilles making an irritated noise. Something was forever irritating the man. Dee turned to see what it might be this time.

Gilles was gazing to that place across the broad dark river opposite the Spheres.

Two shapes of men stood together in the dusk, watching from the banks after the travelers. One, a strongly-made man in mid-life. The other must have crossed that river slightly younger. *Gwyl*, though Dee. *It's Gwyl they're watching.*

But why should this bother Gilles so? Dee noticed Gilles's gaze was moving from the younger of these two men to a shadowy figure further off under a tree away from the banks. A dark figure, bent over, alone. A figure Dee knew all too well.

"Gilles," said Mervin, a warning in his voice. He had noticed, too. "There's not a thing you can do about those two men, either one of them. Not Caedon. Not Rafe. You might have controlled them once, or tried to. Not any more. They're out of your reach. Give it up, Gilles."

Gilles turned his malign stare on Mervin.

But Dee was still observing the two on the shore.

Gradually, he saw, the shore had thronged with watchers. First just those two. Then four more: two tall men, and a shorter man, and a slighter, hard-muscled, graceful man who looked to have been taken across the river a little older than the other three.

Then, drifting from the trees, three women, one of them dark-haired; one with a lovely honey fall of hair; one with hair that, even at such a distance, Dee saw glinting red-gold.

One of the two original watchers on the shore, the younger one, detached himself to come to stand by the dark-haired woman and gaze into her eyes. One of the newcomers, the shorter man, moved to embrace the woman with the honey fall of hair. And one of the others, a tall young man with a slight limp, went joyfully to the woman with the glints of red-gold in her hair. As for the other two newcomers, another of the tall men and the older, slighter man, they leaned into each other's arms.

All of them lingered on that shore, watching the little group of travelers go by. The dark haired woman, Dee could swear it, put out a yearning hand to Yann. The man in middle years strode down the bank, keeping pace with Gwyl as far as the river allowed. Only the dimmed-out figure by the tree shrank more and more into himself, alone.

Mervin looked over at Dee with a sigh. He got up and pulled the curtain of the heavens across, blotting out the scene. "Enough, John," Mervin said to Dee.

So the three of them turned in, Mervin, Dee, and Gilles. The next morning, as the sun clicked by again, they resumed living their lives (or existences, or whatever you might call them) happily ever after. Or in torment. Or somewhere in between.

Much like the tiny figures heading west, shadowed by the owls underneath the comet far below.

# ABOUT THE AUTHOR

I hope you have enjoyed *Ghost Bird*, Book Four of the Harbingers series of fantasy novels. Please leave a review of my novel on amazon.com and other sites. I care about what my readers think! Please visit my author page on amazon.com, and my author web site, www.janemwiseman.com. On my web site, you can find a playlist of most of the songs featured in the Harbingers series, including the three prequel volumes in the Stormclouds series. Follow my blog about speculative fiction, www.fantastes.com, or follow me on Twitter, @jane_wiseman. On Pinterest, find my board, Medieval Life—Ghostbird to get an idea about what some of the people, places, and objects in the books may have looked like.

I hope you have read the other books in the Stormclouds/Harbingers series. I've added an excerpt from *The Martlet is a Wanderer*, the first of the Betwixt & Between companion novel, with events that overlap the last few Harbingers novels. You can find the full novel on amazon.com. Have fun! Jane

*Jane Wiseman splits her time between Albuquerque and Minneapolis. She loves fantasy in all its forms, enjoys her family, reads all the time, tries to write the kind of stuff she'd like to read, and paints.*

# A note of acknowledgment:

Thanks first of all to my wonderful editor and daughter, Margaret Govoni. You steered me away from many mishaps and missteps. All the rest are mine alone.

Thanks to Bob, marvelous beta-reader.

Thanks for all the helpful suggestions I've gathered from a number of online Litreactor workshops, www.litreactor.com, and from the writing workshops at the Tinker Mountain Writers' Workshop and the (sadly now defunct) Taos Summer Writers' Conference. The instructors' comments and suggestions were of course incredibly helpful, but I have valued beyond measure the comments and suggestions of my fellow workshop attendees. Thanks to all of you! You may not have been able to save me from all my writing sins, but you saved me from many. Thanks also to Anamcara, a wonderful writing retreat on the Beara Peninsula of Ireland. What a peaceful place to write! Thanks, Sue.

And thanks to all you Norrathians out there, especially a few special battle buddies of mine. You know who you are. You are my fantasy friends in the purest sense of all.

# A special thanks to the artists whose public domain work contributed to the composite graphics of the cover:

Image by <a href="https://pixabay.com/users/ArtsyBee-462611/?utm_source=link-attribution&utm_medium=referral&utm_campaign=image&utm_content=921863">Oberholster Venita</a> from <a href="https://pixabay.com/?utm_source=link-attribution&utm_medium=referral&utm_campaign=image&utm_content=921863">Pixabay</a>

and

Image by <a href="https://pixabay.com/users/ArtsyBee-462611/?utm_source=link-attribution&utm_medium=referral&utm_campaign=image&utm_content=2214015">Oberholster Venita</a> from <a href="https://pixabay.com/?utm_source=link-attribution&utm_medium=referral&utm_campaign=image&utm_content=2214015">Pixabay</a>

and

Image by <a href="https://pixabay.com/users/dannymoore1973-1813225/?utm_source=link-attribution&utm_medium=referral&utm_campaign=image&utm_content=1107397">danny moore</a> from <a href="https://pixabay.com/?utm_source=link-attribution&utm_medium=referral&utm_campaign=image&utm_content=1107397">Pixabay</a>

# READER, Before you go!

The sweep of the nine novels in the **Stormclouds/Harbingers** series, including the two companion novels (**Betwixt & Between**) starts with the sighting of the comet of 976 CE, recorded in the British Isles. Except for that one reference, we know almost nothing about this hyperbolic comet, known as x976, but it did show up, and you can read about it in the historical record.

The events of the nine novels progress from the appearance of x976 to the famous sighting of Halley's Comet in 1066 CE. Halley's, one of the most-studied comets in human history, seemed to the people of the British Isles in 1066 to presage the regime change ushered in by the Norman Conquest, and it was observed in the Americas, too. These two comets frame my series of novels—with this difference, that the sightings of the two comets in my novels occur in the fantasy-verse, not in real-life history!

The nine books of the three interconnected series are all available in print or for Kindle through www.amazon.com. For more information about the novels in the series, and for a playlist that includes many of the songs the characters play and sing, go to my author web site, www.janemwiseman.com. To see the way people, places, and things may have looked in the Stormclouds/Harbingers world, go to my nine Pinterest boards: *Medieval Life—Gyrfalcon*, *Medieval Life—Shrike*, *Medieval Life—Stormbird* (for the **Stormclouds** series); *Medieval Life—10*[th]

*Century* (about *Blackbird Rising*), *Medieval Life—Halcyon, Medieval Life—Firebird, Medieval Life—Ghost Bird* (for the **Harbingers** series);. *Medieval Life—Martlet* and *Medieval Life—Nightingale* (for the **Betwixt & Between** companion series).

The "flavor" of the three series varies a bit. The novels of the **Stormclouds** and **Betwixt & Between** series are a bit darker and more adult, while the novels of the **Harbingers** series are a bit more YA/NA in flavor. Even though, chronologically, the **Stormclouds** novels come first, you may begin either with the **Stormclouds** novels or the **Harbingers** novels, and may want to read the **Betwixt & Between** novels last. And now, for those interested in the origin story of the villain Caedon and his brother Maeldoi, read *Dark Ones Take It*.

## The Novels:

*A Gyrfalcon for a King (Stormclouds, book 1)* : King Ranulf is cursed, a curse of his own making, through his own misdeeds. Which of his sons will redeem him and which will be his undoing? Artur, the crown prince, scholarly and retiring? Audemar, the second son, conspiring to unseat him? Avery, the third son, alert to the dangers that surround the throne? Or John, Ranulf's bastard son—John the minstrel, John the mage.

*The Call of the Shrike* (Stormclouds, book 2) : Ranulf's true-born son Prince Avery and his bastard son John band together with three friends in the guerilla action they name The Rising. The young warriors of The Rising set out to right a great wrong that threatens the realm. They face a mighty enemy—not the enemy they thought they were fighting, but one more dangerous than they could ever have imagined.

*Stormbird (Stormclouds, book 3)* : The ragtag band of The Rising faces near-impossible odds in its quest for justice. How can the Six hope to prevail when they fight without resources; when they are picked off one by one? When they face an evil man backed by an unimaginably evil force? John's young brother Wat must take up his brother's fight, struggling against not only the powerful enemies of The Rising but his own self-doubts. Meanwhile, in the grasp of Caedon, their enemy, the Princess Diera must do the same.

*Blackbird Rising (Harbingers, book 1):* An orphaned young girl, a band of spies and assassins, a sister lost, a queen found—in the midst of chaos and treachery, Mirin must somehow learn to trust. Only then can she fulfill the mission John the minstrel left her. Only then can she live up to the promise and the magic of her music.

*Halcyon (Harbingers, book 2)* : On the run, Mirin and Wat try to carve out a new life together. But when everything is taken from Mirin, she must find the strength to go on alone. Her music sustains her, and so does the mysterious power of the fisher-bird, the harbinger of her god.

*Firebird (Harbingers, book 3)* : Keera has one goal—avenging her parents—and boundless confidence. After all, she has her magic powers, and they are second to none. When she finds she must fight her battle with only her wits and her grit, how can she possibly prevail? But the girl has friends: an old mage who helps her, a young man with a twinkle in his eye who can't get her out of his mind—and a ghost.

*Ghost Bird (Harbingers, book 4)* : Keera and Gwyl voyage in Gwyl's dragon ship to the heart of a new continent. But their enemies from the world left behind are not done with them yet. The two of them have to fight for the life they want, pursued by a powerful evil, relentless and closing in. Lucky for them Keera is an ornithomancer like her mother, Mirin, and like her uncle, John—the kind of mage who calls upon the mysterious powers of birds.

*The Martlet is a Wanderer (Betwixt & Between, book 1)* : Who is Silence? He can't speak to tell anyone the role he played in the conspiracy called The Rising, and he can't remember it anyway. He knows only that he needs to find two people: a friend, and a woman who means more to him than life itself. How can he possibly carry out this mission? Especially since he might be dead. (The events of this novel take place in parallel with *Halcyon*.)

*The Nightingale Holds Up the Sky* (Betwixt & Between , book 2) : Say you've been kidnapped and dragged to the underworld. Say the man who loves you wanders the realm looking for you. Say he finds a way in. But suppose you don't want to be found. As for the fate of the realm in the grip of evil, the fate of the world underneath the Spheres; as for justice—what if you forge your own? (The events of this novel take place in parallel with *Halcyon*, *Firebird*, and *Ghost Bird*.)

And finally: *Dark Ones Take It* , *being the origin story of Caedon and his brother Maeldoi.* Caedon and Maeldoi are gwrgi--creatures who look like the rest of us, except for their amber eyes. When they get into a rage, they transform. Like werewolves? Not exactly. To an out-of-control bestial form of themselves. As they reach manhood, the dangerous age, the brothers are separated. Caedon is adopted by Gilles de Rais, a powerful mage with powerful secrets, a sorcerer who values Caedon's rage and schemes how to use it. Maeldoi is taken off by his fellow gwrgi to be taught how to control the rage inside him. BROTHER AGAINST BROTHER. When Caedon and Maeldoi meet again, the fate of the Spheres Themselves hangs in the balance.

# NOTES ON Ghost Bird

## from the author

THIS NOVEL IS A WORK OF FANTASY , not historical fiction, although it is indebted to history. I have striven to be respectful of Native American/First Peoples traditions and cultures. Characters based on these cultures are not intended to represent any particular tribe or group. These fantasy characters native to the Unknown Lands, like the fantasy characters loosely based on European medieval culture, are not intended to be savages, or even noble savages, just people.

THE TIME-PERIOD of the novel is roughly early medieval. The characters of this novel look back to a geopolitical environment resembling several of the Frankish, Anglo-Saxon, and Scandinavian kingdoms vying for power in the 10th and 11th centuries. The first landscapes of the novel vaguely resemble Viking Age Greenland (the Cold Lands), and later on, the Viking settlement in Newfoundland (and, presumably, further south), Basque communities established on the St. Lawrence River in the medieval period (the New Found Land stands in for all of these places), as well as pre-Columbian North America south of the Canadian border, such as the Mississippian Culture city of Cahokia (across the Mississippi from present-day St. Louis, Missouri) and the Mayan city of Chichen Itza in the Yucatan peninsula of Mexico. You will also encounter a strange little episode in 21st century St. Louis.

Twelve Realms:

THE SCEPTERED ISLE stands in for the united Heptarchy (seven main kingdoms) of mainland Anglo-Saxon England, but also includes the northern part of the realm (Scotland), the Western Isle (Ireland) and the northern isles (islands off the coast of Scotland— Inner and Outer Hebrides, Orkney, and Shetland Islands). It does not include the area around Lunds-fort (London), however.

THE EASTERN BARONIES stands in for a loose confederation of powerful feudal lords spreading across medieval France and parts of Germany. In my tale, the Eastern Baronies also own territory on the mainland of the Sceptered Isle—the land around Lunds-fort

(London) and along the eastern edge of the mainland—in addition to their strongholds across the Narrows (the English Channel).

THE SOUTHERN PRIMACY stands in for medieval territories in Italy (as well as Portugal and Spain), the homeland to which the Old Ones (ancient Romans) pulled back as their empire dwindled.

THE LYRE-LANDS stands in for the vestiges of ancient Greece and the lands rimming the Aegean in the medieval era, including that vast metropolis the Vikings knew as "the Great City," Constantinople (earlier called Byzantium; later, Istanbul).

THE REALM OF THE ASP: the ancient Near and Middle East.

THE BURNT LANDS is a vague concept to people of the Sceptered Isle and similar northern realms. It stands in for North Africa and below, through Sub-Saharan Africa, but people in the northern realms know little of these lands.

THE ICE-REALM stands in for medieval Norway and, in a loose sense, the other parts of Scandinavia. Its king wants to add the Cold Lands (Greenland) to his realm.

THE FIRE ISLE stands in for medieval Iceland.

THE MOUNTAIN FASTNESSES: the Alpine regions of Europe.

THE TRADE ROAD FORTIFICATIONS: the old Silk Road of the late ancient world through the Renaissance, stretching along the Eurasian steppes.

THE SILK LANDS: China and southeast Asia.

THE FORGOTTEN KINGDOM: the Indian subcontinent.

ALSO—AND MOST IMPORTANTLY IN THIS NOVEL OF THE SERIES:
UNKNOWN LANDS (the Americas) across the Great Sea stretching to the west. Travelers have come back with tales of these lands. Now people in the Ice-Realm, the Fire Isle, and other northern realms,

including the Baronies people straddling the westernmost mountainous Baronies/Southern Primacy border, know they really do exist, and have set out to explore them. The New Found Land is based on the Newfoundland/Labrador area of Canada, the place where the Vikings established at least one archaeologically proven settlement (L'Anse aux Meadows), and undoubtedly more.

THE OVERALL CONCEPT OF MY NOVEL'S UNIVERSE is Pythagorean: nine revolving crystalline spheres carry the heavenly bodies (sun, moon, stars, planets) around the earth at their center. This idea from the ancient classical Near East was widespread in the medieval period, obviously long before anyone knew anything about the way the physical universe really works.

ONE FOR SORROW is a traditional nursery rhyme of the counting type, often sung (Roud 20096), usually about magpies. I have repurposed it and changed the wording a bit. In Keera's world, the rhyme is about owls, especially the barn owl (ghost bird or ghost owl). The version by the Unthanks is my favorite, although it's about magpies and the words are different. The tone is exactly right, though:
https://www.youtube.com/watch?v=_fPbWEa1cyg

KEERA is a transliteration of the Irish name *Ceara*. Too many people pronounce it like *Sierra* for me to use it in its correct spelling. *Ceara* should be pronounced either *Keera* or *Ky-era*. My character's name is pronounced like *Keera*, so in my fantasy world, that's her name.

THE TRISKELION is an ancient symbol common in many parts of the world, especially Brittany in northern France. It is a triple interconnected spiral, sometimes represented as three running legs. Sometimes the ends of the spiraling lines resemble the heads of birds of prey. Black and white is a good traditional color for a Breton flag or pennant. Gwyl and Yann come from that part of the world.

SHIP-BUILDING IN ANGLO SAXON AND VIKING CULTURES is a complex topic. Apologies for any technical details I've gotten wrong. Likewise, navigation in the 10th and 11th centuries has attracted a great deal of archaeological and scientific research. The compass and magnetism were unknown, and even the astrolabe, but many authorities on Viking-age navigation think Viking mariners might have used so-called sunstones and similar devices to tell the position of the sun even in overcast conditions: https://www.livesci-ence.com/44366-vikings-sun-compass-after-sunset.html

Here's an interesting video that explains Viking navigation and the possible use of the sunstone. I like this video especially because of its very useful set of links to more resources (at the end of the video): https://www.youtube.com/watch?v=eq9NE2qQzT0

On the other hand, this extremely useful web site about Viking ships and navigation, http://hurstwic.org/history/articles/manufacturing/text/norse_ships.htm maintains that the idea of the sunstone is likely a modern flight of fancy. Perfect for a fantasy novel!

A great deal of evidence shows that Vikings navigated using natural aids, as well. A finely-honed sense of smell, for example, alerted mariners to the proximity of land, and well-known landmarks were much easier to spot from far away in the unpolluted environment of the era. Even animals played a part, such as birds that, when released, would fly toward land.

VIKING SETTLEMENTS IN THE NEW WORLD: I am indebted to web sites such as https://whc.unesco.org/en/list/4 and sources such as Graeme Davis's *Vikings in America* and Anders Winroth's *The Age of the Vikings*.

THE WORD "WRETCHES" that some of the European settlers pejoratively use for the native peoples in the New Found Land is a translation of the Norse (Viking) term *skraeling*. Some translators don't regard it as necessarily negative; some think the name meant "small men," or "the others"—"those not like ourselves," "those who don't speak in the same way we do," much like the Greek term "barbarian."

THE BRETON HARP, hugely important in early Breton culture, is an instrument that faded away after the medieval period. It's not the same as its Celtic harp cousins in Scotland and Ireland. It's a wire-strung triangular harp that was apparently played by a plectrum, although Alan Stivell and other contemporary musicians who have revived Breton music do not adhere exactly to these medieval descriptions, which are obscure. This is the type of harp played by Yann. The whole topic is quite technical and beyond me, but here are some sources, including a link to Stivell's beautiful music: http://www.standingstones.com/bretonharp.html#telenn http://www.cgh-poher.org/telechargement/kaier29/9-ALAN%20STIVELL.pdf

https://www.youtube.com/watch?v=s4pbYbY5iVA

NATIVE AMERICAN GROUPS depicted in this novel: As my novel describes them, the relations between competing groups of Europeans in the New World, and between European settlers and various Native American groups, are pure fantasy, and while I have interjected bits of history into my novel, they are interlarded with fantasy. As far as reality is concerned, there's no evidence French explorers or settlers were in the New World during the time period of my novel. There's convincing evidence Viking explorers and some settlers from Scandinavia were, but the evidence is scanty and dubious south of Newfoundland, Labrador, and areas of the High Arctic. There's convincing evidence Basque whalers settled in fishing outposts along the Gulf of St. Lawrence and some way up the St. Lawrence River. Everything else is fantasy.

A NOTE ABOUT THREE STRIPE'S GROUP: these people occupy the fantasy territory physically closest to the homeland of a group loosely known, in the real world, as the Lawrentian Iroquois. Historical consensus has long held that this group bore little resemblance archaeologically and linguistically to the Iroquois Confederacy and the Huron, finding that these earlier people, encountered along the St. Lawrence River by the very first European explorers, had disappeared by the 16th century and French exploration. But new evidence disputes this: https://www.ontarioarchaeology.org/resources/Publications/OA96-12%20Warrick%20Lesage.pdf .

This paper by Gary Warrick and Louis Lesage, published in *Ontario Archaeology* in 2016, makes a cogent argument that the Lawrentian Iroquois didn't go extinct but were instead absorbed into other Iroquoian groups, and that the descendants of these people, not archaeologists and linguists, are in the best position to determine this. I do not dispute their argument (and am not qualified in any way to do so) and make no claim that my fantasy group is this group, although I have been inspired by a few aspects of its culture known to historians and other experts—for example, a list of around 200 words from the group (see http://www.native-languages.org/laurentian_words.htm). In most other ways, my fantasy characters have nothing to do with this group. For example, the real group seems to have been matrilineal (see http://www.virtualmuseum.ca/sgc-cms/expositions-exhibitions/iroquoiens-iroquoians/grande_epo-pee_peuple_iroquoien-epic_story_iroquoian_people-eng.html), which is not the case with my characters.

SO-CALLED "CAPTIVITY NARRATIVES" from the Americas attest to the troubled situation arising when Native Americans captured European interlopers. Narratives such as that of Hannah Duston (highly fictionalized for propaganda purposes: https://web.archive.org/web/20100725225259/http://iws2.collin.edu/lrdavis/Cutter%20on%20Dustan.pdf) emphasize the brutality of captivity and the savagery of the captors, while narratives such as Mary Jemison's https://www.gutenberg.org/files/6960/6960-h/6960-h.htm reveal the humane way captives often became assimilated into a captor's group. Another source I found interesting depicts the North African Barbary pirates' captivity of Europeans, especially the experiences of a Cornishman whose natural coloring and the strong sun to which he was exposed ended up making him indistinguishable from his captors except for the color of his eyes: Giles Milton's *White Gold: The Extraordinary Story of Thomas Pellow*. I read that book after I had written mine, and I was struck right away with how closely imagination can sometimes parallel reality.

BOAT-BUILDING IN THE PRE-COLUMBIAN AND COLONIZED AMERICAS, especially in the northeastern parts of North America, is a topic just as daunting as Viking ship-building. My apologies for anything I got wrong there, too. I am using the word *canoe* for convenience, even though it is a word from the Caribbean. For information about building birch and elm canoes, I am indebted to web sites such as:
http://firstpeoplesofcanada.com/fp_groups/fp_groups_travel.html

THE BARN OWL, disseminated world-wide, is an owl with, usually, a buff body and a white, flattened, heart-shaped face. It has been termed the ghost owl or ghost bird because of its silent flight, its deadly predation, its nocturnal habits, and the eerie, pale appearance of its face. Some cultures have considered it a bird of ill omen; other cultures consider it a helpful messenger from the realm of the dead. Pairs of barn owls usually mate for life. Females lay their eggs in hollow trees or other protected areas where they can create a roosting area. They don't build nests. They do not show up in flocks in the daytime. Not real ones, anyway.

BASQUE PRESENCE IN THE NEW WORLD: I am indebted to web sites such as https://www.smithsonianmag.com/arts-culture/the-basques-were-here-43953489/

The evidence described there comes from much later than the time period of my novel, but in my fantasy world, the Basques got there early.

NATIVE AMERICAN CULTURES FURTHER SOUTH : I am indebted to sources such as Charles Mann's *1491: New Revelations of the Americas Before Columbus*, Arthur Demarest's *Ancient Maya: The Rise and Fall of a Rainforest Civilization*, and *A Forest of Kings: The Untold Story of the Ancient Maya*, by Linda Schele and David Freidel.

HUMAN SACRIFICE to a sun god in North America, at least as I imagine it in this novel, is pure fantasy. The evidence for human sacrifice along the northern tier of North America is weak and sketchy in general, although there are documented practices among Plains Indians, such as the Pawnee Morning Star sacrifice:
https://nativeamericannetroots.net/diary/1994
Among the Cahokia mound builders of the Mississippian culture further south in North America, and even further south in the Mayan culture of Mesoamerica, however, human sacrifice was a deep-rooted cultural practice. Historians and anthropologists do not consider such sacrifices to be acts of unprovoked brutality but as part of belief systems that honored the courage of the victim or other characteristics of the victim that benefited the community. Here's a quick read on Cahokia, an ancient city on the banks of the Mississippi opposite present-day St. Louis, MO that may have been home, at its height, to 100,000 people:
https://www.washingtonpost.com/wp-rv/national/daily/march/12/cahokia.htm

The carving that unsettles Gwyl near a fantasy-Mayan city is based on a real Mayan carving:
https://en.wikipedia.org/wiki/Human_sacrifice_in_Maya_culture#/media/File:Madrid_Codex_sacrifice_scene_p76.jpg

While these events may seem grisly, they are not unique to the Americas. Celtic, Scandinavian, and other European archaeological sites (the burial places of the so-called "bog men," for example—here's a synopsis from the PBS television show Nova: https://www.pbs.org/wgbh/nova/bog/iron-nf.htm ) give plenty of evidence that the practice was widespread in the Europe of prehistory. I hope the reader will see that European practices during the historical era too seem equally grisly to modern eyes—for example, the medieval execution method of disembowelment. Here's a good quick read, if you are interested in the topic:

The incidents in my novel are not intended to disparage any ethnic group but to add dramatic weight to my story. Human beings seem to me to be a violent lot, however and wherever that violence is practiced, so that's what I have depicted in my novel. Humans are also capable of great love and generosity as well, and I've tried to depict that too.

Groups of human beings coming in contact with other groups frequently misunderstand them, their cultures, and their intentions. That too I have tried to depict.

I'm going on about this at such length because I myself represent an infinitesimally small sliver of humanity in gender, culture, and race. I can't possibly speak for all cultures, of course, but as a fiction writer, I can respectfully imagine other peoples and cultures. Today, such imaginings have become contentious. Some think only a member of a specific culture can or should write about that culture. By such a standard, with no scope for the imagination to do its work, no writer of fiction confined to her own tiny demographic sliver would be able to write at all, except perhaps autobiography. The ability to imagine beyond our own small place in the universe is part of being human too, and I stake my claim to that.

Why have I not felt equally leery about playing fast and loose with the history of the fantasy-European characters in the rest of the series? I suppose because they reflect my own ancestry. However, I have tried to be just as respectful there as I have in this book. After all, I'm an American, not a European.

**Two competing religious groups among the European characters** , worshippers of the Lady Goddess vs. worshippers of an elemental universe controlled by earth, sea, fire, and sky, is fantasy but based on some actual bits of information about belief systems in the post-Roman British Isles and medieval beliefs in general, especially medieval ideas about the body and healing. These derived from very ancient sources such as the Greek philosopher Empedocles. The head of these elemental gods, in some sources, is Trioditis, the Three, the goddess of the crossroads. For Empedocles, the three faces of this triple godhead are Strife, Love, and the overarching Harmony that binds them together. For others, they are the three faces of Hecate, or the Triple Goddess Selene, Artemis, and Hecate. (Present-day astrologers and neo-pagans have their own settled ideas about these matters, as do anthropologists and folklorists. I know nothing about their ideas, or nothing deep, and don't pretend to—I'm writing fantasy, not philosophy or theology or anthropology. Besides, I'm situating the Triple Goddess in Meso-America—not exactly historically accurate. Apologies too, Matthew Arnold!) There is a sense that older gods once ruled the lands, but no one remembers much about them.

SUN GOD: Among the native American characters, the worship of a sun god reflects real practices at Cahokia, and perhaps elsewhere in the Americas, but not in the way I imagine it, and there is of course no worship of a Sky Child or the triad goddess called The Three. There's a real Temple of the Owls in the ancient Mayan city of Chichen Itza, though, and the big pyramid there really is a pyramid within a pyramid. I have been in it back in the day when you were still allowed to do that, and there is a real, magnificent, and extremely fierce-looking jaguar altar or bench at the top of it. Recently, an even smaller pyramid was found inside the inner pyramid: https://motherboard.vice.com/en_us/article/z4384j/a-secret-pyramid-was-found-inside-an-ancient-temple-in-mexico

ORNITHOMANCY is, literally, divination using birds, a practice that goes back to ancient times and exists in many cultures and religions. I have broadened these practices of sortilege (telling the future) to include all sorcery based on and using birds.

THE RULES OF TRIAL BY COMBAT vary from culture to culture and place to place. The rules evoked here would be fairly accurate for combatants in the medieval Frankish fiefdoms.

HALLEY'S COMET was seen in 1066, at the very end of the time period of my series of novels. The word "comet" literally means "hairy star." The appearance of Halley's Comet in 1066 was documented most notably by William of Malmsbury's *Gesta Regum Anglorum* (Deeds of the Kings of the English) written in 1125 (I've used the J. A. Giles 1847 translation). In Book I, Chapter 13, a monk variously known as Elmer or Eimer or Oliver exclaims over the dire sight, which was later thought to presage the death of Harold II at the Battle of Hastings and the success of the Norman Conquest, in words that I have borrowed to put into Mervin's mouth. Halley's Comet would have been seen in North America in that year too. There is evidence pictograms in New Mexico's Chaco Canyon dating

from around 1066 depict it, so it was probably not only seen but noted in the Americas, as this web site contends:
http://www.astronomy.pomona.edu/archeo/outside/chaco/nebula.html

APOLOGIES FOR MY PETTY AND NOT-SO-PETTY THEFTS! (As always, lawyers, I am playfully using the word "theft" for the literary figure of speech known as "allusion.") In this book, I stole from the traditional folklore of the British Isles; from seventeenth century poets John Donne and Andrew Marvell (and a bit from Milton); from *Monty Python and the Holy Grail* and from the MGM 1939 film version of *The Wizard of Oz* (again—just kidding, lawyers—I didn't steal, I alluded); from the mmorpg *Everquest*, variously published over the decades by Verant Interactive, Sony Online Entertainment, and Daybreak Games; from Ecclesiastes 10:1 (KJV); from 12th century English historian William of Malmsbury; from Jonathan Swift's *Gulliver's Travels*, Part II (and "gull," for Swift, doesn't mean the bird—by extension, it means a very naïve person. In *Gulliver's Travels*, this gullible guy wanders from one strange place to the next to the next, a gawker and outsider bumbling around in someone else's culture).

I also borrowed from and was inspired by a variety of sources on Arthurian texts and lore, especially the lore surrounding Merlin the Magician, his connection with Brittany, and legends that have him imprisoned, variously, in an oak tree or a rock; from the life of Dr. John Dee, a real mathematician, astrologer, proto-scientist, believer in all manner of crazy mystic theories, and advisor to Queen Elizabeth I during the English Renaissance; from the life of Gilles De Rais, a real fifteenth-century French baron who supported Joan of Arc but later became fascinated with the occult, going down in history as one of the most prolific and chilling serial killers (especially of children) the world has known.

Finally, I stole one of my brother-in-law's best jokes. Sorry, John! Huge apologies to nineteenth century poet Matthew Arnold, whose lines from *Empedocles on Etna* I swiped and butchered for the ending of this novel.

And a final thank-you to Warren Robinett, the inventor of the easter egg.

Excerpt from **Betwixt & Between** , Book I
The first book of the companion series to the
Stormclouds/Harbingers  fantasy novels

# The Martlet is a Wanderer

The man wasn't sure where he was or even exactly what he was. He was positive he did not know who he was, but that question came later.

He only knew that he was covered in some kind of filmy material, and that he was in some kind of long narrow box made of sweet-smelling wood. And that the world was rocking back and forth, first gently, then more and more urgently.

It made him feel a little sick.

Now, through the filmy material covering his face, he saw the outline of a woman bending over him, murmuring something. He wasn't sure what she was saying. It sounded rhythmic, like a kind of chanting.

He tried to raise his arms to cast the cloth away from him, but for some reason his arms wouldn't move. He tried to speak, but no word came from his lips.

This woman had in her left hand some kind of light, maybe a rush light. She was raising the light and coming nearer. The light diminished and he heard scraping sounds as the light bobbed about overhead; she was fixing it into a bracket, perhaps. She returned. Now her left hand hovered just above his face, as if she were about to draw the filmy material back. She was lifting something, long and narrow, in her right hand. Even through the filmy material, he could see that this object glinted in the rushlight. Something made of metal. Maybe a knife.

He hoped she would take the filmy material away. Maybe she was about to cut it away, with the knife. He was feeling suffocated in the layers of cloth, and he suddenly realized he was very thirsty.

But then an obscure banging became a loud banging, and the rocking motion became a bounding, twisting, vicious careening.

The woman screamed. The torch must have fallen from its bracket, because the world around him plunged into darkness. He heard a clatter as something dropped on the floor—*the knife*, he thought—and a scrabbling sound, and a shouting. A door crashing open, quite close by. Another light, but dim and further away.

"Mistress, come with us. Up on deck. We're feared we may break up. You must come!" An urgent male voice.

The door clapped to, and this dimmer light disappeared as well. In the darkness, he felt the emptiness of the rocking, bucking room that contained him. He was alone.

With a mighty effort, he did manage to raise an arm. As the heaving and swerving of the room increased a hundred-fold, he fought in a panic out of the folds of cloth. Grasping the sides of the narrow box in which he lay, he hauled himself upright. But before he could try to clamber out (and he had his doubts whether he'd be able to do that, his limbs felt so weak), a tremendous crash threw the box sideways, with him in it. The box upended on the floor below. Lying half-stunned with the kindling of broken shards of boards shattered around him, he realized the box had been set up on a kind of frame, and it had tipped over and spilled him out onto the planking of the room's floor.

Now, though, the hurtling of the ship quieted. That, he realized, was where he must be. Not in a room. Not on a floor, but a deck, in a ship's cabin. The ship rode more steadily.

He crawled from the wreckage of the box, scraping himself on splintered wood, and then he fought his way from the cloth tangled about him. Putting out a hand in the dark, he found a stable strut of some type, and after many attempts, he hauled himself upright, using it as a support.

He wondered if the woman, or the men who had summoned her, would come back. He hoped they would. He was full of questions now. How was he here? Where was he? Why? Too many questions to take in, just at the moment, as he stood unsteadily, holding onto the strut, his head swimming.

From far away, he heard voices.

*I must get out there*, he thought. *I must let them know I'm here. They'll help me.*

He began feeling his way through the dark toward the place where he thought the door of the cabin might be. The motion of the ship was still heaving, and his head was still swimming, so he grabbed on to handhold after handhold—the strut, the ladder back of a chair, some other solid object—and made sure not to let go of one until he had securely grasped the next.

Now he saw the door. A dim line of light from underneath it showed him where it was, and let him know that outside the door he'd be able to tell more about his surroundings.

He got to the door and pushed at it. It opened out easily into a narrow corridor where he could support himself with both hands on the closely-opposing walls. At the end of the corridor, rushlight flickered. He knew he must be on the ship's lower deck. Probably a fairly large cog, the kind used for shipping.

He stopped to listen. He kept hearing the voices. They weren't near. He must make his way in their direction.

As he lurched along, he saw he was nearly naked. A brief white cloth was drawn about his loins. He leaned to catch his breath against one of the heaving corridor walls, and looked down at himself. His rib cage was bandaged tight. He felt the bandaged area and winced. There was a wound there. Underneath the bandage he could feel the edge of some long straight gash down the middle of his torso.

Around his neck was a thong, and from it dangled a small object.

He put his hand to his head. It pounded, as if a tight band were being screwed tighter around his skull.

*I've been injured*, he thought. The woman bending over him must have been tending to his wounds.

But how had he been injured, and when? Judging from the seepage into the bandage, it might have been days ago. At least a day ago. A few days. That's what he decided.

He had the eerie notion that the bandage was keeping his body from falling apart into two halves. That the long straight cut down his torso had been made to slice him apart.

He managed to stagger to the end of the corridor where he heard voices just at the place it teed into another. He made his way as hurriedly as he could toward the voices.

Two men. As he approached them, they turned, and their eyes widened.

"What's this, then?" one of them said.

"Good sweet Lady's tits, did the hold burst open too?" said the other, his tones weary and exasperated. He looked to be a sailor. He grasped the man, bandaged, bloody, nearly naked, by the elbow. "Come with me, fellow. Back to where you belong."

This sailor pushed the man along stumbling ahead of him down another corridor, curved with the hull of the ship. The two of them pulled up short before a square hole in the planking of the deck.

"Pirtle Jailer," the sailor holding the man called out.

A head popped up from the hole.

"You're missing one of your prisoners," said the sailor. He gave the man a shove, and now this other one called Pirtle had him and was hustling him down a ladder into the hole.

The man looked over his shoulder puzzled at the sailor who had led him there. He opened his mouth to say—

*To say what?* He wasn't sure what to say. *I'm not a prisoner?* But what if he were? That's when he realized. He didn't know what he was. He didn't know who he was.

By the time these thoughts had swarmed like bees into and out of his head in a confused buzzing, the man named Pirtle had thrust him roughly into the stinking dark and had withdrawn up the ladder, slamming the trap door to the square hole shut behind him.

A groaning came from all around.

As his eyes adjusted to the dimness, he made out huddled bodies. Scores of them. Prisoners, it seemed. And he was one of them. What had he done, he wondered. And why hadn't he been down here before? What had he been doing up above? What had he been doing in that box?

Before he could think much about these disturbing notions, he felt himself lapsing back into the dark he had come out of not too long before. Not the physical dark of the fetid space into which he had been cast. A darkness lapping at him from inside his head, taking him off to some unknown place of oblivion.

How much later before he came back to himself again? It was hard to tell, but a watery green light was filtering into the room, so the world underneath the Spheres had moved from darkness into daylight. Now he could make out the tumble of bodies, largely naked, mostly male, that lay in the room.

He retched a little at the smell and also because he knew he must not have eaten for days. The thirst was the most overwhelming of all the feelings that assailed him. He tried to call out for water, but only a dismal croak came from his mouth.

"Child keep you, I thought you were one of the dead ones," said a voice. "You certainly were sweet-smelling when they pushed you down here. Someone rubbed you all over with spices, like. Less sweet-smelling now."

The man looked toward the voice. A large powerful fellow, one of the prisoners, lay near by. This big man raised himself up on an elbow. "Name's Kipp. And you are?"

He opened his mouth to reply but closed it again. He knew he couldn't say his name. He didn't know it. But he wanted to tell this man Kipp, *I don't know it.* Maybe somehow Kipp could help him find out what it was. He opened his mouth again to speak, to ask for Kipp's help, and he found he didn't know how. *Strange,* he thought. *I don't know how.*

Now this man Kipp changed to the speech of the Baronies and asked again.

Another prisoner had gotten up and had moved over to them to crouch down and look into the man's eyes. "Think he fought for their side? Are you crazy, man? Why would he be in here with us if he fought for the barons."

The prisoner named Kipp shrugged. "Worth a try. He could be a deserter."

"Could be," said the other one. He peered harder into the man's face. "Tell you one thing," he said to Kipp. "He's the Sea Child's for certain."

"Looks like it," said Kipp. They were speaking of the man as if he were some inanimate object. "But if he is, what's this, then?" This man, the one called Kipp, reached over and tugged at the leather thong about the man's neck.

He heard himself making an inarticulate soft sound of distress. He didn't want these others touching it.

Kipp dropped it and regarded him with interest. "Some sort of amulet. A bird."

"Blackbird," said the other prisoner. "Ours."

"Not a blackbird. Look at it." Kipp reached out his hand again, and the man shrank back. "Don't worry," he said with a kind look. "I promise not to touch it. But look at it," he said to the other prisoner.

"Not a blackbird," said the other one, grudgingly, peering at it in the dim light. "Like a blackbird, sort of."

"But different," Kipp insisted.

"Different," the other one agreed. "Sea Child eyes for certain, though."

"Whoever and whatever he is," said Kipp, "I think he can't speak."

"Master Silence, is it?" said the other man.

"Don't mock him. Who knows what he has seen?" said Kipp.

But from then on, the man's name was Silence.

Silence fingered the amulet on the thong about his neck. He didn't know what it was, either. Just that he didn't want anyone touching it.

For the few remaining days of their voyage, Kipp appointed himself Silence's protector.

The next time Pirtle came through with pieces of bread, Kipp made sure Silence got one as the others in the hold pushed and shoved to grab their share.

Kipp made sure to go to the water butt with the ladle and come back with water for Silence, again and again, until Silence had drunk his fill.

He sat by sympathetically as the bad water and the wormy bread ravaged Silence's starved skinny body, leading even the foulest of the rest of the prisoners to edge away from him in disgust.

*If I had ever been sweet-smelling,* thought Silence, *I'm not now.*

Kipp helped Silence take the bandage off his wound as the cloth became dirtier and dirtier.

"Any protection that bandage gave you has long been lost," he told Silence. Then he examined Silence's wound. "You're lucky, man. It has healed up nicely, no festering. You must have had a good healer. If it had started to fester, you would have gone fast down here." He considered it for a while. "It's an odd wound, though. What weapon and what kind of thrust would make a long straight wound like that one?" After a while, he asked, "Do you know who you are, and who you fought for?"

Silence looked at him in confusion. Had he fought? He must have. How else explain the wounds.

One of the others, overhearing, laughed. "That dummy lost his speaking, and he lost his mind with it, looks like," he said.

"He's not stupid," said Kipp. "He may not be able to speak, but he knows things as well as we do. Ordinary things. I think he may have been knocked in the head, though," he agreed after a moment, "and his memory knocked out of it." Kipp considered

Silence carefully and gave him an encouraging smile. "He doesn't know his name, I don't think. Not just that he cannot speak it. He doesn't know it."

Silence looked at him and at the others. He shook his head.

"You see?" said Kipp. "He knows what I'm asking him. He may not know who he is, but he knows ordinary things. He does. We're on a ship, aren't we?" he said to Silence.

Silence nodded.

"You see?" said Kipp.

"You told him we were on a ship," the other man argued. "You just did," he insisted. "He's a dummy. He's no use. They'll kill him when we get to port."

"He'll be very useful to some master," said Kipp. "They won't kill him. They'll get good coin for him. You watch."

But Silence saw Kipp wasn't very certain about what he was saying. Silence saw he was saying it to be reassuring and kind.

He summoned up a smile for Kipp. He rubbed his two fingers together, miming the fingering of a gold piece.

Kipp laughed, delighted, and nudged Silence.

Silence laughed too.

"You see?" said Kipp. "He can laugh." Kipp peered through the dimness at Silence. "He has good teeth, too. Maybe he's a gentle."

"Nah," said the other one. "If he was some gentle, do you think he'd be down here with us?"

*Will they?* Silence was thinking, ignoring all the rest of it. *Will they kill me? And who are they, and why would they want to?*

Made in the USA
Monee, IL
26 August 2020